The Classic American Novel and the Movies

The Classic American Novel

and the Movies   EDITED BY

Gerald Peary and Roger Shatzkin

WITH HALFTONE ILLUSTRATIONS

Frederick Ungar Publishing Co. / New York

Copyright © 1977 by Frederick Ungar Publishing Co., Inc.

Printed in the United States of America

Designed by Irving Perkins

Library of Congress Cataloging in Publication Data
Main entry under title:

The Classic American novel and the movies.

   (Ungar film library)
   Filmography: p.
   Bibliography: p.
   Includes index.
   1. American fiction—Film adaptations. I. Peary,
Gerald. II. Shatzkin, Roger.
PN1997.85.C55   791.43'7   77-3139
ISBN 0-8044-2681-3
ISBN 0-8044-6647-5 pbk.

*T*O KARYN AND KATHY WITH LOVE

ACKNOWLEDGMENTS

Elizabeth Dalton and the staff of the Wisconsin Center for Film and Theater Research, Mary Ann Jensen, Curator of the Theatre Collection, Firestone Library, Princeton University, and the staff of the Theatre Research Collection, New York Public Library at Lincoln Center, all helped us in our investigations into the subject of film adaptations; J. Dudley Andrew, David Bordwell, Marshall Deutelbaum, and John Cawelti led us to many of our fine contributors; Gerald Priesing of Universal Sixteen and Doug Lemza of Films Incorporated came to the rescue in making films available for viewing; Janet Abramson spent a good part of her summer typing; Paula Horvath provided general assistance in preparation of the manuscript. Katherine Koch gave us extra special help in the closing weeks of the project and Karyn Kay aided also; Stan Hochman and Ruth Selden of Frederick Ungar proffered their patient support and intelligent advice throughout the project. Finally, we would like to thank our contributors, all of whom spent many hours involved in this undertaking.

PHOTO CREDITS

The International Museum of Photography at George Eastman House provided the stills on pp. 13, 23.

The Wisconsin Center for Film and Theater Research provided the stills on pp. 33, 45, 65, 75, 97, 107, 117, 127, 135, 145, 155, 167, 179, 209, 221, 229, 259, 271, 299, 307.

Other stills from Cinemabilia and Movie Star News.

Contents

Introduction

I

The volume in hand shows thirty of our most engaged film historians and/or literary critics attempting to bridge the formidable gap between a "classic American novel" (defined expediently by chronology—as published prior to 1930) and its cinematic adaptation: deciding by what tortuous paths Nathaniel Hawthorne's *The Scarlet Letter* became the silent Hollywood film called *The Scarlet Letter*, and so on.

Perhaps a tiny minority of writers herein serve one medium to the detriment of the other: they are visual junkies, who dance merrily upon the Gutenberg grave; or they are proudly out-of-fashion literati, who think almost any transformation from print to celluloid inherently sinister. Most contributors, however, are tempered in their judgments. While friendly to the novels—or else why write about them?—they do not insist on the automatic sanctity of the printed word. And if they are learned about the cinema and spend an extraordinary amount of time in the dark, they would just as soon pass that time . . . absorbed in a book.

Such catholicity and common sense, obvious as they might appear, are more rare than typical. There can be no denying the hegemony that literature, and especially the novel, has held over the cinema in traditional critical circles. Nor is the prejudice without its reasons. Who of us would not join with Stanley Kauffmann in demanding "What is missing?" of the 1959 film version of *The Sound and the Fury* and then echoing his harsh rebuke, ". . . Faulkner is missing"? Who can find patience when Hollywood, gross Hollywood, stumbles to rationalize its improvisation of a brother named Howard to add spice to filmdom's Compson family? Alas, something is rotten in Yoknapatawpha County. And there is deep trouble on the high seas when a frisky Ahab kills the whale and then gets married in Warners' "upbeat" 1930 version of *Moby Dick*.

Cinematic adaptations are rarely so silly as these two examples or so openly inviting of ridicule. But even in cases where the translation has been accomplished with sophistication and care, the bias in favor of the book persists. The cinema stands suspect, regarded as a flashy but floundering and intuitive child, clinging hard to literature's coattails and hoping to achieve, through association with an established art, a modicum of respect and some purpose. According to this view, the film medium began at rock bottom, as a sub-art, a play thing for idiot savant wizards and tinker-toy technologists, zoetrope to kinetoscope. This gave way to burly primitivists carrying about magic boxes, photographing crude people waddling out of factories and waving at the cranking cameras. It was only when a genuine literary man, D. W. Griffith, entered the scene with *Oliver Twist* tucked beneath his arm, that an Art was made even vaguely possible. Adopting Dickens as his muse and novels as practical teaching tools, Griffith conjured up from his Victorian brow editing, parallel montage, and the close-up. That is the way one legend of the Birth of Movie Art goes, fostered by Sergei M. Eisenstein himself in the essay, "Dickens, Griffith, and the Film Today" (*Film Form*, 1949).

Film can learn much from literature, especially when taken up by such a clever craftsman as a D. W. Griffith. But does film ever catch up? Prevalent among literary-minded critics is the distinct feeling that a lag is permanent. Even at the cinema's most lucid and profound moments, where is the complexity, the sheer density, of the simplest prose metaphor? Film can be a rare diversion but it is too "easy," too ephemeral, a seductive narcotic that puts minds to rest like a smooth-spoken bedtime tale. Simply, all the directorial Scheherazades of the world cannot add up to one Dostoevsky.

This bleak view of cinema finds allies in the strangest places, even among committed film critics. Pauline Kael, who confounds

the more delicate *New Yorker* readers by her weekly champion-
ing of visceral, charismatic, "popular" movies, nevertheless makes
this tough judgment:

> If some people would rather see the movie than read the book,
> this may be a fact of life that we must allow for, but let's not pre-
> tend that people get the same things out of both, or that nothing is
> lost. . . .
>
> Movies are good at action; they're not good at reflective thought
> or conceptual thinking. They're good for immediate stimulus, but
> they're not a good means of involving people in the other arts or in
> learning about a subject. The film techniques themselves seem to
> stand in the way of the development of curiosity.
>
> Movies don't help you to develop independence of mind. . . .
>
> *(Deeper into Movies, 1976)*

George Bluestone in *Novels into Film* (1957) articulates the
most basic way in which film and literature are different: "We
observe that the word symbols in written language must be translated into images of things, feelings and concepts through the
process of thought. Where the moving picture comes to us directly through perception, language must be filtered through the
screen of conceptual apprehension." Perhaps it is the apparent
absence of this filtering process, the inoperativeness of mind on
movie matter, that causes many to regard film viewing as an over-
whelmingly banal intellectual activity.

This elitist position on attending the cinema takes humorous
forms: the ashen-faced scholar who journeys forth from his study
once annually to do combat with some abstruse, dragon-like
filmic puzzle (a Bergman perhaps, or a *Barry Lyndon*) lying
across the local screen; or the campus brain, turned self-conscious
barbarian, who wanders into popular movies precisely because
they are vulgar and "meaningless." There is also a position in
between, less overtly hostile to the cinema but not much different
in its conclusion: a nervous apologia for the abysmal state of
current film-making combined with a firm promise that this still
youthful, unlearned medium will shed its delinquent wings in
the future. Robert Richardson, in *Literature and Film* (1969),
typifies this line of thought:

Film language, which is the basis of film as a narrative art, seems to be evolving, and it would be premature and rash to suggest that it will not eventually develop language with the force, clarity, grace, and subtlety of written language.

It is at this point that, as editors, we must show our hands. Although we agree that film is ever-evolving, as evidenced in its current post-Godardian self-reflexive and modernist phases, we are skeptical of the idea that aesthetic evolution necessarily means "better and better." There is no intrinsic reason for a film or a cinematic adaptation of today to be any less accomplished than some corresponding film ten years hence. *When* a film is made should be no more a factor in ascertaining quality than when a novel was written.

For an informal test case of this proposition, we invite readers to open this book to its first essay, a discussion of the silent adaptation of James Fenimore Cooper's *The Last of the Mohicans.* The film was made in 1920 and thus is disqualified as a highly "evolved" work of art in Richardson's sense. But to the eye of critic Jan-Christopher Horak, there is a subtlety in cinema director Jacques Tourneur's complex mise-en-scène and metaphoric spatial composition that results in a richer and more densely unified artifact than the original "classic" novel. Fully aware of the heresy implied in his statement, Horak nevertheless claims that "it could be possible to argue that Tourneur 'improves' on Cooper's novel."

Whether Horak is right or wrong is a minor issue. What is significant is that he, like many younger film critics, is examining film in a different way than the person trained only in literature —and perhaps that is why he is arriving at such radical conclusions. The point is almost self-evident: film is and always has been a more complicated and multi-layered medium than most people concede. Often it is not the film-makers who have been negligent at their task but critics who have been indolent about creating a vocabulary to articulate the characteristic qualities of the cinema. In the past several years we have witnessed at last the new wave of movie methodologists, spreading the descriptive tools of structuralism and semiology, the theory of psychoanalysis and, very occasionally, Marxism, into the study of film-making. Again, we ask readers to turn to Keith Cohen's essay contrasting Theodore Dreiser's *An American Tragedy* with the scenario devised for it by Eisenstein. Cohen reveals the strong potential of such analysis by beginning to show empirically what we know by lip service: that film and literature are not quite twin bedfellows. As George Bluestone explained it:

> It is insufficiently recognized that the end products of novel and film represent different aesthetic genres, as different from each other as ballet is from architecture. . . . It is as fruitless to say that film A is better or worse than novel B as it is to pronounce Wright's Johnson Wax Building better or worse than Tchaikowsky's *Swan Lake*. In the last analysis, each is autonomous. . . .
>
> (*Novels into Films*)

II

Briefly and unsystematically, let us consider some of the tendencies in the movement from novel to film noted by contributors to this volume:

1. Scope. Almost all films reduce the dimensions of the novels upon which they are based. With the exceptions of once-a-century monumental attempts at literal transposition from page to screen, such as Erich von Stroheim's forty-two-reel *Greed*, ambitious novels cannot be presented in their full historical expanse and accretion of detail. However, as Albert J. LaValley points out about the film version of Sinclair Lewis's *Dodsworth*, compression may have its rewards. LaValley finds scenarist Sidney Howard's principle of "dramatizing by equivalent"—reducing novelistic events to a fewer number, consolidating several characters into one—an advantageous method. One scene in the film detailing Dodsworth's return home from Europe certainly is more evocative than the longer treatment in the novel.

Ray Bradbury, in his explanation of writing the film script for John Huston's *Moby Dick*, presents his own, probably less persuasive case. In order to make a "coherent," conventionally organized film of Melville's sprawling novel, Bradbury had to condense, reshuffle events, and restructure the original plot. "What you want to do is build the tension, build the tension," Bradbury admonishes. "So I went through and I tried to line up all the scenes." Unlike earlier versions, Bradbury does not toss out the whale with the sea water. However, he does empty Melville's ocean of "most of the documentary . . . and the philosophical dimensions of the novel . . . leaving behind the adventure story . . . ," according to Brandon French. Moby Dick, yes. But Moby Dick speared by Gregory Peck. Though the film has its virtues, one is tempted to invoke Ishmael (as French does) to the effect that the film version is cut off from "the real living experience of living men" and turned toward straight melodrama.

2. The question of melodrama. Is Bradbury's method of streamlining *Moby Dick*, creating a film with discernible beginning, middle, and end, and traditional patterns of rising and falling action, endemic to the translation from page to screen? One should consider Erwin Panofsky's contention in "Style and Medium in the Motion Pictures" (*Critique*, January–February 1947), that the film developed less from "highbrow" literature than out of diverse media with a popular body of established conventions that tended toward melodrama. These conventions have continued to dictate the shape of mass-market motion pictures. At the least, to violate these patterns is to tamper with public expectations and taste—and to threaten the all-determining box office.

The injection of cheap melodrama into so-called serious films springs up most noticeably, and disconcertingly, in the preponderance of "happy" endings sneaked in where none existed on paper, or in the addition of cinematic romance where it too was lacking in print. The adaptations of Nathaniel Hawthorne's works treated here, *The Scarlet Letter* and *The House of the Seven Gables*, present interesting examples of such transformations. In both instances, the film-makers chose to accentuate the strain of melodrama that Hawthorne freely acknowledged to be a part, but only part, of his method. As E. Ann Kaplan points out, the filmed *Seven Gables* converts brother and sister into marriageable cousins tragically kept from wedlock; in the screen version of *The Scarlet Letter*, the relationship of Hester Prynne and Arthur Dimmesdale often gets reduced, in Mark W. Estrin's words, to "boy-meets-girl," confusing "Hawthorne's idea of the Romance with Hollywood's notion of the romantic. . . ."

3. Ideological content. As Nancy L. Schwartz shows in her discussion of *Alice Adams*, the substitution of a benign ending in a film adaptation can have disorienting political implications. Alice's joyous romantic union with Arthur at the close of the film completely undercuts her potentially bleak fate in the Booth Tarkington original, a fate meant to question the American dream of happy marriage and upward mobility. Schwartz also indicates the total absence of commentary about social class in the movie, a smoothing over of those inequities Tarkington revealed through the painful plight of his black people.

Are all Hollywood films necessarily less politically progressive than their novelistic sources? Despite its primary allegiance to big business interests, Hollywood is anything but monolithic, even in as hypersensitive an area as ideology.

The film of *The Sea Wolf* becomes, according to Tom Flinn and John Davis, more directly antifascist, than Socialist Jack London's conceptually murky political novel. The Warner Brothers movie was made on the brink of World War II, so that the Nietzschean philosophy of Captain Wolf Larsen, so close to Nazism, needed to be clearly debunked.

In another broadly political way, the process of adaptation can go to the heart of cultural and societal change. The chronological dislocation of certain movies from their points of origin as novels creates new texts that are historically revealing. Joseph F. Trimmer, writing on *The Virginian*, argues that shifts in the Virginian's image from "cowboy Romeo" in 1929, to "capitalist" entrepreneur in 1946 (and, if we can extrapolate, to chairman of the board of a corporate family in the television series of the 1960s), mirrors the cultural context within which each vehicle appeared. Likewise, Carolyn Geduld demonstrates how Dreiser's turn-of-the-century Sister Carrie bends to the ethos of the American 1950s in William Wyler's film, becoming a suburban housewife-in-trouble because she does not conform. Gerald Peary shows how the novel *Little Caesar*, written in 1928, becomes a metaphoric text of Depression America in its late 1930 film incarnation, made a year after the Crash.

4. The question of qualitative judgment. Like the nearly iden-

tical Prince and Pauper described in Peter Brunette's essay, who are endlessly fascinated by their similar visages in the mirror, comparing novels and films has its own beguiling appeal. But in such a complex and evanescent process as the translation from novel to film, how are we finally to evaluate the success of an adaptation? One provocative standard is proposed by Keith Cohen in his treatment of Dreiser and Eisenstein: "Adaptation is a truly artistic feat only when the new version carries with it a hidden criticism of its model or at least renders implicit (through a process we should call 'deconstruction') certain key contradictions implanted or glossed over in the original." That this rigorous prescription has not often been fully met is hardly surprising. Hollywood production is not the same as Brecht's experimentation with the Berliner Ensemble, taking John Gay's *The Beggar's Opera* and reworking it as *The Threepenny Opera*. Subverting the world's masterpieces (both an intellectual and a decidedly political act) is not any way to keep a movie company financially afloat. Moreover, Cohen's criterion has found few allies among mainstream cinema critics. Most essays up to this time have put forth the notion that an appropriate adaptation offers an "equivalent" of the book instead of a critique.

III

In any collection such as this there must be regrettable omissions—eccentric adaptations not discussed (such as a recent experimentalist version of Henry James's *What Maisie Knew*, 1975), certain film versions of a particular novel not included, and so forth. Just to mention one notable example; though there have been at least four film versions of *Huckleberry Finn* we found in none sufficient merit to warrant an essay. Better to stick to Twain. Although we have limited the topic to the discussion of American novels and their filmed adaptations, even that boundary proved too large. A second volume of essays on filmic adaptations of novels written after 1929 will follow publication of this volume.

The strict narrowing of our topic necessarily precludes discussion of the role of American short fiction and drama as film sources. More to the point, our contributors had little forum to explore the question of dramatization as an intermediary step in the film adaptation of a novel. (*The Virginian, The Great Gatsby, Dodsworth, Washington Square/The Heiress* are only a few instances in which a stage version of a novel preceded at least one version of the film. This topic no doubt deserves a study of its own.)

Regardless of the limitations, we believe that the present study provides detailed pragmatic analyses of many individual cases of adaption, a task often overlooked in more theoretical approaches. We are proud of the number of original pieces written especially for this volume. Twenty-one essays appear for the first time in print.

GERALD PEARY
ROGER SHATZKIN

The Last of the Mohicans (1826), James Fenimore Cooper

Maurice Tourneur's Tragic Romance

BY JAN-CHRISTOPHER HORAK

Almost before James Fenimore Cooper's grave had settled, Mark Twain attacked his fellow literateur. He deflated Cooper's reputation on all accounts, including succeeding at this simple requirement of fiction: "that the personages in a tale shall be alive, except in the cases of corpses, and that the reader shall be able to tell the corpses from the others."

In our century, the devaluation has continued on course. R. W. B. Lewis, in *The American Adam* (1955), characterized Cooper's *The Last of the Mohicans* as "violent and incredible, and the style unbearably sentimental." Even Leslie Fiedler, whose psychoanalytic and mythic approach to Cooper in *Love and Death in the American Novel* (1960, 1966) brought extraordinary insights into the darker side of our national psyche, admitted that "Cooper had, alas, all the qualifications for a great American writer except the simple ability to write."

Still, many adults harbor sympathetic childhood images of Natty Bumppo, trader, trapper, pathfinder, "a man without a cross," America's first nonconformist hero. Memories linger also of the noble Chingachgook and his doomed son, Uncas, gliding across a wooded lake in their birchbark canoe or following the trail of some Huron into the deep expanse of American forest. White woodsman, Indian father and son, all have fled the encroaching restrictions of "civilization"; the Mohicans are remnants of a race doomed by the very culture that Natty shuns. They are men of action, terse but eloquent. Their idealized isolation holds the key to their mythic stature. A more disciplined reading of *The Last of the Mohicans* notices the tensions and contradictions within the text. For one thing, an uneasy balance is struck between the noble Mohican chiefs and the implicitly racist portrayals of the other Indians, who are either twisted and evil Hurons like Magua or weak and senile Delawares like Talemund. As Twain remarked: "In the matter of intellect, the difference between a Cooper Indian and the Indian who stands in front of the cigar store is not spacious."

Cooper can be linked politically to the hard line that rationalized Indian genocide in America during the 1800s, philosophically to a reactionary trend in nineteenth century American formula westerns. In his *Six-Gun Mystique* (1971), John Cawelti paraphrases popular culture historian Roy Harvey Pearce, pointing out that

> the various seventeenth and eighteenth century views of the Indian with their complex dialectic between the Indian as devil and as noble savage quickly gave way in the nineteenth century to a definition of the Indian way of life as an inferior and earlier stage in the development of civilization.

Though the earlier dialectic still remains in Cooper's novels, the tension for the modern reader lies in Cooper's undeniable belief in the superiority of Christian-white culture, and the ineluctability of manifest destiny regardless of its tragic consequences.

Another tension derives from Cooper's adolescent archetype of idealized and isolated heroes. When Cooper created a new American romance filled with wild adventure, last-minute rescues and exotic locales, he deemphasized the classic love interest of the European gothic novel. Male-female romance becomes always secondary to a central drama of male bonding. Cooper's women are held in awe for their purity, goodness, and virtue. They are images without flesh and blood, even when the plot centers on their rescue. The real empathy lies with the men of the mostly womanless wilderness. Understandably, Leslie Fiedler sees

Cooper's failure to deal with heterosexual love as symptomatic of America's psychic regression into an asexual (or latently homosexual) world of male violence and death. This failure is especially clear in *The Last of the Mohicans*, where Cooper barely touches upon the romance of Cora and Uncas. Yet it is this subplot that many readers recall—a love affair the author refuses to acknowledge at the novel's end. And it is this classical romance which forms the mature center of Maurice Tourneur's and Clarence Brown's 1920 silent version of *The Last of the Mohicans.*[1]

Maurice Tourneur, a Frenchman by birth, was until the mid-1920s considered the artistic equal of Griffith. Yet prior to Richard Koszarski's perceptive appreciation in *Film Comment* (March-April 1973) several years ago, his reputation had gone into eclipse. Koszarski proclaimed Tourneur a visual stylist, capable of manipulating his mise-en-scene for both depth (realism) and flatness (fantasy), and possessed of an awareness of the "dramatic potential of editing through the use of off-screen space." Tourneur films have recently begun to resurface, and in 1976 there was a limited retrospective at the Museum of Modern Art. Such works as *Trilby* (1915), *The Pride of the Clan* (1917), *The Poor Little Rich Girl* (1917), and *The Blue Bird* (1918) have revealed a major *auteur*.

It is *The Last of the Mohicans* that stands as Maurice Tourneur's greatest work, and certainly one of the great films of the silent period. It would be possible to argue that Tourneur "improves" on Cooper's novel. When Cooper's action gets bogged down in turgid prose, Tourneur's narrative is always swift and concise. Where Cooper's landscapes, for all their details, remain abstract, Tourneur's landscapes are lyrical in their pictorial ambiance as well as properly abstract in their meaning. While Cooper's narrative oscillates uncomfortably between adventure and thinly achieved romance, Tourneur's adventure is consistently and intensely romantic.[2]

[1] As early as 1909, Griffith adapted *Mohicans* for his Biograph one-reeler, *Leatherstocking*. In 1911, two versions were released by Powers and Tanhauser respectively. The most notable sound version is the 1936 George B. Seitz film, with Randolph Scott.

[2] One historical issue concerning authorship of the film and the relationship between co-directors Tourneur and Brown must be dealt with. Brown,

Uncas (Albert Roscoe), Cora Munro (Barbara Bedford), Hawkeye (Henry Lorraine) and Chingachgook (Theodore Lerch) hold the line of defense as Heyward (Henry Woodward) looks on and Alice Munro (Lillian Hall) ministers to the wounded David Gamut (Nelson McDowell). The Last of the Mohicans *(1920)*

In *The Last of the Mohicans* Tourneur's distinct visual style is immediately recognizable. The typical Tourneur composition includes a dark foreground of silhouettes, humans, doorways, or cave entrances, to frame a highlighted middleground, which finally recedes into a dark background. The placement of actors in this three-fold layering of space is in direct relation to their dramatic importance within the shot. For example, in the Delaware council tent Tourneur puts Cora, Alice, and Heyward in the lower right foreground; Magua (left) and Uncas (right) at the edges of the middleground, and the three wise men in the middle (upper right quarter); a group of Delawares fill out the darkened background. The shot makes clear not only that the Delaware chiefs are about to decide an issue concerning the two rival warriors, but also that the women's sympathies lie with Uncas.

Tourneur's narrative dexterity is evident as he establishes the major characters. First we see Chingachgook and Uncas looking over the valley below. There is a cut to Fort Edward, and then to an interior where Cora Munro is playing the harp for a group including her sister Alice, Cora's nominal beau, the slightly effeminate Captain Randolf (created for the film), and Alice's fiancé, Major Heyward. Uncas arrives at the door with news of enemy movements, followed by shots of the renegade Indian runner, Magua, arriving with a message from Colonel Munro. Through an economical use of close-ups Tourneur establishes the central relationship between Cora and Uncas, as well as Randolf's contempt and jealousy, while his mise-en-scene confirms Magua as a primary threat by having him nearly assault the camera.

The first half of the film roughly follows the first half of the novel. We see Magua's betrayal of Heyward and the Munro women; the Huron attack near the falls; and finally, the group's rescue and safe arrival at Fort Henry; the next third of the film

---

while always acknowledging his debt to Tourneur, has usually claimed credit for much of the film. Stating that Tourneur was injured early in the shooting, he told Kevin Brownlow that, "I made the whole picture after that." The film's art director, Floyd Mueller, corroborates that Brown was responsible for all location work. But one must assume that Tourneur, as a producer-director who insisted on retaining total control, reviewed Brown's rushes daily and gave orders for the next days' shooting.

(only chapters XV to XVII in Cooper) follows Randolf's treason, the subsequent slaughter at the fort, and Magua's recapture of Cora and Alice; the last reel brings the climactic trial at the Delaware camp, the final confrontation between Uncas and Magua on the cliffs, and the burial of the lovers.

Of primary importance to Tourneur's scheme vis-à-vis the novel is the relegation of Cooper's central characters, Hawkeye and Chingachgook, to minor roles. They appear only after Magua's desertion, and are nowhere in sight during the fort intrigue or final chase. At the last moment they arrive (like avenging angels) to kill Magua and bury their dead. Of course, in the novel they take part in the chase, and Hawkeye especially is involved in the climactic battles between the Delaware and Huron camps.

Stills of Alice, Heyward, and "a bear" (Hawkeye) in a Huron tent, indicate that some of the novel's long section concerning the captivity of the Munro sisters was in fact shot. Yet all that remains of this portion, in which Hawkeye and Chingachgook play major roles, is the Delaware council scene, when Talemund awards Cora to Uncas and Alice to Magua. Tourneur necessarily plays down the roles of Hawkeye and his Indian counterpart, since his Cora Munro, and not Cooper's Hawkeye, will unite civilized and natural culture in her person. Rather than getting involved in Cooper's plot machinations, then, the director crystallizes the triangle involving Magua, Uncas, and Cora.

Tourneur's Magua is a solitary renegade inciting the other Hurons to slaughter the defenseless British. In the novel Magua, as a chief of the Hurons, acts almost always within a group (even during the life-and-death struggle on the rocks with Uncas). He is driven as much by revenge against Colonel Munro (for a whipping) as by desire for Cora. The revenge motive is dropped entirely from the film, although stills again indicate that scenes of Magua's whipping (showing Munro) were shot.

Magua finds his opposite in the aristocratic Uncas. In these two characters we see the positive and negative images of Rousseau's noble savage: one controlled by the dark demonic forces of nature, the other living by the natural codes of a civilization in harmony with the environment. Both are creatures of the forest, and show intelligence, cunning, and ingenuity. Yet whereas Uncas uses his gifts with dignity (Tourneur's Uncas, instead of Cooper's Hawkeye, shows compassion for a wounded Huron by shooting him with his last powder), Magua is obsessed by his lust for the white Munro women.

Tourneur's Europeans, Heyward and Randolf, also stand in a polar relationship. Thus, Randolf illustrates the weak, cowardly, effeminate, and degenerate European, while his positive image is found in Heyward who, in the course of the narrative, adapts himself to, and copes with, the dangers of the forest.

With Alice and Cora the polarity becomes more complex, modified by the sense that the sisters' relationship is more akin to mother and child. Alice is childlike, capricious, and totally helpless in the wilderness. Cora is adult, self-sacrificing, and strong. At the blockhouse in the forest, Magua asks Cora whether she would consent to Alice being his squaw. There is, in Barbara Bedford's performance, a sense of melancholy, an acceptance of suffering totally lacking in Lillian Hall's Alice.

In Cooper the mother-daughter relationship is modified by a degree of sexual tension between the siblings. Both are emotionally attached to Heyward, yet the fairer Alice is obviously favored. Cora's tainted racial purity (her mother was West Indian), imbuing her with a headstrong nature uncommon to white ladies, makes her apparently less desirable to whites, and conversely more attractive to the Indians. Ultimately, Cora's (and Alice's) position in Cooper's male-oriented universe remains secondary, so that even Uncas's attempt to save her on the cliffs seems more a matter of duty than sexual attraction.

In contrast, Tourneur's Cora is undoubtedly the moral center of the film around which the other characters are defined. Placing the safety of Alice above her own happiness, Cora consistently suppresses her own sexual inclinations. At the same time, as a sexually desirable woman, she becomes the catalyst for three of the major characters: her attraction to Uncas precipitates Randolf's treason and finally becomes the logic for Uncas's and Magua's mythic struggle on the rocks.

Cora's centrality to Tourneur's romance is most clearly established in her movement toward a more complete persona in harmony with both the wilderness and civilization. This evolution of her character is only alluded to in Cooper's narrative through the Indian maiden's eulogy:

> That she was of a blood purer and richer than the rest of her nation, any eye might have seen; that she was equal to the dangers and daring life in the woods, her conduct had proved. . . .

But the thought is uncomfortable for Cooper and he cannot bring his alter ego, Hawkeye, to translate the pagan song to the mourning father and sister. It is Tourneur who, through his mise-en-scene, celebrates Cora's growth and final union with the earth.

From the very beginning, Tourneur establishes specific areas of space, which not only define the central romance between Uncas and Cora, but also Cora's movement from artificial culture to a natural state. Space breaks down into a set of polarities which we may designate as inside space and outside space; safety and danger; civilization and wilderness; rationality and instinct; civil law and natural law; Europe and America.

Our first glimpse of Cora is as she plays the harp, surrounded by finely dressed ladies and officers. At the lovers' first encounter, Cora looks out the door at Uncas, who remains resolutely outside. When they spend the night by the falls, Cora again gazes at him in proud silhouette standing in the cave entrance, as the sun sets behind him. After their arrival at Fort Henry, Cora turns briefly to Randolf, but much to his chagrin, turns again to look out the window at Uncas. Later that night when the lovers chat, Uncas remains sitting outside on the window sill, while Cora stands inside. Thus, although Cora keeps her own space, her rejection of the degenerate European in favor of the natural Indian is reflected in her movement to the window, and by extension the border between civilization and nature.

The final movement occurs after we see Cora outside, and Uncas inside the Delaware tent. She must leave with Magua, while Uncas is bound by the Indian laws of sanctuary. Here, then, Cora visually steps over the invisible border between culture and nature. In the next scene she actively resists Magua by climbing the mountain—despite her premonition of doom.

In the film generally, and particularly for Cora, high space affords an unobstructed view, suggesting knowledge and certainty. It is light, the mountain, the sky, life itself. Low space, on the other hand, brings the darkness of the forests, with intonations of ambiguity and death. As Chingachgook tells Hawkeye in the novel: "I am on the hill-top, and must go down into the valley; and when Uncas follows in my footsteps, there will no longer be any of the blood of the Sagamores."

The editing of Cora's fall into the valley is extraordinary. As she sits on the cliff's edge, her face half covered by the shadow of death, Cora fights off sleep, while Magua waits with "the patience of an Indian." We cut to Uncas who sees them from far below. At the next moment Magua grabs her, as we cut to an extreme long shot of Cora dangling from the cliff's edge, at the very top of the frame. Struggling not to fall, she suddenly stops as she sees Uncas climbing up behind Magua. Magua pulls a knife and repeatedly stabs at Cora's grasping arms, while Uncas, within range but helpless, fears his least movement might jeopardize Cora. Finally, Cora's body plunges to the earth below in a silhouetted extreme long shot.

Then Magua and Uncas battle, rolling down the mountainside, over rocks, past streams, until finally Uncas is vanquished and dies grasping Cora's already cold hand. (In Cooper, Uncas and Cora die on the ledge.) At the next instant Hawkeye shoots Magua at the top of the falls, and Magua's corpse glides over and down the thunderous waterway. Thus, in different ways, all three characters fall to their death. (Ironically, the ignoble Randolf dies literally under the ground, when he hides in an ammunition dump at the fort and is blown up.)

Faced with this contrast we cannot help but acknowledge the archetypal associations that come to mind with the image of the fall. Are we to see the deaths of Cora, Uncas, and Magua as a kind of Faustian fall? What tabu have they transgressed? Perhaps Tourneur's mise-en-scene supports a thought that comes covertly from Cooper, the horror of miscegenation. Leslie Fiedler's explanation of Cooper's rationale might extend to Tourneur: "The last of the Mohicans is portrayed as the last, the Vanishing American shown to have vanished because . . . the color line is eternal and God-given."

Uncas and Cora, the noble Indian and the white maiden, are doomed for their willingness to break the tabu against race mixing. Not even the purity of their relationship, as natural lovers without a sense of guilt and sin, can change their fate. Twice Uncas must helplessly stand by while Cora's life is threatened—almost as if exterior forces really were in control.

Likewise, Magua must fall because of his indiscriminate lust for the fairer skin. Magua finds a watery grave among the fish, a fate, Cooper tells us, the mere thought of which no Indian mind can endure. Yet, while we gleefully approve of Magua's damnation, we find it difficult to accept the same harsh judgment accorded the lovers.

Ultimately, though, Tourneur celebrates what Cooper cannot: the lovers' *Liebestod*. Tourneur crosscuts between the Indian burial on the mountain, and the Christian burial of Cora in the valley. Uncas's grave is shot from a low angle against the "masculine" sky, while Cora is photographed from a high angle, her body resting in the "feminine" earth. The film ends with Chingachgook in silhouette, standing vigil by Uncas's grave and looking left to his son and the past (a mirror image of the film's first shot). He utters Talemund's immortal words: "In the morning I saw the sons of Unamis happy and strong; and yet, before night has come, have I lived to see the last of the Mohicans."

By 1920 the genocide of the American Indian was a *fait accompli*; thus, the proud figure of Chingachgook stands as a true symbol of the sole survivor—emerging alone from both history and the complex mise-en-scene of *The Last of the Mohicans*, Maurice Tourneur's greatest achievement.

The Scarlet Letter (1850), Nathaniel Hawthorne

"Triumphant Ignominy" on the Screen

BY MARK W. ESTRIN

Henry James recalls, in his well-known analysis of Hawthorne's fiction, that as a child he had been deemed too young to read *The Scarlet Letter*, about which so many adults were talking. He wondered how a letter—thinking of "one of the documents that come by the post"—could be of such a strange color. But the mystery of Hester's A was partially clarified by a visit to the National Academy to see an exhibition of paintings, where the young James encountered

> a representation of a pale, handsome woman, in a quaint black dress and a white coif, holding between her knees an elfish-looking little girl, fantastically dressed and crowned with flowers. Embroidered on the woman's breast was a great crimson A, over which the child's fingers, as she glanced strangely out of the picture, were maliciously playing. I was told that this was Hester Prynne and little Pearl. . . . [T]he picture remained vividly imprinted in my mind. I had been vaguely frightened and made uneasy by it; and when, years afterwards, I first read the novel, I seemed to myself to have read it before and to be familiar with its two strange heroines.
>
> *Hawthorne*

Editors' title. This is an abridged and revised version of " 'Triumphant Ignominy': *The Scarlet Letter on Screen*," by Mark W. Estrin, which originally appeared in *Literature/Film Quarterly*, Vol. 2, No. 2, Spring 1974, pp. 110–122. Reprinted by permission.

This reminiscence offers more insight into Hawthorne's art than James might have thought in that precinematic era. For the painted image that so impinged on the child's consciousness, and remained with him as an adult reader and critic, suggests why certain sections of the novel, resembling as they do tableaux or static pictures, often remind us of a photographic sensibility.

Indeed, the novel may be approached as a series of visual, dramatizable images or scenes reflected through the consciousness of a cameralike observer. Citing Hawthorne's use of the mirror in the novelist's own introduction to the book, Richard Chase suggests that Hawthorne's "fictions are mirror-like. They give a static and pictorial version of reality" (*The American Novel and Its Tradition*, 1957). One thinks of moments among the most penetrating in the novel: the three scenes on the scaffold; Hester, Pearl, and Dimmesdale in the forest; Dimmesdale contemplating the meteor as a great red A. These episodes are successful illustrations (literally) of what James regards as Hawthorne's obsessive search "for images which shall place themselves in picturesque correspondence with the spiritual facts with which he is concerned."

Such sequences are translatable, in the hands of an effective director and his skilled photographer, into cinematic terms. In Victor Sjöström's* 1926 silent film version of *The Scarlet Letter*, these static moments photographed out of time, without dialogue, provide the most satisfying scenes. If, as Harry Levin claims in *The Power of Blackness* (1958), "the interrelationship between open shame and secret guilt in *The Scarlet Letter* is dramatized by a tense alteration of public tableaux and private interview," then the scenes that linger longest from this "moving" picture are those that recreate Hawthorne's resonant but static tableaux, without resort to cinematic motion or montage. Like the scaffold scenes, they are in fact still-lifes made coherent and artful by the composition, the sharpness of blacks and whites and the expressions on the faces of the actors.

* The Swedish emigré Sjöström directed in America as Victor Seastrom between 1923 and 1930. Afterward he returned to Sweden as an actor for a career culminating in the role of the aging professor in Ingmar Bergman's *Wild Strawberries* (1957). He died in 1960 at the age of eighty.

Consider as an example that moment in chapter XIX, "The Child at the Brookside," when Hester and Dimmesdale watch Pearl playing on the far side of the brook. Two people, whose guilty secret we share, sit and watch their daughter as both the manifestation of that secret and of something strangely beautiful, too. The scene as conceived by Hawthorne is designed in terms that would not be alien to a camera. Hester and Dimmesdale sit and watch "Pearl's slow advance" toward them.

. . . Pearl had reached the margin of the brook, and stood on the farther side, gazing silently at Hester and the clergyman, who still sat together on the mossy tree trunk, waiting to receive her. Just where she had paused the brook chanced to form a pool so smooth and quiet that it reflected a perfect image of her little figure with all the brilliant picturesqueness of her beauty, in its adornment of flowers and wreathed foliage. . . .

Pearl fixes "her bright wild eyes" on her mother and father; Dimmesdale moves his hand over his heart in habitual, involuntary gesture; Pearl points her outstretched arm toward her mother's breast and that image in turn is mirrored in the brook. In Sjöström's film, the sequence above from Chapter XIX is combined in a single scene with the contents of chapters XVII and XVIII, and includes the revelation from chapter XX that Hester intends to leave with Dimmesdale and Pearl for the Old World aboard a Spanish ship. Dimmesdale (Lars Hanson) reports that he is too ill, too broken to go. "We shall be with thee," responds Hester in a title, as she removes the A from her breast, and, in essentially the same words that appear in chapter XVIII, avows "With this symbol I undo the past and make it as if it had never been." The camera holds on her as she takes off, in Hawthorne's words, the "formal cap that confined her hair." Hester and Dimmesdale embrace, Lillian Gish as Hester looking lovely as her hair falls upon her shoulders. Pearl plays at the brookside as Hester puts the A back on, and both of her parents watch her until the sequence ends. Although the scene at the brookside is quite brief, drastically synopsizing the events of three chapters, it is hauntingly beautiful and oddly faithful to

Hester Prynne (Lillian Gish) cradles the dying Reverend Dimmesdale (Lars Hanson) on the scaffold as Pearl (Joyce Coad) and the townspeople watch. The Scarlet Letter *(1926).*

the exquisite visual sense of Hawthorne. Thoughts unspoken are revealed in the faces and vivid gestures of the characters and, in Chase's terms, by the "mirror-like" portrayals of a camera viewing persons in turn viewing others.

But the scene has a jarring note, one that typifies the nature of the film's difficulties as an adaptation. Not only do we see Hester and Dimmesdale watching Pearl, we also observe Roger Chillingworth (Henry B. Walthall), undetected by the others, watching the three of them. The intrusion of Chillingworth into this tableau is not intended to explore some further cinematic delineation of mirror images. He is used solely for purposes of turning the plot. Chillingworth must be present in this scene in order to overhear Hester's plans for the escape and, thereby, to raise the audience's expectations that he may "foil" these plans. As a "movie-villain" antagonist to Hester and Dimmesdale, he possesses none of the complexity of the novel's characterization. And the adaptation slips away from faithfulness toward simplistic genre formula.

How else to explain the fact that Chillingworth does not make his entrance until approximately two-thirds of the film have elapsed? His identity and a hint of the transformed role he must play are immediately revealed. When he signs the official account of his captivity by the Indians, the camera shows us the page as he writes "Roger Pr—," breaks off, crosses out the beginning of Prynne, and writes Chillingworth over the name. No attempt is made to develop Hawthorne's subtlety of characterization; we are not even made conscious during the course of the film that Chillingworth has, after all, been at the wrong end of Hester's unfaithfulness. Hawthorne, in potently conveying Chillingworth's diabolical methods, also makes it clear that this is not simply an evil man. An *idée fixe* has ballooned within him from which he cannot be set free "until he has done all its bidding." He changes from his entrance in the novel as a "calm, meditative, scholar-like" figure, until he becomes "a striking evidence of man's faculty of transforming himself into a devil, if he will only, for a reasonable space of time, undertake a devil's office." Allotted a brief appearance in the film, Chillingworth can only be seen therein as a one-dimensional, formulaic malefactor.

Indeed, the first forty minutes of the film seem shaped by similar exigencies of formula. The movie's opening section details events that never take place in *The Scarlet Letter*, in effect providing a "beginning" for a story that starts *in medias res*. Not only is the chronology straightened out for the sake of simplicity, but screenwriter Frances Marion makes the narrative a more conventionalized love story by providing the background of how our hero and heroine had come to meet and mate. For a novel that is in an important sense about the concealment of emotion, the film substitutes courtship rituals; Hester and Dimmesdale's clandestine romance becomes boy-meets-girl.

Put in stocks for "running and playing on the sabbath," Hester is given water by the kind reverend. He soon releases her and walks her home. Their next encounter is set in motion by a camera shot of a law in the statute books forbidding the public display of undergarments. Hester is then shown washing clothes in the privacy of the woods. Along comes Dimmesdale. She tries to run away, while hiding her underclothes, but a bemused Dimmesdale, pretending to be stern, orders her to stop. Soon they are hand in hand, walking into the woods. Hester tells him, "It would be pleasant, sir, to walk beside thee and hear thee condemn me for my sins"; she ultimately confesses her love for him and tells the minister not to feel guilty about any feelings he holds for her. He promptly makes the admission toward which the entire sequence has built: "Hester, I have fought against it but I love thee." They embrace. The touches of humor work surprisingly well in the context of this sympathetic love story. Miss Gish and Lars Hanson—despite occasional resemblance to poor waifs being pursued by a villainous monster—are quite winning. Yet the tone of the scene remains alien to our literary expectations.

Another quite remarkable scene further illustrates the dual feelings evoked by this adaptation. Dimmesdale has come to ask for Hester's hand in marriage. He is being sent to England as emissary to the King and wants her to accompany him. At this point, she confesses to him (and us) her earlier matrimony. Dimmesdale angrily chastises her, while, on her knees and kissing his hands, she pleads for his forgiveness. As he begins to stalk out of the house, Hester emphatically defends herself: her father forced her to marry a wealthy surgeon; he has not been heard from for years; she never loved him and told him so; she was never a *wife* to him. Dimmesdale relents, holds her as they sit before a flickering fire. We are given a shot of a town crier outside, a striking black figure against the snow, announcing that all is well. When shortly thereafter, Dimmesdale leaves, Hester rushes after him but stops abruptly. The camera focuses upon her as, silhouetted against the snow, she watches Dimmesdale going off, another dark figure against the white ground. Dejected, she re-enters the house and the scene fades. Boy still loses girl, but the visual power of the sequence transcends the banality of the conventionalized action.

That this scene is moving is the more astonishing in light of the one-dimensional, melodramatic characterizations. The Hester of the film lacks any real toughness; Dimmesdale, more seriously, is softened into a man who does wrong only by chance, not because of his lack of backbone. Not only does Dimmesdale offer to marry Hester early in their extratextual relationship, but upon his return from England, learning that Hester is in prison for having given birth to his child, he rushes into her cell and *demands* that he be allowed to stand with her on the scaffold. "Thou hast no right to tear down ideals of thy followers who look to thee for guidance," she answers, adding that she wants him to atone for both of them through his good work. Although he remains silent during the effective scaffold scene which follows (the point at which the novel begins), this Dimmesdale genuinely wants Hester to tell the truth. The film offers no gradation of Dimmesdale's torment and guilt, just as there is no progression in the development of Chillingworth's vengeance. Without any warning, with half the film over, Dimmesdale becomes instantly riddled by remorse.

The flattening of the major characters gives way to outright caricature in the supporting roles of the Puritans. If the reader of *The Scarlet Letter* is occasionally permitted to feel morally superior to the Puritan community whose rigidity forms the backdrop for the novel's drama, he still perceives that this specific historical context might be enlarged to envelop any society and any age. The Puritans in the film, however, are delineated in the clearest derogatory terms. They are foolish and contemptuous and "bad" for wanting to take Hester's baby from her. Typically, an obnoxious town gossip, Mistress Hibbins (who bears no resemblance to the "reputed witch lady" of the novel), is given a sound ducking in the village pond by Giles the barber, a stock figure of comic relief. Hawthorne's Puritans could never be the butt of such an audience-pleasing joke. The actions of Hester and Dimmesdale must be understood as growing out of Puritan culture and its moral outlook; they should not be romanticized as the antithesis of a vicious and silly society. As Richard Chase observes, "the moral and psychological results of sin—the isolation and morbidity, the distortion and thwarting of the emotional life . . . results not of man's living in sin but of his living in a Puritan society, and thereby, to some extent, in *any* society."

Even the use of titles to represent dialogue moves the film necessarily toward melodrama. Because of the need to condense events (even more acute in a silent film, where the titles must be kept to a minimum and must be printed in groups of no more than two or three sentences), Hawthorne's characters become like the figures in comic strips who always speak in exclamatory declarations and in sentences packed with punch. Thus what might in the original text be several lines that encompass melodramatic elements seems, in the film titles, to be melodrama only because the fuller context and accompanying distancing by the narrator have been stripped away.

By the end of the novel, when he confronts Dimmesdale on the scaffold, Chillingworth's language has descended to outright villainy: " 'Hadst thou sought the whole earth over . . . there was no one place so secret,—no high place nor lowly place, where thou couldst have escaped me,—save on this very scaffold!' " As Dimmesdale expires, his head supported against Hester's bosom, the physician repeats several times, " 'Thou hast escaped me!' "

Just before Dimmesdale mounts the scaffold in the final minutes of the film, Chillingworth tells Dimmesdale: "The ship that takes thee and Hester away takes *me*; I shall always follow thee." These are his last lines in the film. The further dialogue of Chillingworth is omitted. As the movie villain he is "foiled," his function completed, so Chillingworth's becomes but another face in the crowd while the focus of attention shifts back to hero and heroine.

Hester and Dimmesdale, in the film's closing moments, are pushed to vociferous melodramatics (but again, this is tempered by the visual depth and aura evident in the movie's other "tableau" scenes). As Dimmesdale collapses in Hester's arms, she shouts that he is innocent, that his mind is unbalanced. He bares his chest and shows the A quite literally carved into his skin. Totally distraught, he falls to the ground, still cradled by Hester, and lies in her lap as she calls for a doctor. "I love thee so," she tells him, "I cannot face life without thee." "That is as God wills and God is merciful," he answers. He touches the A on her dress and it comes off in his hand. "Is this not better freedom than any we have dreamed of?" he asks her, to which she responds with a kiss as he dies. The camera shifts to Giles, the barber, whose previously estranged girlfriend takes his arm in a fleeting but obtrusive gesture of reconciliation; the crowd doffs its hats out of respect to their dead minister, and the film is over.

With its additions of extraneously coy and comic scenes, its softening of Dimmesdale and gross simplification of Chillingworth, its extractions of the most exaggerated bits of dialogue from the novel—or insertions of completely new dialogue—the film misses the mark. And yet, it remains a significant event in our cinematic past. It is true that the very ambiguities with which Hawthorne structures his novel—and which he defines in his preface to *The House of the Seven Gables* as prerequisite for romance—have been resolved in favor of conventionalized solutions. But the movie keeps surprising us, especially when those moments in the novel described by Richard Chase as "frozen, muted and remote" are transformed legitimately into cinematic terms.

At its best, Sjöström's *Scarlet Letter* reminds us of the way in which the young James identified the pictorial brilliance of this novel. At its worst, it recalls, in its confusion of Hawthorne's idea of the romance with Hollywood's notion of the romantic, something James Agee once wrote: "Most movies are made in the evident assumption that the audience is passive and wants to remain passive; every effort is made to do all the work—the seeing, the explaining, the understanding, even the feeling" (*Agee on Film: Reviews and Comments* [1958]). Accordingly, into the scenario for this adaptation went "background" material which reduces the mysterious to the rationally explainable, thereby allowing the audience to retain a sense of what is visually moving, while it remains morally unmoved. This film version of *The Scarlet Letter* entertains by providing bright images to remember— particularly in Gish's luminous performance—without offering dark truths to ponder.

The House of the Seven Gables (1851),
Nathaniel Hawthorne

Hawthorne's "Fancy Pictures" on Film

BY E. ANN KAPLAN

With *The Scarlet Letter* (1850), Nathaniel Hawthorne rested his study of the Puritan past that had preoccupied him in the tales. In *The House of the Seven Gables* (1851), he began to pursue an interest in the American present. But he was faced immediately with two interlocking problems: first, how to find an authentic language and literary style to write about the present since the predominant American form—the romance, with its morbid exaltation of time gone by—seemed unsuitable. (The standard literary conventions hedged in a writer as much as did social traditions, preventing fresh explorations of lived reality.) Second, how was he to resolve his own conflicting attitudes toward the past? Hawthorne valued certain traditions and institutions and wished to retain them, yet he also desired to overthrow outmoded values and social forms that lay like a stifling weight upon the present.

In attempting solutions for his problems in *Seven Gables*, Hawthorne tended to distance himself from the old conventions at the very time he was employing them anew within his text. He thus strove to expose their limitations. However, as his prefaces show, he was uneasy about what he was doing, fearing that his efforts would be judged negatively. In theory then, Hawthorne still clung to the romance, claiming allegiance to a form that gives the writer the freedom "to manage his atmospherical medium as to bring out or mellow the lights and deepen and enrich the shadows of the picture." And he ostensibly rejected the novelistic form because it would contaminate his romance "by bringing the fancy pictures almost into positive contact with the realities of the moment" (preface to *The House of the Seven Gables*). In practice, of course, there were more realist elements in his work than Hawthorne himself suggested. Romance is mingled with realism, the mixture reflecting Hawthorne's struggle to understand the nature of reality and how it can be captured in fiction. By transcending the romance or any other single literary mode, Hawthorne prepared the way for realism without writing realistic novels himself.

The House of the Seven Gables, as a result, functions as both novel *and* romance, each distinct literary mode presenting one side of a conflicting attitude toward the past. It will be easier to show how this formulation works in the novel after becoming familiar with the larger shape of the plot.

The novel concerns an old New England family, the Pyncheons, who trace their ancestry back to Colonial times. The narrative follows the continuing conflict between the respected Pyncheons and the humble Maules. In the sixteenth century, Colonel Pyncheon had seized the land of carpenter Matthew Maule solely because the colonel had determined that it was the right location for his family mansion. Fearing reprisals, Colonel Pyncheon had Maule executed as a witch, illicitly using his authority to cover his misdeeds. Maule reputedly cast a curse on the Pyncheons before he died, and on the day of the opening of the House of the Seven Gables, the colonel is discovered dead in his chair with blood all over his beard and "the print of a bloody hand on his plaited ruff." From that time on, the Pyncheons had rarely experienced good fortune, and often died in the same inexplicable manner as their ancestor.

After the first chapter, which reprises the past, the bulk of the novel takes place in Hawthorne's present. The major characters are the descendents of the Pyncheons on the one hand, and Holgrave, last descendent of the Maules, on the other. There is Jaffrey, the chief heir of the Pyncheon family, obsessed with finding an old claim to land that Matthew Maule was said to have hidden in revenge for the seizure of his land; Clifford, Jaffrey's cousin, who, as a result of Jaffrey's treachery, has languished in jail for thirty years, framed by Jaffrey for his uncle's murder; Hepzibah, Clifford's sister, who has lived alone many years in Seven Gables, working for Clifford's freedom and withering away while awaiting his return; and Holgrave, a daguerreotypist who is taken in as a lodger by Hepzibah and who is involved in radical causes. Significantly, as the last of the Maules, Holgrave is the main character in opposition to the Pyncheons.

Also counterpoised to the Pyncheons is Phoebe, who though their distant relative, stands untainted, committed to the present and to undoing the evils of the past. Although connected to the feuding families, Holgrave and Phoebe don't belong to their worlds; and together they stand in contrast to the wickedness of the old order. Most of the novel, then, concerns itself with establishing every character's place in the Pyncheon-Maule feud and articulating their subsequent points of view regarding the relative values of past and present. The climax of the novel occurs when Jaffrey attempts to force Clifford, finally released from jail, to give him the lost deed to the Pyncheon land. As he awaits Clifford's appearance, Jaffrey dies choked in blood in true Pyncheon fashion. Phoebe and Holgrave discover him, and the end of the curse—actually a form of hereditary stroke—is symbolized in the union of the two young people.

This literal plotline allowed Hawthorne to express his contradictory attitudes to the past, and to raise issues related to fictional style. There is, to begin with, the attitude represented by the Pyncheon family, which is essentially a providential notion of the Christian pattern of sin and redemption working itself out through the history of man, while institutions and social organization are regarded as fixed and divinely ordered. This first view of history, familiar from the historical romance, is fittingly expressed through the gothic literary mode.

A second view of history, represented primarily by Holgrave in *Seven Gables*, developed out of nineteenth-century transcendentalism in its relationship to Jeffersonian ideas. Romantic reformers, following Jefferson, attacked the whole idea of inheri-

Two faces of the Pyncheons, Jaffrey (George Sanders) and an ancestral look-alike. The House of the Seven Gables (*1940*).

tance (literally and figuratively). Their optimism about America's future was linked to an impatience about ties with Europe and the past it represented. Fittingly, Hawthorne used the mode of realism for the characters connected with this view.

The two literary modes and differing manners of interpreting reality exist side by side in the novel, linked by a complex structure of imagery. The first chapter surveys the Pyncheon family from the sixteenth century to the middle of the nineteenth and establishes Hawthorne's procedure. On the one hand, there is reverence and awe for the past, presented as shadowy, mysterious and sinister, with a heightened sense of doom pervading the house and its inhabitants, the Pyncheons. The gothic atmosphere precipitates (perhaps) the eerie and preternatural death of Colonel Pyncheon, and the narrator points out with relish such items as the strange mirror in the house that supposedly reflects images of all the departed Pyncheons "not as they had shown themselves to the world . . . but as doing over some deed of sin. . . ." The writing is purely in the romance mode. Hawthorne brilliantly evoked a mood of terror and doom as he would do again toward the end, in the chapters describing the death of Jaffrey.

But at the same time he created a gothic atmosphere, Hawthorne had his narrator undercut the voice of awe, reverence, and excitement about the past by presenting a rational, commonsense, and political alternative. The narrator questions the fantastic events he has just described so vividly, suggesting that it is all mere rumor, and that the events may be accounted for in rational terms. He also takes an ironic stance toward the Pyncheons and their despicable treatment of the Maules, so that doubt is cast on their role as societal leaders and on the institutions that they uphold. The Pyncheons emerge, through this voice, as hypocrites who abuse their power and oppress the innocent. Privilege and inherited rank are ridiculed so that the reader finally must question the whole concept of accepted authority.

A series of character confrontations extends the contrast of past and present beyond the first chapter. Hepzibah, described as "a dark-arrayed, pale-faced, ladylike old figure," represents the decaying gentility of old-line New England. She is pitted against Holgrave, who stands for radical notions—democracy, freedom, and the overthrow of tradition. When contrasted with Phoebe, Hepzibah represents the decadence of the old way of life, pathetic in her "rustling and rusty silks, with her deeply cherished and ridiculous consciousness of long descent, her shadowy claims to princely territory."[1] Phoebe is by comparison "like a bird in a shadowy tree" when living at Seven Gables. Hepzibah's narrow rigidity is complemented by her brother Clifford's aestheticism—from Hawthorne's point of view the most positive aspect of the old order and the one he is most reluctant to see disappear.

Within the aristocratic old guard there is a subtle separating off of Hepzibah and Clifford on one side, and Jaffrey Pyncheon on the other. Of all the Pyncheons, Jaffrey is most related to evil and the supernatural, and is also most severely judged on the socio-political level for his gross materialism and hypocrisy. Holgrave and Phoebe are together offset against all the older Pyncheons; only visitors at the House of Seven Gables, they confront the entrenched decadence of the longtime denizens. Representing "intellect" and "heart" respectively, they form a strong barrier against the prevailing decrepitude and malevolence. Fulfilling the expectations of gothic romance, they rid the house of the curse that has plagued it when they marry. But their union also has realist-political implications, for it re-establishes the Maules's rights to the property and vindicates them after years of illicit oppression.

Thus, in *The House of the Seven Gables*, Hawthorne established a precarious balance between the novel as a form of social criticism and the romance with its providential acceptance of the status quo as divinely ordained. He dealt with the Pyncheons as an historical family of a privileged class at the top of the hierarchically ordered community; but he also conceived of the Pyncheons in gothic terms, placing them within a sinister and

[1] With the description of Hepzibah, as with that of Jaffrey, Hawthorne's ambiguity about the value of tradition is evident. He is impressed with the grandeur and antiquity of the Pyncheons, but ridicules their pomposity, insensitivity, and rigidity.

mysterious world whose chief image is their foreboding house—as gloomy and otherworldly as any castle in gothic novels. Hawthorne's stance, apart from the process of the fiction making, focused attention on the devices of the romance form and set this mode up against the pragmatic, unheightened, and more realistic vision that Holgrave represents. While allowing us to see how the imagination may be used to render things mysterious, awesome, and dramatically depicted in hectic colors, Hawthorne also showed us that this may be neither the only, nor even the best manner of perception.

The year 1940, when Joe May made *The House of the Seven Gables* at Universal, is a fascinating time in film history, since it represents a bridge between the essentially optimistic realist style of the Roosevelt thirties and the "black" cynical realism of the war and postwar forties (now being termed the *noir* style). Films made in 1940 often seem tenuous and schizophrenic, as though the director is trying to retain the optimism of the thirties while knowing in his heart that it will not work. Sometimes this intuitive sense of a worsening future intrudes on the visual style. The lighting begins to darken, with looming shadows and asymmetrical composition within the frame; the plot may change unexpectedly from lighthearted and frothy to pessimistic and somber.[2]

Looking at Hawthorne's novel in 1940, Joe May and his scenarist, Lester Cole, may have sensed that *Seven Gables* could fall one of two ways: they could choose to emphasize the supernatural, fantastic elements of the novel, or stress its more realistic, socio-political aspects. Given Universal's position as the studio of horror—*Dracula* (1931), *Frankenstein* (1931), and all the others—and given May's background in German film and work in thrillers and science fiction (he had already made *The Invisible Man Returns* in 1940), one might have supposed the production would lean toward the gothic elements in Hawthorne's novel.

[2] Raoul Walsh's *Strawberry Blonde* (1940) fits this formula instructively. The film starts as light period comedy, until Jimmy Cagney is framed and sent to jail unjustly (a situation repeated with Clifford's jailing in *Seven Gables*). Of course, Welles's *Citizen Kane* (1941) links realism and expressionism in the depiction of Kane's life, and represents one of the few films that achieves a synthesis of these modes in the period.

May (Joseph Mandel) was one of a long line of German and Austrian-born directors who worked in Germany during the "golden age" of the expressionist period, but found their way to Hollywood in the thirties as Hitler came to power. In the Germany of 1911, May had become his own director-producer with the Continental Art Film Company, where he discovered Fritz Lang and employed him as actor and scenarist. Later May was to give Conrad Veidt, Lya de Putti, and Emil Jannings their first big screen roles. In the 1920s he had his own studio and received offers from Hollywood; after several refusals, he finally came to study American production methods in the late twenties. Then, in the early thirties, he took a contract with Universal where he made films in diverse genres—musicals, mysteries, "message" films, and Dead End Kids potboilers, and labored in an obscurity out of keeping with his prominence in Germany.

Despite his expressionist background, May chose to stress the social and political levels of *The House of the Seven Gables*. (At times though, his visuals lean toward a dark and shadowy style that belies the film's optimistic notion that social justice triumphs in the end.) May's move to the social instead of the supernatural may have been influenced by screenwriter Cole, a man known for his political beliefs and, later in the decade, for his membership among the unlucky "Hollywood Ten," jailed for being uncooperative Congressional witnesses in the search for Communists in the movie industry.

May and Cole effected many changes in the novel to conform to thirties formulas and commercial expectations, as well as to make manifest the political content they wished to emphasize. To begin with plot, Hepzibah became the cousin of Jaffrey and Clifford's lover instead of sister, while Clifford was changed into Jaffrey's brother. This increased the romantic interest in the film by making two of the major characters eligible mates; the competition of Jaffrey and Clifford was also intensified as sibling rivalry. As another concession, the novel's chronology was collapsed to preserve the attractiveness of Clifford and Hepzibah, who never age to the degree they do in Hawthorne.

The changes in narrative structure are not so out of keeping with Hawthorne's tone and mood, and are justifiable inasmuch as Hawthorne's complex pattern of symbolic confrontations was

unlikely to work in film. May substituted a simple, logical structure for the original complex one: he took the latest parts of the
historical account in the first chapter—beginning in 1828—and
simply started the action there, enacting events that are merely
described by the narrator in the original. The film thus falls neatly
into three sections: the period before Clifford's fight with his
father (his uncle in the novel); the period of his subsequent trial,
conviction, and jailing for murder; and the period following his
return from prison to Seven Gables. It is only in the film's central
section that anything approaching the novel's meditative and
symbolical dimensions are attained. But even here, as in the rest
of the movie, May's real focus is on the literal action of the novel
that corresponds with his social concerns.

May and Cole were bold in inventing scenes to buttress the
social commentary of their work. In the film, the dispute between
Clifford and his father the Judge about selling Seven Gables to
pay debts turns into a conflict of life styles and values. Clifford
is presented as a musician,[3] full of vitality, and longing to go to
Europe to be among artists who share his enthusiasms. Judge
Pyncheon is embittered and rigid, a believer in upholding tradition at all costs. In an interesting scene a crowd of local people,
viewed from the vantage of an open window in Seven Gables,
gather to watch father and son quarrel. (This scene and others
showing the house, streets, and people of the town prefigures
Welles's *Magnificent Ambersons* (1942) in the use of a "chorus"
of townspeople commenting on the action and in its emphasis
on locale.) At the high point of their quarrel, Judge Pyncheon
has a seizure and dies upon the spot. Jaffrey comes in, and, within
hearing of all outside, holds Clifford responsible for the death.
Enraged and unheeding of the hard, intolerant faces seen through
the window, Clifford grasps Jaffrey by the neck and threatens to
strangle him if he dare make such an accusation of murder again.

An effective trial scene (discussed later) in which Clifford is
unjustly found guilty for his father's murder is followed by a

---

[3] Incidentally, the music Clifford is playing in an early scene has an anachronistic swingtime beat that fits in nicely with the optimistic thirties sections
of the film. It is quite anomalous, however, to see Vincent Price's Clifford
in Victorian attire, sitting in a colonial setting, pounding out light jazz.

further addition to the novel, an episode of Clifford in prison. We
see a jail corridor in long shot, the lighting, the bars, and the
black-clothed policemen recalling the portentous atmosphere of
Lang's *You Only Live Once* (1937). A young man, struggling
against his captors, is brought into a cell wherein we see Clifford,
now aged considerably. The man turns out to be Holgrave,
Maule's descendent, and he is agitated about his arrest, declaring
that "the prison is not yet built than can stifle man's cry for freedom." He goes on to decry his imprisonment "for the crime of
defending freedom in a land that stood for freedom." It turns
out that Holgrave is an abolitionist who asserts that his group
will remind Americans of their heritage. Clifford shares his in-
dignation because, as he says, he "stood before a jury whose mind
was made up before it stood." Eventually, understanding that
they are descendents of families who have been at odds for cen-
turies, they shake hands in delight, implying that they will work
together to end the feud. In fact, their alliance will bring about
the denouement in the film rather than the union of Holgrave
and Phoebe as in the novel.

The middle section of the film, set at Seven Gables while Clifford is in jail, starts, at least stylistically, to undercut the socio-
political mode that has preceded it. This portion of the movie
picks up some of Hawthorne's gothic elements (and, interestingly,
seems the least dated part of the film today). One senses here
that May was working with a congenial visual style. A scene that
marks the transition to a somber mood occurs after Hepzibah
learns unexpectedly that she and not Jaffrey has inherited Seven
Gables. She pushes Jaffrey out of the house and sets about closing
all the shutters, as if the broad light of day was too painful to
endure during Clifford's imprisonment. We see people gathering
outside to watch (the "chorus" again), then we catch her inside,
the bars of a shutter across her in shadow as she bends down to
open a trunk and caress the folds of a dress obviously intended
for her abortive wedding to Clifford.

Another effective sequence follows: a montage marking the
passage of time while Clifford is away. The house is shown in
various seasons, decaying rapidly. A winter scene is particularly
memorable. Snow falls lightly on a fallen shutter that is quickly

embedded in white, a fitting corollary for the desolation of Hepzibah and Clifford. (The image reminds one uncannily of the snow falling on young Kane's sled in Welles's still future *Citizen Kane*.) The mailman is seen in several shots taking and leaving letters to and from Clifford, his horse carriage replaced by a sledge as the seasons change. The entire atmosphere of this montage evokes feelings of loneliness, and the despair of lost time (and again prefigures the mood of much of *Citizen Kane*).

The scene where Clifford returns at night from prison (one of the best in the film) recalls the earlier sequence where the young Hepzibah put aside her wedding gown. The paired scenes express the pain of lost opportunity, separation, and departed romance. A series of cuts between Hepzibah in her darkened room, again pulling out the wedding gown, now in shreds, and Clifford sitting at the piano unable to play a note, present a poignant moment.

In the final section of the film that follows Clifford's return, the mood brightens and there is a rather jarring return to the predominance of the social themes of the start. Holgrave, now living in Seven Gables, is shown at a meeting of an antislavery society (another added scene). In place of Holgrave's developing relationship with Phoebe in Hawthorne's novel, we see him overtly engaged in radical activities. The addition of a subplot implicating Jaffrey as a financier of the slave trade and subverter of the abolitionist group renders him even more despicable than in the novel. When his treachery is revealed, Jaffrey succumbs to apoplexy. He dies as did all his Pyncheon forbears.

A quick cut to the double wedding of Holgrave and Phoebe and Clifford and Hepzibah ties things up neatly. The union of the older couple provides real satisfaction after their long separation. The two couples leave the House of Seven Gables forever and go off to a country home. The happy ending concludes the socio-political thrust of the movie. The middle pessimistic section is completely repressed, and the film never addresses itself to the providential working out of the Pyncheon curse, central to the novel's exploration of conflicting views of the past.

Only on occasion is May able to effect a mingling of modes that is such a crucial part of what Hawthorne attempts. A rare sustained example is the courtroom scene where Clifford is unjustly sentenced for his father's death. The rigid design of the mise-en-scene seems to represent tradition and the stolidity of entrenched power. May has two huge windows in the rear of the frame spilling diffuse light into the room, while, in the foreground, the intolerant townspeople are arranged in dark clothes against the light walls. Two candles flickering on the magistrate's desk add a note of insecurity to the otherwise impassive scene. The legitimacy of this bastion of the establishment is shattered by the director's sympathetic focus on Clifford's outcry against injustice. (One can surmise that his speech might have pleased both May and Cole, the refugee from Nazi Germany and the American leftist, especially in light of the Nazi successes at the beginning of the 1940s.)

But the gothic-realist synthesis of the courtroom sequence is rare. May's film has its visually arresting moments and holds fascinating social, political, and cinematic implications for its time. But in the last resort, it has only partly to do with Hawthorne. For May's and Cole's unambiguous stand for democracy and against tradition, power, and privilege emerges precisely because they omit the notion of evil working itself out through time according to divine, rather than human will. But the omission eliminates the ambiguity that enriches Hawthorne's fiction. Hawthorne shows past and present, existing together and vying for dominance and value. As Holgrave perhaps dimly understands at the end of the novel, there is a complex dialectical relationship between past and present, so that the past informs the present as surely as the present moves on beyond the past.

Moby Dick (1851), Herman Melville

An Interview with Ray Bradbury

BY THOMAS ATKINS

John Huston's *Moby Dick*, for which Ray Bradbury wrote the script, is a flawed but valuable attempt to adapt a classic work of American fiction to the screen. Two earlier Hollywood adaptations, *The Sea Beast* (1926) and *Moby Dick* (1930), have little to recommend them aside from the fact that both feature John Barrymore as the one-legged whale hunter. But the Huston-Bradbury collaboration is the first serious effort to capture on celluloid the authentic spirit of Melville's novel.

Released in 1956 as a big-budget epic, Huston's film was three years in the making, including one for research and writing, another for shooting, and then an additional year for editing and scoring. In this interview Bradbury discusses the experience of working with the director and the creative ordeal of condensing the original 1,200 pages of outlines and screenplay to the final 140–150 pages used for the actual shooting script.

"Our biggest problem," Huston has said of the adaptation, "was to turn Melville's expositional passages into characteristic dialogue.... While *Moby Dick* has some tremendous action sequences it has little actual plot. For dramatic purposes we had to make some changes in Melville's construction.... Ray and I tried to be

From "The Illustrated Man: An Interview with Ray Bradbury," by Thomas R. Atkins, *Sight and Sound*, Vol. 43, No. 2, Spring 1974. Reprinted by permission. With a new introduction.

as faithful to the meaning of the book as our own understanding and the special demands of the movie medium would allow." A small Irish port served as New Bedford in the 1840s, and an 110-foot squarerigger was equipped like the *Pequod*. Huston shot as much as possible on location in order to give the film a realistic sense of being at sea; several times, while filming in stormy weather, the *Pequod* was nearly lost. Whaling scenes were filmed at Madeira, using Portuguese fishermen who still hunt from longboats in the Atlantic. The leviathan was created at Elstree Studios near London; life-size sections of the whale and small-scale models were filmed in a specially constructed water tank.

Oswald Morris was responsible for the cinematography, which is often stunning. In an attempt to give the picture "a harder texture" than that provided by ordinary technicolor, Huston experimented with a processing technique that involved overlaying a color shot on a black-and-white duplicate of the shot. Consequently, many sequences have the sharp, well-defined look of an engraving.

Orson Welles gives a brief yet memorable performance as Father Mapple. Richard Basehart is effective as the narrator Ishmael. As many critics have pointed out, Gregory Peck is too soft to convey the demonic aspect of the obsessed Ahab. Bradbury feels that the role should have been taken by an actor like Laurence Olivier, who is capable of portraying a truly frightening madness. The critic Andrew Sarris, on the other hand, suggests that Ahab should have been played by Huston himself and that Welles should have directed the movie.

Moby Dick earned Huston the New York Film Critics Award for Best Director, and he ranks the film among his most important accomplishments. Describing the adaptation as "almost magnificent," Bradbury remarks that he and Huston aimed to combine "the Shakespearean approach which is pure language and the cinematic approach which is pure image." He adds: "It is a pretty good blend. It almost worked."

The film's conclusion, which is different from the ending of Melville's novel, appears to have influenced Peter Benchley's novel *Jaws*. Just as in the Huston movie the giant white whale carries Ahab into the depths, ensnared in harpoon lines, so at the close of the Benchley novel the great white shark slips away into the ocean, trailing the body of the fisherman Quint.

I have deleted my questions from the following talk, which was recorded in Los Angeles in November, 1972.

Ray Bradbury:
The reason John Huston selected me to write the screenplay of *Moby Dick* is that he saw in my own books a kinship with Melville. Melville is a poet and a Shakespearean, and I've been influenced by poetry and Shakespeare all my life. In high school I was an actor, and I read all Shakespeare and was influenced by the wonderful sound and look of his plays. Huston had enough sense to see the poet in my writing.

I wrote the first pages of the screenplay, which have never been changed, on the way to Ireland. The opening sequence with Ishmael coming over the hills and down by the waterfalls and streams—that was written on the train and revised on the boat. I finished reading *Moby Dick* on the third day out at about two o'clock in the morning, in the midst of a 90-mile an hour hurricane out on the back deck of the boat.

We met Huston in Paris before we went to London and then on to Dublin. The first thing I said to John was, "Do we get rid of Fedallah? He's a bore. He's horrible. He's the thing that ruins the whole book. I don't care what the Melville scholars say, he's the extra mystical symbol which breaks the whale's back, and he would be unbearable on the screen." He said, "Oh, yes, let's pick him up and throw him right overboard." So, together in our conversation, we grabbed Fedallah and threw him overboard, because we knew if we put him on the screen the picture would never work.

You have to be careful always on the screen not to overload your circuits, because there's a certain point in any tragedy, high tragedy like this, where people simply will not take what you are giving them. They're going to pull back in their seats and say, "Oh, no, now you've gone too far! Now you're funny!"

I had learned a good lesson which I remembered, because about two or three years earlier O'Neill's *Mourning Becomes Electra*

Ahab (Gregory Peck), Ishmael (Richard Basehart), and Queequeg (Frederick Ledebur) chase the white whale. Moby Dick *(1965).*

Queequeg (Frederick Ledebur) confers with Ishmael (Richard Basehart) on the deck of the Pequod. Moby Dick *(1956).*

had been made into a film at RKO with Rosalind Russell and Kirk Douglas and, I think, Michael Redgrave and Raymond Massey. Very interesting cast. A lot of different qualities. But it didn't work because they put the whole goddamn thing on the screen. And O'Neill never works when you do all of him on the screen because it's too close to you; it's too intimate. You back off just like someone breathing in your face who's had too much onions or garlic the night before. They say, "Boy, is that real! That's too real!"

You can accept O'Neill on the stage because you are removed from it. Stage is fantasy; film is reality. The stage should never be real. That's why the realistic playwrights really don't work. They pretend they work, but they don't because we don't go to the stage to see what we already know. To hell with that! We go to see things that we *don't* know. See if you can build an illusion there!

The stage is the art of the impossible. Cinema is the art of the possible; it's always the super-real. You've got to be careful when you do any sort of fantasy or anything that's fancy or baroque not to carry it too far because it's right there, shoved right into your eyeballs. That's why someone like Fedallah, when he comes on with his mysticism and astrological signs and all that, can be mildly or completely ridiculous.

I did twenty or thirty outlines trying to understand this book. Then I went to London finally for the last three weeks of work, which turned out to be the best three weeks in the whole six or seven months experience. I got out of bed one morning in London, looked in the mirror and said, "I am Herman Melville." On that day I rewrote the last thirty-five or forty pages of the screenplay—in just a few hours, seven or eight intense hours of banging away like crazy because I was inspired. I truly was. The ghost of Melville was in me. I ran off across London to Huston's hotel and I threw the script at him. I said, "There! I think that's it!" And he read it and said, "Jesus Christ, Ray! This is it. This is the way we'll shoot the ending."

My inspiration was to have Moby Dick take Ahab down and wind him in the coiled ropes and bring him up among the harpoons on this great white bier, this great cortège, this funeral at sea. Then we see, "My God, these two should be together for ever through eternity, shouldn't they—Ahab and the white whale?" I like to believe, in fact I do believe, that Melville would have approved. I'm proud of that touch. Then the motion of the whale in the sea causes Ahab's hand to beckon the men. They get maddened again and they charge in and are destroyed. Well, it's not in the book.

As a result of that I went back and rewrote some of Elijah's predictions; I went back to the start and said, "What do we need here that will clarify Elijah's predictions?" I changed that to indicate what will happen later at the end of the film and then halfway through when Ishmael remembers the predictions. So it all ties up very nicely. Then I had to go through the whole book, of course, and reorder the structure in cinematic terms. Melville gives away a lot of his climaxes too soon for motion picture purposes. It doesn't matter . . . you can do anything in a novel and it will work if you're good enough, but that's not true for films. If you blow your hunt halfway through the film or if you have the encounters with the various ships lined up incorrectly . . . it won't work.

What you want to do is build the tension, build the tension. So I went through and tried to line up all the scenes. I took some sections of the book which were late or which came earlier and I put them in the middle. I took things from the middle and put them towards the end. The encounter with the *Rachel*, the hurricane, the becalming of the ship—these are all separate entities in the book. I fused them together. I tried to build.

When the man went up and Ahab rededicated the men to the hunt and nailed the coin to the mast—that's a separate incident in the book. Then the man goes up and falls overboard; and that's a separate incident. Now I fused those together so that when he falls overboard, the ship is becalmed. I took that from another section and added that, you see, so that it has meaning. The sea is devouring him. The sea is in a way warning them to turn back from the hunt. Then they are becalmed; that's a separate section, too. I added that. In the middle of that they look at the coin on the mast and say throw it overboard and get us out of here. In the middle of that I put Queequeg's going into his trance. That's another whole section later on in the book. I borrowed that and brought it up so that you get this tight fusion of symbols and ideas and emotions that work. All of these are separate entities in the book; they do not occur that way.

Then I thought to myself, how in hell do you get Queequeg out of his trance? My recollection of it is that he just sort of comes out of it for no reason. My reasoning to Huston was there's only one way to get Queequeg out of that trance: if his most beloved friend is endangered. Death can only counter death. Queequeg is dying in the trance. How can you get him out of that? Well, if someones tries to kill Ishmael, that will bring him out. Only something as violent as that. I added this—it's not in the book. They come up and cut Queequeg, and Ishmael sees it. They have a fight and at the moment when the knife touches Ishmael's throat, Queequeg comes out of his trance and begins to crack the man over his knee to kill him, at which point Moby Dick makes his first appearance. That isn't in the book. Again we have a fusion of images, and they have a first glimpse of this great white thing going off away and they follow.

We have a series of encounters. We've had one encounter with the captain of the *Enderby*, who is jolly and has lost an arm. The *Rachel* comes on scene. The calm is over and the *Rachel* comes looking for her lost children. The captain turns them away. Starbuck says, "For God's sake, Captain, don't do this. Our name will be a curse in every seaport of the world, knowing that we haven't helped a man search for his own sons." They say, "Turn away," at which point the hurricane arrives, you see. This is punishment; this is separate in the book and not connected with the *Rachel*. I fused those two things together.

I'm making a rising line of events here—the *Rachel* comes into focus, Ahab turns away, God warns him that he shouldn't have done that, he then does a satanic thing, he has the harpoon in his hand which is glowing with St. Elmo's fire. Starbuck tells Ahab that the fire is a warning too. Ahab says, "No, it lights our way to the whale," and then he puts out the fire, damps down the fire symbolically. They put up new canvas. The hurricane goes away and they start their final pursuit of Moby Dick. All this doesn't occur in that sequence in the novel.

Then we had to decide what to do about the three lowerings for Moby Dick in the novel. That's too many for the screen. You can't lower three times; people are going to go to sleep on you. So we packed everything into one titanic lowering at the end when the whale is sighted and Elijah's prediction is remembered by Ishmael just before the sighting (which is not in the book). Then they set out and are destroyed.

It was a huge challenge, and I'm very proud of the screenplay. If somone were to ask me what my gift was, it's to make metaphors that are clear and that fuse many dissimilar things together. The longer I live the more I see that this is what I've been doing, but I didn't know I was doing it.

The film's plot is easy to tell. Once you've seen *Moby Dick*, you can go out and tell that screenplay very easily to people—I tried to write a silent screenplay as much as possible, with strong visual images. That gave me enough room here and there to be Shakespearean.

It's interesting . . . after I finished work on this film I discovered, of course, that Melville had been influenced by Shakespeare the same way I had been, except that Melville's influence came late. Melville had rather bad eyesight, and as he was writing *Moby Dick*, someone gave him an edition of Shakespeare with large type. For the first time in his life he read *Lear* and *Othello* and *Hamlet* and fell in love, madly, with Shakespeare. He picked up his whale and threw it away. His first version of *Moby Dick* he threw completely away. He rewrote it in terms of what he learned from Shakespeare.

While I was writing the screenplay I went back to Shakespeare myself and got reinfected with my fevers. His texture is so thick that he's always fresh. You must see Shakespeare dozens of times in your life to begin to hear new things. Then you say, "I don't remember that line. Was that really in there all the time?" It was, but what happened is that the line before it was so beautiful that you gonged it inside your head; you rang it around in there; you ricocheted it and you savoured it, to change the metaphor. While you're busy savouring it, the next two lines go by you. It's only the next time around that you hear the second line and then the third time around you hear the third line. Most of us don't have the capacity to take in thick poetry like that, thick, beautiful textures of poetry all in one fell swoop.

There are three or four long scenes in the film where you have a lot of poetic texture, where we dared to be brave and say a lot—with Ahab and the mild, mild day speech and his rededication of the men and the scene in the cabin where he describes Moby Dick. We've used a combination then of the Shakespearean approach which is sheer language and the cinematic approach which is pure image. It is a pretty good blend. It almost worked. The film is almost magnificent; I wouldn't say it's a failure.

It misses because Peck couldn't bring madness to it. A dear sweet gentleman, but he's not mad. Olivier is a madman to begin with. There's always been that quality of madness there in many things he did. He can call on that madness. Well, Greg Peck is never going to be a paranoid killer or a maniac devourer of whales. He can play in *To Kill a Mockingbird* and make a beautiful film. That's a different quality there.

In some scenes it works. The quiet scene in the cabin where Ahab is awakened from a nightmare and he in very quiet terms madly describes his obsession with Starbuck. That's a good scene because he doesn't have to go too hard with it. If I'd been old enough to advise Huston, which I wasn't (I can look back now and advise him but it's too late), I would have advised him to play the whole thing that way, a quiet madness that's very inner, very intense, so that you don't have to try for the big thing. I think Peck could have carried that off and you'd have had a different kind of Ahab.

I saw in Huston the same confusion I suffered. We were two blind men leading each other. We were way out over our heads and it took six or seven months for me to find myself. Huston had enough sense, at that moment, to say, "Yes, what you've just done is it." He didn't know where we wanted to go, and I didn't know. We were hoping somehow to blunder through and we did. John, in other areas, on other kinds of projects, I'm sure can be a great help to people, but we're both children at sea.

Huston tried, God knows, to help me, and when the outlines began to get better he said, "Yes, yes." Let's say that he could be a good influence in saying, "No, that doesn't work. Throw that outline away." That's very helpful, because sometimes, just out of frustration, you'll latch on to something that's not good because you're tired. You don't want to do any more work. He sent me back again and again until finally these little bits began to add up. I did around 1,200 pages of outlines and screenplay altogether in order to get the 140–150 final pages that became *Moby Dick*.

I think Ahab is the most American character in all our literature. He stands as the American character who says, "I will deal with the universe on the terms which it presents to me—death, annihilation, mystery, afflictions, paradoxes, evil. I would strike against it." He works against nature to survive. There are all kinds of ways of approaching nature, and the two halves of our nature are Melville's Ahab on one side and Jules Verne's Nemo on the other. Captain Nemo is the constructive side of a scientific experiment which says I will go with nature instead of striking against it. Find ways of using our blood to cure us. Ahab is the self-destructive side, the demonic side.

Moby Dick (1851), Herman Melville

Lost at Sea

BY BRANDON FRENCH

How can we begin to come to grips with the meaning of this novel? The madder among us behave like Ahab, the serenely certain like Starbuck, the eclectics like Ishmael, and the casual adventurers like Stubb. But it seems impossible, even for so staunch a critic as F. O. Matthiessen, to wrap one's mind around the whole leviathan. And so *Moby Dick* always escapes us in the end.

Except in Hollywood. In the first and second adaptations of the novel to film (*The Sea Beast* in 1926; *Moby Dick* in 1930), Warner Brothers not only got the better of the whale, it reduced him to a cameo role. A human villain named Derek and a conflict with Ahab for a woman named Esther (probably concocted from Melville's references to Ahab's wife) were substituted. Both these versions end happily, with Moby Dick and Derek done in and Ahab reunited with Esther. Terrible. But understandable. After all, what could Hollywood do with a whale who allegedly represents nature, all evil, the invisible forces of the universe, Truth, the white soul of America, the superego, and God? What could they do with a democratic Everyhero-Satanic Archvillain Antichrist who supposedly symbolizes a mindboggling amalgam of Adam, Prometheus, Don Quixote, Ulysses, Jonah, and the biblical king of Israel who, seduced by false prophets, went to his death in battle?

An additional problem. As Alfred Kazin puts it in his introduction to the Riverside Edition (1956), "everything in *Moby Dick* is saturated in a mental atmosphere." Half the novel is concerned with "invisible spheres" and invisibility does not lend itself easily to a photographic medium. Moreover, in the process of creating an epic, Melville gathers poetry, facts, ideas, history, myth, legend, and folklore into a highly complex narrative which moves freely in time and space. Such a novel requires radical condensation if an adaptation be braved at all.

In Ray Bradbury's screenplay for the most recent film of *Moby Dick*,[1] John Huston's version of 1956, there are, according to my calculations, fifty-four plot events (*i.e.*, Ahab in the moonlight, the first whale chase) which extend over 148 pages, in contrast to the 135 chapters of Melville's 724 page novel (in my Library of Literature Edition, Bobbs-Merrill, 1964). What Bradbury deleted are most of the documentary (whaling as a commercial occupation and industry) and the philosophical dimensions of the novel, leaving behind the adventure story with "enough room here and there to be Shakespearean" ("An Interview with Ray Bradbury," reprinted here, pp. 42–51).

In the most general terms, these deletions cut the story loose from its moorings as "the real living experience of living men" in Ishmael's words, casting away the novel as allegory of the American nineteenth century capitalist spirit, as the balanced account of nature's epic adversaries (*i.e.*, whales as well as men), and as the adventure of the human soul in a chaotic universe of indeterminate morality.

The universe in the Huston-Bradbury production of *Moby Dick* has firm moral polarities. One side joins together Father Mapple, chaplain of the whalemen's chapel who preaches against Jonah's defiance of God, and Starbuck, first mate of the *Pequod*. They are adherents of traditional Christian morality, an obedience to God's will and a respect for His mysteries. On the other side is Ahab, who in defiance of the will of God and his commitments to his employers is demonically obsessed with a desire for vengeance against the whale who took his leg. In the middle are Ishmael and the crew of Ahab's ship. Eventually everyone, in-

---

[1] Mr. Bradbury has kindly supplied me with a copy of his unpublished screenplay.

cluding Starbuck, is seduced by Ahab's charismatic madness to pursue the whale. As a result all are destroyed but Ishmael, the narrator of the story, saved presumably by his love of the pagan harpooner Queequeg, whose coffin provides a life raft. Whether Moby Dick is good or evil is not clear in the film, any more than it is in the novel. The difference is that this ambiguity is largely ignored as unimportant in the movie, whereas it is the central focus of the novel.

Charles Feidelson, Jr., in my Library of Literature Edition introduction to *Moby Dick*, writes: "Certainly no interpretation is adequate which fails to take into account the multiplicity of possible meanings in the white whale and in *Moby Dick* as a whole." In fact, since the novel is a quest for meaning itself, no interpretation which fails to acknowledge clearly the struggle between ambiguity and meaning makes fundamental sense. And it is on that fundamental level which the Bradbury-Huston adaptation ultimately founders.

Let us compare the opening of the movie with Melville's first chapter, "Loomings." After the film titles, we see a man in long shot walking along a winding road amidst a "sea of hills." We come closer to this man, silhouetted against the sky, and in voice-over we are told, "Call me Ishmael." Ishmael tells us that when he feels "a damp, drizzly November in my soul" it is time to go to sea again. This is followed by a montage sequence of ponds, lakes, pools, a creek, a river, each bigger, each running faster, juxtaposed with Ishmael walking faster. In voice-over he tells us that all paths lead to the sea since "the sea is where each man, as in a mirror, finds himself." Ishmael comes over the rise of a hill and below him lies the sea, bordered by the town of New Bedford. We are told, voice-over, that the year in 1814 and that Ishmael stands "letting the flood gates of the wonder-world of the sea swing open in my soul." He then proceeds down into town.

The novel begins in limbo—nowhere, no time. "Call me Ishmael. Some years ago—never mind how long precisely . . ." Ishmael refers to going out to sea as "my substitute for pistol and ball. With a philosophical flourish Cato throws himself upon his sword." He then adds that almost all men, sometime or other, "cherish very nearly the same feelings toward the ocean with me." But what feelings are these? A desire to escape one's dreary existence on land, or a desire for suicide? He alludes to both, acknowledging at the same time that he is like "all men," that what he says is universally true, and most significantly, that he is like the reader.

Both this ambiguity and the transformation of Ishmael's thoughts and feelings into universals are continued a few pages further on. "Why is almost every robust healthy boy with a robust healthy soul in him, at some time or other crazy to go to sea?" Is this craziness a passion, or is one literally crazy to do it? "Why," Ishmael adds, "upon your first voyage as a passenger [implicating the reader with the pronoun "your"], did you feel such a mystical vibration [positive or negative?] when first told that you and your ship were now out of sight of land?" "Surely," Ishmael says, for the first of three times in 46 pages, "all this is not without meaning." Still deeper, he says, is the meaning of the story of Narcissus, who, because he could not grasp his image in the fountain, plunged into it and drowned. "But that same image, we ourselves see in all rivers and oceans." Notice he does not say "we see ourselves," as Ishmael says in the movie. "It is the image of the ungraspable phantom of life; and this is the key to it all." At the end of the chapter he refers to the flooding into his soul of "endless processions of the whale, and, mid most of them all, one grand hooded phantom, like a snow hill in the air." Thus he links the phantom of life, which we all seek, with the quest for Moby Dick.

Bradbury's Ishmael is drawn to the sea for adventure and his quest is for his own identity. Ishmael in the novel is lured to the sea, like all men, he insists, both by the promise of adventure and by some suicidal passion. His quest, the universal one for the essence of life itself, is, if Narcissus serves as example, potentially deadly. Finally, his quest has a shape suggestive of Moby Dick himself ("a snow hill"), which links him, and us, to Ahab.

I want next to compare the film's treatment of Father Mapple's sermon with Melville's original. The movie's Father Mapple (Orson Welles) says ". . . He spoke and the whale came breaching up from shuddering blackness toward all the delights of the warm sun and earth and 'vomited out Jonah on dry land.' " The sermon stops here. But in the novel, the notion of delight is carried on into a litany. "On the starboard hand of every woe, there is sure delight." The word "delight" is then used nine more times in a single paragraph which ends with the promise that "Delight is to him, whom all the waves of the billows of the seas of the boistrous mob can never shake from this sure keel of the Ages. And eternal delight and deliciousness will be his, who coming to lay him down, can say with his final breath—O Father!—chiefly known to me by Thy rod—mortal or immortal, here I die. I have striven to be Thine, more than to be this world's or mine own. Yet this is nothing; I leave eternity to Thee, for what is man that he should live out the lifetime of his God?" What is all this about?

In chapter 131, the *Pequod* passes "another ship, most miserably misnamed the *Delight* . . ." which has been destroyed in its attempt to harpoon Moby Dick. One can perceive this destruction as an omen of the delight which Ahab is about to destroy in his defiance of God, but why should an ordinary ship piloted by an ordinary captain ("those who by accident ignorantly gave battle to Moby Dick," as Ishmael says) merely pursuing his trade be destroyed by a great white whale? In what way has it transgressed against God? Is the destruction of delight an act of divine justice, the act of wicked gods, or an arbitrary event in an amoral universe? Such a question never arises for a viewer of the film since, along with most philosophical speculation, delight is deleted from the movie.

The movie does, toward the end, raise the question of fate vs. free will. Ahab, echoing Gloucester in *King Lear*, says:

> Oh, how the Gods enjoy playing with us. We are the wooden pieces they move about. What's the point of the game, I wonder? Sometimes I'm on the very edge of knowing; and then they toss me back in the box . . . a voice within me says, "Ahab, all that has happened, all that is to happen, was immutably decreed. It was rehearsed for thee a million years before this ocean rolled. You are the Fate's lieutenant. You act under orders. It could not be otherwise."

Ahab, as in the novel, sees himself as the victim of playfully perverse gods of Fate, not a defier of an almighty God but an obedient pawn of Providence. But this possibility is not developed in the film, not attached to any larger philosophical fabric. Whereas the idea of how man comes to live his life is introduced by Ishmael in the novel's first chapter:

> And, doubtless, my going on this whaling voyage, formed part of the grand programme of Providence that was drawn up a long time ago. It came in as a sort of brief interlude and solo between more extensive performances. I take it that this part of the bill must have run something like this:
> "*Grand Contested Election for the Presidency of the United States.*
> "Whaling voyage by one Ishmael.
> "BLOODY BATTLE IN AFFGHANISTAN."

Although the film retains Ishmael as the narrator of its story, his role as the mediating consciousness, which can accommodate contradictions and identify paradoxes, is eliminated along with most of his charm, wit and humor. It is the Ishmael of the novel, and *only* the novel, who can perceive Queequeg as "George Washington cannibalistically developed." It is the Ishmael of the novel who sees, *and who can make us see*, Ahab's madness and his tragic grandeur simultaneously:

> . . . moody stricken Ahab stood before them with a crucifixion in his face, in all the nameless regal overbearing dignity of some mighty woe. . . . Now, in his heart, Ahab had some glimpse of this, namely: all my means are sane, my motive and my object mad. . . . Here, then, was this grey-headed, ungodly old man, chasing with curses a Job's whale round the world, at the head of a crew, too, chiefly made up of mongrel renegades, and castaways, and cannibals. . . .

Although Ishmael is "a good Christian" who believes in Divine— not demonic—Providence, he grants Ahab the possibility of some "infernal fatality." He realizes that "though in many of its aspects this visible world seems formed in love, the invisible spheres were formed in fright." And in the central philosophical chapter of the novel, "The Whiteness of the Whale," he presents the possibility that there is no Providence at all and that the world's meaning, like its beauty, is an illusion:

But not yet have we solved the incantation of this whiteness, and learned why it appeals with such power to the soul. . . . Is it that by its indefiniteness it shadows forth the heartless voids and immensities of the universe and thus stabs us from behind with the thought of annihilation . . . or is it, that as in essence whiteness is not so much a color as the visible absence of color, and at the same time the concrete of all colors; is it for these reasons that there is such a dumb blankness, full of meaning, in a wide landscape of snows—a colorless all-color of atheism from which we shrink? And . . . consider . . . that all other earthly hues—every stately or lovely emblazoning—the sweet tinges of sunset skies and woods; yea, and the gilded velvets of butterflies, and the butterfly cheeks of young girls; all these are but subtle deceits, not actually inherent in substances, but only laid on from without, so that all deified Nature absolutely paints like the harlot, whose allurements cover nothing but the charnel-house within. . . .

In addition to Ishmael's expansive philosophical orientation, the language of the novel is a constant reminder of the struggle between absolutes and oppositions and the resultant ambiguities. To begin with, we have what Charles Olson, in *Call Me Ishmael* (1947), calls "patterned contradiction": *a dumb blankness, full of meaning; a colorless all-color; a mighty mildness of repose in swiftness.* It is as if Melville is striving to create a new language out of the old one by means of contradictory juxtapositions, a language in which paradox is the central fact, the rule, a language which accommodates Melville's vision of the universe. John Huston in the film version of *Moby Dick* provides no equivalent for this dialectic. And without Ishmael, without a visual language, whatever contradiction and complexity Bradbury tries to retain in his script seems forced, heavy-handed, out of place; ideas spoken but not visually nor even narratively intrinsic. A film such as *Jaws* (1975), which unloads everything but the collision of simple absolutes—a reckless boy wonder, a terrified but honorable landlubber, a spiritually twisted, arrogant captain, and a demonic shark—and feeds the devil to the shark and victory over evil to the landlubbing audience, provides a better, less pretentious analogue for the "invisible spheres formed in fright": the terror of meaningless annihilation, of random disaster; the horror beneath the seductively smooth, blue surface of the sea.

Ironically, two of John Huston's earlier quest films, *The Maltese Falcon* (1941) and *The Treasure of Sierra Madre* (1948), provide more interestingly ambiguous objects of pursuit, the values of which remain pointedly indeterminate; a more exciting use of mythology about the objects; more effectively ambivalent portrayals of the characters and their morality; much more charm; and a far greater visual sophistication which includes a choreography of shifting perspectives as a stylistic analogue for some of Huston's thematic preoccupations: life's moral ambiguity and reality's instability.

But the tragedy and poetry of spiritual torment have never formed part of Huston's ironic, disillusioned romanticism. In fact, they are alien to American film as a whole. One must look to foreign directors for success in the treatment of this subject: Robert Bresson (*The Diary of a Country Priest* [1950], *Balthazar* [1966]), Carl Dreyer (*The Passion of Joan of Arc* [1928], *Vampyr* [1932], *Ordet* [1955], and Ingmar Bergman (*Wild Strawberries* [1957], *The Magician* [1958], *Persona* [1965], and *Shame* [1968]). These directors share a gift for investing real objects with complex abstract meaning, the gift of effective cinematic symbolism; and an exquisite ability to maximize the expressiveness of the human face.

Because Ray Bradbury counted upon Ahab's face to express a world of meaning, the script holds on his countenance during the entire second whale chase:

> We HEAR their voices off-scene, we HEAR the sounds of preparation, the ten thousand large and small sounds of rope and wood and feet and boats and harpoons, much cursing and swearing, more running of feet, Ishmael's voice, Queequeg's voice, the panorama of it all is in Ahab's face, each and every small bit and part of it is reflected there. It is obvious that Ahab sees Moby Dick pulling away from him, and that the great shout of the whalers had drowned out, for a time, the sound that might be Moby Dick beyond the horizon. For a full minute we dwell on Ahab's face and see there reflected the activities of all his men. . . .

One need only try to imagine Gregory Peck, who plays Ahab in the film, as King Lear, the dominant model for Melville's characterization, or as a replacement for Victor Sjöström in *Wild Straw-*

berries or Max Von Sydow in *The Magician* to recognize how impossibly miscast he was. As Bradbury himself admits: "[The film] misses because Peck couldn't bring madness to it. A dear sweet gentleman, but he's not mad."

There is no way to calculate how much of the film's failure is attributable to miscasting (not only Peck, but Richard Basehart as Ishmael), but the greatest burden of responsibility must fall upon the adaptation itself. Bradbury, persuaded that the ghost of Melville was in him—see the accompanying interview—made changes that are difficult to account for, under even the most generous scrutiny.

Why, for example, does Bradbury transform Captain Boomer of the *Samuel Enderby* into a caricature? He is used by Melville to illustrate what a normal attitude toward Moby Dick might be, for Boomer has lost his arm to the whale as Ahab lost his leg. In the novel, Boomer says:

> No thank ye . . . he's welcome to the arm he has, since I can't help it, and didn't know him then; but not to another one. No more white whales for me; I've lowered for him once and that has satisfied me.

In the film, Boomer says:

> It's a beauty, eh, Captain? (Holding up his ivory arm) Better than flesh and blood. Like mine so much, think I'll have me other arm cut off. . . . Lubbers with four limbs don't know what they're missing, do they, captain? In other words, sir, them as have, haven't, have they? And we as haven't have! Oh, I had me doubts, when I lost me old arm. I was downright disgruntled—but when I got this ivory jib all spanking new and shapely, why I could've thanked that whale!

Bradbury's scene, in exaggerating its point, makes Boomer appear mad—as Ahab is—so his reaction to his loss cannot be viewed as normal. One is torn in the novel between attraction to Boomer's sanity and recognition of Ahab's lunatic heroism. Boomer himself acknowledges it indirectly: "There would be great glory in killing him, I know." But in the film, one can't really appreciate either character's perspective.

Another perplexing change in the movie is Starbuck's "conversion," his sudden adoption of Ahab's quest after the captain is killed by Moby Dick:

> Yes—now I'm captain. Turn the boats around. . . . We're going back for the whale. . . . Any whale could have [killed us], any year. We went to sea knowing that. Moby Dick is no devil. He's a whale. A monstrous big whale, aye, but a whale—no more. And we're whaling men—no less. We don't turn from whales; we kill them. We'll kill Moby Dick.

Again Bradbury sacrifices character credibility to make a point. In the novel, Ahab and Starbuck are increasingly drawn to one another in mutual compassion. But Starbuck, as stable as the land values he represents, is incapable of executing a 180° turn into madness. "Oh! Ahab," he cries, "not too late is it, even now, the third day, to desist. See! Moby Dick seeks thee not. It is thou, thou, that madly seekest him!" And his last act is to try to steer the *Pequod* out of the whale's murderous path.

But the most disturbing adaptative change is that Starbuck in the movie actually succeeds in *killing* Moby Dick. (The black blood in the film and a reference in the script to "the dying whale" confirm the murder.) One can't kill the phantom of life in the novel, but evidently in Bradbury's estimation, Moby Dick was, after all, just a whale.

And in that light, all the madness, all the melodrama, all the dramatic monologues and Shakespearean paraphrases and philosophical pretensions left over from the novel become absurd. They are merely camouflage behind which Hollywood once again gets the best of Melville's masterpiece.

Little Women (1868–69), Louisa May Alcott

Life with Marmee: Three Versions

BY KATE ELLIS

In times of economic and social upheaval, the sphere of home and mother is always there to fall back on. This at least is what popular literature and the media would have us believe. Yet war and economic depression often necessitate changes in the family that bring reality into conflict with the ideal of a single male breadwinner and his flock of happy dependents. Men in wartime leave home to fight, while female members of the household are drawn into the labor force—paid and unpaid—in support of the war effort. And when employment is scarce, women's menial jobs do not disappear as quickly as men's work. It is therefore not surprising that, in the aftermaths of wars or depressions, books and films idealizing the domestic sphere should find an especially receptive market. It is in this light that I would like to look at Louisa May Alcott's novel *Little Women* and its two film versions, appearing in 1868, 1933, and 1949 respectively.

The novel *Little Women* opens in the middle of the Civil War. Father is away, and does not appear until the middle of the book, after which his presence is confined mainly to his study—"off-stage," so to speak. His ineptitude as a breadwinner is mentioned in the opening chapter, though none of the daughters makes an issue of it the way the spoiled, selfish Amy (played by Elizabeth Taylor) does in the 1949 film version. Fiscal authority in the March family lies mainly with the women throughout the novel, and Meg and Jo are proud to contribute to the family income, though neither particularly likes her work—as governess and paid companion respectively.

This deviation from the ideal is rectified by the preeminence of Father as the source of moral authority, a role that he can play from a distance since Marmee is the agent through whom his wisdom is transmitted to his four "little women." We can see this downward flow of authority in the scene where Marmee reads Father's Christmas letter to his daughters and wife, written from the front and quoted in full, incidentally, in both film versions.

> Give them all my dear love and a kiss. Tell them I think of them by day, pray for them by night, and find my best comfort in their affection at all times. A year seems a very long time to wait before I see them, but remind them that while we wait we may all work, so that these hard days will not be wasted. I know that they will be loving children to you, will do their duty faithfully, fight their bosom enemies bravely, and conquer themselves so beautifully, that when I come back to them I may be fonder and prouder than ever of my little women.

This letter, replete with Biblical echoes ("a cloud by day and a pillar of fire by night"), suggests a modern Christ urging his faithful disciples to love one another, to carry out his work in his absence, and to await with patience and hope his return ushering in the millenium.

Father does communicate directly with his family after he returns, but Alcott reproduces almost nothing of these conversations. Those she does show us are between Marmee and her girls, where father is a supreme but absent God who teaches gently and by example. We see this in a conversation between Jo and Marmee about anger, the "bosom enemy" that Jo must conquer if she is to be a source of pride to her father. "You think your temper is the worst in the world," says Marmee to her daughter, "but mine used to be just like it." Jo is astounded, since she has never seen her mother show anger, but Marmee insists that she feels anger every day of her life, and felt it particularly strongly when Father lost his money and she had four small children to deal with, economically and emotionally. "Poor mother!" Jo exclaims. "What helped you then?" to which Marmee replies:

> Your father, Jo. He never loses patience—never doubts or com-
> plains—but always hopes and works, and waits so cheerfully that
> one is ashamed to do otherwise before him. He helped and com-
> forted me, and showed me that I must try to practice all the virtues
> I would have my little girls possess, for I was their example.

Marmee exemplifies a warmth and openness with her daughter that is a departure from the Puritan model of child-rearing, where the emphasis was on "breaking the will" of the naturally willful, intractable, sinful child. Observers from Europe coming to America after the Civil War noted the precociousness of American children, to whom their parents were companions rather than distant authorities. The frequency with which American mothers and children were thrown on their own resources while the males of the community were engaged in "civilizing" a new land undoubtedly laid the groundwork for this development even before the Civil War took men from their homes in a systematic way. But it was in the 1860s that the new freedom began to attract comments, most of them unfavorable. One American observer in 1863 warned his fellow citizens of "an irreverent, unruly spirit [that] has come to be prevalent, an outrageous evil among the young people of our land."[1] The demise of family discipline, in other words, was lamented in the same language that we hear used today.

What Alcott did in her novels about children was to show how this method of teaching by example rather than by severity could be made the basis of a new family ideal: a modified "little commonwealth" that might reflect the democratic spirit stirring in the larger society, and which might at the same time preserve the moral preeminence of Father even in his physical absence. Previous children's literature had presented life as a grim Pil-

---

[1] Quoted in John Demos and Virginia Demos, "Adolescence in Historical Perspective," in *The American Family in Social-Historical Perspective*, edited by Michael Gordon (New York: St. Martin's Press, 1973), pp. 211–12.

Gathered in song, Alcott's "little commonwealth": Marmee (Spring Byington), Amy (Joan Bennett), Meg (Frances Dee), Beth (Jean Parker), and Jo (Katharine Hepburn). Little Women (1933).

Marmee (Mary Astor) and her daughters read Father's Christmas letter. Beth (Margaret O'Brien), Meg (Janet Leigh), Jo (June Allyson), and Amy (Elizabeth Taylor). Little Women (1949).

grim's Progress, as the title of one frequently reprinted work, first published in 1700, suggests:

> A Token for Children; Being an Exact Account of the Conversion, Holy and Exemplary Lives and Joyous Deaths of several young children. To Which is added A Token for the Children of New England of Some Examples of Children in whom the Fear of God was remarkably budding before they died in several parts of New England, Preserved and Published for the Encouragement of Piety in Other Children.

The spirit behind this document was softened slightly over the next century and a half, but religious tracts conveying essentially this message remained the principal reading material for children up to the time that Alcott began writing.

In *Little Women* we see her making conscious use of this exemplary tradition of her predecessors. The Christmas letter, the references to John Bunyan's *Pilgrim's Progress* in the early chapters, and the use of his characters and place names for chapter headings ("Playing Pilgrims," "Burdens," "Beth Finds the Palace Beautiful," "Amy's Valley of Humiliation," "Jo Meets Appolyon," "Meg Goes to Vanity Fair") all suggest a spiritual progress that ends, for three out of the four girls, in the presence of a husband who takes Father's place as their moral authority. It is significant, I think, that Jo's Professor Bhaer, the most overtly paternal of the three husbands, is first shown romping spontaneously with children. He thus has character traits that make him eligible to head the kind of modified patriarchal family that Alcott accommodates to her other vision of economically capable, self-sufficient women.

Writing at a time when the Civil War had not only loosened the bonds of parental authority but given impetus to the movement for women's rights, Alcott endowed the March women not only with an appreciation of female earning power but with the high spirits that tend to accompany such competence in the world. All the girls dream of fame and wealth, building "castles in the air," and Jo and Amy do more than dream: they work hard at their writing and painting. Moreover, the negative side of these high spirits is neither whitewashed nor turned into trivial bickering, as it is in both film versions. Rather, it is expressed in real temptations that are portrayed vividly before they are overcome. For instance, Amy burns a notebook in which Jo has been writing her stories, and Jo in retaliation allows Amy to skate where the ice is thin, with the result that she falls into the freezing river and risks drowning. Amy's anger has been set off by the discovery that her older sisters have excluded her from an expedition they were planning. The painful lesson she is resisting, and which Jo resists right up to her meeting with Professor Bhaer, is that exclusion is part of growing up, that the four sisters cannot do everything together as they did as children. Yet her feelings, as Alcott portrays them, are simultaneously childish and serious, and set off a chain of increasingly severe retaliation that ends only when Jo turns to Marmee for help and they have the talk about anger mentioned above. In presenting family harmony as a product of struggle against strong negative emotions that would have condemned children in earlier literature to the fires of everlasting damnation, Alcott made a real contribution to the representation of children in fiction.

What makes *Little Women* more than an innovative book for children is Alcott's portrait of Jo as an economic force in her family's household and later behind her husband and his school. Before Jo leaves for New York she has won a hundred dollars in a short story contest, published a novel that receives mixed reviews, and tasted the joys of self-sufficiency. Her father's advice, which he probably follows himself, is to "aim at the highest, and never mind the money," but Jo's head is not so far in the clouds. Alcott comments:

> Wealth is certainly a most desirable thing, but poverty has its sunny side, and one of the sweet uses of adversity is the genuine satisfaction that comes from hearty work of head or hand; . . . Jo enjoyed a taste of this satisfaction, and ceased to envy richer girls, taking great comfort in the knowledge that she could supply her own wants, and need ask no one for a penny.

Later in New York, "her emaciated purse grew stout," and fed her dream of "filling home with comforts." These comforts may be seen as luxuries and thus not a threat to Father's position as prime breadwinner, but a trip to the seaside for her mother and dying sister, Beth, is hardly a "frill." Jo's role in the economy of her household is one of the contradictions of the March ménage, as it was of the Alcott home.

At the end of *Little Women* Jo apparently gives up her writing and thus her access to money of her own. Yet it is her inheritance of Aunt March's house that provides the building for her husband's school for boys. She may become "Mother Bhaer" to the pupils he teaches, but she does not become his economic dependent. Much later, in *Jo's Boys* (1886), the school runs into financial hard times and she takes up her pen to earn money. After having lost her girlish dream of success and fame, she becomes a celebrated American author, a New England tourist attraction, in fact. She is thus always, either potentially or actually, the economic moving force behind whatever household she is in.

Alcott is able to get away with this partly because Bhaer, like Father whom he replaces, is so clearly the moral authority in Jo's life, particularly when it comes to ending her career as a writer of sensational stories. But also Alcott was writing at a time when the feminist movement, though small, was strong and growing. In the 1930s, when the first film version of the novel came out, feminism was perceived to have run its course and died. By 1949 there was strong backlash against the idea of women working outside the home at all. Moreover, the portrayal of working women by Hollywood has always been somewhat ambiguous. The thirties produced the most serious and extensive treatment of the subject, but the focus of many thirties films on stage careers is not accidental: actresses and chorus girls were not taking jobs from men. Katharine Hepburn could therefore rise to stardom in *Stage Door* (1937) without upsetting the all too visible apple cart, while *Gold Diggers of '33*, though it focuses on the plight of unemployed chorus girls, ends with a moving plea by Joan Blondell for full male employment.

It is not surprising, then, that Hollywood had difficulty both with the unfeminine exuberance of young Jo and with her later earning power as a writer. The problem with both of these attributes is that our culture views them as masculine qualities, and did so particularly in the periods of difficult social adjustment when the two films appeared. This was also true in Alcott's day, though the fact that the economy was still for the most part rural gave a scope for female competence that waned after World War I with the advent of home appliances and processed foods, and had all but disappeared in the suburban home of the late forties. This development affects not only women but also children who, having no useful economic function in relation to their families the way children in a rural economy do, are reduced to paradigms of cuteness. The media contributed to this new image of the cute child and the child-centered family, giving us the "Our Gang" series in the twenties, Shirley Temple in the thirties, followed by Mickey Rooney, Margaret O'Brien, Roddy McDowell, and a host of other child stars. The problem with Jo March is that she is not merely cute, yet Hollywood found it difficult to deal with any other qualities in children. This impoverishment of the media notion of family life is particularly visible in the later version of the book, which is simply a showcase for stars as stars: Janet Leigh, June Allyson, Elizabeth Taylor, and Margaret O'Brien, with Peter Lawford adding a heavy dose of precocious virility.

Unlike media adolescents in the twentieth century, Alcott's Jo is both a serious person and a tomboy. She is also quite maternal, and the first time she visits the orphaned Laurie she gives the gloomy living room of the Laurence mansion the benefit of a woman's touch. When he tells her his mother died, and turns away "to hide a little twitching of the lips that he could not control," Alcott comments:

> The solitary, hungry look in his eyes went straight to Jo's warm heart. She had been so simply taught that there was no nonsense in her head, and at fifteen she was innocent and frank as any child. Laurie was sick and lonely; and, feeling how rich she was in home love and happiness, she gladly tried to share it with him. Her face was very friendly and her sharp voice unusually gentle. . . .

The George Cukor version of 1933 has some of this innocence in it; but the Mervyn Le Roy remake (1949) with June Allyson and Peter Lawford is a stereotyped boy-meets-girl encounter, and at no point during the youth of Jo are the sharp voices of either actress who played the role "unusually gentle." Apparently a tomboy cannot walk or talk normally, let alone gently. She must be constantly swaggering, stomping, thrusting out her chin and exclaiming, "Christopher Columbus!" Then to offset Jo's masculinity and give us a hint of things to come, both directors give us a touch of comic eroticism. Hepburn and Douglass Montgomery fence in the style of Hamlet until Hepburn falls and the audience, along with Laurie, get a brief view up her skirt until her gallant partner helps her up. June Allyson, a little more restrained, burns her skirt, falls to the ground face down, and lets Peter Lawford beat the back of her skirt with a broom.

For Hepburn this boyish image changes dramatically and without explanation in the last third of the film, as the heroine who has sold her hair to help finance Marmee's trip to Father's sickbed in Washington, and who climbs out of windows and talks out of the side of her mouth, suddenly becomes (such is the transforming power of the right man) the subject of dreamy, soft-focus close-ups. She positions herself next to the piano while Professor Bhaer is singing "None But the Lonely Heart" (a scene not in the novel) and leans back in a way that allows his head to be outlined against her breast and torso. Later, when they return from the opera, she who vowed to wear her hair in pigtails till she was twenty is wearing a low-cut dress and leans back seductively against the bannister while she responds to the professor's broken English. From being Hepburn the tomboy she suddenly becomes, under Cukor's loving direction, Hepburn the star, as Alcott's image of the true-woman-as-mother gives way to the glamorous image of escapist thirties films: top hats and evening dresses.

June Allyson's portrait of adolescence is more consistent, but reflects the increasingly stereotyped view of adolescence. Despite the period costumes, she is a suburban teen-ager on her way to the altar. This effect is created partly by Allyson's acting style: she is one of those wholesome actresses, perpetually virginal and smiling, who gave to the forties and fifties films in which they starred their peculiar brand of premarital unreality. It is also created by the sets, which were not researched as Cukor's were, and have the low-ceilinged coziness of suburban colonial living. Further, even the few references to the world beyond the home that appear in the novel and the Cukor film are cut out of this one. The Cukor film begins, for instance, with soldiers marching through town and Marmee at the commissary giving a coat to an old man who has lost four sons. In 1949 studios were discreet about invoking the war dead on screen.

One other unmentionable in both 1933 and 1949 was the pride of a woman at the sight of her "emaciated purse" growing stout. In the earlier film, the first money Jo receives for a story is not a hundred dollars but a dollar fifty. In 1949 the value of that first check has dropped to a dollar! When Professor Bhaer confronts Jo with his opinion of her stories (something that does not happen in the novel: he only suspects, and, like an understanding father, forgives a poor girl her desire to make money), Katharine Hepburn mentions briefly and apologetically the things she has been buying for her family. June Allyson does not mention her purchases, but simply resolves to Rossano Brazzi (one could not have a real German in this romantic role in 1949) never to err again. In the novel, the "simple stories" that Jo writes after she returns home from New York are sent by her own hand to a publisher, and win her some real success that she can acknowledge to her family. In the films, she sends everything she writes to Bhaer, and he takes care of her career, bringing her finally a copy of the novel for which his friend has "great hopes," but which do not translate, as far as we can see, into cash for his author.

One final eradication that is performed in the 1949 version, but not in the earlier one, is the passage of time itself. In the Cukor film, Spring Byington is a not very intelligent looking middle-aged Marmee who wears her gray hair in the style we find in photographs of nineteenth-century matrons in their fifties. A nineteenth-century woman whose oldest daughter was fifteen would probably be in her late thirties but no attempt is made by Cukor to make Marmee look youthful. The same is true for Father, who comes home from the war emaciated and white-haired. It seems that such an image of a returning soldier was not acceptable to those in charge of casting the later film. In this version Leon Ames as Father looks only a few years older than Peter Lawford, his daughter's admirer, while Mary Astor's Marmee has exquisite red hair with not a streak of gray to be seen.

This attempted annihilation of the generation gap is in part a by-product of the fact that all members of the younger generation except Beth are played by adult actors trying to look ten years younger than they are. But I suspect that a large part of the message of this film to its postwar audiences was that home was a place where men could return to wives who had not aged, and where wives could greet men whose experiences overseas could be wiped out and forgotten. Home, then, was a place where both parties could begin again as if time had stood still for five years, and where Father's preeminence was not only economic and moral. It was physical as well, which meant that he wanted his "little women" to have become in his absence not so much virtuous as attractive. It was in the early fifties that Ivory Soap ran a series of ads which pictured a mother and a daughter and asked if you could tell the difference. If you look at Jo and Marmee in this film it is, in fact, hard to tell which one is more successful in canceling out the effects of time.

The Adventures of Tom Sawyer (1876), Mark Twain

Tom Sawyer: *Saturday Matinee*

BY DAN FULLER

Mark Twain has always been among the most hospitable of American authors, often providing us with instructions as to how his novels should read. Occasionally, as in the case of *Huckleberry Finn*, he even confronts the reader directly: "persons attempting to find a plot in it will be shot." In his preface to *The Adventures of Tom Sawyer*, he informs us that "Although my book is intended mainly for the entertainment of boys and girls, I hope it will not be shunned by men and women on that account. . . ." Henry Nash Smith points out in *Mark Twain: The Development of a Writer* (1962) that the germ of the novel was a burlesque of an adult love story. Following a common nineteenth-century practice, Twain reduced his principals to children. In so doing, he apparently "was not clear in his own mind whether he was writing a story for boys or a story for adults." The events of the book are the stuff of juvenile fiction, but the point of view is not merely omniscient, but also looks backward from an adult vantage. The tone is nostalgic—and nostalgia is solely the province of adulthood. It is precisely at this point that the novel and John Cromwell's 1930 motion picture diverge. The book contains much that could only be intended for a mature reader; except for the opening scene, however, the film is aimed strictly at a juvenile audience. Only the atmosphere of nostalgia is retained for the occasional adult viewer.

While novel and film are often antithetical, it is equally clear that some novels are, according to George Bluestone, more "nearly like shooting scripts." In *Novels into Film* (1957) Bluestone notes Edmund Wilson's observation about John Steinbeck's *The Grapes of Wrath*—that it seems to have been written with the screen in mind and ". . . was probably the only serious story on record that seemed equally effective as a film and as a book." Bluestone subsequently disputes this view, but one may still conclude that there are novels that lend themselves more easily to adaptation —those objective in point of view, episodic in structure, and divided into fairly distinct scenes with something visually interesting in each.

In composition, *The Adventures of Tom Sawyer* seems particularly filmic. Twain's river books were, in the main, generated by a trip back to his childhood home in Missouri in preparation for *Old Times on the Mississippi* (1875). The *Boy's Manuscript*, as the first version of *Tom Sawyer* was known, drew upon boyhood reminiscences, scraps from Hannibal history, and the atmosphere of the antebellum South. Twain would record episodes as he remembered them, shelving the project whenever "the tank [ran] dry." This method of composition obviously leads to a fragmentary structure; and, in fact, the novel contains at least three distinct plots, a number of episodes essentially unrelated to the narrative—all promising raw material to be shaped into an adaptation. The more sophisticated or "adult" portions of the novel—social criticism and satire, the parodies of sentimental literature and reform movements—are, for obvious reasons, omitted from the movie.

The various plots of the novel all revolve about Tom. He contends with unrequited love and a variety of frustrated reformers on the one hand, and the more serious threats of Injun Joe, McDougal's cave, and his conscience on the other. The novel is a compendium of almost every adolescent fantasy, schoolboy prank, and emotional crisis that could occur to a dozen boys in half a dozen summers. Indeed, one of the reasons that *Tom Sawyer* is so satisfying a novel is that not only does Tom triumph over many tormentors who would squelch his enthusiasm and stifle his boyish exuberance—this would be good enough—but

Becky (Mitzi Green), Tom (Jackie Coogan), and Huck (Junior Durkin) in McDougal's cave. Tom Sawyer (1930).

he also realizes the romantic fantasies of rescuing and winning the maiden, finds a fortune in honest-to-goodness buried treasure, defeats Injun Joe and his malevolent plans, and basks in the absolute adulation not only of his peers but of the whole community.

But Tom "was not the Model Boy of the village. He knew the model boy very well though—and loathed him." Tom is contrasted with his half-brother Sid, the apple-polishing and well-behaved—hence loathsome—"good boy." (John Cromwell also directed the 1936 *Little Lord Fauntleroy*—perhaps that is Sid's film.) Many situations characterize Tom effectively—bartering tickets to win a Sunday-School Bible under false pretenses, challenging a well-dressed new boy to a fight, feeding vile patent medicine to a cat, running away to play pirate, and more. Tom is a rebel, "full of the Old Scratch," but he is also an "acceptable" rebel, contrasted with his goody-goody brother on the one hand and the socially ostracized Huckleberry Finn on the other. At the novel's end, it is Tom who emerges both rich and a hero—in the best Horatio Alger tradition. Sid is left to savor sour grapes and Huck simply wants to leave. The premise seems to be that, his boyish exuberance once over, Tom Sawyer will grow up a well-to-do, respectable member of the community. Romantic dreamer though he may be, most of his dreams are borne out in reality.

Tom Sawyer is puckish and lovable and contends with real dangers. He bears only slight resemblance to the amoral manipulator of the same name who dehumanizes Jim and drives the reader to distraction in *The Adventures of Huckleberry Finn* (1884). (If Tom differs, so does Huck. Although he takes one deliberate risk in warning the Welshman of Injun Joe's plans for Widow Douglas, he runs from the scene of that action and actually falls ill from the excitement. He also regrets the fact that he has no good home or family, and is generally insecure and afraid. There is little similarity to the self-reliant, curious adventurer of the immortal trip down the river.) The temptation is always to evaluate *Tom* as an adjunct, a companion piece, an apprentice preparation for the superior *Huck*. But *Tom Sawyer* is considered here out of the shadow of its ostensible sequel (the subtitle of *The Adventures of Huckleberry Finn is* "Tom Sawyer's Comrade").

Paramount's 1930 film *Tom Sawyer* was the second of at least four adaptations (the first was in 1917) and was greeted enthusiastically by the *New York Times*. Mordaunt Hall notes that "adults and children" howled with delight at an afternoon screening. Both Hall and a second, unsigned review endorse the film for its superb casting and fidelity to the source. Hall notes some "small discrepancies" and "certain omissions," but both reviews give unqualified praise to the actors, director Cromwell, and the faithfulness of the adaptation (this latter concern and the undemanding acceptance of all facets of the picture are typical of the fledgling film criticism of 1930). And it is an easy film to like for the same reason that the novel is easy to like. There is much appealing in a story of universal boyhood set on the romantic Mississippi before the Civil War; here is a kind of collective unconscious of the nostalgic as Tom and his friends act out the fantasies and adventures of the childhood all adults would have liked to remember having had.

The first two-thirds of the film follows the novel closely, faithfully reproducing many significant scenes even as to dialogue. There is some condensation of events and details in this section, but the leisurely pace and important occurrences follow the book closely—although there is more emphasis given to the high jinks of Tom and his friends than to the involvement with Injun Joe. The final third of the film, however, changes speeds, telescopes scenes, and makes significant alterations in both the cave episode and the death of Injun Joe, as well as omitting Huck's role almost entirely. It is in this last third that the film falls short even as juvenilia because it lessens the suspense, changes the conclusion, and eliminates much of the satisfying denouement. Not only is mature material missing, but an apparent desire to keep the film morally fit for a juvenile audience resulted in a number of alterations even on the level of boyish fun.

While the book opens with Aunt Polly calling for an absent Tom, the film, borrowing perhaps from the memorable beginning of *Life on the Mississippi* (1883), opens aboard a steamboat about to land at St. Petersburg. We see the sleepy hamlet awaken to the vessel's arrival, followed by two nostalgic vignettes. In the first sequence, two residents express amazement at the speed of mail delivery from California (three months). In the second, a housewife scoffs at the newfangled paraffin wax for canning. These glimpses of rural America in 1850 are clearly intended to establish a mood of retrospective longing for a slower and simpler time.

This introduction appeals most to a mature audience, but it is the only place in the film where such an obvious concession is made. Whatever else is for adults is atmospheric not concrete, evocative not direct: a reminiscence of boyish fun and golden summers. (Not that it is Arcadia. The whims of nature can be precarious along the Mississippi, and here is the home of immanent evil in the person of Injun Joe. The film, like the novel, is, in Bernard DeVoto's words, an "Idyll enclosed in dread.")

The film then makes the first of a number of thematic transitions to introduce us to Aunt Polly and her high-spirited nephew. This transition is achieved by cutting from a sign hawking paraffin to a shot of Tom, trapped into helping Polly in the kitchen and struggling with old-fashioned sealing wax. Tom's penchant for daydreaming is introduced immediately as he allows the kettle to boil dry while he drifts off into the first of several superimposed reveries—this one of being a pirate. The sequences original to the film quickly establish the uneasy relationship between the perpetually exasperated and practical Aunt Polly and the undisciplined dreamer Tom. Jackie Coogan's performance in the title role is one of the outstanding features of the film. Coogan earlier had played *Peck's Bad Boy* (1921); now, as the saying goes, he *is* Tom Sawyer. (In general, the casting is effective—Mitzi Green is plump and appealing as Becky Thatcher, Clara Blandick is bespectacled, befuddled, and often beside herself as Aunt Polly, and Charles Stevens is an appropriately villainous but underplayed Injun Joe. In fact, it was the cast, and especially Coogan, that drew most of the contemporary notice.)

Following the introduction of Huckleberry Finn (played by Junior Durkin) and the establishment of his unsavory reputation, Tom is found to have stolen Sid's crabapples. Sid (Jackie Searl) is an appropriate goody-goody, crybaby, tattletale, and an even greater thorn in Tom's side. In the book, Tom runs afoul of Aunt Polly for many reasons; in the movie, Sid is almost always involved. In the crabapple case (new in the film) Tom's punishment leads to what must be the best-known scene in juvenile literature—whitewashing the fence. Not only is Tom's clever ruse reproduced, but the camera eye adds a dimension the novel cannot possess. The brief shot of a dozen St. Petersburg youths scrambling to do their part communicates the success of Tom's venture at least as effectively as the original prose. Even the *Times* noted that the "episode is admirably pictured for, through the camera, the full length of the fence on two sides of the house comes to the screen." (In general, Cromwell maintains a light touch technically. Where the camera can reinforce the material, particularly in background and atmosphere, it is effectively used—as in the opening scene of the great river and the small town. Tom's ideas, Aunt Polly's aggravation, and the boy's terror are conveyed naturally, if conventionally, through close-ups. Only the several superimposed fantasies seem self-consciously "cinematic," and even they can be justified in their successful characterization of Tom as a romantic daydreamer.)

Tom avenges himself on Sid with a ripe tomato and then, in a scene from the book, he picks a fight with a new boy who is dressed like a "dude." They huff, threaten, and brag their way through the puffery of adolescent ritual before actually coming to blows. Tom wins the fight but he befriends his opponent the next day at school. In the novel, the new boy is unnamed, but in the film he transfers into Joe Harper, Tom's best friend in the book. The change is reasonable and an example of a successful condensation of two characters.

With the social milieu introduced by the opening vignettes, and Tom's character established, the film moves to the first of the extended plots. Tom sees and immediately falls in love with Becky Thatcher at her window. Again material is modified and compressed. Tom sees Becky the second time in grammar school not, as in Twain, in Sunday school, and their relationship goes from introduction through declaration of love to engagement and jealous breakup in one scene. It is late in the novel when Tom cavalierly takes a beating for the anatomy book that Becky has accidentally torn, but it is early in the film and for a different reason: she has drawn an unflattering caricature of the master.

The nobility of Tom's sacrifice is somewhat lessened by this change in circumstance. There can be no repeat of the scene in Twain where Becky's father, Judge Thatcher, compares Tom Sawyer to George Washington and envisions for him a great future.

The beginning of the second major plot comes to the screen intact and even almost word for word in the dialogue. Tom and Huck take a dead cat to the graveyard in search of a cure for warts, but they witness instead the murder of Dr. Robinson and the framing of Muff Potter by Injun Joe. The cutting back and forth from the boys' view of the events in the desolate graveyard to close-ups of their wide-eyed wonder infuses the scene with an eeriness beyond Mark Twain's prose. The subsequent writing and signing in blood of an oath promising never to reveal what they have seen is reproduced exactly. The effect on Tom's conscience of knowing Muff Potter's innocence is also well handled in the film. When he hears townspeople in the general store talking about hanging Potter, his fear and guilt are communicated not only by facial expressions but, in another Cromwellian borrowing from the special syntax of the cinema, by a superimposed image of the blood oath. While the original signing of the oath may seem boyish fun in both novel and film, the superimposition effectively informs the viewer of the seriousness of the oath and the boys' awesome respect for it.

Tom escapes his guilty conscience by leading Huck and Joe on a pirate trip to Jackson's Island. The film handles the three-day "pirating" excursion and the boys' dramatic return to their own funerals with much allegiance to the novel. Tom's solitary night-time journey home, his birch-bark message to Aunt Polly, and his nocturnal kiss are reproduced in scenes with very little dialogue or sound.

A great friendly roar greets the boys' return, but Tom's anxiety is brought back as he and Huck overhear the falsely accused Muff Potter consulting with his attorney. (The device of over-hearing significant conversation seems overworked in the film, but it occurs just as often in the novel.) Finally, while Huck flees in terror of the broken oath, the truth about the murder is re-vealed to Muff's lawyer. There is a rapid cut to the courtroom where Tom identifies Injun Joe as the murderer. The scene ends with the culprit escaping.

It is at this point that the film begins to deviate significantly from the book. The condensation and alteration of events in the first two-thirds are justified and generally effective; however, the changes in the finale seem to work less well. Gone is the boys' lengthy but abortive treasure hunt, the shadowing of Injun Joe, and the bulk of Tom's social triumph after the trial. The film moves right to the episode at McDougal's cave.

As the children enter the cavern, Tom and Becky make up, and in their rapture, they wander off and become lost. Yet, their predicament does not convey the sense of terror or hopelessness found in the novel. Twain develops their dilemma slowly, building tension as they nibble the crumbs of their "wedding cake," nurse the final bits of candle, and try bravely to retain their spirits. Phrases such as "sunk into a dreary apathy" and "tortured with a raging hunger" have no counterpart in the film where the couple are found almost as soon as they know they are lost. Obviously, the length of time necessary for proper building of tension and also the morbid aspects of the situation, would have unbalanced the film both structurally and atmospherically. While looking for a way out, Tom happens upon Injun Joe gloating over his treasure. Despite Twain's attack on Fenimore Cooper for breaking twigs when "absolute-silence" is worth "four dollars a minute," the cinema Tom Sawyer is unable to stifle an exclamation, and the Hollywoodian chase is on. From this point, any resemblance to the novel is coincidental as the renegade pursues Tom madly through the cavern and corners him at the end of a ledge overlooking a deep chasm. In his desire for revenge upon his accuser, Injun Joe slips from the ledge and falls to his death. Tom returns to Becky with no problem and they are found by rescuers, including Huck, who has located the treasure while searching for Tom and Becky.

Since the mythic overtones of the novel's cave sequence are outside the scope of the film, and perhaps because Hollywood was not ready to let a boy and girl spend the night together— even lost in a cave—the highly dramatic and frightening incident is significantly altered. Instead of Tom and Huck returning to the cave to dig up the treasure in true romantic fashion, it is sitting in plain sight for the taking. Again, the demise of Injun Joe is considerably less grotesque that Twain's depiction of his starvation behind the locked door of the cave. The Welshman is forgotten and Widow Douglas (Jane Darwell) appears only to adopt Huck. The film ends with an incident from the middle of the book. Aunt Polly does not believe that Tom cares enough about her to have explained his absence in a message that he intended to leave on his nocturnal visit home from Jackson's Island. He tells her the birch-bark missive is in his coat pocket, she finds the message, and is overjoyed. Although the event is out of place, it provides the way to a satisfactory conclusion. Tom steals Sid's fishing pole and when Sid runs crying to Aunt Polly, her happiness with Tom is so complete that she slap's Sid's face and the film ends.

There are, of course, other alterations and omissions. The most significant of these are the satirical passages that ridicule the human race and its institutions. The parody of young ladies' literary production could not, of course, fit into the film, and the industry's prohibition of religious satire obviously accounts for the elimination of the rather extensive parodies of Sunday School, the Temperance movement, evangelism, and preaching. Again, apparently in deference to the potential corruption of children, the memorable episode on Jackson's Island in which Huck introduces Tom and Joe to tobacco is omitted. Even the dead cat appears only inside a bag. And Twain's criticism of "sappy" women who go from wanting to lynch Muff Potter to coddling him is ignored. Superstition plays a significant role in the film as it does in the novel, but there is not even the book's veiled suggestion that the boys' superstitious rites are to be equated with the community's religion.

But the omissions do not seriously detract from the level of boyish fun or, for that matter, from the more adult mood of nostalgic optimism. Within limitations, Cromwell's *Tom Sawyer* is successful as an adaptation, and in its own right—essentially as a children's film.

Daisy Miller (1878), Henry James

An Interview with Peter Bogdanovich

BY   JAN DAWSON

With an eleven-week shooting schedule, a budget of over four million dollars and permission to shoot in the story's authentic locations (including the Pincio and the Colosseum in Rome, the Château de Chillon, and the exclusive Hôtel des Trois Couronnes in Vevey), Bogdanovich had already completed the Italian footage for *Daisy Miller* and had just started shooting in Vevey when he spoke about the film last October [1973]:

"What preoccupies you is telling a story about some people that interest you: characters that move you, that you find sad or funny. I think the most exciting thing is if you can tell a story that's funny and sad alternately, or hopefully both at once. The ending of *Daisy Miller* is the most painful thing I ever shot. In fact it's only the second time I've cried while I was making a scene. But *Daisy Miller* is also very funny. Anyway, we intend it to be.

"I know that I'm going to get an awful lot of questions about Henry James, but that doesn't really concern me. I read a story that I thought was very interesting, very *sketchy* . . . he himself called it a study. And he meant it, I think, not as a study of the American girl but in the way a painter would refer to a sketch

Editors' title. From "The Continental Divide: Filming Henry James," by Jan Dawson. *Sight and Sound*, Volume 43, No. 1, Winter 1973/74, pp. 14–15. Reprinted by permission.

as a study for a larger canvas. I think he did do larger canvases on the same theme all through the rest of his career. *Daisy Miller* is in fact a kind of sketch. It's only about fifty or sixty pages, and it's like a very good treatment for a movie. Just enough to make it damned interesting to make as a movie, because you can fill in certain nuances or explain certain things that he leaves totally unexplained. Or at least imply certain things that he leaves even unimplied.

"In other words, I don't think it's a great classic story. I don't treat it with that kind of reverence. If James hadn't written *Daisy Miller*, I wouldn't be making it. So one is in debt to the author. On the other hand, if Shakespeare hadn't written *Othello*, Verdi wouldn't have written the opera. I don't mean to compare myself to either Verdi or Shakespeare; I'm just saying that I'm sure Verdi didn't go around worrying about Shakespeare. And I don't want to spend too much time worrying about Henry James. Except to take whatever I can from the story that I like. I mean, one is making a movie, not a *Classics Illustrated* comic-book. And whether or not I put in the movie what James meant to say with the story doesn't really concern me. The social aspects of it don't really concern me. The thing that interests me *least* is what James saw in it. Though on the surface I think we've been very faithful to the story." . . .

Bogdanovich was actively involved on the screenplay, for which he will share a credit with Frederic Raphael. "He and I worked out the structure together, and then he wrote a script. He wrote one draft, and then I rewrote it three times. And then he made some comments on my second version, and I incorporated some of his comments into that. And then there was a third draft, which I did. I did a lot of writing on this picture. Some of James' dialogue sounds a little bit like an Englishman trying to write in American. Even though he was an American, he'd spent a great deal of time in foreign parts. So one had to try to make it sound a little more American. There's a lot of dialogue in the movie, but it doesn't seem talky, although it is almost all talk. I also think it's rather marvellous to have a costume piece in which nobody behaves as though he's in a costume picture. I didn't want the actors to be afraid to be casual about overlapping or stepping on

Daisy (Cybill Shepherd) and Winterbourne (Barry Brown), Americans in Rome. Daisy Miller (1974).

Daisy (Cybill Shepherd) strolls with her Italian suitor Giovanelli (Duilio Del Prete). Daisy Miller (1974).

each other's lines. Everybody talks very fast, and it might as well be *What's Up, Doc?* in terms of the pace. It's very fast. I think the whole picture will only play at about 95 minutes.

"But I also want the film to be beautiful. It's the first chance I've had to make a movie which would be beautiful on purpose as opposed to bleak. *What's Up, Doc?* and *Targets* were purposely ugly; in terms of the lighting and the clothes I tried rather strenuously to make them as ugly as possible. Whereas in *Daisy Miller* the tragedy of the film is that anything as sad as this could happen to such beautiful people in such beautiful settings. Of course the film has two definite segments: one in Switzerland and one in Italy. And the first section is more romantic, so to speak, than the second. I can't begin to describe it. All I can say is that there is a big difference, pictorially, between Switzerland and Rome; not so much in the camerawork, but in the texture and colour. Though since we are telling one story, it's not a question of suddenly changing styles in midstream. The people change, but the change is more subtle than doing anything as obvious as a Fellini kind of Rome.

"I've noticed about myself that I'm not terribly keen on gratuitous atmosphere. I hope you can get the feeling of what's going on by following the characters. But what I have managed to do in *Daisy Miller* is to get a depth-of-field, a depth-of-focus, in colour that you usually only get in black-and-white. We did one sequence, the evening party where Daisy is given the cold shoulder by Mrs. Walker, with absolutely extraordinary depth-of-field. We had a room with eight mirrors (the room was already there, but we used it, because it seemed to fit the story and to fit Mrs. Walker's world), and it's really a wonderful scene because you never lose sight of anybody. You see people walking away in the mirror, then you cut and they're coming towards you. It sounds confusing, but it has a beautiful flow to it. You're not aware of it being a trick. We'd have a close-up of somebody, and in the mirror behind him you'd see what he was looking at. And they would both be in focus, which is exceedingly difficult to do. Plus it was all supposedly by candlelight. It took, I don't know, four or five days."

For his previous films, Bogdanovich has tended to take recognisable sounds (including radio and TV programmes) from the period in question and weave them into a kind of music track. I asked whether he was going to resort to a score for *Daisy Miller.* "No. We're doing the same thing. It's going to be Mozart and Verdi and Handel and Schubert. Some people will recognise it, though not the Hank Williams fans. There's music all the way through, but it's not a score. You see the musicians mostly. For instance, Giovanelli sings an aria from Verdi's *Masked Ball* at Mrs. Walker's party; and later Winterbourne goes to the opera and sees *A Masked Ball* (nobody will notice that, because we don't make a point of it). Then there's a string quartet at the party; there's a pianist at the tea; and there's a band at the Pincio which was actually there, we didn't invent that. Daisy (Cybill Shepherd) in fact sings in the picture. We've dramatised the scene that James mentions but doesn't discuss, the scene where Winterbourne comes to her hotel and finds Daisy and Giovanelli at the piano. Daisy sings an American song, "When You and I Were Young, Maggie," which was popular in about 1870; and Giovanelli sings an American song in that scene, which I think is rather funny. He sings 'Pop Goes the Weasel.' "

Apart from dramatising some of the incidents to which James only alluded, Bogdanovich also admits that he has modified some of the characters, shifting the emphasis or developing their motivations. His screenplay opens with Daisy's younger brother Randolph indulging in an early morning practical joke in the hotel corridors; and Randolph, hidden in the branches of a tree, is now also a witness to Daisy's nocturnal flirtation with Winterbourne in the hotel grounds. "We've made Randolph" (played by Larry McMurtry's ten-year-old son James; Bogdanovich finds professional child actors odious and lacking in spontaneity) "a little more interesting than he is in the story, a bit more devilish from the start."

Bogdanovich has also made the character of Winterbourne's severe aunt Mrs. Costello "quite a bit more human than she is in the story . . . I don't think I have a rosy view of life. I think the idea of villains is rosy, because it simplifies. People aren't good or bad, they're people. I don't like obvious heavies; they're boring. So in the movie Mrs. Costello is rather likeable, she's rather funny too. One of the reasons I cast Mildred Natwick is because I think it's impossible not to like Mildred Natwick." Perhaps the most audacious change to the James purist is the fact that the likeable Mrs. Costello no longer keeps herself and her migraines to her rooms, but displays her hypochondria in the thermal baths, from which public place she explains to Winterbourne the social niceties of the Miller family's vulgarity.

"The story gets darker as it progresses. And it seemed to me that if we began at the baths with Mrs. Costello, we'd have somewhere to go. I was worried about it and almost changed it back. But I left it that way, first of all because I thought it was funny. The mixed bathing is authentically of the period. And they're not really undressed; they are even more absurd-looking because they are dressed so much. I felt that, if it could be pulled off, it would be very amusing to see people having tea and playing chess and chequers while immersed in water. And I also thought it was a light way to introduce Mrs. Costello that would contrast with how accurate she is in her predictions of what's going to happen. So that one would be sort of amused and feel that this was a ridiculous woman (though Mildred Natwick is so dignified in the way she plays it that it's almost as though she were in her parlour); and then one would come to realise that she may be ridiculous, but she's also quite astute.

"Mrs. Walker is the biggest change in the movie. I thought she was a bit melodramatic in the story; I found her difficult to accept because she seemed rather unmotivated except for her social reasons. And I thought there should be more beneath that. I think all that stuff is based on some other kind of repression anyway. So although James didn't talk about it, it seemed implicit that there was something else at work there, some threat that Daisy posed. So I've changed her. In the way I've cast it and the way she's played, she's rather heavily motivated sexually. She's quite attracted to Winterbourne. Eileen Brennan is wonderful in the part.

"Winterbourne, in the movie anyway, is also exceedingly jealous. James doesn't even mention the word jealous and neither do I. But I think it's quite clear that part of what's bothering him is that he's jealous. In a sense, he's a typical Victorian man with a lot of hang-ups. None of which we detail. It's not a Buñuel movie.

"I sort of treated it as a suspense story . . . in the sense that there is a feeling of mystery about the whole picture. One has the feeling that something terrible is going to happen, but you don't know where it's coming from." From its light beginnings, the screenplay in fact builds to Daisy's funeral (the third that Bogdanovich has shot), with which the picture closes. "It's a sad story. Somebody's dead who should be alive. In fact, more than the main character is dead at the end of *Daisy Miller*.

"I make an active effort, and it becomes more active on each succeeding picture, to preserve my innocence about the story as well as about the film-making process; to rely on my instinct and listen to my instinct as much as possible." Asked whether he feels that, in venturing into Europe and embarking on a literary classic with instinct and innocence as his main guides, he runs the risk of being compared to one of James' characters, Bogdanovich replies: "I'm not one who lives too long in foreign parts. I can't wait to get home . . . I sort of don't like expatriates."

Daisy Miller (1878), Henry James

An International Episode

BY KATHLEEN MURPHY

Henry James took as one of his major themes the amusing—more often, tragic—encounters between representatives of the Old and New Worlds. His Americans were brash, uncomplicated, crudely ignorant, or gloriously innocent. He pitted them—sometimes on their own ground, sometimes overseas—against European complexity and wisdom that occasionally ran to decadence. If the New Worlders looked optimistically towards a utopian future, the denizens of the Old were the products of an immensely rich past, and layers upon layers of civilization provided them with a patina of cosmopolitan sophistication and worldliness that the parochial inhabitants of the new Eden could either admire or outrage, but never hope to equal. In a sense, Peter Bogdanovich is similarly caught between two worlds: as a director who admittedly admires the great film-makers of the past—Ford, Hawks, Welles—his films have been, to a greater or lesser degree, *hommages* to classical direction, to genres made generic by Pantheon auteurs. But Bogdanovich also lives in the here and now, and his work must look to its future. For he can never really reattain the innocence of those early halcyon days of making movies: he knows too much, is too self-conscious to successfully recreate what the masters originally conceived. Howard Hawks made

"An International Episode" originally appeared in *Movietone News*, No. 33, July 1974, pp. 13–16. Reprinted by permission.

movies for the fun of it long before the French critics "discovered " and enshrined his films in learned exegesis—and the tone of director-critic Bogdanovich's films, for me, has always been less fun, more learned.

Perhaps it is Bogdanovich's innate respect for a past master that makes *Daisy Miller* the successful portrait in miniature that it is; perhaps too it is that respect, that painstaking effort to capture another artist's nuance and style which prevents the film from transcending itself, becoming more than a tasteful, sometimes brilliant visualization of James's superbly succinct novella. The very first shot of the film is an obeisance to Welles's *The Magnificent Ambersons,* but it also represents a visual announcement of Bogdanovich's informed reading of James: the camera pulls away from screen-filling textured gold to reveal the ceiling of what we come to realize is a luxurious hotel; moving, disorienting, it travels down through dim, hushed *étages* to finally come to rest outside the door of the Miller suite. The door opens, a child immediately identifiable as a brat emerges into a corridor discreetly punctuated by pairs of shoes left out to be polished. Switching shoes the length of the hall, sliding down an elegant bannister, boosting a walking stick under the very noses of properly respectful hotel staff, Daisy Miller's little brother spreads disorder and impropriety as though to herald the more serious breaches of Old World protocol that his sister will eventually perpetrate. The Millers—Americans on the Grand Tour—are clearly out of their depth in the layers-deep, complexly architected system of rules and customs that governs the behavior of Europeans, and more importantly, the American colony in Europe—who ironically, but understandably, exceed even their hosts in punctilio.

One of these expatriates, Frederick Winterbourne (Barry Brown), is a typically unreliable Jamesian narrator through whose biased eyes and limited sensibility we come to recognize what Daisy Miller (Cybill Shepherd) is and is not, what Winterbourne, who "has lived too long in foreign parts," seeks only to formulize, and in so doing, kills. Brown's Winterbourne oscillates between faith in the innocence of this perfectly unself-conscious creature who chatters breathlessly on as though all the world were her oyster, and disenchantment with her "want of finish," her periodic crudities, and worst of all, what appears to him to be her promiscuous intimacy with socially unacceptable Europeans. Though Bogdanovich uses practically every word of dialogue (and description) from James's story, he is forced, by the very nature of film, to have Brown act out the ironies of behavior and perception that on the written page create quite a different impact. Thus, over and over, we *see* Winterbourne's errors in judgment: Barry Brown's face must express what James imbeds in prose so cool and civilized that the small horrors it conceals are all the more terrible. Also, in the story, we are locked into Winterbourne's mind, and his failures in perception are revealed in his own words and thoughts, whereas in the film we can see independently so that Daisy is not just the creature of his imagination, but ours as well. Our sympathies are thereby enlisted much more on her behalf, while James makes us feel for and with a man who misses the point even when Daisy's deathbed protestation of innocence makes him think he has been enlightened.

Under Bogdanovich's direction, Cybill Shepherd brings off Daisy Miller to near perfection: not only does she manage James's difficult dialogue with admirable authenticity, but her very complexion seems to pale or color in response to the delights and cruelties Europe offers her. That "perfectly direct and unshrinking glance," which so disconcerts Winterbourne in his search for a "formula" in which to contain Daisy, telegraphs the self-absorbed innocence that Shepherd expressed so naturally even in her modeling days. The open-flower quality of that face and personality soon wilts under the wintry weight of blanket disapproval and ostracism, so that it's not so much the "Roman fever" of which Daisy dies, but Winterbourne's final "relieved illumination" concerning her heretofore disturbingly ambiguous character: "She was a young lady whom a gentleman need no longer be at pains to respect." Bogdanovich makes his Winterbourne much less lethal, more vulnerable to Daisy's charm. James's character remarks of Daisy's death from a distance (literal and figurative): "A week after this the poor girl died; it had been a terrible case of the fever." Bogdanovich brings it into closer focus, and in so doing slightly shifts our assessment of Winterbourne. The camera remains outside the door of Daisy's hotel watching through a curtain of ivory lace as Winterbourne, carrying a cheerful bouquet, buoyantly swings through the lobby and is halfway up the staircase when, still outside, we hear a murmured "*E morta*" and he stops, frozen in midstep. That complexly fashioned lace, like the first shot of the film, accurately indexes the long-established intricacies of custom and mores adhered to by those who have misunderstood and betrayed Daisy to death. (The falling of just such a lace curtain signals the death of Isabel Amberson in *The Magnificent Ambersons.*)

Bogdanovich also significantly alters James's conclusion. In the novella, a year after Daisy's demise, Winterbourne confides to his "exclusive" aunt (who did not care to know the girl) that he has finally understood Daisy's dying message (that she was not engaged to the odious Italian). It meant that "She would have appreciated one's esteem." A lesson learned so late, and so badly, for again Daisy's life and personality have been reduced to one of Winterbourne's comfortable formulas. "Nevertheless" (a wonderfully ironic and quintessentially Jamesian word), Winterbourne returns to Geneva to continue his "studies" . . . of the very clever foreign lady with whom he was linked at the beginning of the story. Bogdanovich is rather more sympathetic to Winterbourne as he stands stricken at Daisy's grave, learning of Daisy's innocence from the Italian he so despised, cut dead by Daisy's unforgiving little brother. He remains after the other mourners have departed, a lonely figure among the cypresses, slowly lost to view as the camera recedes and the frame is gradually suffused by the rich gold with which the film opened. Here, Winterbourne seems more a hapless, helpless victim of his upbringing, to have loved and lost, while James indicts him as a co-conspirator and lets us know the full extent to which he misinterprets his entire experience and how very much he loses, not only in love, but in life, by that misinterpretation.

On the whole, however, Bogdanovich has meticulously followed James even to the reproduction of marvelous details like Winterbourne's affected curling of his mustache when he denies his aunt's "You are too innocent." (She ripostes, "You are too guilty, then!") Andrew Sarris remarked that there is a great deal of

Daisy Miller in Peter Bogdanovich. I would add that he contains more than a little Winterbourne as well. For, like James's character, Bogdanovich studies rather than grasps instinctively, is so refined in his cinematic sensibility that he never seems to direct spontaneously, by the seat of his pants. Which is not to say that I don't think he makes good movies. Only that, like some enormously talented student, he has yet to find his own mode, a style that is inspired by its own momentum, rather than an impetus out of the past.

Washington Square (1881), Henry James

Washington Square *and* The Heiress: *Comparing Artistic Forms*

BY JERRY W. CARLSON

How fair is it to compare a film adaptation with its literary original? In the case of William Wyler's *The Heiress* (1949)[1] from Henry James's *Washington Square* (1880)[2] the matter is more than usually complicated. First, the screenplay by Ruth and Augustus Goetz is not based directly on the novel but derived from their play, *The Heiress*, produced on Broadway in 1948. Second, as the Goetzes claim in the play script[3] and in the title sequence of the film, both the play and its cinematic rendering are only "suggested by" the James novel. Third, there is the additional knowledge that James's own dramatizations of two of his novels—*Daisy Miller* (1878) and *The American* (1877)[4] —seem best described also as "suggested by" their antecedents. In each adaptation, to summarize, the characters who suffer tragic fates in the novel find happy endings in the play. Hence the radical transformation of materials in adapting from one medium to another is practiced willingly by Henry James himself.

---

[1] I would like to thank Mr. William Wyler for his courtesy in sending me a copy of the shooting script of *The Heiress*. Hereafter cited as *H*.

[2] Ed. by Gerald Willen (New York, 1970). Hereafter cited as *WS*.

[3] New York: Dramatists Service, 1948.

[4] Leon Edel, ed., *The Complete Plays of Henry James* (Philadelphia, 1949).

A comparison of *The Heiress* and *Washington Square*, then, must not concentrate on how the film violates the original, thereby ignoring the stated principle of the adaptation: "suggestion." Nor must it look on one as the translation of the other. Instead, it must weigh the inevitable alterations and transformations in terms of their appropriateness to the individual artistic wholes.

But how do we begin the weighing? One way—endorséd by the popular sloganism of Marshall McLuhan—would seem to be a comparison of the relative impact of the artistic medium on the works: film vs. prose narrative. But this is a false starting point —however popular it may be—insofar as it takes as an implicit assumption that medium is a *determinant* of artistic creation, not a *variable*.

Again, how do we begin? To start, we may note that what one critic has recently observed about the novel seems equally applicable to narrative film. In his study *Hawthorne, Melville, and the Novel* (Chicago, 1975) Richard Brodhead makes this point:

> Nothing in a novel exists in itself; each included element has its being—its relative massiveness or slightness, its relative significance or insignificance—in its relation to the novel's whole configuration of elements. A novel's form is the system of relations in its created world, the elementary laws of conservation and interaction that structure its behavior and govern the potentialities within it for meaning and for action. (p. 9)

Thus, inasmuch as we experience these works not as simple determinants of medium but as artistic wholes—as unities of matter, means, and medium of expression—we can compare their synthesizing powers or, in a more familiar though frequently vague critical term, their "forms."

What, then, are their respective forms? Most generally, both works are embodiments of the same proto-story. Catherine Sloper, a dull and plain but pleasant young woman, is courted by Morris Townsend, a handsome world traveler and fortune hunter. As the story advances, Catherine slowly discovers not only that Morris's sincere attraction is confined to her fortune, but that her protective father, Dr. Austin Sloper, a well-respected physician

Catherine Sloper (Olivia De Havilland) is courted by Morris Townsend (Montgomery Clift). The Heiress (1949).

and wit, has no more human feeling for her than does her mercenary suitor. Eventually, Catherine is rid of them both. Morris jilts her. Somewhat later, her father dies of natural causes. Later still, Morris returns with a second offer. Catherine, full of her past experience, rejects him. Finally, Catherine lives out her days as a spinster, somewhat crippled by her experience but continuing admirably within her limits.

James's shaping of the proto-story—his overall design to hold the parts in relation to the whole—is to work toward an increasing respect for Catherine's moral integrity. As his heroine moves from naiveté to experience, James is careful to assure us that her movement is not from innocence to bitterness, but from moral simplicity to moral understanding, a transformation the more impressive because it is not suggested in any of the other characters.

Perhaps the most important indexes of Catherine's moral superiority are her dealings with her father and Morris after she discovers their true natures. When Morris reappears after many years of absence, she recognizes that "the story of his life defined itself in his eyes: he had made himself comfortable, and he had never been caught. But even while her perception opened itself to this, she had no desire to catch him; his presence was painful to her, and she only wished he would go" (WS 167). Furthermore, when Morris makes a rhetorical appeal to her feelings by pleading for forgiveness, she replies, "I forgave you years ago, but it is useless for us to attempt to be friends" (WS 168). Her answer certainly shows what Morris calls a "confounded dry little manner" (WS 167), but it is laconic and tactful, without illusions, not bitter or nasty.

Catherine shows comparable moral integrity in dealing with her father. To save Catherine from Morris, Dr. Sloper takes her to Europe, and there, in a barren Alpine valley, he rages against the love affair and all but deserts her to the elements (WS 112–113). But Dr. Sloper's viciousness is not characteristically so blunt. More typically, when Catherine claims that *she* has broken off her engagement, thereby hoping to cover up the obvious and embarrassing fact that Morris has jilted her, Dr. Sloper replies with his most calculated irony:

"How does he take his dismissal?"

"I don't know!" said Catherine, less ingeniously than she had hitherto spoken.

"You mean you don't care? You are rather cruel, after encouraging him and playing with him for so long!"

The doctor had his revenge after all. (*WS* 151)

Yet despite her father's malice and sarcasm, Catherine maintains gentle relations with him. When Dr. Sloper talks of dying, she replies, "I hope you live a long time" (*WS* 157). And when he enters his final illness, she is "assiduous at his bed side" (*WS* 159). Importantly, her gentleness of manner is not cowardice, a failing of moral integrity, but an aspect of her discerning and forgiving moral intelligence. When she must stand up for herself, she does so. Thus, when she realizes that her father's deathbed wish—a promise that she will never see Morris again—is an "injury to her dignity" (*WS* 158), she decides not to honor the request.

Ultimately, our respect for Catherine rests not so much on the small acts she does do as on what she chooses *not* to do. She never stoops to conquer. She is superior because she refuses to use language or emotion to injure others in her own service. Moreover, the credibility of Catherine's accomplishments remains high because James is careful to measure its painful cost. We are told that she "rigidly" averts herself from other possibilities of marriage and that, in her spinsterhood, she becomes a "person to be reckoned with" (*WS* 154; 160). Nonetheless, such a fate at such a cost stands superior to the cut-rate charms and the moral diffusion which surround her.

While James's treatment of the story emphasizes the complexity and limitation of moral triumph, William Wyler's faithful handling of the Goetz script offers a different focus. Wyler's overall design—his synthesizing principle—is to secure a sense of vengeful satisfaction for Catherine as she metes out appropriate justice to those who have injured her. Thus, like her Jamesian incarnation, she moves from naiveté to experience, but whereas James's heroine shows internal moral development, Wyler's heroine displays an abrupt reversal of character: first she is a duped innocent, and then she is a stoic domestic warrior returning injury in kind. Or, to put it differently, whereas James's narrative is based on a line of moral development, Wyler's film is based on the symmetry of revenge. Once again, the most important indexes of Catherine's character are her dealings with her father and Morris after she discovers their true natures.

As in James, Dr. Sloper (Ralph Richardson) takes Catherine (Olivia de Havilland) to Europe to protect her—in his own fashion—from Morris. Father and daughter's most brutal face-to-face meeting is saved for later, in the back parlor of their house the evening they return from Europe. Catherine announces that she hopes to marry Morris (Montgomery Clift) after all.

> DR. SLOPER: Catherine, I've tried not to be unkind, but now it is time for you to realize the truth. How many girls do you think he might have in this town?
> CATHERINE: He finds me—pleasing. . .
> DR. SLOPER: Yes, I'm sure he does. A hundred women are prettier, and a thousand more clever, but you have one virtue that outshines them all!
> CATHERINE (*fearfully*): What—what is that?
> DR. SLOPER: Your money!
> CATHERINE (*horrified*): Oh, father. What a monstrous thing to say to me. . .!
> DR. SLOPER: I don't expect you to believe that, I've known you all your life and have yet to see you learn anything . . . (*he rises and sees her embroidery frame*). With one exception my dear . . . you embroider neatly. (*H* 123–124)

Soon afterward, Catherine lets Morris know that her father "despises" (*H* 130) her. Rapidly—probably too rapidly for credibility—she changes. A scene later, the sheepish daughter has joined the predators and is ready for revenge—that is, to elope with Morris against her father's wishes. To an observation that Dr. Sloper will be shocked by her action, Catherine replies: "Father . . . (*laughs ironically*) . . . He finds me so dull. It will surprise him to have such a dull girl disgrace his name" (*H* 134). Yet she is hopeful as she looks out on the Greenwich Village street: "Think of it, I may never stand in this window again. I may never see Washington Square on a windy April night" (*H*

135). Catherine, who talks so little, talks too soon. Morris, having learned that Catherine will make no effort to secure a portion of her father's estate, abandons her there and journeys alone to California. As her elopement fails, so does her initial scheme of revenge. Injured by her father and her suitor, she remains at Washington Square waiting to strike back.

Catherine's continued proximity to her father only exacerbates her new-found capacity for malevolence. As her father makes a self-diagnosis and announces the onset of his final illness, she remains rigid and emotionless at her embroidery—an action particularly chilling because it is measured against the gushing reaction of the maid Maria in the background of the deep-focus frame. Where for James's heroine passivity is a sign of moral strength, for Wyler's protagonist it is an instrument of icy retribution. Soon, however, Wyler's Catherine acts out her vengeful impulses. While her father's illness overtakes him and drives him to seek comfort and sympathy, she taunts him with his own cruelty: she tries to force him to change his will so she may be disinherited!

Even more cold-heartedly, Catherine saves her final revenge for her father's deathbed. In his last hours she sits in the park across the street from their house. To Maria's announcement that Dr. Sloper is "very low" and wishes to see his daughter, she remarks: "I know he does. Too late, Maria" (*H* 153). Her refusal is appropriate, vicious, and pathetic. It is appropriate because it mimics Dr. Sloper's initial manipulation of Catherine, forcing her to leave the sanctuary of the house. (Significantly, we only see her away from home twice before Dr. Sloper's death: with her father at the party where she meets Morris and again with her father, in Europe.) Thus, her revenge is perfect because it fulfills her father's fondest wish in exactly the wrong way. Still, it is vicious: Dr. Sloper is Catherine's father and he is dying. And it is also pathetic because, finally, it is pyrrhic. When Catherine returns to the house, it is for life.

Catherine's life in the house is only interrupted once: when Morris reappears after several years' absence. At the onset of their reunion, he tries to intimidate Catherine with his physical bearing—just as he had done during their first romance. She feigns

compliance and promises to elope with him later that evening.
After he leaves to pick up his luggage, Catherine acidly remarks:
"He came back with the same lies, the same silly phrases. . . . He
has grown greedier with the years. The first time he only wanted
my money, now he wants my love, too" (*H* 170, 171). How well
Catherine is capable of acting upon her bitterness is clear in the
last dramatic scene.

Interior of the front parlor
The sound of hoofs and the carriage stopping outside is heard.
Catherine is still; she is not surprised; she has expected it. We hear
the sound of the doorbell as it rings. Maria comes by the front parlor
door on her way to answer the bell. Catherine calls to her.
CATHERINE: I will attend to that. It's for me.
MARIA (*stops*): Yes, Miss.
We hear the sound of the bell as it rings again. Catherine takes a
last stitch and breaks off the thread [of her embroidery—author's
note]. Maria, puzzled, watches Catherine for a moment. Then we
hear the sound as Morris uses the knocker.
MARIA: Miss Catherine?
CATHERINE: Bolt it. Maria.
MARIA: Bolt it?
CATHERINE: BOLT THE DOOR, MARIA!
MARIA (*weakly*): Yes, Miss. (*H* 172)

Morris is left standing at the door, frantically knocking.
This revenge, though frightful, is satisfying, too, because it
answers in some detail what Morris did earlier to Catherine. It
was in the same parlor, on her return from Europe, that she
waited for Morris to come with a carriage for their elopement.
Now, years after, Catherine responds in kind. Yet her reprisal is
as much a transformation as a repetition. She makes the house
over from a prison partially created by Morris into a fortress
against him.
It is here, however, that the film's design most clearly shows
its weakness. The implications of Catherine's actions are far from
necessarily admirable. Unlike her Jamesian sister, she *always*
stoops to conquer. Because her imagination is used for imitation
rather than transcendence, she, in exacting her revenge, becomes

like her torturers. Of course, telling a story of moral corruption can be as admirable as charting a moral development. But, although Catherine's actions invite—indeed, beg for—a close look at her process of moral corruption, that is not what Wyler gives us. His stress is the satisfying shape of the plot. In the last scene Catherine emblematically rids herself of her father's image by finishing a piece of embroidery—that which her father feared would be her "life's work"[5]—and announcing that it *will* be her last. Moreover, in the same sequence, by giving the returned Morris the set of buttons she had bought as a wedding present she rids herself of the final sentimental reminder of their romance. These details reenforce, point by point, the cathartic symmetry of Catherine's revenge. Therefore, when, in the last moments of the film, Wyler shoots Catherine ascending the stairs to her bedroom (and does so with a tracking camera which makes us ascend the stairs with her as we hear Morris's knocking at the door and harsh brass music from Aaron Copland's score), her revenge is triumphant and complete.

But William Wyler's triumph is less than complete. In choosing to leap from Catherine as tortured to Catherine the torturer, in the way of the Goetz play, he sacrifices both moral complexity and dramatic credibility. Catherine's humanity pales before the mechanical demands of a well-made plot. Thus, if judge we must, we can say that *Washington Square* is superior to *The Heiress* not because narrative prose is inevitably superior to film nor because James as an artist is always superior to Wyler (*The Heiress* is arguably better than, say, James's *Confidence*), but because, in changing James, Wyler settles upon a form less complex in its human representation than its novelistic relative.

Still, with this said, much remains to be explored about the relationship between *Washington Square* and *The Heiress*. How, for example, does Wyler's cinematic style differ from James's prose style in convincing us of the relative merits of the main characters? How does Wyler take elements from the novel—most notably, the house—and use them as metaphors for the internal states of the characters? Furthermore, to what degree is

[5] Dr. Sloper's remark appears in the film, but not in the shooting script.

The Heiress, like *Washington Square,* not only the story of Catherine Sloper but criticism of an entire genteel tradition? There are many more questions to be asked. But the point here is that because individual elements cannot be understood outside of their relation to artistic wholes and because form is our critical mirror of those wholes, whatever further questions we ask must be related to the formal similarities and differences of the works. Formal comparison is not a mere companion for other kinds of comparative studies in adaptation. It is a prerequisite for such studies. As James tells us, "Form alone *takes,* and holds and preserves, substance."[6]

[6] Leon Edel, *Selected Letters of Henry James* (London: Rupert Hart-Davis, 1956), p. 202.

Faces in the Mirror:
Twain's Pauper, Warners' Prince

BY PETER BRUNETTE

Warner Brothers' 1937 adaptation of Mark Twain's potboiler, *The Prince and the Pauper* (1882), is that rare thing in American cinema, a movie that betters the "classic" book on which it is based. For Twain the novel was a somewhat regrettable departure. After his rowdy early successes, *The Innocents Abroad* (1869), *Roughing It* (1872), *Tom Sawyer* (1876), and *A Tramp Abroad* (1880), he now apparently wrote, in Maxwell Geismar's words, for "that audience of 'good little children' (and good parents) he had previously mocked." The results were spotty at best. And although certain genteel authors like William Dean Howells praised *The Prince and the Pauper*—"It breathes throughout the spirit of humanity and the reason of democracy" —the book was greeted by a considerably larger outpouring of critical disapproval, which hurt and dismayed Twain. Reviewers called it "a prolix work singularly deficient in literary merit" and "a heavy disappointment," and one commentator went so far as to say that "of [Twain's] many jokes, *The Prince and the Pauper* is incomparably the flattest and the worst." Modern critics have tended to agree, even with the totality of Twain's erratic output to consider.

Although such masterpieces as *Huckleberry Finn* (1884) and

A Connecticut Yankee (1899) were still in the future in 1882, the early books were already a rather difficult act to follow. Twain, of course, was expected to be nothing less than Twain, and his critics were perhaps overly demanding. Yet, in spite of the initial disappointment, *The Prince and the Pauper* managed over the years to worm its way into the American collective unconscious, so thoroughly in fact that many seem to have absorbed the tale without ever having read the book. (I suspect that most Americans under thirty-five know the story through *Classics Comics* rather than through any other source.) The Warner 1937 film seen today can take advantage of this familiarity and favorable predisposition without arousing the more exacting expectations of critics weighing Twain's prose.

The tale concerns two boys born on "a certain autumn day in the second quarter of the sixteenth century," one, Tom, the lowliest pauper in England, and the other, Edward, the Prince of Wales. Through various twists of the plot, they meet one day ten years later in the prince's chambers and, for a lark, exchange clothes. Astonished, they realize that no physical change at all has occurred, for underneath their finery and rags they are startling look-alikes. They are inadvertently separated, still dressed in each other's garb, and each spends the rest of the book trying to convince the denizens of his double's environment that he is not who or what he seems. The true prince finally reestablishes his identity and, with his father's death, is crowned king at the end. Chastened by his recent harsh experiences among the unfortunates of his domain, he frames a new code of generous and merciful laws.

Twain committed more than his usual share of literary sins in telling his tale; a tight plot, for example, with complications proceeding from character rather than from the vagaries of purest chance, was never very important to him. Even *Huckleberry Finn* and *Connecticut Yankee*, much better books, are episodic and loosely structured to an extreme. Mercifully, though, most of the narrative faults of *The Prince and the Pauper* are not translated to the screen. Scenes that Twain leaves inconclusive in the novel or that are repeated without significant variation at ten- or twenty-page intervals, are collapsed in the movie. And where

The crown prince and Tom Cantwell (the Mauch twins) exchange knowing glances in the throne room, while the wicked Earl of Hertford (Claude Rains) lurks in the background. The Prince and the Pauper (1937).

Twain disconcertingly doubles and redoubles minor examples of the poor boy's initial discomfort in Edward's presence and later at court, the film simply shows him not knowing which piece of fruit offered by the prince is a pear.

Nor does Twain hesitate to stop the action for lengthy descriptions of Renaissance curios—such as a peeress's hairdo—totally divorced from the advancement of plot or character. These passages, even if their peculiar information does add some sense of "atmosphere" to the narrative, still are vastly out of proportion to the more organic elements of the story. The film, on the other hand, can utilize its simple but fundamental visual power to place all this scene-painting instantly before us within an establishing long shot. At the same time, the foreground of the film is kept uncluttered for the unraveling of plot and filling in of character.

Still another weakness of Twain's narrative technique is his penchant for narrating in his authorial voice sequences that would have been better dramatized. The film remedies this common shortcoming of nineteenth-century fiction by constantly isolating the gesture, phrase, or visual detail that will perfectly summarize the point. In the very beginning, for example, the movie offers images of happy London crowds, joyous over the birth of the new prince, which are linked through matched dissolves to the more private joys of the palace. This scene is contrasted, through another unobstrusive dissolve, with Tom Canty's humble birth. A whole cosmos is expressed in his father's righteous anger that the newly born is so healthy—and thus not much prospect as a beggar.

A few more minor faults are remedied as well: Twain's verbal effusions ("the Prince of Poverty" vs. "the Prince of Limitless Plenty"), his inordinately long quotations from the chronicles of the sixteenth century, his awkward time shifts backward and forward, his blatant intrusions to escape technical culs-de-sac ("Let us change the tense for convenience") all disappear in the Warners version.

More important changes occur in terms of characterization, but not all are beneficial. In the movie, for example, the rough and ambiguous edges of Tom Canty's character are smoothed over in the interest of greater simplicity and directness, but he becomes a much less fascinating character in the process. In Twain, Tom begins to fall ever more comfortably into his newly acquired princely role, until he is brought up short by his mother's recognition of him on the way to his coronation. This compelling scene is omitted in the movie—along with Tom's mother. The only Tom we see is unrealistically right-minded and unwavering in his desire to have the true king receive the crown.

Another character, King Henry VIII, is made much less monolithically evil in the movie (Claude Rains as the Lord Protector, the Earl of Hertford, assumes most of his heinous aspect) and is given an expanded part filled to bursting by the convincing histrionics of actor Montagu Love. In a very well-done scene between the king on his deathbed and the child prince (perhaps suggested by Shakespeare's *Henry IV*, Part II), the audience is treated to a delightfully complex view of the practice of statecraft. The king gives the prince a contradictory crash course in kingship, explaining that he should remember three things: politics, which is cutting off the right heads at the right time; patriotism, which is remembering to govern with the consent and support of the people; and power, which forbids conscience, love, or trust, because the exigencies of political life may force a betrayal of those closest. This cold message is expounded quite ironically by way of a warm domestic scene, with the king smiling in his nightcap and pajamas and the prince lovingly hanging on his every word.

Miles Hendon, the unsuspecting, idealistic soldier of fortune who protects the real prince during his picaresque wanderings, also undergoes a major alteration. (He is played in the movie by Warners' rising star, Errol Flynn.) In a miscalculated subplot which Twain introduces near the end, we see Miles attempt to claim both his birthright, Hendon Hall, and his true love, Lady Edith, who has been forced to marry Miles's evil younger brother. All who knew Miles are now forced to deny his identity, so that his situation parallels young Edward's. But, despite its resonance, the new plot is simply too complicated for this late introduction. Besides, the little prince is hardly involved in these scenes at all. His thoughts are quite logically focused on a larger matter taking place in London—the impending coronation of the imposter. This entire subplot simply disappears in the film, and the role of Hendon is made thoroughly subservient to the main plot. In the end, he proves to be much more realistic than Twain's Hendon, refusing the new king's grateful largesse. He chooses rather to continue the life of a soldier of fortune, unencumbered as he is by the book's country manor and loyal sweetheart.

The single most important character change is in the Lord Protector. Twain's creation plays little more than a bumbling, contradictory minor role in the book; in the movie, he is elevated into an Iago-like, malevolent figure of splendid proportions. Discovering Tom Canty's unwilling imposture, he forces the boy to remain silent under threat of death so that he, the Lord Protector, can run the kingdom. To assure his wicked scheme, he dispatches the compromised Captain of the Guard, initially responsible for the mixup of identities, to assassinate the real king—a key plot transformation that gives the whole a suspenseful life-and-death cast almost from the beginning.

The true king is thus put to the test of the knife in both versions, but in vastly different circumstances. In one of the more exciting (and more improbable) episodes of Twain's version, the royal child is bound, gagged, and menaced by a mad hermit, formerly the abbot of a monastery and cruelly dispossessed by Edward's father, Henry VIII. The crazy priest now insists that he is an archangel who has met God and all the prophets. This scene must bring pleasurable fright to younger readers, but its primary reason for inclusion seems to be the expansion of the identity motif. Again, the encounter appears more a contrived event in Edward's perilous journey than a logical part of the web of cause and effect.

The film's writers, Laird Doyle and Catherine Chisholm Cushing, chose to exclude this scene, probably both because of its tenuous link with the overall plot, and the natural disinclination of Hollywood to pursue anticlericalism for its own sake. Instead, they chose to have the Captain of the Guard catch up with the child-king and prepare him to meet his death, so that the Lord Protector's scheme will succeed without interference. The scene is quite touching because the Captain is nearly overwhelmed at the prospect of harming the master he is sworn to protect. For his part, Edward is able to demonstrate his true nobility and loyalty to his Tudor blood, as he bravely offers up his quivering body to the Captain's knife. Naturally, Errol Flynn arrives on the scene at the last possible moment. It all has a curious inevitability, at least up to the point when Flynn begins to wield his rapier to the accompaniment of the full-volume Erich Wolfgang Korngold score.

In addition to character and plot, the film is also successful in some of its specifically visual images. The Walpurgisnacht ambience of the robber's den is emotionally effective, and the director, William Keighley, was able to get some of the mixture of delight and dread that Minnelli later achieved magnificently in the Halloween scene in *Meet Me in St. Louis* (1944), and which Twain himself got in parts of *Tom Sawyer*. This episode also contains a very well-staged mock coronation parade (in derision of the unrecognized king's claims to royalty), which is reminiscent of Quasimodo's parodic exaltation in *The Hunchback of Notre Dame*—both, of course, ultimately alluding to the cruel mockery of Christ's kingship. Even the central motif of the story, the striking similarity of the two boys, seems more effective on the screen through the constant visual presence of either Billy or Bobby Mauch, the twins who played the roles. The novel must rely on our residual memory of passages describing their similarity, whereas the film literally *shows* us this similarity, nonstop, from beginning to end. Further, Twain's ponderous parody of aristocratic titles and the decadent court are translated into snappy visual jokes, e.g., the endless string of useless courtiers ceremoniously passing along each item of the king's *toilette*, transforming the simplest act into a grueling ritual. The apotheosis of the visual imagery comes with the lavish Hollywood-style coronation scene, from which is squeezed every drop of gaudy "grandeur." We are treated to long shots of the magnicent nave arching up into the incense-filled ogives as the full-throated boy's choir sings the false king's praises.

In terms of theme, the novel and the film are substantially different, primarily because, in the movie, the themes are stripped down to their functional essentials. Twain's profoundly democratic views are here taken for granted, as is his often blind, stubbornly melioristic view of human history. His belief in the innate goodness of children is also vaguely present, muting his normally antimonarchical stand in the warm, favorable portrait of the child king. The film, however, is less intent on being a political tract, more genuinely concerned with being a good adventure story, and thus most of its energies are aimed in that direction.

One major exploration the novel and the film do share, so typically American, is that of the rise of the poor boy to a position of eminence. Granted, in both versions of *The Prince and the Pauper* this happens almost entirely by chance, without any real effort on the part of the boy, but Tom has learned enough about royalty to make him intensely dissatisfied with his own lot in life, and perhaps this is enough. In *Mark Twain: An American Prophet* (1970), Maxwell Geismar opines that "the central fantasy of the barefoot boy become proxy king was Sam Clemens' own dream, no doubt, and in his case a fact," but the fantasy goes beyond Twain and is clearly a fundamental American myth.

In the Depression film version, the recognizably Horatio Alger elements have been strengthened, though not enough to do violence to the basic story. Thus we see the book's briefly mentioned liaison between the priest Father Andrew and the pauper Tom Canty blown up into a scene of major proportions. Like Pat O'Brien's priest in *Angels With Dirty Faces* (1938), which came out the following year, and so many other rise-out-of-the-slum figures of thirties' movies, Father Andrew wants to help Tom Canty escape. There is but one proper way in Alger—hitting the books "to make something of yourself," for the short-range attractiveness of crime ultimately does not pay. So the priest teaches Tom his Latin and tells him that's the way "to escape Offal Court."

Another shared theme, even more fundamental, or at least more deeply philosophical, is the question of "true" identity mentioned earlier. The key moment in the film occurs during the exchange of clothing between the ragamuffin and the royal prince. They laugh and giggle through the whole thing, the pauper properly imperious in spite of his rags and charcoal-smeared face. They go over to the mirror, still laughing, and in a very well-timed and well-executed set of gestures, they stare wide-eyed at the incredible resemblance between them. For the audience, and perhaps for the boys as well, the moment has even deeper significance, for called into question is the very basis of identity itself. What makes one boy a prince and the other a pauper if only mere externals separate them? Throughout the film each boy continues to insist that he is not what he seems—and each is thought crazy. Is there then a "true self," or is what we call the self merely a random assortment of purely arbitrary externals?

Near the end, during the great coronation scene, Edward reclaims his identity and his throne by remembering details of his father's room and most importantly, the original location of the Great Seal, which Tom had been using to crack nuts. We learn again that we are, in essence, that which we remember, and we are *because* we remember.

Twain spends a lot more time developing and echoing this theme—Miles Hendon's identity is denied by his brother and his lover (a related, equally pervasive theme of the book is that of betrayal in the sense of Peter's betrayal of Christ), Tom Canty's father changes his name and the little king's while trying to escape the constabulary, the hermit insists that he is an archangel, and not what he seems to be (as the king has been doing all along)—but the whole contraption, interesting and inventive as it often is, doesn't add up to the power of that one simple shot of two astonished faces in the mirror.

The Red Badge of Courage (1895), Stephen Crane

Uncivil Battles and Civil Wars

BY FRED SILVA

John Huston's 1951 adaptation of Stephen Crane's *The Red Badge of Courage* represents an instance of a talented, sympathetic director reworking a widely heralded classic novel that in filmic terms is highly problematic. Crane's adherence to a subjective point of view with particularly strange and vivid imagery would not lend itself for easy screen adaptation under any circumstances. But Huston's efforts were encumbered, beyond the elusive qualities of the novel, by the complex power struggle enmeshing the top officers of Metro-Goldwyn-Mayer, for whom he worked. Although not as notorious a studio reconstruction as von Stroheim's *Greed* (1925) or Welles's *The Magnificent Ambersons* (1942), Huston's *Red Badge* can be seen nevertheless as a case study of how corporate demands affect aesthetic intentions. As shall be seen, MGM's timid brass decided to transform Huston's movie, conceived as a war film, into what audiences would recognize as a "filmed classic."

One of the surprising truths that emerges from Lillian Ross's *Picture* (1952)—her justly famous account of the production of *Red Badge*—is that, as limited as as the MGM producers were, they *were* correct in diagnosing Huston's failures in his version of the film. Metro took seriously a preview audience's comments that the original full-length cut was hard to follow. They then asked Huston to clarify the inner responses of the protagonist Henry Fleming. During months of delay, confusion, and a growing communication gap between director and studio, MGM executive Dore Schary took charge himself in shaping Huston's footage into a more direct and discernible narrative structure.

MGM-instituted "improvements" began with the programmatic Bronislaw Kaper score and James Whitmore's voice-over narration of passages from Stephen Crane's novel, both devices meant to help an audience understand Henry Fleming's subjective condition at critical moments. (The hallowed pages of Crane's novel turn behind the credits as Whitmore's voice tells the audience that they are about to witness a great work of literature translated into a film: "Stephen Crane wrote this book when he was a boy of twenty-two. Its publication made him a man.")

Dissatisfied with Huston's major battle episode, Schary had declared that "the construction of the sequence, in which the troops are withdrawn is bad. . . . You can't have 'em going back and forth, back and forth. You've got to get the audience worked up and then you've got to deliver. . . . Get them ready and charge!" Huston's charge-retreat-second charge became a single forward movement. Another prime cut of original footage was the deletion of the famous scene where Henry encounters the dead man propped up against a tree in the forest. Most devastating, Schary altered the context of the dramatic death sequence of the Tall Soldier and the Tattered Man (which Huston recalled in a 1973 interview as "the best scene in the film"). Schary removed the Tattered Man's death completely but arbitrarily retained the Tall Soldier's demise. This still effective vignette is nowhere near as "shocking" or "emotionally taxing" as the double death, which, as Huston remembers, propelled one-third of the film's first preview audience out of the theater.

Although not as individually damaging as these changes, a number of minor cuts were affected: removed were a cavalry charge, an artillery scene as Henry flees, an old soldier digging a foxhole, and veterans gibing at the recruits before their first major battle. A number of shots, including the final one, were shortened. Thus, the released version of *The Red Badge of*

Courage (still circulating in 16mm) contains sixty-nine minutes of John Huston's material augmented and rearranged by MGM under Dore Schary's overall supervision. Even with this truncated version, we can still sometimes locate a directorial artist transforming another man's delicate literary vision to the screen, an intricate problem of adaptation that did not depend on the simple adding of music and narration and restructuring of footage.

Stephen Crane works almost entirely within Fleming's consciousness, that of a very young soldier thinking in adolescent and bloody fairy-tale images. Looking across a river, he sees the red flashes of an engagement and "conceived them to be growing larger, as the orbs of a row of dragons advancing." The regiment marches on "like one of those moving monsters wending with many feet." Later he notes the men are totally absorbed in their thoughts about the battle and thinks that "they were going to look at war, the red animal, the blood-swollen god." He thinks of one of the later skirmishes as "an onslaught of redoubtable dragons."

Crane controls the reader so that he sees Nature, a matter of obsession to Fleming, very much in the protagonist's vacillating terms. At times Henry shares with Crane the idea of Nature as unconcerned with men's actions, but at other times Fleming transforms it under the impact of his fearful imagination. As Henry marches toward the first battle, the group encounters a dead soldier in the road, and soon after he begins to reflect on his situation. "Absurd ideas took hold upon him. He thought that he did not relish the landscape. It threatened him." After a skirmish Fleming looks with astonishment at the blue, pure sky and the sun gleaming on the trees and fields. "It was surprising that Nature had gone tranquilly on with her golden process in the midst of so much devilment."

Fleming's perception of this general indifference of Nature does not apply to all specific contacts. Walking through the forest he must overcome saplings and the like, but realizes that "he could not conciliate the forest." At another point, "It seemed now that Nature had no ears . . . ; He conceived Nature to be a woman with a deep aversion to tragedy." Throwing a pine

*Henry Fleming (Audie Murphy), the Loud Soldier (Bill Mauldin),
and The Tall Soldier (John Dierkes) await the battle.* **The Red Badge
of Courage** *(1951).*

cone at a squirrel who scampers away, he wishfully and erroneously concludes that "Nature has given him a sign. The squirrel, immediately upon recognizing danger, had taken to his legs without ado." Later as he runs away from the battle through the forest: "Sometimes the brambles formed chains and tried to hold him back. Trees, confronting him, stretched out their arms and forbade him to pass. After its previous hostility this new resistance of the forest filled him with a fine bitterness. It seemed that Nature could not be ready to kill him." Preparing for the battle: "The youth stared at the land in front of him. Its foliage now seemed to veil powers and horrors."

Similarly charged images chart Fleming's growth toward acceptance of his role as soldier. Rationalizing his initial cowardice, he thinks of himself as a "man of experience. He had been among the dragons, he said, and he assured himself that they were not so hideous as he had imagined them." Before the battle in which he achieves "manhood" he sees his surroundings with heightened clarity: "It seemed to the youth that he saw everything. Each blade of the green grass was bold and clear. He thought he was aware of every change in the thin, transparent vapor that floated idly in sheets." This sense of intense participation in reality accentuates his fears as he enters the final battle of the novel.

These few examples illustrate Crane's thorough control of the novel's point of view. Except for occasional intimations of Crane's narrative presence we are given no consciousness other than Henry's. Nature, the army's activities, his companions' speeches and behavior are all presented as Henry reacts or reflects upon them; and all are depicted in Crane's characteristic vivid hues and often eccentric metaphor.

Thus we have Huston's complex problem: how to transform a tightly controlled point of view conveyed with a highly individual impressionistic style into a series of images for a medium of objective reality; and also, for the necessities of film genre, how to get outside of Fleming's mind and into where war films are usually found—the outdoors.

From the beginning of the project Huston wanted to shoot the film in a dramatic black-and-white Mathew Brady style. (Huston asserted in a 1965 interview that the control of chromatics had always been central to his work as director.) The Brady tone seems appropriate as most people's visual images of the Civil War conform to Mathew Brady photographs of it. (Huston shared this view with D.W. Griffith, who had the same effect in mind when he shot *The Birth of a Nation* [1915].) Part of Huston's attraction to black and white for *The Red Badge of Courage* may have been also his desire to continue the style of his government work in World War II, particularly the powerful *Battle of San Pietro* (1944). The choice of the black-and-white photography for *The Red Badge of Courage* created a natural and somewhat stark effect, a photographic style which, coupled with the camera's inherent objectivity in recording the surfaces of reality, renders it almost impossible to duplicate the colorful expressionistic subjectivity of Henry Fleming's first engagement in war. Crane colors Fleming's world with blues, golds, reds, browns, greens, and fills it with dragons, flashes of light, ominous, threatening clouds, as well as the sounds of exploding shells, popping rifles, yelling rebels, and dying moans.

Even without Huston's final cut, or all of the footage he shot, we can see clearly enough in the released version what he wanted. While the movie explores Henry Fleming's interior struggles, Huston did not constrict the point of view as tightly as Crane and consequently relaxes a good deal of the novel's tension.

Huston communicates his widened point of view in the camaraderie between Henry Fleming and his regiment, a pattern that emerges with the opening shot of the 301st Regiment marching out of the woods along a road toward the camera. (The film closes with a shot of the same regiment marching back along a road into another woods, but after Fleming and his comrades have undergone battle.) The opening sequence of shots establishes the importance of the group. The lights of the encampment are seen across the river, and companies drill on a dusty marching ground, establishing the boring routine of the regiment when it is not in battle. These shots are followed by a two-shot of men discussing the information about the impending battle. They leave the river bank and bring the message back to the camp group.

The frame begins to fill with men as the camera cranes back

to show the enlarging effect of the news of upcoming combat. At this point we first see Henry Fleming. The camera picks him up looking very anxious and moves him away from the group. At the very least, the shot establishes Fleming's isolation from the rest of the regiment and implies a narrowing to his point of view. Afraid that the image would not convey the idea, Dore Schary added a voice-over in the release print: "There was a youthful private deeply troubled. They were so sure of their courage. . . ." an unnecessary comment since we next see Fleming writing a letter, part of which reads, "I hope my conduct will make you proud of your loving son." As Henry composes that letter, Huston indicates a special relationship among him, Jim Conklin, and Wilson, who enter Henry's tent to comment on the rumored encounter. Huston extends the connection beyond these three men to encompass the whole regiment by shooting the scene generally from Henry's point of view in the foreground, with Jim and Wilson in the middleground, and members of the regiment shown in the deep background through the flap of the tent.

Huston uses conventions of the war film genre to expand this relationship between individuals and the group. Frequently he singles out soldiers for a close-up and a spoken line (often a complaint or a gibe) as the men march along or drill. The effect here, as in other war films, is to show that a group comprises many individuals. The model here could easily be *Guadalcanal Diary* (1943) or *The Story of G.I. Joe* (1945). By alternating long shots and close-ups, Huston conveys the idea that although armies wage war, individuals fight battles. At the first sign of a fight, the men lie down behind their dugout protection, waiting for the battle to start. Huston cuts from a long shot of the men to individual close-ups of the men holding their triggers or sighting their guns. Extending the center of consciousness from Fleming to these other soldiers with the close-ups, Huston inevitably individualizes the characters Crane originally generalized through such abstract names as the Tattered Man and the Tall Man. In addition, Huston removes the concentrated focus from Henry Fleming. In short, Fleming becomes the most important *one* of a number of men faced with war—a significant departure from Crane's novel.

Huston's battle sequences, essential for a war film, more closely resemble Crane's material than do his directorial attempts to give us Fleming's adolescent world view. Transforming the broader tableaux into visual images obviously presents less of a problem than externalizing the details of Henry Fleming's mind. Crane's skirmishes generate much smoke and haze. Early in the novel Henry's brigade stops at the edge of a grove and peers into the smoke ahead: "Out of this haze they could see running men." In that same episode: "The battle flag in the distance jerked about madly. It seemed to be struggling to free itself from an agony. The billowing smoke was filled with horizontal flashes. . . . Wild yells came from behind the walls of smoke. A sketch of gray and red dissolved into a moblike body of men who galloped like wild horses." At one point in the film the wounded of both sides emerge from the haze as if it had in fact produced them. (Actually Huston's military encounters were so filled with haze from smoke machines that some MGM brass complained that they couldn't see what was happening on the screen!)

The battle scenes work well in the way in which Huston alternates objective and subjective points of view. Generally he renders men's activities as matter-of-fact and ordinary. The final battle in the film, for example, occurs on an open field dotted with a few haystacks and broken farm wagons. The men seek protection behind the most humble sort of pasture walls. No panoramic charges, no spectacular explosions, just an ordinary group of soldiers all of whom run the risk of achieving their Red Badge of Courage.

This sense of the ordinary permeates the film. In one sequence the regiment stops to entrench themselves in a grove dappled with sunlight. Unable to appreciate the setting, however, they must dig into the earth as much like animals as men. One grizzled soldier refuses to dig, declaring that he "sure ain't gonna lie down before I'm shot. It ain't a natural way to fight." They don't fight then, but the placid background foreshadows the arena of their first battle, a gently rolling field that seems more appropriate for picnicking or strolling than fighting and dying.

Henry *in battle* experiences an occasional subjective vision plucked more directly from Crane. Frequently, Huston shoots the enemy in long shot from Henry's point of view, making them impersonal and distant, and very menacing. (Crane writes: "The youth turned quick eyes upon the field. He discovered forms begin to swell in masses out of a distant wood.") A subjective camera also operates at the end of this first skirmish. After the rebels have retreated, the voice-over intones, "So it was all over at last . . ." at which point Henry Fleming looks over his shoulder, whereupon the film cuts to an extreme low shot of the sun's light radiating through a tall tree. Clearly Henry's happiness and relief have been projected onto the world around him.

But Huston does not sustain these effects. When Henry flees the next charge in the battle, even the woods he runs through have none of the subjective menace that the woods have for Fleming in Crane's novel, where they seem to Henry to grab him and impede his progress. In the film we see him from an objective point of view as he runs past trees and bushes but with no sense of his being pulled at by the foliage. Only once in this extended sequence does the film project surreality, but within the confines of Huston's cool and objective camera. In what remains of the original footage of the almost concurrent deaths of the Tattered Man and the Tall Soldier, Henry encounters a stream of badly wounded and dying men slowly marching to the rear lines. The area has much long haylike grass through which the wounded march downhill along a strange zig-zag path. The Tattered Man (who will not be shown dying and is in no way individualized in Schary's cut), strides along marking time with a long branch and singing a madly strident version of "When Johnny Comes Marching Home." Jim Conklin appears, obviously badly wounded. He stops to speak to Henry, but almost immediately begins to run crazily up a hill. When he reaches the top, he totters for a few moments and then drops over dead—all shot from an accentuated high angle. Thus is something like Crane's nightmare vision achieved, despite Schary's tampering with what William Wyler thought one of the best sequences of Huston's career.

Huston's sense of the mundanely natural returns at the end of the film once the battle stops. Henry and the troops have repulsed the rebels. Henry in particular has behaved well by carrying his own flag and capturing the enemy standard. As the men sit around and chat about the battle with some of the prisoners, the subject that comes up—suggesting normality, renewal—is spring planting. John Huston's Henry delivers a line directly from Crane: "It takes no time for the birds to start up singing, as soon as the shooting stops. . . ." Nature remains a totally indifferent constant, always there but generally unmoved by men's subtle activities, be they the confusion of Henry Fleming's early fears or his subsequently courageous behavior.

Huston's *The Red Badge of Courage* does preserve much of Crane's general statement of the war as an initiation into manhood. The film does not communicate, however, the intensity of Crane's view of that experience. We can see from the way in which Henry reacts to the group and in the emotions displayed in the numerous close-ups given Audie Murphy, who plays Fleming, that he fears the battle, but we have only occasional sense of what images run through his mind. The objectivity of the camera and Huston's use of genre elements create a more usual war film than one might have expected. Doubtless some of this conventionality was exacerbated in constructing the sixty-nine-minute, studio-trimmed release print. One must say, however, that this version contains so much evocative photography and so many better than passable sequences that it is to be hoped the rumored reconstruction of the film may one day occur.

Billy Budd (posthumously published 1924),
Herman Melville

Melville's Sailor in the Sixties

BY ROBERT L. NADEAU

The 1962 film of *Billy Budd* is a one-man show—Peter Ustinov helped write the script, served as producer-director, and played the role of Captain Vere. Although his technicians were aware of the fetching possibilities of color in a movie featuring an eighteenth-century British man-of-war on the high seas, Ustinov insisted on using black and white as his medium. The choice is consistent with Ustinov's stripped-down interpretation of Herman Melville's sea novella, but it is also indicative of his decision to swim clear of the more profound and disturbing aspects of the Melville masterpiece.

Ustinov's Billy is a paragon of innocence and virtue victimized by the very embodiment of moral depravity (Claggart) and the fierce, unbending principles of social justice (Vere). A college sophomore might arrive at this interpretation after a brisk reading of *Billy Budd*, but any serious effort to study the narrative would immediately undermine it. In Melville's vision the conflicts that arise are so troubling precisely because they cannot be resolved in terms of black-and-white, either-or morality.

Although Melville's characterization of Billy is enriched with associations to the Christ figure, his Billy is definitely not intended to be a personification of innocence and virtue. Christ, as far as we know, was not crude like an upright barbarian, childlike in his interactions, or doglike in intelligence, and yet Melville describes Billy in precisely these terms. The infamous vocal defect, which makes Billy less than a perfect specimen of physical beauty, is, says Melville, "a striking instance that the arch interferer, the envious marplot of Eden still has more or less to do with every human consignment to this planet of earth." Billy's curious asexuality, most evident in the absence of normal erection upon death by hanging, is also indicative of physiological or psychological deformity.

The only personal liability of Ustinov's Billy, played by Terence Stamp, is that he seems too perfect to survive in an imperfect world. This Billy, extraordinarily intelligent and extremely adept in interpersonal behavior, not only proves an astute political theorist but an amateur psychologist as well. When first impressed into His Majesty's service, Billy perceptively notes that it is wrong to flog a man because "it is against his being a man"—thinking quite foreign to Melville's Billy. In an extended conversation with Claggart, which owes nothing to Melville, Billy draws his nemesis into the startling admission that his social isolation is a consequence of his inability to accept himself. (The psychotherapist Carl Rogers could not have done it any better!) The vocal defect, which assumes such philosophical importance in Melville, appears little more in the film than the response of a sensitive individual to stressful situations. If speech therapy had been available in this bygone era, the tragic ending, we conjecture, might have been avoided.

There are rare moments in the movie, like the shots of Billy prior to execution, which recall the image of Melville's sailor. But Peter Ustinov as Vere fails at all times to conjure up the dark and brooding presence of the novella's captain. As Pauline Kael pointed out in *I Lost It at the Movies* (1965), Ustinov is "too much the relaxed and worldly European to share Melville's American rage." Even when he portrays himself as the rigorous purveyor of societal law, his sweet visage and refined paternalistic manner belie his commitment. Ustinov is more a benevolent British headmaster chiding his favorite pupil than the captain of a British man-of-war willfully sacrificing the innocent for the sake of some imagined greater good.

In the trial scene, Vere appeals to a junior officer, as Melville's captain never would, to posit a legal argument that would obviate the death penalty and "save us all." Similarly he confesses "revulsion, shame, and rage" in being forced to play the role of societal henchman, and laments, rather pitifully, after the execution that "I'm only a man, not fit to do the work of God or the devil." The Vere of the novella never indulges in such disingenuous emotionalism.

If Melville's Vere conveys the impression that he is the impersonal instrument of societal law and institutions, there is much in his behavior inconsistent with his public posture. On occasion, he appears to be motivated subconsciously by the same malevolent feeling toward Billy that he consciously finds so despicable in Claggart. He insists, for example, that Billy be precipitately tried by a drumhead court even though further action should properly be postponed until the case is referred to the Admiral. Vere's rhetorical pretrial indictment of Billy over the body of Claggart—"Struck dead by the angel of God. Yet the angel must hang!"—combined with his insistence during the trial that hanging *must* be the verdict also suggest darker and seamier motivations. Nothing of this is hinted in the film.

Ustinov, to his credit, cast the role of Claggart so as to suggest that "depravity according to nature" that Melville's character consistently exudes. The commingling of pain and pleasure in Robert Ryan's face as he oversees the ritualized brutality of the flogging scenes and the curious smile that an expiring Claggart bestows on Billy are nicely consistent with the terrible malignity felt by Melville's master-at-arms toward a human being whose seeming goodness is such a painful reminder of his own debased nature that he is willing to sacrifice anything, including his own life, in an effort to destroy it. Although the film viewer is made to understand, in deference to contemporary psychology, that Claggart's problems are primarily a consequence of unknown traumatic experiences in the past, he remains sufficiently repulsive to suggest that evil is an irrevocable aspect of the human condition. Claggart's superior intellect and education also come to life in Ryan's notable performance.

Dansker, played by Melvyn Douglas, bears little resemblance to the silent, illiterate old salt created by Melville. In the film

Terence Stamp as Melville's sailor. Billy Budd *(1962).*

he is guru, prophet, and seer rolled into one. He appears at all times somehow above and unrelated to the tragic drama he so knowingly interprets for lesser intellects. During a funeral, Dansker steps forward to recite verbatim the lines of the Anglican funeral service, forcing the "erudite" Captain reading these lines into awed and respectful silence. In testimony before the drum-head court, he discourses upon flaws in Claggart that caused him to "bear malice toward a grace he could not have," offers a detailed and entirely credible analysis of the history of the relationship between Billy and Claggart, and concludes with an extremely sophisticated statement on the nature of collective moral responsibility.

It may be that the peculiar treatment of the role of Dansker was a half-hearted and ill-conceived attempt by Ustinov to get more of Melville in the film. Vere, as Ustinov plays him, is con-stitutionally unequipped to perceive anything but the obvious. Some spokesman, then, was needed to suggest that Melville at least was not so stupid. Although Dansker's moralizing is in no way consistent with the understanding of moral ambiguity found in the narrative, it does pay lip service to the fact that Melville believed in its existence.

It is the chaotic ending of Ustinov's *Billy Budd* that tries the patience of anyone with respect for the integrity of Melville's work. The Captain, emotionally unhinged by Billy's final declara-tion "God bless Captain Vere," refuses after the execution to dismiss his men. When that order is finally given by the Captain of the Marines, the crew does not obey in spite of the fact that a French man-of-war, which miraculously appears out of a nearby estuary, is now blasting the British vessel right out of the water! The enlisted men, in an inexplicable outburst of nationalistic fervor, decide to fight, but the battle is lost in record time. A well-placed French cannon ball somehow dislodges the royal seal from the ship's bow, at which point the symbol for that law which has our hero dangling from a hangman's noose on the foredeck plunges unceremoniously into the briny deep. As the camera surveys the deck strewn with corpses, broken spars, and disheveled sail, and withdraws to a long shot of the decimated ship bobbing in a vast sea, a voice-over ponderously intones, "The rest belong to naval history, but if the sacrifice of Billy Budd has served to make men more conscious of justice then he will not have died in vain. Men are perishable things, but justice will live as long as the soul and the law as long as the human mind."

Melville does say in the epilogue sections of *Billy Budd* that the *Indomitable*, significantly renamed *Avenger* in the film, engaged a French battle ship *Atheiste* during its return passage to join the British fleet. Captain Vere, who remains always the responsible leader, is mortally wounded and dies several days later on the shore in Gibraltar. Melville then describes how the Billy Budd incident is utterly distorted in an authorized weekly chronicle on naval affairs, and concludes with a ballad derived from a song created by another foretopman entitled "Billy of the Darbies." As Melville notes, the ballad is the product of an "artless poetic temperament" and does little more than express affection for an extremely likeable shipmate executed and buried at sea.

Melville was far too skeptical to assume, as Ustinov does, that Billy's death can make men "conscious of justice." Nowhere does Melville indicate that if Billy's case had been held over for litigation by the Admiralty the penalty would have been anything less than death by hanging. Vere's desire to reach an early verdict may be reprehensible, but there is no reason to doubt the correctness of his interpretation of the legal aspects of the case or his assessment of the consequences if the law is not strictly obeyed. Melville's concern was not to question the efficacy of laws and institutions, but rather to attempt to fathom the unfathomable depths of human character in a fallen universe.

Although what is most conspicuously absent in the film of *Billy Budd* is the richness, variety, and terrible ambiguity found in Melville, the Ustinov production is not completely without its appeal—especially if we remember why this film was so enthusiastically received, particularly by college-age youths, in the year of its release. In 1962 we witnessed the vague beginnings of social unrest that would quickly escalate into what we now call the counter-culture revolution. On the one hand the face of the nation appeared placid, undisturbed, and self-satisfied: John F. Kennedy and his photogenic family were reigning in Camelot; liberal representatives of the law on *The Defenders* spoke out on the television screen; the crew-cut and the Twist were still in vogue; and the gross national product was growing at an unprecedented rate. There were other indications, however, that things were not quite what they seemed: the undeclared war in Vietnam was escalating; the newly formed Student Nonviolent Coordinating Committee began organizing sit-ins, demonstrations, and boycotts in the deep South to force integration; James Meredith tried to enroll at the University of Mississippi; and the Cuban missile crisis left many unenthusiastic about the prospect of continuing the nuclear arms race.

For those of us just developing an awareness of problems on the national and international scene there was the nagging sense that those in authority were not as infallible as we had been taught to believe. It was not difficult, therefore, to identify with a central character whose honesty, disarming directness, and respect for the essential goodness of others seemed so consistent with our own idealistic prescription for the cure of civilization. Billy's removal from the *Rights of Man* and his conscription into involuntary servitude readily brought to mind the local draft board and the possibility of becoming involved in a military action just as remote and meaningless as the Napoleonic wars. Paternalistic Vere, willing in the final analysis to sacrifice youth and innocence to preserve a corrupt world order, conjured up associations of parents and other authority figures who spoke against civil disobedience and for American military intervention abroad. When Vere told Billy that grown men were no longer capable of explaining the necessity of war and injustice, we could nod a ready assent.

Perhaps in fairness to Ustinov we should note that 1962 might have been too early for a film that asserts that either-or, black-and-white morality is often the servant of unconscious, alogical, and malignant forces in the human psyche. It was no accident that American intellectuals appreciated Melville's art only after the disillusioning experience of World War I had undermined their belief in the moral universe. If there has been any truly significant development in American culture since 1962, it is the growing mass awareness of how the night side of psychological reality affects behavior at even "the highest level" of societal functioning. The opportune moment is now for some bold director to translate Melville's painfully conceived and uncompromising literary vision into a film of the seventies.

Turn of the Screw *and* The Innocents: *Two Types of Ambiguity*

BY JEANNE THOMAS ALLEN

Few students of Henry James today take seriously his comment to H. G. Wells that *The Turn of the Screw* is "essentially a potboiler," a trap "to catch those not easily caught" among a popular audience. The author's careful revisions of the original *Colliers'* serial for his 1908 edition surely belie his offhand self-denigrating remarks. The modest little ghost story manifests far more of the modernist complexities of the later James than its early critics avowed.

Edmund Wilson launched an extended scholarly fascination with James's novella about the young governess who grows convinced that her two charges are possessed by the demonic spirits of their former gardener and governess. In "The Ambiguity of Henry James," printed in *Hound and Horn* (1934), Wilson opened the critical Pandora's box by suggesting that the governess-narrator was sexually repressed and that she hallucinates Quint and Jessel because of her own obsessions.

According to Wilson's view, she harbors subconscious desires for her employer, the children's uncle. Her wish to prove worthy of his trust clouds her judgment and leads her to perceive great opportunities for heroism. She sees herself as a savior, courageous and self-sacrificing, and shows a pronounced determination to leap to irresponsible conclusions. The absence of any substantive evidence of the children's malevolence accentuates her seemingly dubious evaluations of evidence. For Wilson, not only is the governess an unreliable narrator, but it is she, not ghosts, who is responsible for destroying the children in her charge.

In the next decades the governess's detractors and defenders lined up, pointing to evidence in the novella, in James's prefaces and letters, and in the proliferating James criticism. Their contentions were well summarized in Wayne Booth's *The Rhetoric of Fiction*. But James's careful manipulation of a limited point of view makes it impossible safely to confirm any interpretation. When we become involved with the governess and her story, we fall into a self-enclosed cell. There can be no appeal for outside corroboration because the governess's testimony is all we have; James's marvelous joke on those of us obsessed with "proving" our interpretation of fictional events continues.

The primary experience of *The Turn of the Screw* is one of ambiguity. We are torn between believing that (1) the governess has discovered some hideous truth that the children are possessed and (2) that her misguided suppositions and neurotic drives have turned *her* into a possessive demon who destroys them. The recent critical trend has been away from the question of which interpretation of the governess is more satisfactory and toward appreciation of James's masterfully ambiguous presentation. (See Susan Crow, "Aesthetic Allegory in *Turn of the Screw*," in *Novel*, Winter, 1971, for a good example.) The questions have become: *how* did he achieve this balance of mutually exclusive options? How did he utilize the techniques of narration at his disposal?

The increasing interest in "how" the story "means" makes a comparison with Jack Clayton's 1961 film *The Innocents* (scripted by William Archibald and Truman Capote) especially attractive.

As we have noted, the novella's self-enclosed point of view creates in the reader a troubling inability to know the truth of what has transpired as recorded by the narrator. With *The Innocents*, we witness what has happened but remain uncertain how to interpret or how to judge the governess's behavior. The viewer is constantly forced to weigh each piece of evidence against another, to see, for example, if there is *enough* malevolence in Miles to warrant the risks taken by Miss Giddens (as James's nameless narrator is called in the movie) in forcing Miles to call forth (and perhaps exorcise) the demon she believes possesses him.

Throughout *The Innocents* the see-saw bounces between governess and children with the viewer's sympathies vacillating between them. *The Innocents* moves from question to question: if this is so, then is that merited? Is there something wrong at Bly? Are the ghosts real for the children? Is their influence bad? Can the children be safely removed from their influence? Is the attempt worth the risk involved?

Still this is a different level of anxiety from that in *The Turn of the Screw*, where the reader cannot know whether Miles is malevolent at all, or whether the governness's attempt to force from the children a confession of complicity with Quint and Miss Jessel is not just less than optimal but wholly unwarranted. It is quite possible that Miles is neither possessed nor necessarily even bad, that his dismissal from school was not on such severe grounds.

Anxiety is intensified because the possible options are mutually exclusive in the novella. As the governess herself expresses it, "If he were innocent, what then was I?" One or the other of them is "possessed." The tension in James is larger than the interpretive and ethical considerations of *The Innocents*. It involves an epistemological quandary, for given the expertly balanced and irresolvable ambiguity, the reader cannot be certain of what has actually happened.

Several narrative aspects of *The Turn of the Screw* contribute to .this fundamental ambiguity: certain characteristics of the governess's character; the laconic dismissal note; the strange structure of the story line. In the novella, the governess's capacity for self-criticism in relating the past events at Bly produces typically contradictory reactions. (1) We believe her arguments are reliable because of her detachment from the events. She offers revelations of details that a purely self-justifying narrator never would offer. (2) We see her judgments as unreliable because at times she inadvertently supplies information which

Giddens (Deborah Kerr) forces Miles (Martin Stephens) to confront "the existence" of Quint. The Innocents *(1961).*

builds to conclusions she either does not share or never has reflected upon deeply enough to reach.

In *The Innocents* ambiguity about the governess does not pivot on the limits of her self-awareness. Miss Giddens does sense that both Mrs. Grose, the housekeeper, and the children's uncle have reason to regard her as slightly insane, but she understands this to be the consequence of being the exclusive witness to the horrors at Bly. Since the film viewer is locked into this otherwise solitary experience with her (though perhaps with occasional distance established because of the variables in the film conventions that convey it),[1] ambiguity shifts to observing her response to events.

How is the film viewer to regard Miss Giddens's sensitivity? Is it unusual perception, giving her special access to truths others are missing,[2] or neurotic imagination turned to melodrama in which she figures as heroine? Deborah Kerr is uniquely fitted to convey this ambiguity. Even apart from her gifted acting in this particular film, she brings to the role accrued resonances from the dependable and charming governess in *The King and I* (1956) to the repressed neurotic pining for love in *Separate Tables* (1958). The viewer's faith vacillates with her subtle but erratic moods, both as they appear in this film and as they recall the Deborah Kerr of other films.

Another ambiguity of the novella stems from the fountainhead placement of the letter of dismissal. The letter states only that the headmasters express their regret that "it should be impossible to keep him [Miles]." The governess concludes that this can have but one meaning—that he is dangerous to others. On this questionable assumption the governess builds her entire house of cards, concluding that Miles is evil because of the influence Quint continues to have on him. The precariousness of this reasoning is reduced in the film by having the letter explicitly state that Miles is "an injury to the others."

[1] The film alternates between presenting Quint and Jessel from the subjective point of view of Miss Giddens to including her in the frame with Quint and with Jessel.

[2] The first words after the opening frame sequence are the uncle's "Do you have an imagination?" When Miss Giddens replies in the positive, he is pleased.

But ambiguity concerning the ordering of events is found in the film at other points if not at the arrival of the letter. Are events merely sequential (that is, arbitrary and/or motivated independently of the governess's consciousness) or are they causal (linked to the governess's perceptions)? In both novella and film, the impetus remains ambiguous for critical sequences: when the governess views Quint after catching a glimpse of the statue in the garden; when she sees Miss Jessel at the lake after a fitful night of dreaming, etc. A causal relation is suggested but not confirmed.

An aspect of the novella that does not find its counterpart in the film is the crucial dimension of the overall point of view of *The Turn of the Screw*, located partially in the countervailing balance between the two time perspectives of the narrator— the young impetuous governess in the dramatic present and the mature, somewhat detached older woman who tells the story and comments on her former self.

Temporal distance may argue for credibility; the reader may prefer to believe the more experience-worn thirty-year-old commenting on her younger self. Yet distance is also a measure of the internalization of experience, frequently implying the obfuscating interpretation rather than more objective observation. These contradictory aspects heighten the frustration. The governess's screen is impenetrable.

Distance, both in time and in degree of interpretation, poses several questions: although the specific detail of direct observation is closer to the event than the summary generalization stemming from the governess's later interpretation of her experience, is involvement an asset to truth or a detriment? Does the distance in the governess's narrative really add up to authentic detachment or just the appearance of it?

Although *The Innocents* suggests various shifts between objectivity and subjectivity in its soundtrack and camera point of view, for the most part the film does not blur factual experiences with interpretive response. Clayton's presentation reinforces a one-to-one correspondence between events and the visual representation of them. A viewer is not encouraged (nor completely discouraged) to believe that what transpires is a function of private vision, what Pasolini called the "free indirect subjective." For example, the first sighting of Quint on the tower is a distorted view, but the distortion is on account of the sun which makes Miss Giddens squint. Environment conditions thought rather than vice-versa.

(What seems a major lapse in this correspondence explains the disturbed response of some viewers to the photographically "real" tear on the desk where a weeping Jessel—is she "unreal," [a ghost] or "non-real" [imaginary]?—had just appeared.)

Undeniably, there are moments when Jack Clayton tries to trick the viewer. The use of statues, water, and glass reflections give evidence of Clayton's attempt to instill doubt as to what is "real." That we are conscious of the attempts is the measure of their failure. We do not mistake a statue for Quint, and we really cannot believe the governess does either.

On a thematic level, the notion of reflection is more workable. The imagery conveying a relationship of hunter and hunted is reflected or duplicated many times on different levels: Quint stalks Giddens, Giddens pursues the children at the gazebo and in the conservatory, the children imprison and dominate their pets. Uncertainty stems from not knowing which is the original relationship being replicated. What reflects what?

Although Clayton's film does not attempt to question the objective reality of events, his manipulation of point of view does to some extent simulate the effects of ambiguity; the rapidly alternating perspectives of Giddens and Miles during the final confrontation in the conservatory. Camera movement, editing, lighting, and setting win and alienate viewer sympathies. The viewer is manipulated toward the pursued and away from the pursuer, but the governess and her charge exchange these roles rapidly to catch the viewer between both. The exchange between Giddens and Flora at the gazebo in the rain is a kind of warm-up for this technique of alternation, but it hits its peak in the final moments of the film.

Clayton sought self-consciously for ambiguity in his characterizations, with decidedly mixed results. The children's faces, while enigmatic and eerily provocative (Flora's smile at her bedroom window, Miles's smile while he spins on the piano stool), are really not ambiguous so much as inscrutable, expressing mystery. The most successfully ambiguous visual projection of character is Miles's sling-shot. The suggestion of his cruelty is clear: the cat's scream, the sling-shot on the table, the blinded cat in zoom shot, the cry of the peacock, the broken-necked and yet caressed pigeon. Beyond that, the degree of Miles's culpability is unknown. The sling-shot introduces the ambiguity of whether Miles has the amoral curiosity and adventuresomeness of childhood or already participates in a knowing adultlike sadism.

By far, however, the best approximation of the novella's essential ambiguity—that of whether the reality of the governess's experience has been a subjective or objective one—is carried by the eerie, often unidentifiable soundtrack. The viewer's uncertainty goes beyond the difficulty of identifying a peculiar sound to knowing what the sound signifies within a code system that the film develops for music, echo effects, exaggerated volume, and electronic sound. One sound may further merge into another or two sounds may be heard simultaneously, a technique also used in Hitchcock's *Psycho* (1960).

Several natural sounds are amplified frequently at points when Quint and Jessel appear to Miss Giddens: the plopping of the scissors in the water, the buzzing of flies in the tower and in the schoolroom, etc. This exaggeration may imply either the governess's heightened perception that enables her to apprehend Quint and Jessel, or it may suggest a neurotic hypersensitivity that makes her hallucination-prone. The overlay of natural sound with "supernatural" or at least unnatural sound (as when the governess's fire poker triggers a piano tune or faint crying or when the sash hitting the window frame is overlaid with "love me, love me") seems to confirm the hallucination theory, and the film's emphasis on imagination supports it. Does this mean that during these passages the viewer is given access to the governess's mind and that, like the exaggerated sounds, the apparitions we see are projections of her mind? Clayton has mixed these signals along with the visual conventions for subjective point of view from the beginning to make the code not so much ambiguous as chaotic. Had he clearly established a code and then blurred it, ambiguity might have been better achieved.

That there is more ambiguity in the soundtrack than in the visuals may support the notion that we are conditioned to find our eyes more reliable sensory organs than our ears. Imagining sounds is traditionally easier than imagining full-fledged appearances. Had Clayton chosen to present us with apparitions in a manner similar to Roman Polanski's mirror-reflected assailant in *Repulsion* (1965), whom we see almost subliminally as the door mirror swings shut, probably the uncertainty of not knowing whether we *did* really see or *what* we really saw would have been more horrifying. This is the horror of the Jamesian novel: was it there or were we merely predisposed to hallucinate?

This is essentially what happens in the governess's first experience with the man on the tower in *The Turn of the Screw*. But Clayton has translated the described event in the novella literally into film experience rather giving the filmic approximation of conventions of subjective point of view to counter a prolonged appearance in film. This is why the apparitions' effects are more ominous than their actual appearance. The teardrop is more frightening than Jessel in the schoolroom; the swinging drape more disconcerting than the passing form of Jessel; the rocking puppet head more disturbing than the hostile Miles; and the two demonic points of light in the shadowed face of Quint at the windows far worse than the illuminated head. James knew, as Clayton seems not to have, that the suggestion of evil—a general vision filled out by the horrors of each individual's psyche—is by far the more terrifying.

That is why the electronic and echo effects of the soundtrack are in many ways more upsetting than the visuals. They are more generally ambiguous and suggestive. Is the electronic sound generated by the apparitions or by Miss Giddens's disturbed mind? Is the echo effect a signal of passing from objectively heard sound into an inner chamber of subjective haunting sound? If it is, what do the sounds in the darkened hallways signify? Imagination or supernatural presence?

Less ambiguous but still disconcerting are the questions surrounding Flora's song, which is heard with or without Flora's presence, in natural sound or echo distortion, and the orchestral music accompanying Miss Giddens. The viewer does not know with what point of view to associate the sound: Miss Giddens's, a third-person observer, a relatively neutral omniscient camera-narrator, or some other center? This is partly a factor of the audience's less conscious control over processing sound, but it is also due to the fact that we do not have ways of identifying aural shifts in point of view as we do visual. Is the music an emotive commentary on Miss Giddens's condition from her point of view or from that of an observer? Do we actually hear the absent Flora singing, or an echo effect attributable to a neutral omniscient camera, or the third-person voyeur-narrator who intermittently governs point of view? What consciousness or viewpoint is projecting these sounds?

The Innocents might benefit from the lesson of two other films in its attempt to bring the ambiguous Jamesian terror to the screen. The thematic content of Peter Brooks's *Lord of the Flies* (1963) presents one of two possibilities that are balanced in James. "What if the beast is in us?" asks Simon softly, and no one answers his question. This option is considered in the brilliant final scene of the James novella. By converging strands of imagery that have suggested that the governess has substituted herself for Quint, James brings to excruciating eminence the question of who is the source of Miles's corruption and/or fear of death. Miles offers the name of Peter Quint—ambiguously adding "you devil"—but then cries, "Where?" Does he see him? Is Quint there for Miles? Or is the terrifying specter the governess herself?

The potential for projecting our fears until we make them real for others (or of becoming what we most detest through obsessive preoccupation) is part of the haunting fear of *The Turn of the Screw*. The film that conveys this horror most tellingly is Hitchcock's *Psycho* (1960). The last shot of Bates in close-up with his mother's skull superimposed on his own face is the visual equivalent of one of the alternatives at the end of the novella: that the governess has become Quint, that she and Quint are one. Jack Clayton's ending—where governess and lover roles merge for Deborah Kerr—is so far removed from the tone of the novella's ending that some separate notice should be taken of it.

Miss Giddens cradles Miles in her arms (his eyes are open like those of Quint in death which Mrs. Grose has described as "the eyes of a fox the dogs had hunted down"), caressing him as Miles had caressed his dead pigeon. When she realizes he is dead, she cries out his name and bends to kiss him on the mouth in a necrophiliac embrace. The heavy-handed enactment of Edmund Wilson's Freudian interpretation is resorted to in an attempt to balance (1) Quint's prolonged appearance on the hedge just previous, (2) a camera angle which confirms that Miles looks in Quint's direction, and (3) a shot from behind Quint, not a subjective point of view, which picks up Miles in long shot beneath Quint's extended hand. Once Quint is established as there "seizing" Miles, Clayton hits us with the other barrel. Though his convergence of imagery resembles James's, his ending is not Henry James at all. The two options—possession of Quint and possession by the governess—are neither simultaneous nor mutually exclusive as they are in *The Turn of the Screw*. Dispossessed by Quint, Jack Clayton's Miles become possessed finally and wholly by a new captor. The film's ending, like so many of its other aspects, produces tension, but not the supreme tension of ambiguity.

McTeague (1899), Frank Norris

Frank Norris: His Share of Greed

BY GEORGE WEAD

Film history damns Frank Norris with feigned praise. Norris is (*click*) the novelist whose *McTeague*, a popular "realistic" work published in 1899, was converted into *Greed*, a 1925 masterpiece of the cinema by Erich von Stroheim, who (*click*) achieved a faithful reproduction of the original work, but (*click*) greatly transformed it, giving it layers of meaning that Norris never intended. If any film critic alludes to Norris's style and symbolism, it is to point out what Stroheim's genius improved. And if there are flaws in *Greed*, it is because Stroheim was faithful even to the flaws of Norris.

Writers on *Greed* have been more concerned with rebuilding Stroheim than with assessing Norris, probably because they stand at the ruin of a coherent work of art. Once Stroheim's film was forty-two reels (ten and one half hours) of grand architecture also entitled *McTeague*. Taken from his control by MGM, it became *Greed* in ten reels (two and one half hours). That devastation has cast its shadow over the scholarship that followed, so that many Stroheim commentators now insist that *Greed* itself is a masterpiece. Stroheim had no delusions about the integrity of *Greed*; viewing it, he said, was like looking at a mangled lover in a morgue. A Stroheimist will still claim, however, that "even as a torso, the film insists itself and has a broader impact than the novel."[1]

There is no more to be gained by such cinematic chauvinism. Stroheim's place is secure, his architecture inscribed. It is time to reconsider the logic by which this was accomplished, and Norris's novel is the proper place to begin.

For the story of McTeague, Norris got his inspiration from an 1893 murder in San Francisco. A man mentioned in the newspapers only as Collins and typified as a "brute," stabbed his wife to death over money ("29 Fatal Wounds!" cried one paper) and showed no remorse. Collins was executed. Norris transformed him into McTeague, a slow-witted dentist and ex-miner who has no first name and is repeatedly described as "stupid." His life on Polk Street is described in great detail. There he falls wildly in love with Trina Sieppe. She wins a $5,000 lottery and, after their marriage, becomes a compulsive miser. When McTeague loses his profession, he declines into poverty and drunken sadism, aggravated by Trina's refusal to help. He murders her, takes the money, and returns to gold mining. Just as he discovers a rich strike, a "sixth sense" warns him of danger. He retreats into Death Valley. There Marcus Schouler, once a friend and Trina's ex-suitor, confronts McTeague and demands the money. McTeague kills him, but not before Marcus handcuffs them together. The novel ends with the doomed McTeague, his water supply gone, "stupidly looking around him," with Trina's money useless at his side.

The novel's impact on Stroheim was immediate and immense. In *The Complete "Greed,"* Herman Weinberg recounts that Stroheim, as a poor, newly arrived immigrant, decided on a film career one night while reading a copy of *McTeague*, left by chance in his hotel room. By that time, around 1910, Norris was long dead, but he had left behind a body of work hailed in the critical mainstream as a major example of "American naturalism" —that is, American subjects regarded, in the manner of Émile Zola, as beasts at the mercy of environment and heredity. According to this reading of Norris, McTeague's greed and sadism are

---

[1] François Bondy in *Der Monat*, quoted in Herman Weinberg's *Complete "Greed"* (Arno, 1972).

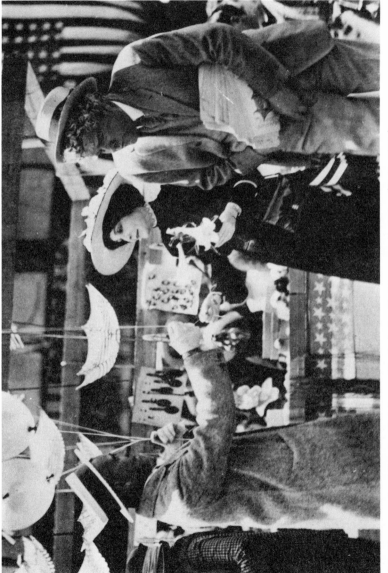

A balloon vender (director Erich von Stroheim) sells his wares to Trina (ZaSu Pitts) and McTeague (Gibson Gowland). Greed (1925). (Still shown is not in release version).

inevitable, granted his "stupidity," his father's alcoholism, and the grasping, middle-class morality of Polk Street. It is easy to assume that Norris's blatant use of gold, gilt, money, canaries, and sunshine symbolize McTeague's lust for acquisition.

The determinism of greed certainly caught Stroheim's eye. Gold color was painstakingly hand-painted into the original film —even for candle flames, says cinematographer William Daniels. ("And all they did was jiggle.") Stroheim intended to open and close his *McTeague* with a quotation from Robert Blair's "The Grave" (1743): "Oh cursed lust of Gold! When for thy sake / The fool throws up his interest in both worlds, / First, starves in this, then damn'd in that to come."

When MGM took over and June Mathis retitled the film, the emphasis was made even clearer, and cruder. *Greed* opens with a quote from Thomas Hood's near-doggerel poem, "Miss Kilmansegg: Her Moral": "Gold, gold, gold, gold . . . Hard to get and light to hold, / Stolen, borrowed, squandered, doled." Thus, one way and another, the meaning of Norris, as filtered through Stroheim, was underlined and passed on. Weinberg states the interpretation most succinctly: "*Greed* is an almost clinical study . . . of *bourgeois* morality—how the idea of wealth so bedazzles its victims that they lose their reason over it and, in a panic at its possible loss, kill each other to prevent that loss."

All this ignores the most striking aspect of McTeague's story. For Norris, McTeague is not greedy. He is a contented innocent who enjoys the regularity of Polk Street life. He longs to have a huge gilt tooth to hang outside his window—not as an emblem of wealth, but of personal achievement. His wants are simple: steam beer, a pipe, a daily nap, keeping his dental equipment clean. Even when he loses all this, he never displays avarice. He comes to hate Trina because she cannot share good fortune. The first money he steals from her is squandered on a spree with others. When he kills her for the lottery money, he is prompted by wounded dignity: she has treated him "like a dog" and sold his concertina, a treasured memento of his happier days. The strongest argument for McTeague's greed is that he hoards every cent of the stolen lottery money. Yet he also gives up a gold strike that would make him a millionaire and follows his "sixth sense." Isn't the novel, then, as much a tragedy of lost values as a clinical study of greed's ravages?

And what of "heredity"? Norris does give Trina "hardy and penurious" peasant blood. He includes an avaricious Jew and a hot-blooded Latin among the residents of Polk Street. He certainly saw McTeague as driven by uncontrollable impulses: "Below the fine fabric of all that was good in him ran the foul stream of hereditary evil, like a sewer. . . ." (Stroheim put the whole passage into a title. Mathis rewrote it, using one idea later in *Greed* for a very ludicrous title. McTeague, courting Trina, says, "Let's go over and sit on the sewer.") The passage above is quoted sometimes to prove that Norris believed in Zola's atheistic determinism. Certainly Norris was affected by Zola, who wrenched people with drama that "works itself out in blood and ordure," as Norris put it. "Terrible things" had to happen in such novels. That attracted Norris, but what he came to say was different from Zola's obsession with doomed beasts.

Raised a Protestant, Norris was drawn to a *theistic* determinism. In college at Berkeley, he encountered Joseph Le Conte's revisionist Social Darwinism, which preached that man evolved in the soul's increasing triumph over his animal instincts. Le Conte offered a special philosophy that Norris would explore in his writings. Man's animal instincts *nourish* his strength; they are good, for without them he is a weakling. But they can clash with his spiritual yearnings. Man evolves through his decision to control his lower instincts.

All this is philosophy, not art. But it tells us that Norris was his own brand of "religious naturalist." He believed in an inherent moral order in nature. He was fascinated with the forces —instincts, "sixth senses," atavisms—that both nurtured and challenged man's social development. And he believed that novels were written from life, not from other novels. A writer, he said, must follow "that nameless sixth sense" he called sincerity. One may read another (like Zola) for methods, but if he is not careful, he will find himself taking "that which he has no right to take; his code of ethics, his view of life."

In his fiction Norris was grappling with his own contradictory, evolving ethics. Thus his McTeague is a complex, confused, and ultimately perplexing character. McTeague doesn't "lose his reason" over money. He is unschooled in "reason," and even criminally inclined. But there is a purity about him that the novelist compliments in contrasting him with the glib Marcus, full of grand ideas and "a passionate readiness to take offense, which passes among his class for bravery." McTeague *is* bravely sexual and sensual. If Norris does not simply *like* him—there is too much troubling and dumb in his protagonist—he does not begrudge McTeague the impact of his primal power. McTeague follows his own "sixth sense"—and how much different did Norris feel that was from a writer's sincerity?

That returns us to *Greed*. Our aim is not to reconstruct Stroheim's faithfulness. Enough damage has been done to film scholarship by the tendency to praise precise literary equivalents for filmic devices. Even Joel Finler, the film scholar most sensitive to Norris, praises Stroheim's passion for accuracy, which took him to the very house where the original murder took place.[2] Yet Norris's style defies such accuracy. Here, as one example, is Trina's death as told in the novel:

> Trina lay unconscious. . . . her body twitching with an occasional hiccough that stirred the pool of blood in which she lay face downward. Towards morning she died with a rapid series of hiccoughs that sounded like a piece of clockwork running down.

The hiccoughs would be easy enough to film, though an audience might be revolted. But that simple shift and blend of time and image in the second sentence baffles film technique. A dissolve to morning? A cut to a clock? Stroheim did not use the scene.

But so what? Stroheim did something *other* than what Norris did. It did not have to be better and therefore was not necessarily worse. The artists' works have different qualities, as we shall see in examining their equivalent symbolisms.

Since Norris came from a background of near-photographic painting (having studied at the traditionalist Académie Julian

[2] *Stroheim* (London, 1967). Actually, the original buildings were destroyed in the San Francisco earthquake of 1906. To get his actors in the right mood, Stroheim reputedly had them live in a similar house, but not in the original.

in Paris), we might expect a "cinematic" eye. As Donald Pizer has pointed out,[3] Norris had a near-matchless sense of the small, telling detail that is far more effective than his massive symbolism. The two sides of McTeague's nature are neatly symbolized by his canary and by references to dogs throughout the novel, but as Norris moves away from such blatant analogues, he becomes surprisingly subtle. Trina loses two fingers because of McTeague's harsh treatment, then later we learn that Marcus, after becoming a rancher, has had two fingers shot away in a gunfight "to his immense satisfaction." The bit of color not only reaffirms Marcus's flamboyant egoism, but allies him with Trina on the side of maiming social convention. At the wedding feast, a champagne cork pops with "a report like a pistol," startling everyone before they drink deeply. In Death Valley a pistol shot will puncture McTeague's canteen, dooming him.

One of Norris's finest passages occurs when McTeague, wishing to observe the correct proprieties, takes Trina, her mother, and little brother August to a variety show. There McTeague delights in the farce of a drunken lodger trying to make love to a girl. Trina is captivated by a "Society Contralto" who sings, "You do not love me—no; bid me good-by and go." Mrs. Sieppe likes the yodlers, and August loses control of his bladder. The passage has richer overtones than even Norris imagined, for one detail is "the crowning scientific achievement of the nineteenth century, the kinetoscope." With deft, ironic foreshadows, Norris parodies both the central characters and the "proper" world they infiltrate.

From all this, Stroheim developed a single skit with drunken knockabouts (which didn't survive into *Greed*) and shots of a clearly distressed August. Arguably, the scene demands sound, as the popping cork does. Arguably, the missing fingers involve too *much* detail.

Elsewhere, though, Stroheim adds his own images and exaggerates Norris's. The famous funeral cortege, which passes by as the McTeagues are married, is pure Stroheim. So is the dwarf at

[3] Pizer is the best single source on Norris. See *The Novels of Frank Norris* (Indiana, 1966) and his edited work, *The Literary Criticism of Frank Norris* (Texas, 1964).

the wedding and the tiny wife seen from behind sitting beside her immense husband. So are the expressionistic sequences of hands caressing money. Stroheim expanded Norris's ten-sentence reference to McTeague's parents into a prologue that makes up twenty-five pages of the reconstituted script. McTeague's canary, an occasional symbol in the novel, is, after the money, the film's most dominant symbol.

Stroheim's fidelity to Norris was his own naturalism on film. He was particularly true to Norris's sexual imagery, but in his own fashion. The public of 1899 had not complained about the sexual implications in *McTeague* (August's weak bladder was their main concern, and later editions removed the incident), though they may seem flagrant today. "Love me big!" cries Trina when McTeague's "huge strength" excites her. When Marcus angrily breaks McTeague's favorite pipe, the phallic overtones are carried over into his whole career: "What did he care about a broken pipe now that he had the tooth?" Whenever Mc-Teague's power is challenged or frustrated he always cries, "Don't make small of me!" If this sounds like schoolboy Freud, at least Norris used it as part of a complicated clash of sexual and social roles. In Norris's society a "proper" wife submitted to the man; he was sexual aggressor and master of the house. Sexually, the McTeagues are happy at first. Socially, however, there is a flaw—and when their fortunes turn, it opens fully. Trina takes mastership away from McTeague, undercutting his sexual complacency and counterposing her own roles. When he leaves her, she reunites her roles perversely: she sleeps nude with her money. When he murders her, McTeague finds his own aberrant sociosexual unity. His brute power overwhelms her as it once did so happily: he beats her to death and takes the money that is his as master of the house. Thus do the tensions between social and sexual proprieties help render them both into "brutes."

Stroheim clearly was taken with the graphic sexual turmoil. Building references to Trina's mouth into a central erotic symbol, he pointed brilliantly to her avarice, too—having her play her finger about her lips when she is scheming to get more money. And the train that comes in when McTeague wins Trina's love is thundering, unambiguous Freud—ahead of Freud.

Such power comes at a price. Thus, Stroheim, no doubt knowing that subtle doubts would mar a scene of innocent lust, omits the moment when McTeague, having aroused Trina to let him kiss her at the train station, immediately "thought less of her," as Norris puts it. There are other nuances in *McTeague* which the silent film cannot bring off in the same way. In the novel, the McTeagues' wedding night arouses fear, then passion in Trina, which Norris connects to primal urges through references to smells, touches, and clamoring instincts that are "strange" (the word he later uses of Trina's masochism). When Stroheim handles the scene he cuts to visual details: Trina covering her mouth, canaries in their cage, her satin slippers standing on McTeague's shoes. Finally, after Trina relents and McTeague closes the bedroom drapes, there is a conspicuous fade-in and -out on a hand sawing wood. (It is no longer in *Greed*.)

Although more than a trifle self-conscious, that is fine direction. Stroheim powerfully exploits the cinema's potential for overwhelming detail. He forces the viewer to look. And so, at "looking" moments, he had intrinsic advantages. Norris's metaphoric intent with Death Valley, for example, is better served by *Greed*'s emphatic geography. But Norris had advantages, too. It is one thing to imagine a brute strength that leaps monstrously to life, "shrill and meaningless . . . the hideous yelling of a hurt beast . . . an echo from the jungle," and something else to watch Gibson Gowland's grimacing. We can see Trina's attraction/ repulsion in Zasu Pitts's pantomime, but, unless we have read the novel, how could we know that Norris, that "pure naturalist," gave Trina's situation evocative classical echoes by nimbly comparing it to Titania's attraction for Bottom in *Midsummer Night's Dream*?

These differences are primary enough, but they have not been discussed in relation to *McTeague* and *Greed*. In reacting to the ruin of Stroheim's masterwork, his commentators have become arch-defenders of his uncompromising moral vision. As a result, we have asked too little about the particular forms his vision took. And, of course, Frank Norris, the ultimate source, a novelist of remarkable moral complexity, has been taken far too much for granted.

Sister Carrie (1900), Theodore Dreiser

Wyler's Suburban Sister: Carrie 1952

BY CAROLYN GEDULD

During the October, 1947, hearings of the House Committee on Un-American Activities, the formidable Mrs. McMath, mother of Ginger Rogers, testified that her daughter had turned down the role of Sister Carrie "because it was just . . . open propaganda." Thus, opposition to Theodore Dreiser's first novel, *Sister Carrie*, was being voiced nearly half a century after its original controversial publication in 1900.

Conservative critics had always been horrified by Dreiser's application of the theories of Charles Darwin and Herbert Spencer to social conditions. *Sister Carrie* contained at least three particularly objectionable ideas: that evolution allows the individual only the illusion of free will; that at the present stage of evolution, the individual is unable to choose between good and evil; and that, in consequence, conventional morality is meaningless.

These ideas were incompatible with the morality that had emerged after 1945 during the Cold War between American "good" and Communist "evil." In the McCarthy era of the early fifties, the idea of producing a film faithful to *any* of Dreiser's works was a strikingly self-defeating proposition. Yet both William Wyler and George Stevens, two liberal directors who had joined Paramount in 1948, made the attempt. In 1951, Stevens's adaptation of Dreiser's *An American Tragedy* (retitled *A Place in the Sun* to distinguish it from the 1931 Josef von Sternberg version) was released, and a year later, Wyler released his adaptation of *Sister Carrie*. The novel seemed a good choice for Wyler, who specialized in literary adaptations like *Dodsworth* (1936) and *Wuthering Heights* (1939) and in narratives colored by social problems like *Dead End* (1937) and *The Best Years of Our Lives* (1946). Still, *Sister Carrie* was not a politically prudent choice during the Hollywood witch hunts. Dreiser's moral ambiguity had to be cleaned up before the film version of *Sister Carrie* could go into production. Scriptwriters Ruth and Augustus Goetz needed to tame a sprawling, often clumsy, over-long story—set in three cities and involving almost every class from aspiring patrician to beggar.

The novel begins when eighteen-year-old Carrie Meeber leaves her small-town home to live with her married sister in Chicago. On the train she meets Charles Drouet, a salesman and "masher," who later persuades her to leave her sister's tenement flat and her grim job in a shoe factory. Under the spell of "the constant drag to something better," Carrie agrees to live with Drouet, justifying herself by his vague promises of future marriage. Drouet introduces Carrie to his prosperous friend, George Hurstwood, the manager of Fitzgerald and Moy's, the best saloon in Chicago. Carrie, always impressed by good clothes, believes the impeccable Hurstwood to be a better man than Drouet. She does not know that Hurstwood is already married—to Julia, an obsessive social climber. The strain of financial and marital pressures and of his infatuation for Carrie compels Hurstwood, almost inadvertently, to steal $10,000 from the saloon safe. He then flees with Carrie to Montreal, where a detective catches up with him and collects the stolen money. Knowing nothing about Hurstwood's theft, Carrie (believing him to be divorced) goes through a bogus marriage ceremony. With only a few hundred dollars, Carrie and Hurstwood move to New York. While she is captivated by Manhattan's wealth and display, Hurstwood goes into rapid decline until he becomes one of the chronic unemployed. When they go into debt for groceries, Carrie auditions for theatrical work. She leaves him once she has achieved success. Hurstwood becomes a street beggar, and eventually commits suicide. Carrie is unable to enjoy her success because a young idealist, Ames, convinces her that money and fame are not "enough"—that her loneliness and dissatisfaction are by-products of the American dream.

While Dreiser's story was based on the life of his sister Emma, Carrie's family connections are de-emphasized. The titular "Sister" is broadened in meaning beyond a single familial relationship. That is: Carrie is a member of the *American* family. Her own personality tends to blur around the edges. Dreiser doesn't even clearly describe what she looks like. What is important is her impact on others—"her look was something which represented the world's longing." In a sense, Carrie is the least important figure in the novel. She is a *carrier*, who primarily functions as a vehicle through which others find expression. She is not a great beauty or an object of intense sexual desire but she has the ability to infect others with desire—for material, rather than sexual, satisfaction. Propelled or "carried" by some uniquely American instinct, Carrie is always on the move, from West to East, and the two trapped men who briefly possess her are attracted by a reflection of their own (weaker) impulses toward motion. This motion is not exactly the equivalent of growth. It is the seemingly aimless motion of the sea—the central metaphor of the novel—in which everything drifts helplessly without a conscious awareness of purpose.

Wyler's decision to drop the word "Sister" from the film's title, ostensibly because the public might otherwise have thought the film was about a nun, is an indication of a shift in balance. Titles consisting only of a woman's name (e.g., *Gilda* [1946], *Harriet Craig* [1950]) generally have been a sign of shallow focus in American films, signaling a concern with a woman who has no context outside of her own psyche and with the men who try to escape, penetrate, or destroy that psyche. The single name title often suggests a strong will, or at least the ability to participate actively in the choices offered by life. The Carrie of the film is neither the helpless woman nor the infectious "carrier" of the novel, perhaps because she is not a "sister"—she is not rooted in the American family and a background of social determinants.

Carrie is a romantic story about the doomed love of Carrie and Hurstwood, rather than the description of a society. Chicago

Hurstwood (Laurence Olivier) admires Carrie (Jennifer Jones) in her finery.
Carrie *(1952).*

and New York are glimpsed only fleetingly in the film. Montreal is dropped altogether. The ambiance of Wyler's version belongs instead to the suburbs. With the exception of the opening scenes, Carrie (Jennifer Jones) is isolated within the confines of the places where she lives—a fate shared by the women who were moving to the suburbs in the 1950s. Unlike the mobile heroine of the novel, the Carrie of the film never joins the parade of strollers along Chicago's Michigan Avenue or New York's Broadway. The stimulating friends of the novel are condensed into a single neighbor, Mrs. Oransky (Sara Berner), a housewife and mother who is a happier version of Carrie's married sister (Jacqueline de Wit) and an example of the alternative that Carrie forfeits by leaving her sister's flat.

In the novel, marriage is never in the cards for Carrie. Dreiser implies that a girl who leaves home without prospects can expect either to become someone's mistress or to starve as a wage slave. Nevertheless Carrie is tough because she continues to struggle despite the hopelessness. For Wyler, Carrie is not hopeless, but weak because she makes the wrong choices—specifically, because she lives with two men without marriage. In her isolation, she is not controlled by social forces or the Darwinian imperative. As a concession to Cold War pressures, the film allows Carrie the possibility of choice and then punishes her—as we shall see—for choosing badly.

The film subscribes to the suburban moral code, in which one's first duty is to appear respectable. In the opening scenes of the film, the Meeber family—people never introduced in the novel—accompany their middle daughter to the railroad station, establishing the conventionality and respectability of Carrie's upbringing. Carrie comes to Chicago with the middle class expectations of an educated woman ("I went through school," she boasts). These expectations are often awkwardly grafted onto the remnants of Dreiser's life-among-the-lower-classes remaining in the script. At best, they force Wyler to invent or dramatize situations to explain choices that might seem inappropriate for a middle-class woman. In the novel, for instance, Sister Carrie loses her job in the shoe factory when she becomes ill for a few days—an expected fate in an expected career for someone of her status. In the film, Wyler has Carrie injure her finger in a sewing machine. This permits her to end the option of a career, a choice she had implicitly rejected already by protesting working conditions. (Dreiser reserves this protest for himself in the third person rather than risk his heroine's job or credibility as a novice.)

Carrie's protest suggests early in the film that she might pose a threat to others. (In the movie, almost every action is threatening to someone. Wyler indicates this in deep focus shots in which the figure in the background poses the threat.) Carrie's aggressive and nonconformist behavior in particular conforms to the 1950s suspicion that the conventional woman is potentially menacing to the male ego. In Dreiser's world, however, men could take refuge from the female threat in such sanctuaries as Fitzgerald and Moy's saloon, where men gather without the company of women. Even in New York, when he is unemployed, Hurstwood finds sanctuary of a poorer sort in hotel lobbies. Sister Carrie, on the other hand, has her own sanctuaries: the department store, the theater, and the restaurant. To underline Carrie's threat in the film, there is a dangerous crossover of these two types of sanctuary. Fitzgerald's is still a man's saloon, but attached to it is a restaurant where the sexes commingle. Carrie enters the saloon side, for men only, attracting the attention of Hurstwood (Laurence Olivier), who directs her to the restaurant entrance. The two rooms are separated by a half wall, allowing the camera to track with Carrie through the saloon. When Carrie stops, astonished, next to a buffet table filled with delicacies, Hurstwood joins her through a gap in the wall. Both sanctuaries are violated, acts Wyler implies are romantic (since Hurstwood is to be the fated love of Carrie's life) and dangerous (since the love affair will end badly).

When Carrie enters the saloon and restaurant through a double set of double doors, it is understood that she has entered a new world. She will not be returning to her sister's tenement or the shoe factory. The symbolic value of doors in *Carrie* replaces the value of walls in *Sister Carrie*. Dreiser describes "walled" cities, where buildings line up like solid walls forming mazes and where economic classes are separated as if by invisible walls. Sister

Carrie finds herself on the right side of the wall when she moves into the theatrical world, leaving Hurstwood on the wrong side, impoverished. But the heroine doesn't get through the wall of her own volition. She is let through magically, for no discernible reason. Wyler puts doors in walls, permitting his characters a freedom of action that challenges Dreiser. Many scenes are staged against doors or in doorways—Hurstwood, separated from Carrie by the door to Drouet's apartment, convinces her to flee with him to New York; he returns the money to the detective (Ray Teal) at the hotel-room door; at the stage door, Carrie is briefly reunited with Hurstwood before his suicide—all such scenes anticipate or recall the door to the café where the film's most critical choice is made. Walls and doors in the film do not divide economic classes: they divide the respectable from the scandalous. The implication is that Carrie can always walk out on the men who won't marry her, and Hurstwood can always return to Julia (Miriam Hopkins).

Respectable options are further reinforced by supporting characters. Carrie's sister, for instance, warns Carrie that "she will regret it all her life" if she takes money from Drouet. Thus, it is immediately after the restaurant scene, when Carrie displays Drouet's money, violating her sister's code as well as a male sanctuary, that she begins her confinement in Drouet's (Eddie Albert's) and later Hurstwood's apartments. Eventually she escapes to the stage, or, since she is never actually shown on stage, to the even more claustrophobic confines of the dressing room. From a 1950s perspective, her confinement alone cannot be considered a punishment: women were supposed to prefer a sheltered life. Carrie never suffers because of her physical isolation, although her moral isolation—from disapproving neighbors, for instance—*is* painful. Wyler suggests that this moral isolation and her loss of self-esteem, strongly felt throughout the film, are punishment for the bad choices Carrie makes.

Dreiser's Sister Carrie lives with Drouet and Hurstwood precisely because they offer an escape from the "confinement" of the sweat shop. They provide both financial security and access to a better class of society—and in the Darwinian struggle upward, the reaction of the neighbors is a minor consideration.

At the same time, she is sexually attracted to both men, although her sexuality is aroused primarily by indications of their material success. Wyler's Carrie offers love to the man who will marry her, who will make her respectable, and withholds both love and sex from Drouet, who cheapens her by refusing to propose. Given the values of the film, Carrie remains sympathetic because she submits to Drouet without passion. Her frigidity is a sign of her virtue, as is her domesticity (she darns Drouet's socks) and her affection for children. Carrie *deserves* to be a wife, something Hurstwood is kind enough to acknowledge when he tactfully calls her Mrs. Drouet, while he openly treats her as his mistress. (In the novel, it is Drouet who has the sensitivity to refer to Sister Carrie as "Mrs. Drouet" in the presence of Hurstwood.)

If the frigidity of Wyler's Carrie partially exonerates her for her relationship with Drouet, her love exonerates her for her relationship with Hurstwood. Typically for the 1950s, there is a split between love, which has enough domestic associations to vindicate the heroine, and sex, which debases her. (Wyler barely hints at a sexual relationship between Carrie and Hurstwood.) Love nullifies the string of deceptions that runs through the film, beginning with Carrie's lie to her sister about Drouet's loan and Drouet's pretense of leaving Carrie alone in his apartment. Hurstwood is the film's serious deceiver, lying to Carrie about his theft of Fitzgerald's safe and about Julia's refusal to grant him a divorce. His most desperate lie occurs just after the theft, when he convinces Carrie to flee with him by telling her that Drouet lies injured in another city. In the novel, Sister Carrie's decision to stay with Hurstwood is made for her by the action of the train moving further and further from Chicago. Meanwhile, Hurstwood, already regretting his flight, tells her any lie just to keep her quiet. Wyler uses the train itself to force Carrie to make her most important choice—significantly, at the door of the passenger car. Hurstwood confesses that he lied to Carrie for love and delivers his ultimatum: "If you love me, stay." When Carrie does stay, her moral struggle is finished. She has acted respectably by (a) leaving Drouet, (b) accepting the man who (she believes) will really marry her, and (c) responding to the higher, maternal demands of romantic love. (Leaving

Hurstwood at this point would be the moral equivalent of leaving an infant to die in the snow.) She no longer needs to choose, although punishment for poor choices in the past will haunt her for the remainder of the film.

The second half of the film and novel belong to Hurstwood. Laurence Olivier's Hurstwood is frail and reserved. Unlike the stout man-among-men of the novel, he snubs Drouet, who reminds Carrie that Hurstwood is, after all, a "high class fellow." Wyler's refinement of Hurstwood makes him an appropriate lover for his bourgeois heroine. Yet, the puritanism of the 1950s demanded a harsher appraisal of Hurstwood's behavior than Dreiser originally intended. In the film, for instance, his desertion of his family for Carrie is morally inexcusable. Wyler omits the unattractiveness of Hurstwood's family and instead makes the Hurstwood children paragons of 1950s virtue. His son (William Reynolds) is a clean-cut tennis champ and his daughter (Mary Murphy) is a sweet debutante. At the same time, Wyler softens the character of Hurstwood by transforming him into a romantic gentleman, omitting the hard manipulative streak suggested by Dreiser. In the novel, Hurstwood "wins" Carrie by arranging for her appearance in an amateur theatrical and then by stacking the audience to ensure her a successful reception. In the film, there are two amateur theatricals. Drouet is ridiculed by Carrie and Hurstwood for *his* appearance in one, and Hurstwood impresses Carrie with his tears when he merely accompanies her to the other.

Hurstwood's theft of Mr. Fitzgerald's money represents the most demanding adaptation of Dreiser's Chance into Wyler's Choice. In the novel, the slightly intoxicated Hurstwood discovers that the safe is unlocked and, his reason numbed by alcohol, he takes out the money. "While the money was in his hand the lock clicked. It had sprung! Did he do it?" Without stopping to wonder or consider alternatives, Hurstwood immediately makes plans to leave Chicago. With the click of a lock, he has become a criminal. In the film, Hurstwood, who does not drink (although his wife taunts him for being "in the liquor business"—a tainted profession in the film alone), also finds the safe unlocked. He takes out an envelope containing money as if to check it, drops the envelope, and while bending to pick it up, inadvertently pushes the safe closed. Not knowing what else to do, he puts the envelope in his pocket and goes home, where Julia is waiting with Mr. Fitzgerald. As he is in the process of turning the envelope over to his employer, the three begin to quarrel about Carrie. With the envelope still in his fist, Hurstwood runs out of the house and down the street. The camera tracks with him, associating his run with Carrie's long walk through the restaurant with Drouet's money clutched in her fist. The tension is maintained by the inference that Hurstwood could return the money at any point, if he were not distracted by the quarrel, just as Carrie could have returned Drouet's money if she had not been distracted by the atmosphere of the restaurant.

A third tracking shot occurs just prior to the third exchange of money at the end of the film. Hurstwood, thoroughly broken, is followed by the camera past the theater lobby, where Carrie's name and picture are prominently displayed, toward the stage door where he begs Carrie for money to buy food. (This recalls Fitzgerald's, where money and food were originally associated, and also the hotel, where Hurstwood had returned the stolen money to the detective just as a waiter passed with a dinner cart.) In the novel, Carrie gives Hurstwood a few dollars and leaves him, fearing the publicity of being seen with a beggar. It is their last meeting. The film, however, gives the couple a final opportunity to legitimize their relationship in accordance with 1950s morality. Carrie takes Hurstwood into her dressing room and (reversing their roles) *begs* him to share her wealth. He, however, has decided to commit suicide and leaves with the smallest coin from Carrie's purse in his fist.

While both novel and film are structured around exchanges of money, the value of money differs sharply in both. In Dreiser's sweatshop society, a wage literally prevents his characters from starving to death. The quest for money is entirely reasonable. In Wyler's suburban and bourgeois society, an educated Carrie is never convincingly portrayed as one of the desperately unemployed. Money, in the film, serves to devalue romance, and the quest for money becomes another indication of an unfortunate choice. After Hurstwood has returned the money taken from the safe, he tells Carrie—by this time his "wife"—that they are broke. Carrie doesn't mind. Lack of money will give her the chance to demonstrate the degree of her love under the "pure" conditions of economic distress. In the novel, by contrast, Hurstwood's bankruptcy changes Carrie's feelings for him from admiration to pity.

Wyler's Hurstwood becomes a man of few words after his "marriage" to Carrie. His decline is expressed through his eyes, narrowed to painful slits, and by the play of light and shadow which convey the state of a character's moral worth. When Carrie betrays Drouet by secretly meeting Hurstwood in the park before the theft, she wears a veil that obscures her face like a shadow. When she embraces Hurstwood on the train, the passing lights flicker across their faces as their moral positions reverse, while the screams of the train whistle suggest both Hurstwood's desperation and Carrie's sexual awakening. In New York, Carrie becomes increasingly a figure of light as she moves toward the stage, while Hurstwood literally becomes the shadow of the man he once was. He often casts his shadow on Carrie and on her photograph in the theater lobby, staining her success with his allusive presence.

The events that mark Hurstwood's decline in the film differ greatly from those in the novel. Hurstwood's unhappy involvement with a leased saloon, his gambling, and his attempt to work as a strikebreaker on the Brooklyn Trolley Line are not included in the film. Wyler substitutes events that are equally humiliating for Olivier's more sensitive Hurstwood and perhaps also humiliating enough for the bourgeois culture of the 1950s: the job in the greasy-spoon restaurant where his elegant manners are ridiculed, the employment agency where he "buys" a dishwasher's job for half the wages he will earn. The relationship between Hurstwood and Carrie also differs in the book and film versions. In the novel, Hurstwood starts ignoring Sister Carrie as he once ignored Julia. Sister Carrie, too, is quickly disenchanted with Hurstwood when he fails to find work. The Carrie of the film blossoms into the ideal 1950s wife, who enjoys fixing up the Lower East Side flat (which would remind Sister Carrie of her sister's dank tenement in Chicago). She soothes Hurstwood, sending him on errands to allow him an escape from the wretched flat. (In the novel, Hurstwood runs errands to obtain control of the grocery money.)

The crisis that destroys their relationship in the film occurs in the space of a few shots. While Hurstwood is ironing his trousers, which have been splattered by a beer truck (a symbol of his demotion in the high-class liquor trade), Carrie enters and cheerfully announces that she is pregnant. Stunned, Hurstwood forgets the iron and burns a hole in the trousers. The destruction of his last good pair of pants makes him weep. The once impeccably dressed Chicago notable now faces absolute humiliation. Carrie —who shares none of Sister Carrie's intense desire for clothes— fails to understand why trousers would matter when their baby is due (a perspective appropriate to the family-oriented 1950s). Wyler allows Carrie her pregnancy only to grant her a miscarriage when she learns that Julia and Hurstwood are still married. Perhaps the miscarriage is the ultimate punishment for Carrie's past mistakes and perhaps it is also a sign of her ultimate virtue— she is physically unable to bear a child out of wedlock. Hurstwood is similarly punished in the film when he loses his child. He attempts and fails to contact his son, whom he will never see again. The loss of their children is more than their relationship can stand. (It also reflects the theme of lost or threatened children that would persist through the 1950s in such films as *Rebel Without a Cause* [1954], *The Night of the Hunter* [1955], and *The Man Who Knew Too Much* [1956].) Ironically, Julia does grant the divorce in the end which could allow Carrie and Hurstwood the option of a legal marriage. Instead, Carrie becomes an actress, appearing in a play significantly titled "Lady in Waiting," and Hurstwood, it is implied, commits suicide.

Hurstwood's actual death was filmed but cut from the released print. In Axel Madsen's *William Wyler: The Authorized Biography* (1973), the director explains why. "The reason for the cuts . . . was the McCarthy era. *Carrie* showed an American in an unflattering light, a very sophisticated and cultured man who sinks to the depth of degradation. . . . This, the superpatriots said, was Un-American, even if it happened every day on the Bowery and even though the story took place 40 years earlier."

The film version of *Sister Carrie* that was finally premièred in July, 1952, two years after production had begun, is thus a perceptive study of the conflict between the conservative forces that controlled a frightened Hollywood and a liberal director's commitment to the work of a leftist author. (Dreiser applied for membership in the Communist Party shortly before his death in 1945.) There can be little doubt that the conservatives ultimately "won" *Carrie*. Yet, despite its obeisance to conventionality, it is as a deeply moving romance—in the best sense of the word—that the film is still memorable.

The Wonderful Wizard of Oz (1900), L. Frank Baum

A Kansan's View

BY JANET JUHNKE

"Tell me about Kansas: all I know about it is from *The Wizard of Oz.*" I have heard those words, or something like them, many times in my life—most recently from my newly acquired New York in-laws. The statement continues to surprise me, not so much because of the ignorance of Kansas it displays (I am used to that), but because it reflects the pervasive power of the Oz legend.

Like Dorothy, I was raised on a small farm in Kansas, but unlike many Americans I did not grow up with *The Wizard of Oz.* The 1939 MGM film I knew mainly by hearsay. And I had never read Frank Baum's 1900 novel *The Wonderful Wizard of Oz* until this year. Coming to the novel and film this late, I must fight against being offended at the picture of Kansas they have left with my out-of-state friends. On this point, the book is worse than the film: the Kansas landscape consists of "nothing but the great gray prairie on every side." There are no trees, only dry, cracked earth baked gray by the sun. Even the grass— and the people—are gray. "When Aunt Em came there to live she was a young, pretty wife. The sun and wind had changed her. . . . They had taken the red from her cheeks and lips, and they were gray also. She was thin and gaunt, and never smiled, now."

Uncle Henry is just as bad off: he "worked hard from morning till night and did not know what joy was. He was gray also." Who wouldn't want to escape such grayness? It is not the Kansas I know.

But the facts of Kansas life are finally incidental to the story. Like all good fairy tales, *The Wonderful Wizard of Oz* is a story of escape: Kansas just happens to be where one escapes from. J. R. R. Tolkien reminds us in "On Fairy Stories" that there is nothing wrong with escape: "Escape is . . . as a rule very practical, and may even be heroic." The wonder of the escape to a land found "over the rainbow" is presented with genius in both novel and film. But since the film is more familiar (at least to non-Kansans), I want to focus first on the book.

Baum's Dorothy is a merry child, not yet beaten down by her harsh, gray environment. "When Dorothy, who was an orphan, first came to her, Aunt Em had been . . . startled by the child's laughter . . . and she still looked at the little girl with wonder that she could find anything to laugh at." This Dorothy is not a frustrated or reflective girl dreaming of a better land. She does not attempt to run away from home: the cyclone takes her by surprise and she confronts her adventures with innocent curiosity.

It is appropriate that Dorothy, "who had lived so long on the dry, gray prairies," should feel with special keenness the wonders of nature in bloom in the Land of Oz. The world she greets as she steps out of her storm-tossed house is a green world— fruitful and fresh and colorful. Noting the fertile fields of the Munchkins, Dorothy remarks that they must be very good farmers. (Perhaps she is contrasting them with her Uncle Henry, who must struggle on a harsher land.) However, even in Oz, nature has a fearful as well as benign face. Take the motif of water— that precious and rare phenomenon in dry Kansas. Dorothy is delighted with the brook that rushes and sparkles along and murmurs to her in a kind voice, and she is grateful for the brooks along her journey that provide water to drink and to bathe in. But water is a menace to the Tin Woodman (the rain makes him rust), to the Scarecrow (he gets caught in the middle of a river), and, more fortunately, to the Wicked Witch of the West (she is "melted" by a bucket of water). The rest of the green

The stalwart cast poses for a publicity still: The Cowardly Lion (Bert Lahr), The Tin Man (Jack Haley), Dorothy (Judy Garland), The Wizard (Frank Morgan), The Scarecrow (Ray Bolger), and Toto.
The Wizard of Oz (1939).

paradise also has its dangers. The forest is lovely but fearful, the flowers can be poisonous and deadly, and the trees can suddenly fight and attack the innocent trespassers. Baum continually shows the ambiguous powers of nature, as friend and as foe.

Like many in myth and legend who go on quests, Dorothy seeks a beautiful city, and Emerald City proves green like the trees and grass she never saw in Kansas. "Green candy and green popcorn were offered for sale, as well as green shoes, green hats, and green clothes of all sorts. At one place a man was selling green lemonade, and when the children bought it Dorothy could see that they paid for it with green pennies." For all this greenness, there is little of nature in Emerald City. No vegetation is mentioned, except for the green flowers on Dorothy's palace window sill, and "there seemed to be no horses or animals of any kind." Furthermore, the green of the city is revealed to be fake, an illusion caused by the green-tinted spectacles all inhabitants and visitors are forced to wear. Perhaps Baum is saying that reality is gray after all, and the return to grayness inevitable —at least for limited human beings. Throughout her adventures, Dorothy does remain an ordinary human with ordinary needs for food and rest and shelter—those "inconveniences" of the flesh that the more privileged Scarecrow and Tin Woodman do not experience. Dorothy's escape from Kansas does not mean an escape from time or hunger or pain: perhaps this is one reason readers find her such a convincing character.

In his preface to *The Wonderful Wizard of Oz*, Baum states that he wished to dispense with "all disagreeable incident," to create a tale in which "the wonderment and joy are retained and the heart-aches and nightmares are left out." Luckily for the reader, Baum is not being quite candid. The book is full of nightmares, frequently taking the form of fearsome animals—beasts with bodies like bears and heads like tigers, attacking wolves, wild crows, black bees, flying monkeys, a spider beast, and creatures with shooting hammer heads. Dorothy's friends must occasionally use violence against the beasts. The Tin Woodman decapitates forty wolves, each with a single blow of his axe, and he also chops off the head of a "great, yellow wildcat" with "two rows of ugly teeth" and red eyes that "glowed like balls of fire."

The Lion kills the sleeping spider monster by knocking off its head, and the Scarecrow twists the necks of forty menacing crows.[1]

Some of the frightening creatures Dorothy meets turn out to be kind and helpful. The Winged Monkeys are really good-natured, though temporarily under evil control; a stork and a troop of field mice help Dorothy out of trouble. But there are other terrors: a fearful cyclone, an arduous journey with chasms and rivers to cross, a mysterious wizard, and a seemingly impossible task—to kill the powerful and wicked witch.

Nor are heartaches, which Baum said he intended to leave out, totally absent from the book. Dorothy's longing for home and the frequent accidents, delays, and threats that keep her from her goal constitute the greatest of these heartaches. The Tin Woodman has an elaborate and affecting history to tell, for though he has no heart he remembers when he did—in Baum, he was once human—and he remembers the love (a beautiful Munchkin girl) he lost because of the witch's jealousy. The story gives no indication that he will ever get the girl back again, even with his new silk heart.

Baum knew better than his preface indicates that fantasy works by a combination of wonder and fear, joy and nightmare. He knew also that the terror must finally be overcome, that the traveler into a fantasy world ultimately seeks recovery of the world left behind, an enlightened return to reality. Along Dorothy's way the Wizard turns out to be a meek humbug of a man, and the Wicked Witch of the West a miserable figure, afraid of the dark, afraid of the lion, powerless against rival magic, and easily destroyed. Dorothy returns to the Kansas prairies as miraculously as she left. And although her magic slippers are lost forever in the desert, Dorothy comes back with a new appreciation of home. "Oh, Aunt Em! I'm so glad to be at home again." Such a safe return, a happy ending, fulfills a deep human need for reassurance, and it succeeds in *The Wonderful Wizard of Oz*

---

[1] These incidents suggest a decapitation motif in the novel. The Tin Woodman cut off his own head by accident (with a bewitched axe) when he was still human. The Great Oz first appears as a giant head without a body. The Scarecrow's head is taken off to have his brains installed.

just as it does in lesser works, such as sentimental novels, and greater works, such as the New Testament.

One somber note, however, is sounded at the ending of the novel. Aunt Em asks Dorothy where she has come from. " 'From the Land of Oz,' said Dorothy, gravely." Why did Baum choose the adverb *gravely* rather than, say, *happily?* Here is proof that, for Baum, Dorothy's adventures have constituted a kind of traumatic initiation. She has experienced terror and death, and she has felt disillusionment and sorrow, and has been forced to assume responsibility. She has begun to grow up—a sobering experience.

The MGM film based on *The Wonderful Wizard of Oz* was, and still is, one of the most successful adaptations of prose narrative to film ever made. It may seem that the material was inherently dramatic and thus a natural for film. However, earlier attempts at adapting the material had failed. The first moving-picture version, a one-reel film produced in 1910 by the Selig Company, was forgotten almost as soon as it appeared. Baum's own film versions—*The Patchwork Quilt of Oz, The Magic Cloak of Oz*, and *The New Wizard of Oz*, produced in 1913 and 1915— also got a poor reception, and a 1925 *Wizard of Oz* starring comedian Larry Semon bombed. What made the MGM film succeed was not simple magic but a lot of money, commitment, talent, and luck.

The principal movers behind the film were its producer Mervyn LeRoy and assistant producer Arthur Freed. In retrospect, each man claimed to have had the idea first and to have persuaded Louis B. Mayer to back the project. Each man also claimed to have insisted on Judy Garland for the role of Dorothy —over the objections of the "front office" (mainly Mayer)—who wanted Shirley Temple for the part. Shirley was owned by Fox, which refused to lend her, so Judy Garland, considered by some too plump and too old for Dorothy, was agreed upon.

The tale of the making of the film is a fantastic prelude to the film itself. The budget was unprecedented—$3.2 million in LeRoy's estimate. The cast was huge, and the full proceedings were spread over twenty-five acres of the studio back lot. Sixty-five different sets and all twenty-nine of Metro's sound stages were used. LeRoy says that a quarter-size model of Oz alone took months to prepare; it contained 122 buildings painted in sixty-two shades of colors by 150 painters. Makeup men and set designers were confronted with unprecedented challenges: how to create a tornado and carry Dorothy and Toto off into the sky on it, how to make people fly without ropes or visible wires, how to melt a witch down to a black pool, how to portray the Tin Man and the Lion. Some of the solutions were brilliantly simple: the cyclone, for example, was created by blowing a woman's silk stocking with a fan. Some solutions were reached through painful trial and error: the aluminum dust sprayed on Buddy Ebsen, the original choice for the Tin Man, put him in an iron lung, so he had to be replaced by Jack Haley, for whom an aluminum paste was created.

The biggest headache for the producers and directors was the Munchkins. Although the screen credits Singer's Midgets with portraying the diminutive ensemble, the fact is that Leo Singer could get a mere 150 midgets together. The 350 needed for the film were really gathered from all over the world by Major Doyle, a midget monologist. Only one-third spoke English (their songs had to be dubbed in), and the group was hard to control. According to John Lahr, *Notes on a Cowardly Lion* (1969), and Mervyn LeRoy, *Take One* (1974), the midgets were uninhibited, wild, even violent; they required constant vigilance by the Culver City police "to keep them from killing each other."

Each principal had a makeup man of his or her own. The Munchkins were made up by twenty artists, each turning out nine an hour. The costumes were hot and uncomfortable for nearly everyone. Jack Haley couldn't sit or lie down in the Tin Man outfit; Bert Lahr in the Lion suit couldn't eat and had to take meals through a straw. Margaret Hamilton's green face was runny and messy. Judy Garland had to be severely strapped in to make her sixteen years look more like the eleven the part required. Her rigors of dieting, going to school on the set, being pepped up with pills, being manipulated by a pushy mother and by Mayer, a sort of grand wizard himself—are all part of the Garland legend. She and her mother together were paid $350 a week, her mother taking the larger share, while Lahr, for example, received $2500 a week. Judy was a relative newcomer, however, and the role not only set her off on a soaring career at MGM but also became an identifying symbol for her the rest of her life.

The film became the most popular of the "Metro musical" genre, described by Anne Edwards as "glossy, Technicolored, dance-packed, song-jammed, star-loaded, chorus-crowded with hundreds of rhythmic robots" (*Judy Garland: A Biography,* 1975). The description is not quite appropriate for this film. *The Wizard of Oz* is spectacular, but not all spectacle: it has moments of quiet humor and pathos. It presents a world of fantasy, but its aim, in LeRoy's words, is that of "putting realism into the fantastic." The music, dance, color, and spectacle are not extraneous additions, but are tastefully woven into the plot. "Over the Rainbow," which was almost cut out of the film at the last moment as too slow-paced, introduces us to the lonely girl's longing for happiness. "Munchkinland" is fantasy land's extravagant welcome to Dorothy. Harold Arlen wrote the music and E. Y. Harburg the lyrics for these and other songs in the film: the triumphal "Ding Dong the Witch Is Dead," the bouncy "We're Off to See the Wizard," the sentimental and nonsensical "If I Only Had a Heart," and "If I Were King of the Forest." Throughout the film, the music reinforces the mood, marking changes in narrative direction, stirring emotions with such contrasts as the harsh, rapid Miss Gulch motif of Glinda's "ethereal" vibrato.

The film of *The Wizard of Oz* appeals to adults because of its cerebral humor—Professor Marvel's lovably obvious fakery, the Lollipop Kids doing their twitching imitation of "tough guys," the Scarecrow's assertion that "some people without brains do an awful lot of talking," the Lion's Brooklyn accent and gag lines like "I can't sleep—I tried counting sheep but I'm afraid of them too," the Wizard's satire of educated men as he offers the Scarecrow a Doctorate of Thinkology and his satire of patriots whose courage is in their uniforms and medals, and the pun on the "horse of a different color." Many children would miss these jokes. Adults also respond favorably to the fine acting and to the film-makers' technical skills. Both children and adults love the music and songs. "Over the Rainbow," especially, appeals to all ages—to all who dream of a happier and more colorful world than their own, like Munchkinland.

Christopher Finch, in *Rainbow* (1975), a life of Judy Garland, asserts that the screenplay for *The Wizard of Oz* "is one of those rare adaptations that is better than the original." However, with two such masterpieces as Baum's book and the MGM film, comparative judgments of quality are meaningless. The two versions are just different; and if the film has touched more people than the book, it is mainly because, through the medium of television, more people have been exposed to the film than to the book. From a film buff's point of view, the book may seem to contain "much superfluous material" and to be "episodic and meandering" (Finch), but the same could be said of *The Odyssey*, *Don Quixote*, *Moby Dick*, and countless other narrative classics. What is good narrative prose is not necessarily good film. Film has an affinity with *drama*, where tight construction, economy of plot, and unity of character are necessary to carry the audience on through climax to conclusion in a relatively brief compass of time. Narrative prose has an affinity with *epic*, which delays the audience with various "retarding elements"—explanations, digressive speeches, stories within the story. Thus the book treats us to full histories of the lives of the Scarecrow, the Tin Man, the King of the Monkeys, and the Wizard of Oz. It marks pauses for eating and sleeping; it takes time to introduce the Kalidahs, the Winkies, and the Quadlings, and to take Dorothy through the Dainty China Country inhabited by easily broken milkmaids and shepherds and by a joker who is cracked in the head.

To be sure, the film's songs and elaborate production numbers "retard" the forward movement of the plot—but much of the book's action is telescoped into a simpler, more unified plot. The film reduces the two good witches to one. The Witch of the North, a little old woman with wrinkles, white hair, and a stiff walk, is omitted, while Glinda, the young and beautiful Witch of the South, somewhat improbably takes the roles both of sending Dorothy to Oz to find a way home *and* of telling Dorothy that the ruby slippers could have got her home anyway. She rather lamely explains why she didn't tell Dorothy the truth right away—because Dorothy wouldn't have believed her. And, of course, without the trip to Oz, there would have been no story. The Witch of the West is treated much more melodramatically in the film. The ugly green face, the marvelous cackle, the periodic threats along the way ("I'll get you, my pretty!"), the fire, the skywriting, the signs in the forest—all are absent from the book. These devices build suspense and fear—and focus the audience's emotions. The book does not use such dramatic tools.

The most striking structural difference between the book and the film, however, is in the frame for the story. In the book, Dorothy's "farm" consists of a small one-room house alone on the prairie, neither prosperous enough for hired hands like Hunk, Zeke, and Hickory, nor near enough to other homes for Toto to bother a Miss Gulch. Those characters—and Professor Marvel —are inventions of the screen writers. The change is significant. In the book, Dorothy is simply carried away to Oz; in the film she tries first to run away from home. In the book she only wishes to escape drabness; in the film, though that drabness is wonderfully emphasized by the black-and-white photography, Dorothy also runs from the cruelty of Miss Gulch, in order to save the life of her only friend, Toto. Professor Marvel's suggestion that Aunt Em is ill adds guilt and worry to Dorothy's later desire to return home.

The reappearance of Miss Gulch, Hickory, and the others in different form in the land of Oz brings delighted recognition to the audience. But when we see them in their "proper" form at the film's conclusion, the "message" of the story is quite different from that of the book. Dorothy hasn't been to Oz at all—it's all been a dream, created out of the fabric of her real life. The book offers no such "interpretation." Baum's Dorothy returns to a new house, built to replace the one the cyclone took away. She has actually been gone, and Aunt Em has missed her. When she runs up the road to the house, she says simply that she's been to Oz and that she's glad to be home again.

It is probably heretical to prefer this simple conclusion to the sentimental ending of the film, which has pleased so many viewers. But the one aspect of the film that seems cloyingly sweet is that tearful repetition: "There's no place like home. There's no place like home. . . ." Such, at least, was the general feeling of my college freshmen (at Kansas Wesleyan, Salina, Kansas) who viewed the film this year. Perhaps the most telling comment came from a nineteen-year-old girl who has since left her Kansas home to make her way alone in New York City: "The ending was a total anticlimax. It stated that this was all a dream, that fantasy is unreal and can only get you in trouble, and boring status quo existence is the right way to live. The moral is 'There's no place like home.' Blah! or Oh, how sweeeet! is how the audience feels. I hate the ending because fantasy *is* real, necessary, and because home is not always the best place to be."

The ending of the film is an adult ending, not a child's. Adults like to dismiss fantasy as "only a dream"; children know that evil witches and animate trees and talking animals are real. Tolkien insisted that in fairy stories the magic must not be explained away. More recently, Bruno Bettelheim argued that fairy tales are important precisely because they show that there *are* evil creatures and that these creatures can be overcome and punished. Explaining the fantasy as a dream negates that moral and psychological function of the tale.

"Toto, I have the feeling we're not in Kansas any more"—this line still gets the biggest laugh in Kansas audiences. But it is serious, too. Kansas is where we all live, whether our address is New York City or San Francisco, and to Kansas we must return, when we become adults and the wonderful and terrifying dream of Oz has ended.

The Virginian (1902), Owen Wister

Three Treks West

BY JOSEPH F. TRIMMER

To paraphrase André Bazin, the Western is America's Odyssey. It is an epic tale of heroic men who live in the timeless world of myth. The Western is also America's myth because it embodies all the aspirations of our national character. It is, after all, the story of a common man who works at a rather menial job; but in the pale half-light of romance, the cowboy can be seen as the equal of Achilles or Roland—the embattled knight defending his code of gallant honor and manly virtue. And like Odysseus, we never seem to tire of hearing our story. It was Owen Wister's *The Virginian* which gave classic formulation to that story. Over the years the novel has enjoyed an incredible popularity; and that popularity has been increased by two adaptations for the screen.[1] What is interesting are the significant alterations. It is not disturbing to learn that Hollywood has not "followed the book."

Editors' title. This article originally appeared as *"The Virginian:* Novel and Films," in *Illinois Quarterly,* Vol. 35, No. 2, December 1972, pp. 5–18. Reprinted by permission.

[1] Of course there are other versions of *The Virginian.* NBC has had good success with two television series using the names of the characters, though little else, from the original story. Fenin and Everson speak of a road company version of the story *circa* 1900 which starred William S. Hart (*The Western,* p. 76). But for purposes of focus, I will restrict myself to the novel and the 1929 and 1945 film versions. [There are also silent *Virginian's* of 1914 and 1923—editors' note.]

What is surprising is the way in which this alteration documents significant changes in the character of the Western myth and our attitude toward it.

One partial explanation for these changes in the Virginian story is that most were implicit in the symbolic content of the novel. The simplest way to read Wister's novel is to see it as a novel of East and West: Wister tested the code of the Western hero by placing it in opposition to the code of Eastern civilization as represented by the schoolmarm, Molly Wood. The sexual-cultural clash produces mutual education for the two protagonists. Robert Warshow has argued in his essay "The Westerner" that "in the American mind, refinement, virtue, civilization, Christianity itself, are seen as feminine and therefore women are portrayed as possessing some kind of deeper wisdom, while men, for all their apparent self-assurance are fundamentally childish." This attitude dominates the early portion of the novel as the Virginian is shown to be wild and given to practical joking. There is, to be sure, much of the romantic primitive in this initial portrait; the Virginian is free, content, and in harmony with his environment.

But we are also aware of the Virginian's potential for education into another kind of life. There is, after all, his name, which not only indicates his origin, but his capacity to apprehend the refinements of "civilization." When the school teacher arrives in town, the Virginian becomes an admirer of Eastern culture; and with her guidance, he reads Shakespeare, Browning, Austen, and Scott. Such an education makes him eventually worthy of the lady from the East. Their three-year courtship is, in fact, a model of Victorian propriety. When they finally return East after their wedding trip, the Virginian is acknowledged as a perfect gentleman by the Vermont social set.

While the Virginian is learning about Eastern culture, Molly is being educated about the Western experience. In this kind of world it is the woman who is childish unless she can develop a sense of quasi-masculine independence and an understanding of the necessity of violence. In the two crisis situations of the novel, the Virginian must make ethical choices that produce moral revulsion in Molly. Initially, Molly believes in law and order and cannot understand why it is necessary to break the law in order to preserve the law. Eventually she is able to acknowledge the expedient necessity of the hanging of Steve—it was for the public good. But the second moral crisis is more difficult since it involves no obvious social benefit. On their wedding day, the Virginian and Molly quarrel over whether he shall answer or evade the challenge of Trampas. What is he fighting for, she asks. "What he defends, at bottom, is the purity of his own image —in fact his honor" (Warshow). And the concept of honor is ironically a virtue associated with the Eastern aristocratic concept of the gentleman. As Warshow suggests, "the Westerner is the last gentleman."

What we have in *The Virginian* is a reassessment of the relationship of East and West. Molly left the East and her rather prudishly cultured admirer because she was looking for a wider world of experience. The West, and more particularly the Virginian, gives her a wider and a revitalized picture of herself. Molly is not alone in sensing that there are deficiencies in her Eastern world. Her great aunt had the opportunity for a similar romantic adventure in her youth. She is therefore capable of recognizing the value and meaning of the Virginian. When she reads his letter of proposal, she responds by saying, "O dear, O dear! And this is what I lost."

What is accomplished in this reassessment of the relationship of East and West is a synthesis of American traditions. Donald Davis has talked about *The Virginian* as a combination of the Western scout of Cooper and the Dime Novel, and a "recasting of the golden myth of the antebellum South."[2] Donald E. Houghton sees the novel as portraying the myth of the romantic primitive, and the economic myth of Horatio Alger.[3] Houghton makes his case even more convincing by showing how the two myths are given separate treatment by the different narrative devices of the novel—the romantic primitive story is told in the first person by a sympathetic Easterner, while the success story is told in the

[2] Donald Davis, "Ten Gallon Hero," *American Quarterly* (Summer, 1954), p. 12.

[3] Donald E. Houghton, "Two Heroes in One: Reflections on the Popularity of The Virginian," *Journal of Popular Culture* (Fall, 1970), pp. 498–99.

The "Cowboy Romeo" Virginian (Gary Cooper) romances the school marm "Juliet," Molly Wood (Mary Brian). The Virginian (1929).

third person. G. Edward White argues that Wister desired "to integrate the Old West and the new order of the East in the person of his horseman of the plains . . . [He wanted] to combine the best features of nature and civilization, rugged individualism and gentlemanliness, past and present, and West and East into a more perfect whole. He suggests in the marriage of Molly and the Virginian that the 'true American' traditions of the eastern seaboard will constantly be revitalized as they pass westward, creating an even stronger and more unified nation."[4] The end of the novel confirms this theory for we see the Virginian turn capitalist "with a strong grip on many various enterprises." The country and the economy are revitalized by strong, rugged men bred in the West and polished by contact with Eastern culture. Surely this is the symbolic point to be made in noting that the novel is dedicated to Theodore Roosevelt, the rough rider turned president.

So much for the implicit and explicit symbolism of the novel. What is now of interest is how the two film versions of this story changed or altered Wister's intended synthesis of East and West. The first sound version of *The Virginian*, directed by Victor Fleming, was made in 1929 and starred Gary Cooper as the Virginian, Richard Arlen as Steve, Walter Huston as Trampas, and Mary Brian as Molly. The film is a curious blend of the authentic and the amateur which makes many films of this period seem ironically realistic. The black-and-white print establishes the bleakness of the Western landscape. Many of the "takes" appear as if they were shot with a home movie camera. Everything is obviously "real": there are no studio shots. The exteriors, the interiors, the costumes, the cows, the dulled report of gunshots, the noise of the train drowning out dialogue, all establish the authenticity of the stark life which is portrayed on the screen.

The film opens with a picture of the Virginian at work, singing in a half-mumbled manner a tuneless cowboy song as he drives his cattle into town. There he meets Steve, his old crony, and they go into the saloon to have a drink. The Virginian is already

[4] G. Edward White, *The Eastern Establishment and the Western Experience* (New Haven: Yale University Press, 1968) pp. 141–143.

a foreman, something it took Wister half a novel to accomplish; Steve, on the other hand, is still "the same." As the two men "dangle" around the bar, slapping each other on the back, drinking toasts to those wilder days when they "pulled that stuff" down by the border, we become aware of the psychological distance between them. Steve remains what the Virginian was before he became a foreman. The Virginian still has a great deal of the wild innocent in him, but becoming a foreman has established him among the ranks of serious citizenry. This membership has not yet been solidified, however, for the Virginian still finds a challenge in competing with Steve for the temporary affections of a barmaid. When Trampas enters the contest for the girl's affection and provokes a near confrontation (which results in the famous line, "When you call me that, smile"), the scene establishes the equality of the three men. Each wants the same object and fights for it in the traditional Western manner. In a sense then, the film remains true to the novel. In the novel the famous line was uttered in a card game when the Virginian and Trampas were competing for the same pot. Barmaids and cards are both entertaining trifles for the men of the West.

The intrusion of Eastern culture in the person of Molly Wood does not alter the mood of gamesmanship, for the Virginian and Steve simply substitute Molly for the barmaid. When Steve bests the Virginian by revealing the Virginian's trick, he is hardly able to smother a childish guffaw. Later, at a party given in Molly's honor, the tricks and guffaws continue as both men become inhibited by the new school marm's culture. Steve dances clumsily and the Virginian cannot carry on a conversation with Molly without excessive stammering. Embarrassment leads to practical joking. The party for the new school teacher is also the occasion for a mass christening of newborn babies. As the ranch hand Honey says, christening is a sign that the country is "getting fancy." Reacting to the frustrations of the evening, the Virginian and Steve switch the look-alike babies from crib to crib and therefore frustrate the christening.

The fact that there was no love triangle in Wister's novel seems unimportant. But that information certainly helps explain Steve's function in the film. He represents the Old West, the unenlightened West, the masculine, anarchistic, romantic, and primitive West of the first half of Wister's novel. He is an image of what the Virginian was, and represents the kind of life for which the Virginian still has affection and nostalgia. But although still childish enough by Eastern standards to be equated with the boys in Molly's schoolroom, the Virginian has demonstrated some interest in education. Immediately after the dance Molly is seen in the schoolhouse attempting to lead a song. She is trying, in other words, to impose the harmony and order of civilization on the children of Medicine Bow. The Virginian sticks his head in the window and Molly, distracted by his presence, waves her hands in such a way as to destroy the harmony and order of the song she was trying to direct. It seems clear then that the Virginian's sexual vitality will eventually make his initial clumsiness insignificant and allow him to conquer. In the next scene the Virginian and Molly go riding into the mountains. When they stop, the Virginian sits on the ground while Molly sits on a rock. Her position above him is appropriate to the discussion of Shakespeare which follows. In the Virginian's eyes Romeo was a fairly decent hero except that he wasted a lot of time around the balcony. "If he wanted Juliet why didn't he take her?"

This picture of the Virginian counters Wister's portrait of him in the novel. The fictional hero accepted the rules of a leisurely and lengthy courtship, was duly impressed by Molly's education and cultural superiority. But Gary Cooper is not interested in play acting. He tells Molly to be real. He stands up, thus suggesting that he has attained, if not superiority, at least equality to Molly. He kisses her and proposes marriage. He tells her that teaching school is not a real woman's job and suggests that they both go West and "do out there what the Judge did here . . . make United States out of prairie land." It is Molly who now feels clumsy. She says she feels like an outsider and realizes that she has more to learn before she can understand the West.

Ironically it is Steve, and therefore the image of what the Virginian used to be, who intrudes on this scene. The Virginian discovers Steve rustling, but their confrontation is easy and friendly. The Virginian admits that they have done a lot of "loco things" together, but "there are some things that are wrong."

He suggests that the whole country is beginning to take things more seriously and that Steve should too. Steve's response is characteristic: "How do I know what I am going to do?" He then argues that the country is getting too civilized, that he will move West, and rides away singing "carry me back to the lone prairie." The importance of this scene is the Virginian's attitude toward Steve. He is not critical, ethical, or patronizing. He simply preaches common sense and implies, in a friendly way, that Steve follow the example he is beginning to set. Steve chooses to leave rather than conform.

The point of all this is that Cooper plays the Virginian as an easygoing Western Romeo completely at home in his own environment. He does win Molly, but he does not need to change his cultural allegiance to the West in order to win her. In other words, we are never aware of that decisive movement toward the Eastern establishment and capitalistic respectability which Houghton identified as a major theme in the novel. Even when the Virginian is forced to punish Steve, forced to become serious, he does so within the context of the Western experience. Steve certainly understands the nature of that experience: when he is captured he utters a soliloquy on the meaning of life. It is, according to Steve, the simple cycle of nature, a few girls and a few drinks and death—"might as well be now as later." But what is dominant in the whole hanging episode is the contrast between Steve's affected jolliness and the Virginian's sudden seriousness. The quail's whistle, which has been their sign of friendship, is heard throughout the scene, thus reminding each of what had been before things got so serious. But the hanging is more a part of the Western ethic than it is a procedure of civilization. Hanging is a custom of the country and it is known and accepted by all. Steve has played the game and lost. To be sure, Cooper's face registers near nausea throughout the hanging, and Honey says that they would rather not hang Steve, but no one suggests leniency. The Virginian directs the hanging, faces Steve and the responsibility for the unfortunate event.

Further proof that the hanging is to be seen as part of the Western experience is documented by the moral revulsion it causes Molly. Soon after the hanging she discovers the children she has been trying to civilize acting out a mock hanging in the schoolyard, and thus hears about what the Virginian "had to do" to Steve. We also learn that both Steve and the Virginian were true to the code of the West because they did not act like "babies" when they confronted death. Mrs. Taylor is given the job of explaining the code to Molly. But she puts the West on a take-it-or-leave-it basis—this is the code; this is why it has to be; if you can't take it, get out. Molly begins by preaching that violence makes people hard—destroys their human feelings—but by the end of the scene she has become the equal of Mrs. Taylor. She argues that her family knows how to do things when they need to be done and offers their gallant deeds in the New York State Indian wars as proof. The scene closes as Molly expells Mrs. Taylor from the house. Molly has become worthy of her Western Romeo.

The final showdown with Trampas produces another crisis. The fight had been inevitable from the first scene of the film. And since that first confrontation was over something neither cared about—a barmaid—we know that neither man needs an issue to provoke the fight. If there is an issue it is vengeance—the Virginian uses Steve's gun to kill Trampas, thus suggesting that the fight is an act of revenge. But really this version of the film makes clear that the duel is about honor. Molly says "it's just pride," but the Virginian says that unless he faces Trampas, he can never face Molly again. When the shooting is over, Molly runs into the street, kisses the Virginian, and the film ends. There is no romantic finale, no sunsets, no music—just the kiss. What this version of *The Virginian* accomplishes, then, is to present us with the romantic cowboy as hero; it gives us a brief glimpse of his move toward seriousness and education, but leaves us with essentially the same character at the end of the film. If anyone has changed it has been Molly—she has accepted the West.

The 1945 version of *The Virginian*, directed by Stuart Gilmore, gives us the other half of the Virginian's character. That is, if the Cooper film shows us the Virginian as cowboy Romeo, the 1945 version, which stars Joel McCrea as the Virginian, Sonny Tufts as Steve, Brian Donlevy as Trampas, and Barbara Brit-

ton as Molly, gives us the Virginian as capitalist. The most
striking difference between the two films is one of tone. The
1945 version is in color and is packaged in the formula of the
1940's melodrama. The film is basically a studio picture: there
are model trains instead of real trains, cowboys talking in front
of a screen on which we see film clips of the cattle they are supposed to be herding, backdrops of the Tetons that resemble
National Park Service postcards more than the real exteriors.
There is also a great deal of emphasis on the ornate. The costumes are done by Edith Head. The homely attire of the 1929
film is replaced by high fashion gowns, suit coats, and black
string ties. The welcoming party for Molly, for example, is no
longer outside at a roughhewn picnic table, but inside in a beau-
tifully decorated Victorian living room. The main feature of the
1945 version, which establishes its tonal aura, is its dependence
on two classic "film noir" techniques—close-up stares into the
camera, and "significant" music. In each case what is being
avoided is any meaningful attempt to resolve tensions, explain
motivation, or render the true context of the inward dilemma.
On the other hand, the use of meaningful and wistful stares into
the camera, the interpretive manipulation of events by music,
may suggest that there are more tensions, motivations, and inward dilemmas than were existent in the 1929 version.

The opening of the 1945 version is symbolic of the change in
emphasis which has been given to the story. We begin in Vermont where Molly is shown leaving her family in search of
adventure. We see her prudish boyfriend, but his comment—"my
family's counting on me marrying you"—suggests his limitations
as a man. We then follow Molly's train west toward her rendez-
vous with romance and self-fulfillment. In the 1929 version, the
eye of the camera, the "I" of the narrative, is certainly the Virginian, which may account for the resolution in favor of the
West. But in the 1945 version it is Molly who becomes the implicit center of consciousness. We should therefore not be surprised when the movie ends not with a synthesis of East and West
but a capitulation in favor of the East.

This capitulation is apparent in the first few scenes of the film.
Steve and the Virginian meet *as* Molly's train pulls into town:

Eastern culture does not intrude on pre-existing relationships as it did in the 1929 version, but is the occasion for bringing people together. After Steve and the Virginian fail in their initial attempt to win Molly, they retire to the bar. But Molly's presence invades the oasis of masculine culture. Trampas tries to send a hospitable drink up to Molly's room. The Virginian takes this as an insult to the sacred institution of womanhood, defends Molly's honor, and thus provokes the near fight and the famous line about "smiling" which was produced in the 1929 version by competition for a barmaid.

This alteration in plot is indicative of a changed Virginian. What we do not see in the 1945 version is that rakish, joking Virginian who would "dangle" around a bar contesting for barmaids. In fact, much of the joking around is eliminated from the 1945 version: the baby exchange is cut, for example. Also gone from the 1945 version is any indication that education is necessary for the Virginian. He is already the cultural equal of Molly. When they go for their ride in the mountains, there is no need to discuss books. They simply sit together by an Edenic pond—The Virginian sits slightly higher—and Molly listens to the Virginian spin his ambitious dream of success. Joel McCrea's Virginian is a serious man, stiff and puritanical in appearance. He is not shy or clumsy; he is a self-assured and confident businessman who will soon imitate the model of his boss, the Judge, and become a capitalist.

Nowhere is this change in the Virginian more evident than in his relationship with Steve. Steve is portrayed as the epitome of childish naiveté; the Virginian's paternalistic didacticism toward Steve shows the extent to which he has become the victim of ultimate seriousness. When the Virginian catches Steve rustling this change becomes manifest. Cooper and Arlen played this scene as equals, but McCrea and Tufts play the scene like Sunday School teacher and truant boy. Steve objects to the inquisitional tone of the affair by saying that the Virginian "takes life too seriously" and besides "you ain't my pappy." But these objections do not register with the Virginian, who has chosen to stand with the forces of law and order, the civilized establishment. His only interest is to impress upon Steve the desirability of making the same choice.

The significance of all this melodramatic preaching reaches a climax when we come to the hanging scene. Suddenly the pace of the movie retards considerably. Steve continues to express carefree courage in the face of death, but the Virginian is significantly changed. In the Cooper film we were aware of the impact of the event because the Virginian suddenly got serious. In the McCrea film we have already seen the Virginian serious. The change in the Virginian's character is registered by his sudden desire to avoid the event which he knew was inevitable. Rather than direct the hanging himself, as Cooper did, McCrea moves on the outskirts of the action in an attempt to shun participation. The close-ups of characters staring meaningfully into the camera, which has been a major melodramatic technique throughout the film, is given an ironic twist in this scene. When the horses are whipped out from under the hanging man, the camera moves in to a close-up of McCrea's back. For all his preaching the Virginian has refused to take ethical responsibility for his actions.

The character of Molly is also changed as played by Barbara Britton. Perhaps a scene from the welcome party is illustrative: a boy, attempting to prove that he can read, recites a label off a baking powder container—"100 Per Cent Pure. Never Varies." Molly comes West looking for adventure, but her character does not vary. Her reaction to the news of Steve's hanging is predictable—particularly since the music interprets for us the meaning of her blank stare. When Mrs. Taylor explains the code, Molly is reduced to tears and wants to leave. Unlike the earlier Molly, who defended herself and then expelled Mrs. Taylor, this Molly tries a weak defense, leaves town, and then is brought back to Medicine Bow by Andy, the stage driver. No resolution is offered; Andy utters some inarticulate sentimentality that evokes the corny reversal. What we see contradicts what we are supposed to see. We are supposed to see that Molly has "spunk" and can learn to accept the code of the West. What we see is a sentimental melodrama where childish emotionalism rather than "spunk" occasions choice.

The ending of the film then is imminently predictable. It is Trampas who has caused all the trouble. And we know from his stereotyped black clothing that he must pay for the evil we see.

There was certainly an element of revenge in the Cooper-Huston duel, but since we saw their initial confrontation over a barmaid we know that finally the duel would be between two men who needed no issue other than their honor over which to fight. Molly objected to this fight because it had no obvious social purpose. But when she saw him in danger she realized, as John G. Cawelti has suggested, "that her love was greater than her genteel antipathy to violence."[5] Since the film ends with Molly awarding the Virginian a kiss as he stands in the street with his gun smoking, we must conclude that the film ends with a confirmation of the code of the West.

The McCrea-Donlevy duel involves more intellectual motives. The Virginian blames Trampas for leading Steve astray, but he also blames Trampas for Steve's death. More to the point, he blames Trampas for his own need to enforce the penalty of death on Steve. But since the Virginian has failed to face that death, his guilt is double—he has failed the code of the East by not enforcing the system of law and order he has preached about, and he has failed the code of the West by not facing death. This multiple guilt is transferred to Trampas. The Virginian has no desire to return to the freedom and violence of the West. He wishes to maintain the order and stability of the East. Trampas then becomes a threat and an unfortunate hurdle that must be overcome if order and stability are to occur. But overcoming this hurdle is only a minor act in a larger drama. As John G. Cawelti again points out,

> This resolution resembled the redefinition of the success ethic worked out under the impact of the new industrial society of the later nineteenth century. In this ethic the aggressiveness of the industrial entrepreneur and the violent social dislocations of industrial growth were seen as a temporary phase; Andrew Carnegie summed up this ethical conception in his own career and in such writings as his famous "The Gospel of Wealth." According to Carnegie the individual should compete aggressively and ruthlessly for power and wealth, which would then be used philanthropically for the benefit of society.

[5] John G. Cawelti, "The Gunfighter and Society," *The American West* V (March, 1968), p. 32.

All this seems to me implicit in the Virginian's execution of Trampas. The manipulation of weather and lighting during the duel—the high winds, the darkness—suggest an event of major importance. But it is only a temporary crisis. Once the violence is over, the Virginian and Molly ride off into the sunset with their goods on an extra packhorse. They are going West to settle and build an empire. But it is the East which has triumphed.

What is also being suggested here is that the Trampas-Virginian polarity is not as clear as it first seems. In the novel, Trampas was simply a ranchhand who had been passed over for promotion. Only after he spent all day drinking "courage" did he challenge the Virginian. In both films he is promoted to a rustler-rancher—a man who has his own brand. In the 1929 version, however, there is a suggestion of equality among the three male characters. Trampas does things which everybody did at one time. But he must cease to do these things since civilization is approaching. In the 1945 version Trampas is villain, devil, nemesis. Yet if this Trampas is antithetical to the Virginian, what is he? The Virginian, as we have seen, is an Eastern capitalist. Does this make Trampas the true Westerner? There is certainly a sense in which Trampas and Steve, if taken together, give us a complete picture of the West. If Steve represents the free individual, the primitive-romantic, Trampas represent the extension of those concepts to anarchism and outlawry. If Steve's wildness is a sign of his vitality, it is also a sign of the potentiality for sudden death which exists outside the secure and stable structure of society. And if Steve is innocence, Trampas is certainly knowledge. Trampas knows that the security and stability of society is only veneer and that no amount of Eastern culture will ever wipe away the realities of wildness and death. He knows that people come West for "health, wealth, and bad reputation." In some ways the serious Virginian is as ignorant as the childish Steve because he refuses to try to integrate this knowledge into a new synthesis of East and West. Indeed, he refuses to face that knowledge. Instead of allowing the West to revitalize the East, he executes it.

The two films have therefore shown us that Wister's intended synthesis is too precarious to be kept in balance. The 1929 Virginian had not reached the point where the East was a significant force in his life. The 1945 Virginian must destroy the West in order that the East may survive. It seems that the further we get from the reality of the Western experience the greater become the changes in the content of the Western myth. The novel, written in 1902, gave classic formulation to the Western myth just as the reality of the Western frontier was ending. In his preface to the novel, Wister acknowledges the passing of the horseman of the plains and his way of life: "Such a transition was inevitable. Let us give thanks that it is but a transition and not a finality."

Wister had hoped that the characteristic virtues of individuality typified by the Virginian would be able to survive in the new century. By the time of the 1929 film, such hopes could no longer be realistically entertained. World War I had initiated Americans into a new age, a complex age where the romantic gestures of individualism produced *nada*. Perhaps it is because of this initiation that Americans were ripe, as Roderick Nash has pointed out, for particular kinds of heroes. Despite the acceleration of life in urban American in the 20s, the most popular writers of the decade, Zane Grey and Gene Stratton-Porter, focused on "frontier and rural patterns of thought."[6] The 1929 Virginian affirmed the traditional frontier virtues in the wake of the growing obsolescence of those virtues.

The 1940s brought deeper disillusionment: World War II, the concentration camps, Hiroshima. Americans were forced out of their isolation and into a full international engagement in order to stop a menace, but overcoming the threat of that crisis did not resolve their problems. As Chester Eisinger has indicated, Americans returned to the

> . . . United States to discover that the corporate character of life here often mirrored the regimentation of the military and demanded much the same conformity. The society seemed to be dominated more and more by great corporate entities—business, government, labor and the peacetime military establishment—that provided a prefabricated place for the conforming individual if he would dis-

[6] Roderick Nash, *The Nervous Generation: American Thought, 1917–1930* (Chicago: Rand McNally, 1970), pp. 126, 137.

guise himself or cut himself to fit such a place, thereby surrendering his individualism.[7]

In 1945, the Virginian is unfortunately at home in this kind of world. He is a disillusioned man who has decided to settle for security.

The Virginian's successive versions have thus documented the alteration in the character of the Western myth and our attitude toward it. In a way that has apparently escaped our conscious awareness, we have changed the myth. Gradually, the virtues of the West have been exchanged for Victorian seriousness, cultural rigidity, and the emerging corporate executive.

[7] Chester E. Eisinger, *The 1940's: Profile of a Nation in Crisis* (Garden City, New York: Doubleday and Co., 1969), p. xvi.

The Sea Wolf (1904), Jack London

Warners' War of the Wolf

BY TOM FLINN AND JOHN DAVIS

The central paradox in the fiction of Jack London results from the clash between his humanitarian, left-political ideals, which have made him an international favorite of socialists, and his frequent use of natural struggle as a paradigm for human action, which inevitably recalls Social Darwinism, the perfect philosophic rationalization for the laissez-faire capitalism of his era. Nowhere are these contradictions more obvious than in *The Sea Wolf*, published in 1904 when London was twenty-eight.

London planned his novel as a frontal attack on Social Darwinism and placed many of the more extreme slogans of the movement in the mouth of his intended antagonist Wolf Larsen, tyrannical captain of the sealing schooner *Ghost*, a self-proclaimed superman who recognizes no law but survival. But Larsen (a master composite of the notorious real-life sea poacher Alexander McLean and such literary prototypes as Milton's Lucifer, Melville's Ahab, and Verne's Nemo) dominates *The Sea Wolf* as he dominates his crew, and few who read the book understood the critique.

Ambrose Bierce wrote ecstatically, "the great thing—and it's among the greatest things—is that tremendous creation Wolf Larsen . . . the hewing out and setting up of such a figure is enough for one man to do in a lifetime." Liberal critics were outraged, and in answering a salvo entitled "American Barbarian" a distraught London wrote:

> You see, all the lessons I've hammered home in my fiction, (my motifs) you've grabbed and crucified me with. I was a socialist before I was a writer. I believe in a culture far beyond present-day culture. I do not believe in war. I am not an individualist. *Sea Wolf*, *Martin Eden, Burning Daylight* were written as indictments of individualism.

In a letter to a friend, London continued to brood further about his frustrations:

> I have again and again written books that failed to get across. Long years ago, at the very beginning of my writing career, I attacked Nietzsche and his superman idea. This was in *The Sea Wolf*. Lots of people read *The Sea Wolf*, no one discovered that it was an attack on the superman philosophy.

The source of London's problem obviously lay in his attraction to the very concepts he professed to detest. He admitted as much when in 1912 he wrote:

> I . . . am in the opposite intellectual camp from that of Nietzsche. Yet no man in my own camp stirs me as does Nietzsche.

Even more revealing was that London liked to be called "Wolf" and named his home in Sonoma Valley "Wolf House." Clearly, London put more than a little of himself into his portrait of Wolf Larsen, which helps explain why Larsen and not his intellectual adversary, Humphrey Van Weyden, speaks the best lines in the book.

Like the poverty-reared London, Larsen is self-made and self-taught. When asked by Van Weyden, "But you who read Spencer and Darwin and have never seen the inside of a school, how did you learn to read and write?", Larsen replies, "In the English merchant service"; and he recites his bootstrap litany: "Cabin boy at twelve, ship's boy at fourteen, ordinary seaman at seventeen and cock of the forecastle, infinite ambition and infinite loneliness, receiving neither help nor sympathy, I did it all myself . . ."

Larsen may be the most complete embodiment of the Nietzschean superman in all literature—certainly Dostoevky's Raskolnikov would have been no match for him in a dark alley! In his first description of Larsen, quoted in part below, London uses the word "strength" no less than ten times:

> It was strength we are wont to associate with things primitive, with wild animals and the creatures we imagine our tree-dwelling prototypes to have been—a strength savage, ferocious, alive in itself, the essence of life in that it is the potency of motion, the elemental stuff itself out of which the many forms of life have been molded. . . .

Unlike an animal, however, and unlike most of the inarticulate humans with whom he mixes aboard ship, Larsen is able to reason philosophically, and he has used this capability to justify his own amorality:

> I believe life is a mess. It is like a yeast, a ferment, a thing that moves and may move for a minute, an hour, a year, or a hundred years, but that in the end will cease to move. The big eat the little that they may continue to move, the strong eat the weak that they may retain their strength. The lucky eat the most and move the longest, that is all.

In spite of Larsen's pernicious philosophizing, Van Weyden can find no evidence of evil etched in the captain's massive features:

> The jaw, the chin, the brow rising to a goodly height and swelling heavily above the eyes—these, while strong in themselves, unusually strong, seemed to speak an immense vigor or virility of spirit that lay behind and beyond and out of sight. There was no sounding such a spirit, no measuring, no determining of metes and bounds, nor neatly classifying in some pigeonhole with others of similar type.

With descriptions so tinged with admiration, it is not difficult to understand why critics of the time missed London's point. More importantly, Larsen's individualist belief that "one man cannot

Aboard the Ghost, *Captain Wolf Larsen (Edward G. Robinson) stares down rebellious seaman George Leach (John Garfield).* The Sea Wolf *(1941).*

wrong another man, he can only wrong himself," is never refuted convincingly by Van Weyden's arguments or by events in the narrative. In the end, Larsen's strength is taken from him by a brain tumor, but, even when blinded, he feels neither remorse for his murderous life nor self-pity for his condition.

Although the heroic stature of Wolf Larsen betrayed London's stated aim, it proved a veritable boon for actors in search of a meaty role. Hobart Bosworth produced and starred in the first film version made in 1913. In what still must rank as one of the most generous settlements for the screen rights to a novel, London received 50 percent of the film's profits. During the same period London won a precedent-setting court case against an unauthorized version, which was forced to appear under the title *Hellship*. Subsequent screen adaptations appearing in 1919, 1920, 1926, and 1930 starred such screen notables as Noah Beery, Ralph Ince, and Milton Sills. In 1937, Warner Brothers obtained the rights from David O. Selznick (who had received them earlier from Fox in a deal involving a Shirley Temple vehicle). Although Edward G. Robinson, long acknowledged as one of the finest actors on the lot, would have seemed the obvious choice for Wolf Larsen, the role was first offered to Paul Muni. Fortunately, Muni decided to impersonate the Mexican President Juarez in a bloated biographical picture.

But the rise of Nazi Germany, with its heinous ideology based on a vulgarization of Nietzsche's superman concept obviously posed severe difficulties for the screenwriters. Certainly Warners, the first of the major studios to openly attack Nazism with *Confessions of a Nazi Spy* (1939), was not about to make a film which might be construed as promoting fascist principles. The first outline of *The Sea Wolf* (by Abem Finkel and Norman Reilly Raine), dated February, 1938, made several important changes in story, the most fundamental being an attempt to provide Wolf Larsen with a worthy antagonist with whom audiences could identify. In the novel, London had made much of the stark contrast between Larsen and Humphrey Van Weyden, a well-born, somewhat effete literary critic who survives a ferryboat disaster only to find himself on Larsen's hellship. Van Weyden serves as the narrator of the novel and an intellectual foil for

Wolf Larsen. "Hump," as he is christened by his snivelling superior, Thomas Muggridge, is a good example of the intellectual "liberal" of his day, and though he remains fairly firm in his idealism, he never seems to be able to win an argument with Larsen. At one point he is even forced to admit that he finds ". . . in Wolf Larsen's forbidding philosophy a more adequate explanation of life than I found in my own." But Van Weyden's non-violent rhetoric seems rooted in weakness, and his obsessively admiring descriptions are tinged with homosexual attraction:

> I must say that I was fascinated by the perfect lines of Wolf Larsen's figure and by what I may term the terrible beauty of it.

and:

> I knew the barbaric devil that lurked in his breast and belied all the softness and tenderness, almost womanly, of his face and form.

London may have merely been trying to emphasize the contrast between Larsen's appearance and his actions. However, such references may also indicate why Van Weyden stands aside at the moment of Leach and Johnson's heroic resistance to Larsen's inhumanity in spite of the fact that he finds in their inevitable martyrdom proof that altruism exists in the world. In these two he sees "men swayed by idea, by principle, and truth and sincerity."

To provide a more worthy opponent for Larsen, Finkel and Raine shifted the emphasis from the passive intellectual Van Weyden (Alexander Knox) to the defiant drifter George Leach. The novel begins with Van Weyden crossing San Francisco Bay on the ill-fated ferry *Martinez*, while the final screenplay (by Robert Rossen, based on the Finkel-Raine outline) begins with George Leach entering a waterfront dive. Described by Finkel and Raine as a "defiant victim" of society, Leach is an ex-convict on the run, who finds on the *Ghost* a refuge worse than prison. The part of Leach was tailored by Rossen to fit the rebellious persona of John Garfield, Warners' fastest rising star. A sure sign of Van Weyden's demotion in favor of Leach is the change in the character of Maud Brewster, his poetess soul-mate.

The Van Weyden-Brewster romance is the weakest aspect of the novel, so ridiculous that even friendly critics gagged. Ambrose Bierce remarked:

> The love element with its absurd suppressions and impossible proprieties is awful. I confess to an overwhelming contempt for both the sexless lovers.

Obviously Hump and Maud would never do for Hollywood romance. The dullest section of the novel during which Van Weyden and Maud enact a Robinson Crusoe-like episode on a barren island (with separate sleeping quarters) was eliminated entirely from the screenplay and the overly idealized figure of Maud Brewster underwent major deflation. "Ruth" Brewster, as she was rechristened by the screenwriters, became a "defeated victim of society," an escaped convict, whose existential despair was interpreted brilliantly by Warners' prime proletarian pixie, Ida Lupino. Ruth and Van Weyden are linked only in that they were both aboard the sinking *Martinez* before rescue by the *Ghost*. It is Leach, not Van Weyden who donates blood when she needs a transfusion. Larsen laughingly suggests Leach as donor since both Leach and Ruth have "jailbird's blood."

The transfusion (which does not occur in the novel) not only connects Leach and Ruth physically, but also provides a crisis for another character added by the adapters: Louie (Gene Lockhart), the ship's doctor, whose whiskey-soaked attempts at medicine provide cruel sport for Larsen and the seal hunters. Louie is a good example of a type of failed professional found in westerns (*Stagecoach* [1939], *The Man Who Shot Liberty Valance* [1962]) and melodramas (*Mandalay* [1934], *Seven Sinners* [1940]). When Ruth recovers, Louie's self-esteem is momentarily restored. He goes on the wagon and demands some respect from Larsen and the crew ("Couldn't they call me Dr. Prescott?"). What he gets, however, is humiliation. Unwilling to go on as before, the somewhat ridiculous Louie throws himself from the main mast—thus attaining a kind of heroic stature, and demonstrating Van Weyden's contention that "there is a price no man will pay for living." Louie is not alone in his self-sacrifice. Leach's friend Johnson drowns himself rather than deplete the meager water supply of a lifeboat on which Leach, Ruth, and Van Weyden are attempting to escape. And Van Weyden, in another significant change from the novel, voluntarily drowns with Wolf Larsen so that Ruth and Leach can make their escape from the sinking *Ghost*. (The repeated theme of self-sacrifice in the face of tyranny would become a central theme in many of Hollywood's anti-Nazi films.)

Although no longer the romantic lead, the Van Weyden of Rossen's screenplay is in some ways a more sympathetic character than London's narrator. For example, he is not the novel's man of total leisure; he earns his living by writing and proves a most effective verbal antagonist for Larsen. Screenwriter Rossen added two original and telling speeches in the form of passages from a book Van Weyden is writing about Larsen. (These replace rebuttals to Larsen only alluded to by Van Weyden in the novel.) The first argues that Larsen only seems so strong because he has surrounded himself with those who are weaker:

> An ego such as this must constantly be fed . . . must constantly be reassured of its supremacy . . . so it feeds itself upon the degradation of people who have never known anything but degradation . . . it is cruel to people who have never known anything but cruelty . . . but to dare to expose that ego in a world where it would meet its equal . . .

"It's a lie," Larsen screams in response, as rage wins out over reason. The other major attack comes in the film's final scene after Van Weyden, Leach, and Ruth Brewster have come back aboard the sinking *Ghost*, deserted except for its nearly blind captain, whom the crew has left to die. Still far from helpless, he manages to lock Leach in the ship's store and to hold Van Weyden at bay with a revolver. Van Weyden uses the occasion to recite the final chapter from his book:

> He saw himself as a great figure. He saw himself to the last, proud, defiant, strong, shaking his fist at the heavens as the waters of the ocean swept over his head. He liked this kind of death. It was fitting that he should die this way . . . dragging his enemies down with

him . . . turning defeat into victory . . . the true death of a superman. As I stood there watching him, I felt sorry for him. In a
few minutes he would be alone, forced to face the truth by himself.
Then he'd see himself as he really was . . . a pathetic, broken
hulk of what was once a man . . . I remembered how he'd reacted
when I once told him that he wouldn't dare to expose that ego of
his in another world . . . Now I knew that I was right. So this
was the end of Wolf Larsen . . . a pitiful, dismal, pathetic finish.

In a rage Larsen shoots Van Weyden, who, however, manages
to convince him that he has not been hit. The writer offers to
stay with the dying captain if the latter will hand over the
key to the room in which Leach is imprisoned. Unable to believe
that true self-sacrifice really exists, Larsen agrees. And when he
discovers that Van Weyden is mortally wounded, he feels vindi-
cated:

> So it was a trick. I did hit you . . . I did hit you . . . I knew there
> was a catch to it . . . someplace . . . I knew it!

The ocean comes pouring in over Larsen's erect, defiant figure.
It is an ending that is just to all the characters and far more
dramatically satisfying than that in the novel.

Almost as significant as the changes from novel to screenplay
are those from the final script to the film as released. The overall
intent of the film-makers was to diminish even further the
stature of Wolf Larsen. Several scenes in the script which might
have allowed audiences to view Larsen in a somewhat more
sympathetic light did not appear on the screen. Missing is a
scene in which Larsen thanks Van Weyden for warning him
about a marlin spike that had been thrown from behind his back.
(Because of the abruptness of the cut to the following scene
this dialogue was almost certainly shot and later excised from
the film.) Also absent from the film is Larsen's monologue of
self-justification in which he boasts of his refusal to work for "a
group of fat shipowners" as his brother does. Such a display of
anti-capitalist independence might have proved dangerously attractive to Warners' traditional working-class audience. A third
important cut occurs after the scene in which Larsen fights his

way out of the hold. The dialogue in the script has Larsen gloating over his strength ("Twelve of them . . . twelve men . . . trying to kill me, and I got out alive. How many men do you know could've done that?"), and this scene of impressive combativeness was understandably removed.

Much of the responsibility for these final changes from script to screen as well as for the overall success of *The Sea Wolf* must go to its director, Michael Curtiz. Curtiz arrived at Warner Brothers in 1926, having already worked in most of the film capitals of Europe. He quickly established himself as the studio's most talented and versatile director, proving himself adept at every genre from horror (*Mystery of the Wax Museum*, 1933) to gangster films (*Angels with Dirty Faces*, 1938) to swashbucklers (*Captain Blood*, 1935, *The Adventures of Robin Hood*, 1938). Though he always modified his style to fit the subject, the basic characteristics of his films—the smooth pacing, virtuoso camera technique, and evocative moods—remained consistent. Undoubtedly one of the most striking aspects of *The Sea Wolf's* mise-en-scène is its all-pervading atmosphere of brooding tension and barely repressed violence. The tone is set in the first scene when Leach emerges from the fog and enters a crowded dockside bar. Inside the smoke-filled room, someone immediately tries to pick his pocket. In quick succession he sees a man being shanghaied, has to hide his face from the police, spies the bartender fixing him a Mickey Finn, and punches the man who gave the bartender the signal to do so. In a matter of moments, Curtiz creates a world consistent with Larsen's vision: a place in which "the big eat the little that they may continue to move."

The fog hanging over this scene never lifts for the rest of the film. It diffuses the sunlight, making it always seem sometime between night and dawn. On board the *Ghost* it will serve to emphasize the remoteness of the ship and crew from the outside world. Almost every shot of the *Ghost* shows it only as a black silhouette against the fog. (The fact that the ship moves silently, accompanied only by Erich Wolfgang Korngold's moody score, makes its appearance all the more sinister.) Indeed, it almost seems inevitable that when we last see the ship it is drifting aimlessly—irrevocably lost in the fog. Responsible for bringing all the characters together—it causes the *Martinez* to collide with the *Ghost*—the fog also seems to isolate them and sap their will to act (with the notable exception of Wolf Larsen). Perhaps this explains why there is never a shot of the crew working topside. None of the montage-sailing images typically associated with Hollywood sea pictures found their way into *The Sea Wolf*. There are no shots of billowing sails or groaning anchor chains or seamen scurrying about in the rigging. Van Weyden's first glimpse of the deck of the *Ghost* sets the tone for the scenes that follow. As he pushes open the louvered cabin doors (the shot is from his point of view) he sees the crew members standing about in sullen unconcern as the first mate dies in a spasm. The only person who shows much animation is Wolf Larsen, who paces the quarter deck in a rage over losing a needed man.

The mood of brooding tension is broken only by eruptions of violence. Although the pressbook publicity claiming forty-seven fights (!) was considerably exaggerated, eleven fights and three suicides do occur. Curtiz, who was justly famous for his skill with action scenes (revealed most prominently in his series of adventure films with Errol Flynn), gushed: "Finally I found my ideal picture, one that is all action." The culmination of all this physical violence comes in Larsen's nocturnal visit to the forecastle following the attempt on his life by Leach and Johnson. This sequence captures the desperate aura of the fight for survival that is so crucial to all of London's fiction. Flailing away with a kind of wild deliberation, Larsen makes every blow count as he retreats toward the hatch through a maelstrom of humanity. The sequence is short, the pace frenetic. Instead of roundhouse punches (with their inevitable hokey sound effects) Larsen uses short powerful jabs, thrusts, and kicks, giving the scene an extremely realistic flavor.

Equally restrained and realistic is Curtiz's handling of the *Martinez* disaster. (An old hand at filming sea-going disasters, in Denmark in 1913 he directed one of the first feature films about the *Titanic*.) The wreck of the *Martinez* takes only ten shots and a little over a minute of screen time. Taking his cue from the novel, in which London repeatedly emphasized "the screaming bedlam of women," Curtiz uses the cries of the female passengers as an overlapping aural "cement" that links the various shots of the panicked passengers attempting to escape the floundering ship. He then ends the swift sequence with a quick dissolve to a stark water level closeup of Van Weyden hugging a timber to stay afloat.

Too much of the writing on Curtiz has centered on his seemingly effortless technique and his adroit handling of action sequences while ignoring his talents as a romantic director— after all, he was the man who gave the world *Casablanca* (1942). *The Sea Wolf's* key love scene (which Curtiz and Rossen rewrote almost entirely after the final script) takes place deep in the hold of the *Ghost* where Leach has been left to lick his wounds after receiving a brutal and "artistic" beating from Wolf Larsen. The sequence begins as Ruth enters to comfort the still defiant Leach. Grudgingly, he accepts a cigarette. As the smoke swirls around the camera lens, they argue, she proclaiming the fatalism of the defeated ("Tomorrow will be like today and the day before"), he still refusing to capitulate ("What I got inside me Larsen will never get at"). Gradually Leach's hostility fades as the two exchange long looks, though Ruth never moderates her pessimism. Curtiz dollies in to a closeup of her as she delivers the film's most poetic speech: "To be free . . . to be let alone . . . to live in peace . . . even if it's only for a little while . . . I don't expect that anymore." Leach listens sympathetically, obviously affected by her words, but determined to prove her wrong and find some happiness for them both. As Leach raises his head and drags on his cigarette, Curtiz freezes the frame for an instant, catching him in a moment of decision and commitment. Though Leach has been attracted to Ruth throughout the film, it is not until this point that he really begins to understand and accept her.

Like *Citizen Kane* and *The Maltese Falcon*, both of which it preceded to the theaters in 1941, *The Sea Wolf* displays the low-key lighting and flamboyant camera technique that was to characterize Hollywood's most stylish decade (though many of the elements of the "high" forties style are found in Curtiz films from the thirties). The development in the late thirties of high contrast super-sensitive film stock encouraged the use of dramatic lighting effects, and *The Sea Wolf* has more than its share. Among the most striking instances is a scene in the almost completely dark hold, where Leach and Johnson are seen in silhouette as they plan their escape from the *Ghost*. (Curtiz had long been fond of such effects, using them freely in such films as *Alias the Doctor* [1932] and *Captain Blood* [1935].)

Camera movement also gained in general popularity during the forties, perhaps because when used in conjunction with wide-angle lenses it eliminated the need for a great many cuts, allowing for a smoother mise-en-scène. A virtuoso example in *The Sea Wolf* occurs when the camera moves in on Larsen the first time he meets and strikes Leach, panning 180 degrees with Leach as he is thrown against the bulwark by the force of the blow. (In this area as well, Curtiz was an early pioneer. He had constructed special camera booms for his first American picture *The Third Degree* [1927], and he was the first to put the soundproof camera booths on wheels in the early thirties.) A comparison of *The Sea Wolf* with other Curtiz films from the forties such as *Casablanca* (1943), *Mildred Pierce* (1945), and *The Unsuspected* (1947), reveals how flexible Curtiz's style was. Though the films abound in similarities of composition, camera movement, and lighting, *The Sea Wolf* has none of the lushness that suffuses the others. The unrelentingly bleak atmosphere of the *Ghost* is a tribute to Curtiz's style in the service of his subject.

But *The Sea Wolf* is linked to Curtiz's melodramas of the forties by more than just technique. In its central concern with the darker side of human nature and the urge toward power for its own sake, *The Sea Wolf* is thematically characteristic of that group of films today known as *films noirs*. Although the majority were set in contemporary America, many like *The Sea Wolf* were concerned with the turn of the century (*Gaslight* [1943], *The Suspect* [1944], *The Lodger* [1944], *Ivy* [1947]). What these films share is a common atmosphere of oppression, as important an element as the obsessed villains who haunt these pictures (the husband in *Gaslight*, the eponymous poisoner in *Ivy*, Laughton's shrewish wife in *The Suspect*, Jack the Ripper in *The Lodger*). Larsen resembles the aforementioned protagonists in his unrelenting urge to dominate, though his sort of dictatorial tyranny had more overt social relevance in 1941 than did the machinations of subsequent villains of the forties dark cinema. (As early as *The Mad Genius* [1931], Curtiz had displayed his penchant for selecting subjects that featured what Siegfried Kracauer referred to as "tyranny figures.") Such films as *Mystery of the Wax Museum* (1933), *Angels with Dirty Faces* (1938), *Kid Galahad* (1937), *The Unsuspected* (1947), and *Bright Leaf* (1950), all concern dominating, compelling protagonists who seem to enjoy wielding power. It is difficult not to see facets of Curtiz's own autocratic personality—particularly his habit of browbeating performances out of his actors—reflected in these characters.

The Sea Wolf then, presents us with a fascinating situation in which a novel is changed, not for the usual reasons of length or conflict with a production code or directorial style, but because of the possible political implications of a major character. Such fears were well founded, as the contemporary reaction to Hitchcock's *Lifeboat* (1944) demonstrated. Hitchcock was pilloried for allowing Walter Slezak's Nazi submarine commander to dominate the film and to appear to be more than a match for any of his democratic adversaries. The film-makers of *The Sea Wolf* made major changes in London's novel, but to their credit, they did not try to downplay or mask Wolf Larsen's intellectual foundations. Curtiz's camera pans deliberately across Larsen's bookshelf past Herbert Spencer's *First Principles* to Darwin's *Voyage of the Beagle*, to Nietzsche's *Man and Superman* and *The Anti-Christ*.

By more than counterbalancing Robinson's still strong and affecting portrayal of Larsen with Knox's sympathetic intellectual Van Weyden, and Garfield's very appealing physical presence as Leach, Curtiz and Rossen could stop short of bowdlerizing or sanitizing this powerful work of philosophic literature. In fact, they sharpened London's paradoxical depiction of Larsen by externalizing his inherent contradictions in conflicting characters, and left little chance that an audience could find him thoroughly attractive. The sense of urgency and relevancy that these changes imparted to the film actually led to a clarification of the issues London had raised in the novel and allowed *The Sea Wolf* to survive the "classic" treatment that proved deadly to so many films in the literary-conscious thirties and forties.

Main Street (1920), Sinclair Lewis

I Married A Doctor:
Main Street Meets Hollywood

BY MAUREEN TURIM

Critics as diverse as Alfred Kazin and Walter Lippman have not failed to remark on the irony of Sinclair Lewis's *Main Street* becoming a best seller upon its publication in 1920. Irony, for the novel broke with a thirty-year tradition in American intellectual history and popular culture of celebrating the American small town "as the home of the purest democracy, the friendliest people, the largest happiness, the sturdiest freedom" (Sheldon Brebstein, *Sinclair Lewis*, 1962). Yet *Main Street*'s popularity and not its iconoclasm is obviously what prompted Warner Brothers to acquire the film rights in 1922. When a silent version (directed by Harry Beaumont and starring Florence Vidor and Monte Blue) was released in 1923, the *New York Times* review of June 12 commented on its commercial potential:

> No book as widely read as Sinclair Lewis's *Main Street* could escape picturization. It would not really matter what was between the covers so long as they could gain possession of the title, a valuable box office asset throughout the country.

When the rights for a sound remake were negotiated, a title change occurred. The *New York Times* of April 30, 1936, said of the sound version (starring Josephine Hutchinson as Carol and

Pat O'Brien as Dr. Kennicott) that "Gopher Prairie has changed its name to Williamsburg and Sinclair Lewis's *Main Street* has become *I Married a Doctor* for the sweet uses of diversity and the Warners. . . ."

The publicity campaign indicates that Warners was not trying to disguise the remake as an original property. The newspaper ads featured the line, "From Sinclair Lewis's most daring novel" and the ad in *Variety* boasted, "Sinclair Lewis's most startling novel is going to make things happen and happen fast at your box office." The subsequent review in *Variety* began with the following assessment:

> While handicapped by the title, *I Married a Doctor*, it should garner good grosses if properly exploited. Despite fact that it may prove disappointing to readers of Lewis's book, stressing the original *Main Street* story in copy should help. Word of mouth will be another factor. (April 21, 1936)

Thus it appears that Warners was hedging its bets with the remake. It hoped to attract the old devotees of *Main Street*, while appealing to a different audience who identified the film through its new title as a "woman's film."

Thirties films are not renowned for their preoccupation with the small town, and it is possible that Warners was unsure how to connect this film to an established genre audience. Interestingly, both William Wellman's *Small Town Girl* and Frank Capra's *Mr. Deeds Goes to Town* opened at the same time as *I Married a Doctor*. While these two films take the small town as their theme, they display none of *Main Street*'s critical stance. They pit the small town hero or heroine against the traumas of the city, while maintaining the traditional view of the small town as repository for all that is friendly, honest, and good. A viewpoint equally at odds with Lewis's perspective in *Main Street* dominated the screen version, *I Married a Doctor*.

In the novel, Carol Kennicott becomes a device allowing Lewis to filter an analysis of the small town into the narrative framework. He pushes the novelistic form toward the descriptive, the contemplative. The social commentary is initiated by Carol's readings, her meditations, and her dissatisfactions; her vision generates the narrative. Such phrases as "Carol admitted," "Carol inquired," "Carol wondered" or "she was thinking," "she knew," punctuate the book.

Chapter 22 provides a good example of how this device operates; it is divided into eight parts quite varied both in topics treated and styles of narration. They are connected by a sustained comparison between Carol and her friend Vida, who shares Carol's desire for town improvement while remaining content with the dominant ideologies. In the chapter, narrative action is minimized to leave room for the sections that discuss the role of books in shaping Carol's critical consciousness, the mechanization and standardization of the small town, the rule of mediocrity and the leveling of foreigners, the commercialization of small-town life and finally, Carol's analysis of small-town ugliness.

The success of Carol as a device for social commentary has much to do with Lewis's depiction of her as a serious, thoughtful reformer, allowing that perhaps her educated style and its strangeness to the Gopher Prairie inhabitant makes it difficult for her to rally others to her cause. *I Married a Doctor* rejects this use of its main character and, in contrast, substitutes a Carol who is a vivacious charmer. The film opts for a more personable characterization and Carol's conflict comes to be less with the mentality of the town than with the jealousy of other women. Carol is told in the film that "You wear clothes that another woman can't forgive —it reminds them that their figures have bumps in all the wrong places."

The film combines this change in Carol's characterization with a shift toward the exploitation of the love intrigues for melodramatic interest. Certainly melodrama can be used as the support of a commentary on interpersonal interaction, as in the films of Douglas Sirk and Werner Fassbinder. We must remember, however, that the novel chose not the manipulation of melodrama, but its denial, as the means of expressing its radical critique. When the film reinstates melodrama, it does so as a substitute— entertainment value *replaces* critical expression. Let's examine specifically how this structural and stylistic transformation occurs.

Carol Kennicott (Josephine Hutchinson) accompanies her doctor husband Will (Pat O'Brien) on a hunting trip. I Married a Doctor *(1936).*

The incident that *I Married a Doctor* elevates to its first moment of melodramatic tension is inspired by one withheld in the book until chapter 21 and then recounted in a totally matter-of-fact manner. We are told in the book that Vida, Carol's best friend in Gopher Prairie, had once been courted briefly by Dr. Kennicott before he met and married Carol. This superficial past involvement is said to have lingered in Vida's imagination, giving rise to her jealous resentment of Carol.

Instead of this toned-down treatment, the film introduces Vera (her name has inexplicably been changed) through the gossip of the other women as they play bridge at the country club with the comment, "She looks terrible—the best catch in town slipped through her hands." With this triangular relationship thus established, the film has Vera attempt suicide the night of Carol's welcoming party. The crosscutting between the drama of the doctor attending Vera and the comedy of Carol, abandoned by her husband, and forced to dance with the town's male buffoons, builds to an initial high point of tension with the film narrative. The concentration on these melodramatic effects is not innocent, since they replace the satire and ideological commentary of the novel and standardize the film as an accessible, entertaining product.

The Vera-Carol-Doctor triangle is resolved when Carol and Vera become friends—but all this is a prelude to the major triangle of the film. While the Doctor and Carol are hunting, she first mentions her project to "make Williamsburg less ugly"; immediately following, the couple collide with Erik Valborg, when the Doctor's dog points him out and the Doctor almost shoots at him. When the Doctor goes off with Erik's father, Carol examines Erik's drawing of the town. Thus this short chain of actions—the announcement of the project, the accidental meeting of Erik, and immediately, the announcement of a parallel artistic and urban interest on Erik's part—sets up the intrigue for the rest of the film.

In the novel, Erik is not introduced until chapter 28. In the film, he is brought on early, both as Carol's partner in her reform efforts and as a condensation of all her love interests in the novel, where she is briefly enamored of Raymie, Vida's future husband,

and then Guy Pollack, a romantic reactionary lawyer. There is further melodramatic compression with Erik's role. The amputation, at which Carol assists Kennicott, is performed on Erik's father in the film instead of on the anonymous Swedish farmer of the book. This change allows the father, raving on the operating table, to denounce Carol in front of her husband for seducing his boy. Another deviation: instead of having Fern, the rebellious schoolteacher, disgraced in a scandalous auto ride with the town's juvenile delinquent, the incident is transferred to Erik. He takes Fern on a drunken spree after Carol refuses his affections. This trip, physically harmless in the novel, ends in the film with a disastrous car crash.

The Erik-Carol-Doctor triangle is played up for full impact by the film. First Erik visits Kennicott to announce his love for Carol, and the Doctor replies that "you must earn your own happiness. Don't spoil the happiness of others." Later Kennicott sends Erik to his wife under the assumption that she prefers Erik, but in the ensuing scene Carol refuses to leave with Erik. There is no room in the film for the understated irony of the novel where Erik simply slips out of town, re-emerging to Carol's view years later as a mediocre actor in a small role in a movie she sees by accident.

If the melodrama of Vera's suicide attempt gives initial impetus to the film's narrative, the triangle involving Erik takes over from that point on and occupies most of the remaining segments. The narrative structure of the film is determined by love conflicts: the universal, dehistoricized theme of the threat to a couple posed by a third party.

Though the film has taken jabs at small town gossiping, touching on the hypocrisy in the treatment of the Swedish outcasts and depicting the lack of intellectual pursuits or aesthetic appreciation in the confined environment, it lacks the conviction to leave even these mildly presented criticisms intact at its conclusion. Instead, Kennicott "teaches" Carol that such foibles as exist in Gopher Prairie are to be found everywhere. The final moment of the film has Carol come back to her husband's arms with the line, "I guess it takes an awful long time for two people to really get married, doesn't it?" How different is the ending of the book, where Carol returns to the small town, to marriage, only in the spirit of compromise. She remains critical of the town and holds onto her convictions, although she believes it will be her daughter who will carry them out. The final section of Chapter 38 ends with Carol exclaiming to Kennicott:

> "But I have won this: I've never excused my failures by sneering at my aspirations, by pretending to have gone beyond them. I do not admit that Main Street is as beautiful as it should be! I do not admit that Gopher Prairie is greater or more generous than Europe! I do not admit that dish washing is enough to satisfy all women! I may not have fought the good fight, but I have kept the faith."

This speech is followed only by Dr. Kennicott's wondering about the storm windows, indicating that nothing has improved for Carol; the mundane and provincial will continue to exert their frustrations. The conflicts remain unresolved, with no easy exit allowing us to leave the book feeling content with small-town American life.

Coupled with the shift in characterization and the standardizing effect of melodramatic formulas, the film is also marked by a change in the treatment of temporal setting. The book covers the years 1906–1920 with the concentration on the time after 1912, when Carol first comes to Gopher Prairie. The film takes place in an indefinite time which appears to be about a year long.

Main Street looks back over the teens, examining how a small town in its traditions, attitudes, and institutions responds to the changes those years impose upon it. As a result the novel takes on numerous issues such as women's suffrage, World War I, immigration and integration, radicalism, and the economic build-up as the nation moves into the development of advanced capitalism. The film avoids any specific historical grounding and thus neglects these issues.

An examination of one of these topics, women's suffrage, reveals the multivaried way this topical commentary is dispersed within the book's narrative. The first reference is a generalized one to women's oppression given as a commentary on Carol's life in chapter 7, section II, including the famous line, "She was a woman with a working brain and no work." The next two references, found in chapter 11, are negative, derogatory statements by other townswomen; in section III, Mrs. Dyer says, "I hate these women politicians, don't you?" while in section VII, Mrs. Stowbody says, "We must oppose this movement of Mrs. Potsbury's to have the state clubs come out definitely in favor of woman suffrage. Women haven't any place in politics. They would lose all their daintiness and charm if they became involved in these horrid plots and log-rolling and all this awful political stuff about scandal and personalities and so on." Then in chapter 16, section V, Carol makes strong statements concerning not only women's liberation, but its connection to class and race struggles: "We're all together, the industrial workers and the women and the farmers and the Negro race and the Asiatic colonies and even a few of the respectables. It's all the same revolt, in all the classes that have waited and taken advice." During Carol's stay in Washington (chapter 37), she moves in with suffragists, which allows her to discuss with one of these women the possibility of moving back to Gopher Prairie. The dialogue that ensues, along with the series of references cited above, puts Carol's personal plight in a specific historic context, broadens her discontent into a large political issue. In 1920 (the year the nineteenth amendment was ratified) great hopes for sweeping social change were tied to women's suffrage. The treatment of Carol's growing awareness is the expression, by Lewis, of this tenet of La Follette's Progressives—the faith in the radicalism of suffrage. Yet Lewis was never so tied to a doctrine that he could not satirize the doctrine itself, as in section V of chapter 38:

> Her baby, born in August, was a girl. Carol could not decide whether she was to become a feminist leader or marry a scientist or both, but did settle on Vassar and a tricollete suit with a small black hat for her freshman year.

The film had the option of being a historical drama set back twenty years and thus maintaining a concern for the same issues as the novel, or of being updated, putting itself solidly in the mid-thirties and doing for that decade what Lewis had done for

the teens. (One can imagine the suffrage issue having been updated to espouse a Molly Dawson–Eleanor Roosevelt position
urging women's participation in popularizing New Deal programs.) The film rejects both options, eradicating any references
to specific historical moments. What survives is a negative comment by a townswoman before Carol's arrival, "She's probably
sweet, but I don't trust an intelligent woman," and Carol's cheerful complaint to her husband during their hunting excursion,
"You can't expect me to be a sit-by-the-fire, kitchen-stove kind of
wife." This weakly voiced protest must come early in the film
since the dutiful wife is indeed the role prescribed to women
by the end of the film. Carol's reform plan is "blamed" on her
husband's inadequacy at the town meeting ("the Doc's to blame
—he can't keep Carey contented") while in the closing shot
discussed earlier Carol's new knowledge of what it means to be
married implies that there will be no more protest or dissatis-
faction with her role. The film ultimately takes a reactionary
position on the role of women in society, quite a transformation
from the novel.

Similarly, the film deletes any reference to a specific economic
context; in the novel the small town is first depicted as part of
a prewar nonindustrial economy in which a petty bourgeoisie
feeds off the farmers who surround it. A few characters have a
decisive role in presenting economic attitudes. Miles Bjornstrom,
the Swedish radical, supplies a working-class and ethnic-minority
analysis of the social and economic functioning of Gopher Prairie.
He is stripped of this role in the film. The film also excludes
Bresnahan, the local man, who left Gopher Prairie to make a
fortune in the auto industry, supplying the town with a Horatio
Alger hero, whose myth allows Lewis to explore attitudes toward
the accumulation of wealth under capitalism. Then in chapter
35, the book takes on the question of the relationship of history
and economic change as it treats the upswing of the postwar
economy:

> The town was booming, as a result of the war price of wheat.
> The wheat money did not remain in the pockets of the farmers,
> the towns existed to take care of all that. Iowa farmers were selling

their land at four hundred dollars an acre and coming into Minnesota. But whoever bought or sold or mortgaged, the townsmen invited themselves to the feast—millers, real-estate men, lawyers, merchants, and Dr. Will Kennicott. They bought land at a hundred and fifty, sold it next day at a hundred and seventy, bought again. In three months Kennicott made seven thousand dollars, which was rather more than four times as much as society paid him for healing the sick.

In the early summer began a "campaign of boosting." The Commercial club decided that Gopher Prairie was not only a wheat center but also a perfect site for factories, summer cottages, and state institutions.

It is in terms of these references to economic history that the question of the sixteen-year time span between book and film is most intriguing. Contemporaneous reviews of the film were quite conscious of the question. *Time* thought a 1936 audience would be antagonistic to the project of remodeling a town and added: "Nor will they feel, when the town banker asks, 'Where is the money coming from?' that he is merely proving himself a worse dolt than the rest of the population." The implication, that the plot is inherently incongruous with the Depression, seems to ignore the reality of the WPA and the struggle for the acceptance of the idea of government funding of work projects in small towns. The fact is that towns like the one Robert and Helen Lynd studied in *Middletown in Transition* (1937) were receiving government funds for such conditions as "the mangy river, the lack of a sewage system, antiquated school equipment . . . things people talked about and editors wrote about as old familiar 'local problems' ten years ago." Some reviewers went so far as to praise *I Married a Doctor* for "going beyond" Lewis's "outdated" criticisms. *Commonweal* proclaimed that "the middle class living in American small towns is no longer warped by willing bigotry, which the producers of *I Married a Doctor* recognize." The *New York Times* echoed this opinion: "Main Street has improved—the influence of radio and movies most likely." Thus the reviewers recognize the ideological transformation, the toning down of the film, but justify it because this supposedly reflects the improved social reality in the thirties small town.

The smugness of this position is easily refuted by turning again to *Middletown in Transition,* where the Lynds find the town's business class offering "impatient characterizations of the working class as having a high percentage of 'intellectually inferior' members." They also note that "the cleft between the white and the Negro populations of Middletown is the deepest and most blindly followed line of division in the community." The Depression may have caused some people to question the traditional values, but the Lynds quote an editorial: "Instead of laying all our troubles upon those who have had the talent and brains to become wealthy, why not each of us assume our share of responsibility for the economic situation of the nation?" And as concerns the role of women, the Lynds find that "there is more indulgent tolerance of a business class girl's working between school and marriage, but when she marries 'all that foolishness stops.'"

The evidence seems to indicate that during the mid-thirties small-town attitudes remained somewhat the same as they had been in 1920—in fact, the chapter in *Middletown in Transition* entitled "The Middletown Spirit," in which the Lynds summarize the axioms of small-town thought, could serve as a catalogue of the responses Lewis assigned his Gopher Prairie characters.

A question always in the back of one's mind in viewing a film adapted from a novel is how would the original author have wanted the film to be. In the case of Lewis and *I Married a Doctor* this speculation is perhaps a bit less tenuous than otherwise, for a curious article that Lewis published in *The Nation* of September 10, 1924, indicates some ways in which he might have approached transposing *Main Street* into a later film. The satiric "Main Street's Been Paved" is based on the extended conceit of Gopher Prairie being a real place to which *The Nation* asks the writer/reporter to return for the purpose of interviewing the inhabitants on their opinions of the presidential campaign.

Among the changes that Dr. Kennicott proudly shows Lewis, besides three whole blocks paved in cement, is "a golf course with an attractive clubhouse . . . and in a pasture beside the golf course rested an aeroplane." Curious that these two changes indicating a more modern appearance for the town should both be incorporated into *I Married a Doctor* and that they are the *only* indications of updating occurring in the film—perhaps the script-writer, Casey Robinson, referred to the *Nation* article. But if he did, he somehow missed the point, for "Main Street's Been Paved" represents an updating of the ideological attack. The radio, for example, is not seen as giving Main Street the culture of the outside world; instead it leads to evenings like the following:

> It was time to tune in on the barn dance music from WKZ, and we listened to "Turkey in the Straw"; we sat rocking, rocking, the Doctor and I smoking cigars, Carol unexplicably sighing.

The prime thrust of the article is to examine and satirize why the Main Streets of America were backing Coolidge over La Follette; if Lewis saw the necessity for treating the topic of *Main Street* again four years later, it was to depict how material changes had not yet provoked a corresponding ideological change, but rather increased the entrenchment. One imagines that Lewis would have had a heyday making Main Street respond to 1936; but in so many ways the Lynds' study did it for him. Unfortunately, *I Married a Doctor* did not.

Alice Adams (1921), Booth Tarkington

From American Tragedy to Small-Town Dream-Come-True

BY NANCY L. SCHWARTZ

Graduating from ethnic low comedy (*The Cohens and the Kellys in Trouble*, 1933) and woeful Wheeler and Woolsey slapstick (*Bachelor Bait* and *Kentucky Kernels*, 1934), director George Stevens made a singularly successful debut into the "A" class in 1935 with *Alice Adams*. The RKO film, starring Katharine Hepburn as Booth Tarkington's eager, posturing heroine, was given a fairy-tale ending to conform to Hollywood's romantic standards, and though not a literal interpretation of its source, it was a fitting celebration of Stevens's own cinematic ascent. The film heralded a return to public favor for Hepburn, whose popularity had cooled in the period after her 1933 Oscar-winning performance in *Morning Glory*. In *Alice Adams*, "Hepburn resumes her high place," said the *New York Times*; she made almost unbearably poignant the hunger of a lower middle-class person yearning for the social status of her well-to-do peers—and miraculously achieving it.

Stevens's *Alice Adams* focuses on the spring and summer of its Indiana heroine's twenty-second year, and her romance with Arthur Russell (Fred MacMurray), who is cousin to the local Brahmins and the incarnation of everything to which Alice aspires. Alice's growing romance fuels the war of attrition her mother wages to persuade her husband to leave his low-level job and strike out on his own. Mr. Adams finally starts a business, hoping to raise his income and social status, and thereby give Alice enough "background" to hook a worthy husband. Alice's burgeoning expectations are juxtaposed against her brother's unfortunate decline, a crossing over onto the wrong side of the tracks that ends in criminal embezzlement.

In the film, Alice is a rural Cinderella, lifted from her shabby existence by her rich Prince Charming, Arthur, who sees through her playacting and discovers the noble girl underneath. The benign ending, so different from the gloomy reality of Tarkington's tragedy of thwarted class struggle, seems a justifiable reward for Alice's basic decency. It is a typical Depression conclusion—the shop girl's fantasy in which economics are forgotten and virtue triumphs. Radio programs of that era spun similar webs: "Our Gal Sunday" never failed to find love and happiness with a titled Englishman.

While the picture was favorably received by critics, they expressed veiled disapproval for the social climbing of Alice and her mother, which struck a rather effete note of poor taste. Social mobility seemed a superficial concern at a time of such terrible national suffering. The *New York Times* critic, André Sennwald, voiced this typical ambivalence:

> It is a temptation in these troubled days to regard Alice's misfortunes as the just punishment of a social climber rather than the stuff of authentic tragedy. But the plight of the Adams family becomes genuinely heartbreaking when we realize how accurately delineated these people are in terms of smalltown life before the depression. (August 16, 1935)

Some critics were more vociferous in their opposition. In 1938 the Commission on Human Relations of the Progressive Education Association, a group that sought to include films in school curricula, published a study guide to *Alice Adams* ("The Human Relations Series of Films Excerpted from Photoplays") that posed questions for the viewer designed to illuminate Alice's character as a vestal of shoddy values. The questions included:

Was Alice realistic about what was important in her community? What factors are most important in determining social position in America today? Are the qualities and characteristics most necessary to the achievement of material success necessarily the most valuable? Do you know people whose lives have been made unhappy because they are poorer than their neighbors? Alice was not hungry, she had clothes to wear and food to eat. Why did her relative lack of money make her so unhappy? Compare the Adams economic condition with that of most people in the U.S. Were they richer or poorer?

Booth Tarkington wrote his book in an earlier epoch, a few years after World War I. Originally a serial in *The Pictorial, Alice Adams* was published in its entirety in May, 1921, then taken to task by critics expecting a book as light and amusing as the earlier *Penrod*. Tarkington responded to these critics in a note to his producer's former associate, John P. Toohey. "This N.Y. reviewer said *Alice Adams* is not so humorous as other stories of mine. Oh Gosh. A.A. was intended to be about as humorous as tuberculosis."[1] Tarkington's purposes *were* serious ones. "*Alice Adams* is my most actual and life-like work," he stated in March of 1921. A few months later Tarkington wrote, "Of course *A.A.* is written to the sophisticated. The girl is drawn without any liking or disliking of her by the writer who is concerned only with making a portrait of her insides and outsides." Tarkington wished to show how Alice was a casualty of the stratifying, rigidifying midwestern society of the late Wilson/Harding era. She is a less ruthless female equivalent of Dreiser's Clyde Griffiths in *An American Tragedy* of a few years later.

Even prior to publication, Booth Tarkington wondered whether *Alice Adams* would make a suitable vehicle for the movies, since the book's downbeat ending (Tarkington's Prince Charming defects) was hardly palatable to audiences craving happily-ever-afters. In February, 1921, he wrote to Toohey, then in the employ of Famous Players-Lasky:

[1] *On Plays, Playwrights and Playgoers*, selections from letters of Booth Tarkington to George C. Tyler and John Peter Toohey, 1918–1925, edited by Alan S. Downer (Princeton, N.J.: Princeton University Press), 1959. All subsequent quotes of Tarkington from this source.

Alice Adams (Katharine Hepburn) is courted on her porch by Arthur Russell (Fred MacMurray). Alice Adams (1935).

Alice Adams might do—since pictures are moving towards realism. I think the end would have to be changed, however. I'm afraid that a second young man of sterling worth—would have to be invented for Alice to fall back on.

Fourteen years later George Stevens's version did little to affirm Tarkington's hope that moving pictures were indeed moving toward realism, although the romantic ending of RKO's *Alice Adams* certainly fulfilled the author's prophecy that a happier cinematic conclusion would be called for.

What does remain consistent about *Alice Adams*, novel and film, is the depiction of the powerlessness of the lower-middle-class woman in the first half of the twentieth century, powerless to change her social position except through marriage or art. When Alice toys with the idea of going on stage, her acting fever is part glamour fantasy and part reaction to her helplessness— she wants to be able to do something, and not have to wait around for her father or for another man to rescue her. (Her father laughingly disparages her aspirations.) In the meantime, Virgil Adams's meagre income makes his daughter a social leper.

Both novel and film, in depicting an environment in which social success is a function of economics, make the point that Alice is as good as any of her tormentors. She's pretty, well bred, a jewel that could outshine the lot of them were she in the proper setting. Her hunger is terribly painful. Her yearning is familiar to every girl who has dreamed of being the belle of the ball; her anxiety is the fear of the insecure woman who dreads the moment the spell will be broken. In Katharine Hepburn's every movement, picking violets for her homemade corsage, playacting before her mirror, yearning for a Prince Charming at the ball, she invests Alice's arrivism with a naive radiance. Alice lives in a fantasy. She's stripped of it in the novel, but Hollywood's forte was making dreams come true. Alice's breathless "Gee whiz" at the end of the film says it all.

Even though Tarkington focused on a period when class lines were hardening, the society he depicted was still flexible enough to allow Alice's father, at fifty-five, an attempt to rise from the rank of petit bourgeois clerk to the level of bold entrepreneur. He does this merely by making the decision to assert his claim on the glue formula he and a deceased partner perfected. Adams, the consummate company man, has allowed the formula to languish for twenty years because it was discovered on company time. Virgil Adams is yoked by the paternalism of the benevolent boss, J. A. Lamb, a nice enough capitalist who keeps on paying Adams his salary throughout his book-long illness and recuperation.

In the novel, J. A. Lamb is kind as long as it's good business, and his ultimate treatment of Adams is casually brutal in a way the film does not depict. Lamb embodies the ruthless elements of the big-business Harding administration glossed over with the folksy veneer of the self-made midwestern industrialist. He buys out the impractical Adams with a show of benevolence, permitting his former employee to cancel out his son's embezzlement debt, right the wrong of "cheating" his employer of a formula discovered on company time, and get himself out of the fledgling industry that supposedly exceeds his capabilities. Lamb leaves Adams broken and his family worse off than before— humiliated, condemned to taking in boarders. The son is exiled from the state and Alice sent off to the declassé drudgery of secretarial school.

In the fairy tale *Alice Adams* that appears on screen, George Stevens cast homespun Charlie Grapewin as Lamb. Grapewin was an actor who represented the virtues of American common sense, his salt-of-the-earth quality reaching its apotheosis in the character of Grandpa Joad in *Grapes of Wrath*. Grapewin-Lamb winds up as a penitent capitalist making amends for his insensitivity to Adams's needs, and the future holds the rosy prospect of his partnership with Adams ("Together we can show the world about glue.") In the film, Lamb represents money that hasn't forgotten its roots, and he's a different breed from the hoity-toity Palmers, who snub the socially unacceptable Alice. In their new society, money breeds class automatically.

Grapewin found a perfect acting partner in Fred Stone, the Broadway musical star who made his talking picture debut at sixty-two as Alice's father. The *New York Herald-Tribune* said of Stone, "He has the sort of role which, in its suggestions of homespun philosophy in action, is inclined to remind one of the Will Rogers type of character." Stone transformed Adams's mildness into an almost tragic quality, and Adams's bitter speech contrasting what the glue formula represents to him (his last chance to make good), as opposed to its triviality for a rich man like Lamb, is one of the most moving sequences in the film. Ann Shoemaker, who played Mrs. Adams, was also a relative newcomer to films, and she conveyed the woman's weary, bitter frustration, without making her seem a shrew.

Beginning with the establishing tracking shot down Main Street, which starts with the sign "South Renford, Ind." Stevens manages to simulate the midwestern atmosphere of Tarkington's world. He even broadens Tarkington's considerable humor on occasion, as in the scene when young Russell (Fred MacMurray) comes to dine with the anxious-to-impress Adams family on the hottest night of the summer. The scene (a reminder of director Stevens's apprenticeship on Laurel and Hardy shorts) is orchestrated with agonized pans from food to sweating guest, and excruciating long takes while Hattie McDaniel, as the maid Mrs. Adams hires for a temporary touch of class, serves dinner with the verve of a hostile slug, chewing gum and making half-hearted efforts to keep her cap on straight.

An earlier scene at a restaurant is reminiscent of Lubitsch in its use of low-comedy domestics to illuminate the interaction of the main characters. For example, the indication that Alice and Russell are falling in love comes from the bandleader's frustration. He is requested by the waiter to play the lovers' favorite song for the sixth time when he obviously can't wait to pack up and go home. The scene is not in the novel, and it subtly places the relationship between Alice and Russell within a conventional social milieu. In the book their courtship takes place almost entirely on Alice's veranda—neither inside nor outside—Tarkington's way of emphasizing the social limbo in which the relationship exists.

One element of Tarkington's novel absent from the film is the aspect of class struggle represented by the blacks in Adams's community. They pose a counterpoint to the social aspirations of the Adams family, for when Virgil begins to manufacture glue, the stench pervades the ghetto where his factory lies. It's a stench with which he himself feels saturated. He washes with the obsessiveness of Lady MacBeth, but he can't seem to get rid of the smell. Actually, and psychologically, Virgil Adams can't dissociate himself from the working class. His glue is packed by the cheapest labor force—black girls. The black people, mute pawns in the game of early twentieth-century capitalism, must bear the burden of even Virgil Adams's enlightened industrial aspirations.

The only blacks seen in the film are menials like Hattie Mc-Daniel; and worse to Alice's mind are the familiars of her brother Walter—the bandleader, the cloakroom attendants he shoots crap with. Alice tries to rationalize her brother's choice of companions to Russell by saying that Walter is literary and intends to write "darkie stories," but Walter's friendships are a harbinger of his inevitable failure in the social struggle, a link with the lower class as irrevocable as the glue stench clinging to Virgil Adams.

The difference between the film as a fairy tale and the novel as tragedy is epitomized by Tarkington's metaphorical structure, which verges on the biblical. The doors to the business college are hellishly viewed as the "portal of doom." The woes of the Adams family are Job-like. "The rain of misfortune," wrote Tarkington, "had selected the Adams family for its scaldings, no question." Alice's misfortune, in this context, seems like punishment for the sin of arrogance. After Russell deserts her, and she decides to go to secretarial school, she compares that course with taking the veil.

Despite the bleakness of Tarkington's saga, *Alice Adams* manages to end on a tiny optimistic note. As Alice mounts the stairs to the dark hell of Frincke's Business College, "the place began to seem brighter. There was an open window overhead somewhere . . . and the steps at the top were gay with sunshine." There's a dynamism to Tarkington's ending which is more enduring than the hearts-and-flowers finish of the film, the coupling of Hepburn and Fred MacMurray. Although she is stripped of her illusions, and her family will never attain higher status, Alice has grown up. She may conceive of getting a menial job as a nunlike alternative for an abandoned woman, but taking the veil is still more active than waiting to be given the veil. The gleam of sunlight at the end of the novel *Alice Adams* shines on a woman taking responsibility for the outcome of her life.

Babbitt (1922), Sinclair Lewis

The "Booboisie" and Its Discontents

BY SANFORD J. SMOLLER

The publication in 1922 of Sinclair Lewis's *Babbitt* caused a storm of controversy on both sides of the Atlantic. Two years earlier, in *Main Street*, Lewis joined Edgar Lee Masters and Edward Arlington Robinson, among others, in what Carl Van Doren called "The Revolt from the Village." Having disabused Americans of the long-cherished belief that small-town rural life was moral, pleasant, and tranquil, Lewis turned his satiric weapons against the middle-class businessman in a burgeoning industrial Midwestern city. Having just undergone the most devastating event in the history of mankind—the Great War—Americans were eager for Harding's promised "return to normalcy." Although the innocence of the late nineteenth century was lost in the Ardennes and at Chateau Thierry, a hope remained that the virtues of the Protestant ethos—hard work, strong family life, and religious observance—would again prevail and engender a new era of prosperity. The middle class resented *Babbitt* because Lewis, in dissecting their morality, mores, rituals, and institutions, revealed that the values around which they organized their lives were at bottom hypocritical and fraudulent. Thus, for many, he removed the last illusion standing between a frightened, insecure society and despair.

But not everyone attacked Lewis. Critics of American society like H. L. Mencken rushed to defend Lewis's portrait of the

American bourgeoisie. To Mencken, Lewis had put flesh and bones on his own abstract image of the "booboisie." As he wrote enthusiastically: "For the first time a wholly genuine American has gotten into a book—not the lowly, aspiring, half-pathetic American of the hinterland, but the cocky, bustling, enormously successful American of the big towns—the Booster, The Master of Salesmanship, the Optimist, the 100 per cent Patriot and Right-Thinker."

Babbitt also found willing defenders in Europe. Already predisposed to castigate America for its barbaric lack of culture and grasping materialism, Europeans had their prejudices confirmed by *Babbitt*. One English observer remarked that "it was *Babbitt* which so impressed its portraiture on this island as almost to create a myth of America as one vast Babbitt warren; and at least replaced the old popular image of the thin American with a goatee beard, by that of a fat American with spectacles." George Bernard Shaw would write in 1931 that "Mr. Sinclair Lewis has knocked Washington off his pedestal and substituted Babbitt, who is now a European byword."

When Lewis was seeking an appropriate title for his book, his co-publisher Donald Brace wrote to say that the general *Babbitt* was better than the specific *George F. Babbitt* "because it can mean Babbitts everywhere, the Babbitt kind of thing, rather than just a character." And so Babbitt, from the title of a book about a fictitious George F. Babbitt of Zenith, U.S.A., passed into the language as a descriptive adjective connoting the pettiness, hypocrisy, materialism, conformity, and chauvinism of a certain kind of American. By the end of 1922 *Babbitt* had sold almost 141,000 copies and Lewis was negotiating with Warner Brothers for the movie rights. Ironically, while the American boob yelped at seeing his reflection in Lewis's mirror, he was obviously willing to pay for the privilege of being ridiculed.

Mark Schorer has pointed out that Lewis originally intended the novel to chronicle a single day in the life of George F. Babbitt. But since Babbitt perceives little besides material objects, business opportunities, and a pretty woman's figure, Lewis was able to record his average day—beginning with his awakening from his comforting dream of the "fairy child" through his petulant family breakfast; his self-satisfied drive to the real estate office; his morning of small business triumphs and defeats; his ample lunch at the Athletic Club; his return home for a dinner of roast beef, potatoes, and stringbeans after an afternoon cultivating prospects and arguing with employees; his evening spent reading the comics, his "favorite literature and art," and pontificating to his son; his soothing shave and bath amid the "splendor" of nickel taps and tiled walls; his ritual of preparing blankets, rug, hot-water bottle, and alarm clock before snuggling into his cot in the sleeping porch and reaching finally, "a blessed state of oblivion"—in the first seven chapters. Thereafter, Lewis roams episodically over what Schorer terms "the sociology of middle-class American life," which includes economics, politics, religion, social life, vacations, businessmen's clubs and conventions, and education. And in all aspects of his public and private life, Babbitt's attitudes and opinions are formed and directed by external forces:

> Just as he was an Elk, a Booster, and a member of the Chamber of Commerce, just as the priests of the Presbyterian Church determined his every religious belief and the senators who controlled the Republican Party decided in little smoky rooms in Washington what he should think about disarmament, tariff, and Germany, so did the large national advertisers fix the surface of his life, fix what he believed to be his individuality. These standard advertised wares—toothpastes, socks, tires, cameras, instantaneous hot-water heaters—were his symbols and proofs of excellence; at first the signs, then the substitutes, for joy and passion and wisdom.

Hence Babbitt provides the classic literary example of what sociologist David Riesman, in the 1950s, called the "outer-directed man."

In his *The Modern American Novel* (Revised 1963), Frederick J. Hoffman discerns, however, the conflicting personalities within Babbitt: the first a "parody Babbitt," the mouthpiece for orthodox clichés, platitudes, and pieties; the second a complex Babbitt, the man troubled by an instinctual buried life struggling to break through years of suppression. As a caricature of the American right-thinker-booster-patriot, Babbitt reaches his apex in a speech

George Babbitt (Guy Kibbee) addresses his family, son Ted (Glen Bales), daughter Verona (Maxine Doyle), and his wife (Aline McMahon). Babbitt (1934).

to the Zenith Real Estate Board, where he defines the "ideal of American manhood and culture" in straightforward, no-nonsense, man-to-man language:

> "[He] isn't a lot of cranks sitting around chewing the rag about their Rights and their Wrongs, but a God-fearing, hustling, successful, two-fisted Regular Guy, who belongs to some church with pep and piety to it, who belongs to the Boosters or the Rotarians, or the Kiwanis, to the Elks or Moose or Red Men or Knights of Columbus, or any one of a score of organizations of good, jolly, kidding, laughing, sweating, upstanding, lend-a-handing Royal Good Fellows, who plays hard and works hard, and whose answer to his critics is a square-toed boot that'll teach the grouches and smart alecks to respect the He-man and get out and foot for Uncle Samuel, U.S.A.!"

But for all his speechmaking, glad-handing, and boosting, Babbitt remains fixed in his station. He fails to realize that he is really a pawn—a front man and shock trooper—of the McKelveys, Eathornes, and Offutts, who, protected by their wealth and status, manipulate impressionable, ambitious underlings into doing the economic dirty work while they reap the profits. The pathetic irony of *Babbitt* is that in blatantly asserting the supremacy of American business practices and ethics in all spheres —in art, religion, politics, education, as well as in trade—Babbitt unwittingly abets the forces that have squeezed out his individuality and almost all natural and spontaneous feelings. For all his insensitivity, avarice, and hypocrisy, Babbitt is not a villain, but a victim.

The other side of Babbitt—and the thing which separates him from Vergil Gunch, Chum Frink, and the others in the herd—is manifested in his friendship with Paul Riesling. A dreamer with an artistic temperament, Riesling is trapped in the roofing business by his unhappy marriage to the shrewish and acquisitive Zilla. Although Babbitt does not understand Riesling's moods and yearnings, he offers his friend, who is clearly an outsider, unaffected sympathy and moral support. When after a good deal of finagling the two men manage to get away from their wives for a fishing trip in Maine, Babbitt experiences perhaps his only moment of freedom and contentment. Sitting with Paul by the sunlit lake and trees, over which seemed to hang "a holy peace," Babbitt is overcome by "the immense tenderness of the place" and wishes he could stay there forever, away from business and family. He asks Paul how the place "strikes" him, and Riesling replies: " 'Oh, it's darn good, Georgie. There's something sort of eternal about it.' For once, Babbitt understood him." But this feeling of release and communion is ephemeral, for when Zilla, Myra, and the children join them Babbitt represses his profound longings and reverts back to his public self. On the trip home he is nagged by guilt feelings at having deserted his wife and angered by being expected to feel guilty.

Paul Riesling's imprisonment for shooting Zilla in a fit of frustration and rage leaves an unfillable hole in Babbitt's emotional life. When Myra goes East to visit relatives, he is assailed by doubts and misgivings:

> It was coming to him that perhaps all life as he knew it and vigorously practiced it was futile; that heaven as portrayed by the Reverend Dr. John Jennison Drew was neither probable nor very interesting; that he hadn't much pleasure out of making money; that it was of doubtful worth to rear children merely that they might rear children who would rear children. What was it all about? What did he want?

Without Paul's presence for emotional sustenance, he fantasizes about the "fairy girl," and discovers that he wanted her "in the flesh." And with this realization, at once "terrifying" and "thrilling," he feels that he has made a "break with everything that was decent and normal."

Though only half-conscious of his motives, Babbitt begins to do things that he long desired but never dared to do: he goes to the movies in the afternoon, makes advances to his secretary and his neighbor's wife, and even arranges a date with a patronizing manicurist. But these efforts to find forbidden love are fruitless, and he curses his folly. Babbitt decides to take his vacation alone in Maine, impelled by a longing to commune with Paul's spirit. Yet the guides are undemonstrative at his arrival; and after a disappointing night camping with Joe, their guide from last year, Babbitt, lonely and desolate, realizes that he can never escape from Zenith—that "merely to run away was folly, because he could never run away from himself."

On the train back he meets Seneca Doane, fighter for liberal causes and the ostensible enemy of right-thinking patriots. Doane recalls that in college Babbitt had told him that he wanted to be a lawyer for the poor and battle the rich. Flattered by Doane's approval, Babbitt, chameleon-like, begins to take on a liberal coloration, professing a belief in healthy opposition and the need for "Vision" and "Ideals." Now Doane replaces McKelvey and Eathorne as Babbitt's symbol of the successful man, and Babbitt defends him when Gunch opines that he "ought to be hanged."

Babbitt is given the opportunity to put his new liberal views to the test when a strike breaks out and threatens to tie up the city. The National Guard is called out, and Babbitt incurs hostile, quizzical glances from the Boosters when he questions the wisdom of violence. Yet these episodes, while estranging Babbitt from his associates, are preliminaries to his major rebellion against the moral and social strictures of the middle class. Through his affair with Tanis Judique, a fortyish widow, Babbitt attempts to discover the emotional and sensual excitement his life has lacked. But after the first flush of repressed passion wears off, he feels that she, too, is directing his actions, and to assuage guilt and weakness he begins drinking heavily. Moreover, through Tanis he becomes embroiled in the shifting liaisons of the "Bunch," a group of her friends whose lives are spent in partying, gossiping, and bickering. Although Babbitt tires of affecting enthusiasm and gaiety, he continues going to their parties because he has no other outlets. Now on the fringe of bourgeois society, cast adrift from family and former friends, Babbitt "walks the streets alone, afraid of men's cynical eyes and the incessant hiss of whispering." Gunch urges him to join the Good Citizens' League—an organization dedicated to protecting American purity from all assaults, foreign and domestic—implying that if he joins his eccentricity will be forgiven but that if he refuses he will be totally ostracized. Here Babbitt comes to the critical juncture in his life: to continue in revolt and become a pariah for a nebulous concept of freedom or to succumb to external pressure and return to a secure but unfulfilling conventional life.

Lewis, however, spares Babbitt the choice. Myra's appendicitis serves not only to reclaim Babbitt's past and sense of responsibility, but also to expiate his guilt for deserting her. In nursing her back to health he reintegrates himself into the family, and from there it is a short step to enlisting in the Good Citizens' League and reintegration into the righteous middle class. Like a fly in a bottle, Babbitt probes to the outer reaches of his enclosed environment, but without the will and moral strength to break through he falls. " 'They've licked me; licked me to a finish!' he whimpered." His future determined, resigned to the onset of uneventful middle age, Babbitt's only real consolation is that his son Ted, who shows his independence by marrying Eunice Littlefield and quitting college to take a factory job, will succeed where he has failed—will attain individuality and freedom.

Lewis's critics have contended, with some justice, that he shared Babbitt's penchant for boosting and realizing a quick dollar, particularly with his own books. His letters to Harcourt, Brace and Company are filled with promotional schemes to push *Babbitt*, and he was very much concerned with getting the highest price for the movie and stage rights. Warner Brothers paid $50,000 for the book and produced a screen version in 1924 that was directed by Harry Beaumont and starred Willard Louis as Babbitt, Mary Alden as Myra, Carmel Myers as Tanis Judique, and Robert Randall as Paul Riesling. But, as with *Main Street,* *Babbitt* was a box-office failure, and Hollywood producers were thenceforth wary of Lewis.

A decade later, however, First National (a subsidiary of Warner Brothers), perhaps hoping to capitalize on Lewis's fame as a Nobel Prize winner, remade *Babbitt*. Written for the screen by Mary McCall Jr. and directed by William Keighley, the 1934 movie version starred the popular comic actor Guy Kibbee in the title role and featured Aline MacMahon as Myra Babbitt, Claire Dodd as Tanis Judique, Minor Watson as Paul Riesling, and Alan Hale as Charlie McKelvey.

As social criticism, the movie is an outright failure. Totally absent from it is the synecdochic quality of the novel in which

Zenith stands for the waxing American industrial giant and Babbitt the little, average man trying to ride its back to personal success. Whereas the novel opens with a sweeping panorama of Zenith's towers of steel thrusting above the morning mist, to symbolize the triumph of the new business spirit of the age, the film pans a small signpost displaying the emblems of the city's service organizations, including the "Zebras," the movie-Babbitt's beloved fraternal order. Whatever satire the movie generates centers on the puerile tomfoolery of the men's clubs, but it remains fixed to that narrow subject and does not push out, as the novel does, to encompass the social, political, moral, and economic values of an entire class. One can, of course, fault the producers and screenwriter for failing to remain faithful to their source, and, indeed, except for notable exceptions like *The Grapes of Wrath* (1939), Hollywood movies based on novels openly critical of the American system are considerably softened versions of the originals. But, timidity notwithstanding, perhaps the major reason for the film's lack of social comment is that conditions had changed radically from the time Lewis wrote the novel. The middle-class paradise that seemed to be within the grasp of every Babbitt in 1922 had been exposed by 1934 to be nothing but a foolish, albeit dangerous fantasy. With the aspiring towers of American capitalism reduced to rubble by the Crash of 1929, what was there left to satirize? Only pompous little men, and fortunately for writers and film-makers they are eternal.

The movie, however, does try to recapitulate the trappings of Babbittry and to suggest the character of the "parody Babbitt." After dissolving from a shot of Floral Heights and Babbitt's house, the camera closes in on Kibbee asleep in his bedroom with his cherubic face wreathed in a beatific smile, which obviously expresses a delightful dream—perhaps of the "fairy child." Jarred awake by the alarm clock, he knocks over a glass of water on the bed stand and trudges irritably into the bathroom. There, his belief in mechanical gadgets is displayed when he straps himself into a reducing machine and endures a few rubs on his ample belly and makes a resolution to go on a diet. At breakfast he grumbles at his family and black cook (in the book she is a

"Lettish-Croat"), who, in keeping with the racist stereotyping of blacks in thirties movies, is singing happily because she has hit the numbers. When Babbitt prepares to go to the office, his wife hands him a telegram. It is from a woman called "Maureen" who demands money or else she will reveal his indiscretions with her. Though he cannot recall the woman, he thinks he must have met her at a lodge party when he passed out from too much booze. This piece of business, which is not in the book, introduces the scheming woman motif and the first of the movie's four main episodes.

Driving to work, the worried Babbitt happens to see Riesling in a pawnshop with his violin. Babbitt dissuades his melancholy friend from hocking the light of his life, lends him fifty dollars, and consoles him with soothing thoughts about fishing in the mountains. (Later Babbitt will be shown in a sporting goods store trying on fishing boots.) At the office he dictates a garbled and simple-minded business letter to his secretary, and after she cleans up the syntax and meaning, beams approvingly at his handiwork. Still worried about the telegram, however, he asks Charlie McKelvey (now a lawyer) for help. McKelvey promises to help him after a bit of good-natured men-will-be-boys ribbing. That evening McKelvey and other Zebras blindfold Babbitt and take him for a ride, ostensibly to settle the "Maureen" affair. He is led into a room and tied to a chair, at which point a high voice begins cataloguing his list of crimes. When he is properly frightened, vehemently protesting his innocence, the blindfold is removed and, wonder of wonders, Babbitt is in the Zebra lodge surrounded by the laughing faces of McKelvey, Gunch, and his other boon companions. Not only is he relieved by this practical joke, but he is positively elated when he learns that the whole thing was to prepare him for the great honor of becoming Grand Ringmaster of the lodge. The scene closes with Babbitt borne aloft to a chorus of hearty male laughter.

The second main episode—Paul shooting Zilla—follows a series of short scenes revealing Babbitt's venality, vanity, pretension, and authoritarianism. After he boosts the public library, Babbitt is invited to the home of big banker Eathorne who, in league with a city commissioner, proposes that Babbitt buy options under dummy names on land meant for a new airport; then he can sell it back to the city and they will all make a killing. Inflated by their sweet talk, Babbitt rounds up a farmer and a black porter to front for him, and when Myra tells him the scheme is dishonest, he replies, "Women don't understand about business." When his son Ted, a clean, upstanding young man, says that he wants to be an engineer, not a businessman, Babbitt snaps, "I'll tell him what's good for him." And after Tanis Judique flatters Babbitt for the manly way he drives a car, he glows with smug self-satisfaction. Thus, with his flaws betrayed, the stage is set for his eventual comeuppance.

Attempting to soft-soap Zilla Riesling into letting Paul go on a fishing trip, the Babbitts invite them out for dinner. But Zilla proceeds to nag her husband, and Myra tries to smooth things over. During the conversation, Babbitt bares his secret longings; materialist to the core, he wishes for a good car and a house with a bathroom for each bedroom. Riesling, the romantic but ineffectual dreamer, asks, "Don't you want anything you can't touch?" This serious questioning of values is not developed, however, for Babbitt here, unlike the figures in the novel, has only one dimension. Nevertheless, he does include friendship—his one redeeming virtue—among his limited attributes. Following Paul's assault on Zilla, Babbitt offers to do anything in his power to free his friend. He even considers bribery despite his son's protests that "it isn't straight." To Babbitt, friendship comes before the law. Paul is sentenced to ten years (in the novel it was three) and Myra, who also places her friendship with Zilla above her husband's protestations, takes Zilla to the country to care for her.

At this point the movie plot diverges widely from the book. Although Babbitt accidently meets Tanis in a restaurant while Myra is away and begins to go to her apartment, his affair has no hint of a general rebellion against moral and social convention. If anything, it is petty revenge against Myra's display of independence. After Gunch sees Babbitt and Tanis together, rumors begin to circulate among the Zebras, and McKelvey cautions Babbitt about the dangers of "stepping out." Matters with Tanis come to a head quickly when Babbitt boasts of a deal that will turn a tidy profit. Tanis, with a little coaxing, gets Babbitt to reveal the scheme, whereupon she reverts to type—the beautiful but destructive "other woman"—and threatens to divulge the deception unless he gives her $10,000. Babbitt pleads that his money is in his wife's name and that he cannot raise that much. Vindictive as well as avaricious, Tanis makes good her threat and notifies the local newspaper of the fraud. Facing ruin and despairing, Babbitt considers jumping from a bridge as this central plot episode concludes.

In the novel Babbitt was manipulated and victimized by powerful social and economic forces; he was, as one critic has pointed out, a pygmy among giants. But in the movie he is directed by women and by similarly weak men who simply seize upon his obvious gullibility and fatuity. If the movie has any moral point, it is that to be respected as a man, a man must act honestly and responsibly. Now impotent, Babbitt can only be saved by the intervention of his wife and son. Myra returns and, with the finesse of a mother changing a baby's diaper, swiftly cleans up the mess Babbitt has made. She dispatches Ted to buy back from the farmer and porter the options (significantly, the shrewd farmer bargains for $500 while the black porter is happy to settle for $100). While Ted gives his father a pep talk—"We Babbitts are hard to lick"—Myra admonishes him for childishly falling into the villains' clutches. Then, demonstrating that she does indeed understand about business, Myra confronts the district attorney and tells him that, far from trying to bilk the city, Babbitt was really buying up the land to protect the city from possible swindle. As proof of his good intentions, she hands him the deeds to the property as a gift from George F. Babbitt, the paragon of civic-minded citizens. In this climactic reversal, another stock comedic convention, Babbitt goes from villain to hero.

That night the Zebras apologize for misinterpreting his motives and welcome him back into the herd. Ecstatic over his reinstatement, having learned his lesson, Babbitt dances ring-around-the-rosy with his family as the screen fades to black.

The years have dimmed Sinclair Lewis's luster, and *Babbitt* is no longer widely read. Nevertheless it remains a minor classic in American literature because, for all its stylistic and structural shortcomings, it pinpoints a seemingly ingrained flaw in the

American character—the compulsion to conform regardless of the moral, psychological, and emotional imperatives to realize fully our intrinsic selves. In a sense *Babbitt* marks the re-emergence of American Puritanism, which was merely covered over—not irretrievably buried—by Emerson, Thoreau, and Whitman. The pressures to conform have increased since Lewis wrote *Babbitt* (as the Watergate conspirators of the early seventies so graphically demonstrated), and in an era when a President could turn the White House into the headquarters of his own "Good Citizens' League," who among us can lightly dismiss the Babbitts and Gunches as cardboard figures from the distant past?

As for the movie, trivial and shallow, it evades the serious issues raised in the novel and makes no claim at all on either our intelligence or our emotions. It eminently deserves its obscurity.

An American Tragedy (1925), Theodore Dreiser

Eisenstein's Subversive Adaptation

BY KEITH COHEN

It might be argued that the scenario for a movie that was never made hardly qualifies as legitimate material for a study of the adaptation of novels to film. When the stymied director is Eisenstein, however, and when the adaptation establishes a fruitfully disorienting relation with the precursor text—to the point of a skillful "deconstruction" of the original—the production becomes most interesting despite its stillborn existence.[1]

I

Dreiser's *An American Tragedy* (1925) is a strongly stated depreciation of American society, in particular its legal and judiciary processes in the first decades of this century, and a psychological case study of an individual who, defying common sense, chooses to act out the American myth of the "self-made man." Here was certainly material that could inspire Eisenstein; though a gracious guest in the United States at the time, he had no intention of forgetting or temporarily reneging his ideological background.

---

[1] Eisenstein presented his finished treatment of Dreiser's *An American Tragedy* to the executives at Paramount and lost the option to shoot it when he maintained that the protagonist, Clyde Griffiths, was essentially innocent. For details, see Bibliographical Note at end of this essay.

As he read the novel,[2] what undoubtedly inspired him to the point of making diagrams of frame compositions in the margins of the book was not simply the driving ambition and inevitable fall of Clyde Griffiths, but the uncannily cinematic appeal of Dreiser's narrative as well.[3] Prior to *An American Tragedy*, Dreiser's prose had been far more leaden, less fluid, his narrative progression more predictable and less subject to anything that might be called a lyric impulse. What Eisenstein read was a highly visual, long, though rapidly paced novel, recounted at points with the rhythm of breathlessness.

Throughout the novel, but especially at chapter openings, Dreiser gives a series of fragmentary sentences that set the decor and atmosphere. Verbs, with the exception of participles, are deleted. The book begins and ends with a brief imagistic passage that starts out: "Dusk—of a summer night."[4] The opening continues:

> And the tall walls of the commercial heart of our American city of perhaps 400,000 inhabitants—such walls as in time linger as a mere fable.
> And up the broad street, now comparatively hushed, a little band of six,—a man of about fifty, short, stout, with bushy hair protruding from under a round black felt hat, a most unimportant-looking person, who carried a small portable organ such as is customarily used by street preachers and singers. And with him a woman perhaps five years his junior. . . .

Over and again Dreiser initiates narrative flow in this majestic manner, shifting activity from the discrete consequentiality of a

[2] Eisenstein's copy of *An American Tragedy*, with copious marginalia, is preserved in the Eisenstein Collection at the Museum of Modern Art. References are to his marginalia in this copy only.

[3] We know that Eisenstein was more than ordinarily sensitive to the "proto-cinematic" devices used by authors since Dickens and even before. See, in particular, "Dickens, Griffith, and the Film Today," in *Film Form*; "Word and Image," in *The Film Sense*, both translated by Jay Leyda, (New York, 1957); and "Lessons from Literature," in *Film Essays and a Lecture*, edited by Jay Leyda, (New York, 1970).

[4] Theodore Dreiser, *An American Tragedy*, (New York: Horace Liveright, 1925; reprinted New York: The Modern Library, 1953), pp. 15, 871. Hereafter all references will be to this edition of the novel.

conjugated verb to the nondelimited action of a participle or the uncontoured directionality of a preposition (such as "up"). The result is a suspension of diegetic action perhaps even more dramatic than ordinary description, like the scenario itself that awaits dynamization by the camera: *cf.*, the start of Clyde and Roberta's fateful trip to Big Bittern Lake (p. 510) and Mrs. Griffiths's train ride to visit her imprisoned son (p. 804).

This sort of sentence fragmentation suspends, holds off; after highly dramatic scenes (the joy ride in a stolen car, the death of Roberta), it also quells, stabilizes, distances (pp. 165, 537). At still other moments the fragmented images add to the breathless concentration of tense moments. When Clyde and Roberta are out on the lake, Dreiser carefully chooses those aspects of Clyde's demeanor that we are to consider: "His wet, damp, nervous hands! And his dark, liquid, nervous eyes, looking anywhere but at her" (p. 529). Eisenstein was apparently struck by the liquidness of both Clyde's surroundings (the lake) and Clyde's attributes (eyes: intention; hands: means of accomplishment). He sketched in his copy of the novel a few frame compositions that suggest a montage progression from eyes (in closeup) to water, one presumably fading into the other. In this way Eisenstein could approximate with the plasticity of the image the conjunctive force of liquidness in Dreiser's scene: a conjunction that works dynamically across the surface disjunction between water (the placid, anonymous setting and eventual veil of the projected crime) and eyes (the most prominent index of that project in Clyde's mind). This counter-disjunctive force of water comes across in the scenario when Clyde, seeing Roberta "playfully letting her hand fall into the water . . . also feels the water. But his hand springs back as though it had received an electric shock"[5] (thus uncannily hinting at the ultimate consequence of this event for Clyde: the electric chair).

---

[5] Sergei Eisenstein, scenario for *An American Tragedy*, in Montagu, *With Eisenstein in Hollywood* (Appendix 2), Reel 10, Sequence 23. The scenario takes the standard form of dialogue and generalized camera directions, plus rather elaborate descriptions of settings and character moods. Hereafter references to the scenario will be given by two numbers in parentheses, the first referring to the reel, the second to the sequence.

Eisenstein elaborates with greater specificity other dynamic aspects of this most dramatic scene. From the time that Clyde, inspired by a newspaper story of a double drowning, conceives the idea of murdering Roberta (especially chapters XLV-XLVII of Book Two), Dreiser portrays the moral battle taking place within Clyde by means of two techniques. First, he endows the forces for and against with voices that loudly debate the feasibility of the project. Even after the two voices have held forth at full center stage, their trace remains in the text, as when, near the climax, Clyde still wavers: "He had come here for what? And he must do what? Kill Roberta? Oh, no!" (p. 528). Secondly, as Clyde rides the train up toward Big Bittern, Dreiser supplies memory-images in italics enclosed in parentheses (pp. 512–17). This technique performs ultimately the same function as the first. The images waver between recollections of emotional indebtedness to Roberta and suspiciousness about people Clyde has encountered so far during the day to recollections of moneyed stability in association with Sondra: "The beautiful Cranston Lodge there and Sondra."

Eisenstein reduces the image content of Clyde's train ride but uses the duel of voices to an even greater extent than Dreiser. What reads as a slightly corny modern version of Everyman beset by the forces of good and evil in the novel can be imagined, on the basis of the scenario, as a technical triumph for Eisenstein's then recently formulated theories of sound montage. Furthermore, at the climactic moment in the duel of voices, Eisenstein re-introduces the Roberta/Sondra dialectic through visual montage.

> "Kill-kill" triumphs and there passes through his mind the memory of his mother, "Baby-baby" comes from his childhood and as "Don't kill—don't kill" rises he hears "Baby boy—baby boy" in the so different voice of Sondra, and at the image of Sondra and the thought of all that surrounds her "Kill-kill" grows harder and insistent, and with the thought of Roberta importunate it grows still harsher and shriller, and then the face of Roberta now, aglow with faith in him and her great relief, and the sight of the hair he has so loved to caress and "Don't—don't kill" grows and tenderly supplants the other and now is calm and firm and final. (10,26)

In other words, Eisenstein picks up the two separate techniques in Dreiser and amalgamates them through the simultaneous use of visual and audial counterpoint. He is not satisfied, however, to leave the Roberta/Sondra conflict expressed through the
duel of voices alone. This conflict of Clyde's allegiance is of
utmost importance, since, as we shall see later, it is the emblem
of the fundamental ideological tension in the work. So Eisenstein
furnishes an additional audio montage during the train ride, when
"the rhythm of the wedding march, the joyous beat, struggles with
the rhythm of death. 'Kill—Kill—' beats the engine to Clyde"
(10,10).

Eisenstein's interpretation of the debate going on inside Clyde
is crucial to the argumentative edge he gives to the scenario.
By underscoring the multilayered conflict by means of visual and
audio montage and by allowing the two sides to remain equally
powerful right up to the end, Eisenstein technically prepares for
his slight though telling modification of the drowning scene.
Dreiser has Clyde become sullen and despondent as the result
of the frustrating irresolution of the two forces. Though he
never makes the frontal attack on Roberta he had once planned,
Clyde yields "to a tide of submerged hate" when Roberta moves
toward him in the boat, sensing now (according to yet another
American myth concerning toughness and masculine aggressive-
ness) "the profoundness of his own failure, his own cowardice
or inadequateness for such an occasion" (p. 530). Eisenstein, on
the other hand, allows the "Don't kill" voice to triumph suddenly
in the end: "Never, never now will he have the courage to kill
Roberta" (10,26). For Eisenstein, it is essential to emphasize
the firmness of Clyde's final decision to spare Roberta and their
unborn child and the accidental nature of what follows.

Fragmentation of images and a decidedly visual orientation
were only one aspect of Dreiser's prose that Eisenstein sought
to exploit by cinematic means. The other aspect has to do with
the discursive experimentation going on in *An American Tragedy*.
What makes this work so much more vivid and electrifying than
Dreiser's earlier, truly naturalistic novels like *Sister Carrie* (1900)
and *The Financier* (1912) is the use of special discursive techniques associated with the limitation and ultimate effacement of

narrative mediation: *style indirect libre* and direct interior monologue. The novel is sprinkled throughout with instances of *style
indirect libre,* and it would not be an exaggeration to say that
what makes Clyde's guilt particularly problematic is the simple
fact that his own consciousness of his reasoning and judgmental
process have been foregrounded by means of this technique,
which precludes narrative and authorial commentary. In other
words, we have nothing more to go on in many cases than Clyde's
own thoughts and recognizance of those thoughts.

No wonder Eisenstein claimed that his meditation on Dreiser's
novel led him to attempt the first "inner monologue" in cinema.
Breaking with the standard Hollywood conception of the origin
and function of sound in cinema, Eisenstein boldly asserts that
"the true material of the sound-film is, of course, the monologue."[6]
It is at this point that he can transform Dreiser's somewhat heavy-
handed internal battle during Clyde's train ride, which Eisenstein accurately categorizes, in comparison with Joyce, as "primitive rhetoric,"[7] into a filmic reconstruction of "all phases of the
course of thought."[8] As noted above, the duel of voices begins
much earlier in Eisenstein's treatment. When Clyde conceives
his murder plan, the scenario reads:

> And from this moment the action begins to work along the line of
> the thoughts of a distracted man, leaping from one fact to another,
> suddenly stopping—departing from sane logic, distorting the real
> union between things and sounds; all on the background of the
> insistent and infinite repetition of scraps of the description in the
> newspaper.
>
> In this scene, in which the idea of murder is born to Clyde, he
> acts separately from the background, which keeps changing after
> him. . . .
>
> With the aid of the technical use of transparencies this effect of
> an inharmony between the actions of Clyde and his surroundings
> can be attained. Around him is first his room, then a street in busy
> movement, or the lake, or the mean dwelling of Roberta, or the
> summer residence of Sondra at Twelfth Lake, or the machines in

[6] Eisenstein, *Film Form*, p. 106.
[7] *Ibid.*, p. 103.
[8] *Ibid.*, p. 105.

the factory, or running trains, or the stormy sea, in each setting of which he now moves, his movements being discordant with the scene.

And the same with the sounds. These are likewise distorted, and a whisper becomes the whistle of a storm, and the storm cries out "Kill," or the whistle of the storm becomes the movement of the street, the wheels of a streetcar, the cries of a crowd, the horns of motorcars, and all beat out the word: "Kill! Kill!" And the street noises become the roar of the factory machines, and the machines also roar out "Kill! Kill!" (9,13)

Here we can only mourn the stillbirth of this incredibly ambitious project. We can only imagine, on the basis of a few such realizations in the uncompleted *Que Viva Mexico* (1931), the astonishing possibilities Eisenstein suggests when he speaks of "distorting the real union between things and sounds" and, referring to the scenario, of nonsynchronized sound, "zigzags of aimless shapes," and "racing visual images over complete silence."[9]

II

Eisenstein's method of reading texts—from the journals and notebooks of Leonardo to the novels of Dickens and the poetry of Baudelaire—was in many ways idiosyncratic. In coming to actual adaptation, he established a kind of relation with the precursor text that is very pertinent to contemporary theories of intertextuality for its deviousness, its uncanny subversiveness. The point in this type of creative and transgressive adaptation is not only that, especially in the case of Eisenstein, conversion must take place across differences of medium, but also that adaptation is a truly artistic feat only when the new version carries with it a hidden criticism of its model or at least renders implicit (through a process we should call "deconstruction") certain key contradictions implanted or glossed over in the original. Of prime interest, therefore, in Eisenstein's scenario is not so much its imitative fidelity or even its cinematic approxima-

[9] *Ibid.*

tion of specifically literary effects, as its pointed distortion, re-orientation of Dreiser's text.

If Eisenstein showed little interest in pursuing the manifestations of the myth of American masculine toughness, he was quite eager to explore the Christian sophistry characteristic of the Evangelical movement. Clyde's father and mother are urban missionaries of this relatively new faith, and the scenario, like the novel, opens on the scene of a street sermon and meeting conducted by the Griffiths. Dreiser uses Clyde's missionary background as a contrasting framework within which to couch the early attractiveness of social success. Clyde's upbringing is not simply poor or working class; his is the willed poverty of a family devoted to self-denial and the salvation of others in the name of their faith. The treatment of Clyde's family in the novel is always sympathetic; his mother is a true Christian sufferer who seems ironically to be chanting at the beginning the very hymn of salvation that she will cry out on Clyde's behalf to the Governor at the end. Clyde's dissociation from his family is seen in the novel as the result of a very human, very American desire to improve the tedious lot that the Griffiths accept with such impassibility.

Eisenstein drastically changes the depiction of these missionaries. The Griffiths' faith is not seen as an honest, if misguided, inspiration springing from traditional Christianity but rather as "a purblind fanaticism."[10] There is thus in no sense a continuity from Clyde's upbringing to his desire for a higher social standing. There is rather a sharp conflict between the self-satisfaction of the Griffiths' evangelism and the self-promotion prompted by the numerous bourgeois temptations lurking around Clyde. This contradiction is built into the sound track of the first sequence with "the infinite contrast between the chant of the sermon and the life of the city" (1,1) and, even more dynamically, in the "discordant dissonance" of a "well-known dance" from a nearby restaurant and the cries of "Hallelujah" from the mission (1,14). Clyde wants to work and learn but is dragged around from mission to street meeting. He cannot be the son of missionaries

10 *Ibid.*, p. 101.

and lead a self-sufficient life at the same time. In Eisenstein's version, consequently, we sympathize all the more with Clyde because we see him climbing out of one trap only to fall into another. His desires to make it in the bourgeois world seem practically commendable, by virtue of the sentimental evangelism on which he has been nourished.

The most brilliant touch in this respect is Eisenstein's augmentation of the mother's role in the final scenes. Eisenstein was not satisfied with Dreiser's initial irony (wherein lies what little venom he shows against Evangelism), by which the doctrine of self-denial and unflagging belief in the Almighty are seen as propitious conditions for the yielding to the temptations of a self-interested murder. He pursues the sophistry implicit in the Jesus-loves-me ideology preached in the midst of a booming capitalist state that gives rise to the most exploitative kinds of individual privation. Deleting the role of Reverend McMillan, which had given Dreiser an opportunity to oppose rather baldly to a fly-by-night Evangelism the healing steadfastness of an established Church, Eisenstein has Clyde confess to his mother: "I didn't do it. . . . I did—think of it, mummy." Upon which, "the mother's caress slows, her fingers have become still and her face set" (14,17). At the crucial moment, then, as prepared by her reaction to her son's words, Clyde's mother falters. In answer to the Governor's question, "Can you, Mrs. Griffiths, can you from the bottom of your soul tell me that you believe him innocent?" she begins, "Yes . . . my son . . . ," but then stops (14,20). Eisenstein sums up his more bitter ironic intention by noting, "The Christian sophism of an ideal unity (of deed and thought) and a material unity (*de facto*), a parody of dialectics, leads to the final tragic denouement."[11]

To return to the initial contention concerning the devious laying bare of implicit elements in the precursor text, we might go even further by saying that the collective guilt characteristic of the moral preachings of American Evangelism backfires in Mrs. Griffiths's assumption of her son's virtual guilt and then is turned into its opposite, on the social plane, in Eisenstein's implications

[11] *Ibid.*, p. 102.

about the collective guilt of American society in Clyde's crime.

Eisenstein uses the scenes of Clyde's apprenticeship to reinforce these specific distortions of Dreiser's text. When Clyde goes out to hunt for a job, his illiteracy, the result of little or no schooling during his family's missionary activity, is underscored (2,3; also 1,37). Once he gets a job as bellboy, Clyde is suddenly exposed to all the luxuries of wealth and position that are to become the primal sources of his future dreams (2,24–3,11). Eisenstein is careful, in particular, to point out the nascent amorality of each of Clyde's employers-of-the-moment in the deluxe hotel—an amorality swept aside, in Clyde's eyes, by the glitter of the decor and the airs of the well-to-do (*cf.* esp. 2,26; 3,6; 3,8): "the moral fact that society presents to him" (3,3).

The first step in eradicating Clyde of any essential guilt is to make of him the *typical* individual: the lower-class *naif* dazzled by bourgeois opulence. Eisenstein accomplishes this by means of iterative-cumulative sequences, a technique of incremental repetition that Metz calls *syntagme en accolade* (bracket syntagma).[12] Clyde grows from a child into an adolescent to the words of his mother's "Life of Man" sermon (1,13), suggesting that he is but one among millions to embark on the illusory road of social ascendancy. During his phantasmagoric first day at the hotel, the gilt surroundings are made representative (by this technique) of all bourgeois decadence: "Through Morocco—through Venice—through rooms in Empire and in Gothic style, through samples of all the world he hurries frantically" (2,30).

Moreover, specific montage devices are used to depict dynamically Clyde's gradual assimilation of the capitalist ethic all around him. Eisenstein lays bare the structures of conquest that underlie Clyde's financial and erotic ventures. As in the novel, his initial shyness is emphasized as he begins work at the hotel, in his uncle's collar factory, or as he begins to court Roberta and then to integrate himself into the society of Sondra. In the scenario, however, Eisenstein again uses sound montage to link

[12] The bracket syntagma presents chronologically disconnected scenettes related by common topic and signifying a general, iterative experience or event. *Cf.* Metz, "Cinema: Language or Language System" in *Film Language*, (New York, 1975).

diverse moments of Clyde's personal conquest. Monetary recompense is connected early on to a musical motif, a swelling "happy march," as Clyde receives his first generous tip in the hotel (2,32). Important in this initial linkage is the further association of the triumphant peals with the music of a "High Mass," by which "the hotel resembles a mighty cathedral." This musical accompaniment, then, becomes a measure of the worldly distance Clyde has already traversed from his parents' mission into society: when the "mighty notes" fade, the mission hall returns, along with "the sound of its congregations singing psalms" (2,33–34). So, when Clyde kisses Roberta for the first time, though she pushes him away in alarm, Clyde is "made happy by his daring, excited by his conquest," and we hear again "that grand music, that majestic—swelling—hymn in the hotel" (5,24). Similarly, once the couple has made love for the first time, Clyde's personal ambition is seen once again as the motive force through the musical metonymy: "Marches of victory. Hymns of happiness are rending the air asunder" (5,23).

We have seen above that, in spite of Clyde's clear intention and careful premeditation, Eisenstein emphasizes the accidental nature of Roberta's death and "the misery of renunciation" in Clyde (10,26–28). This is important in order to appreciate the full force of Eisenstein's ending. As should be evident by now, Eisenstein views as the culprit in the tragedy something far beyond Clyde Griffiths, beyond the shoddy urban missionary environment in which Clyde is raised, beyond even the self-important worlds of the Samuel Griffiths and the Sondra Finchleys. Eisenstein clearly takes aim at American society as a whole and at the inequalities of a legal system founded on capitalist competitiveness. But he is not content, as Dreiser is, to point up the petty intrigues of local politicians, who turn Clyde's case into a vehicle for their election to a higher office. Eisenstein wants more. As in the metaphoric montage of *October* and *Strike*, Eisenstein makes of Clyde's execution a sudden sundering of the bonds between the human and the natural.

Slowly the heavy iron door closes.
And against the background of the spring fields and sky slides

from left to right the barred gate of the prison. And from right to
left the solid inner gate of the prison.

And the blinds and shutters of the windows come sliding down
and sliding down, shutting out the landscapes and the sky—light—
life—

And with their closing, cease the trilling of grasshoppers in the
meadows, the singing of the birds and the sound of human voices,
and as the last sound is gone the last shutter descends closing out
the prison bars against the white and there is blackness.

Blackness and quiet.

A sharp crackle and the sharp light of an electric contact—and
again quiet—again blackness (14,21).

In Dreiser's text, this scene is presented far more paraliptically:
we only see Clyde walking down the hall toward the execution
chamber, then, after a break in the text, Reverend McMillan
leaves the prison, morosely thinking, but in a rather undefined
way, about "The law! Prisons such as this" (p. 870). There is
no "sharp crackle" in the novel. There is no play between opening
and closing, light and dark, sound and silence—finally, most
importantly, life and death.

III

Between the precursor text and the adaptation, then, there
arises a pressing ideological debate. A rift is clearly created between Dreiser's muckraking exposé of Evangelism, urban poverty,
and the petty opportunism of elected officials, and Eisenstein's
bitingly direct attack against the institutional temptations of the
bourgeois world and the inequalities in business and in the law
courts of a system based on cutthroat competition and maximi-
zation of profits. In other words, to Dreiser's depreciation of American society Eisenstein responds with a vividly anticapitalist
document.

While both see guilt arising collectively, conglomerately from
society and the specific social conditions operating on Clyde,
Dreiser stresses Clyde's *innate* desire to get ahead. This comes
to the fore particularly when Clyde arrives in Lycurgus to work

at his uncle's factory. The discrepancy between Clyde's social origins and that of his well-to-do-relatives is never evinced as oppressive to Clyde, but rather as the very gap that Clyde's "natural" ambitiousness seeks to close or to minimize. Thus, a very ironic scene opens up when one of his fellow boarders, Walter Dillard, realizes that Clyde is related to the wealthy Samuel Griffiths. The two young men are depicted by Dreiser as daring free-enterprisers on the social scene. "Equally ambitious socially" to Clyde, Dillard is also like Clyde in being, "because of some atavistic spur or fillip in his own blood, most anxious to attain some sort of social position" (p. 217). Hence, Clyde's own social position is very early obfuscated: Dillard sees Clyde as a stepping-stone into the very world Clyde covets so much himself. And, after the trial, Clyde will remain essentially uncured, never *désabusé* of that central American imperative to "make it," as he remembers "his desire for more—more—that intense desire" (p. 864).

That myth to which Dreiser holds so dearly and which his work propagates itself, revolves around an ideology of opportunity. Clyde is your average American Everyman, except that he just happens to have been born into impoverished circumstances. He is—to use that insidious phrase that indicates all too clearly its point of reference in class terms—"underprivileged." Given the proper opportunities, Clyde will flower into a fine bourgeois cutthroat. Eisenstein substitutes for this doctrine of genetic determinism a concept of social molding. Hence the dialectic presentation of the mission and the world outside, which collapse into an equivalent snare for Clyde; hence the aural and visual patterning of associations for social and amorous conquest; hence the transformation of Mrs. Griffiths into the ultimate tempter and betrayer in her own son's passion. In other terms, while Dreiser merely juxtaposes the formation of the subject with a certain social formation outside that subject, Eisenstein demonstrates the projection of the ideological formation onto the process of subject formation and the subsequent sizing up by the subject of this mold against the now distorted social hierarchies he perceives.

Dreiser demonstrates considerable sympathy for socialist

theories through his negative caricature of Samuel Griffiths and
his son Gilbert:

> As both saw it, there had to be higher and higher social orders to
> which the lower social classes could aspire. One had to have castes.
> One was foolishly interfering with and disrupting necessary and un-
> avoidable social standards when one tried to unduly favor any one
> —even a relative. It was necessary when dealing with the classes
> and intelligences below one, commercially or financially, to handle
> them according to the standards to which they were accustomed.
> And the best of these standards were those which help these lower
> individuals to a clear realization of how difficult it was to come by
> money—to an understanding of how very necessary it was for all
> who were engaged in what both considered the only really impor-
> tant constructive work of the world—that of material manufacture
> —to understand how very essential it was to be drilled, and that
> sharply and systematically, in all the details and processes which
> comprise that constructive work. And so to become inured to a
> narrow and abstemious life in so doing. It was good for their char-
> acters. It informed and strengthened the minds and spirits of those
> who were destined to rise. And those who were not should be kept
> right where they were. (p. 196)

It is difficult to imagine a more concise enunciation of the doctrine of social molding within a capitalist framework. However,
Dreiser does not allow this miniscule "negative moment" to
reverberate through the rest of the novel. He carefully places
both Clyde and Roberta, for example, outside or beyond traditional class stratification. Because he is related to the wealthy
Griffiths of Lycurgus, Clyde cannot identify or be identified with
the workers he joins at the factory: they "were not such individuals as he would ordinarily select for companions—far below
bellboys or drivers or clerks anywhere. They were, one and all,
as he could now clearly see, meaty and stodgy mentally and
physically. They wore such clothes as only the most common
laborers would wear" (p. 215). From the opposite perspective,
once this white-collar no-man's-land has been embraced by Clyde,
he immediately experiences a certain awkwardness vis-à-vis Roberta, a worker at the factory, having to pass himself off "as her

brother or cousin . . . in order to avoid immediate scandal" (p. 332).

Roberta's social class is initially less equivocal. She is the daughter of very poor farmers, to whom coming to Lycurgus for factory work already represents a palpable advancement. However, she, like Emma Bovary, her prototype, dreams from a very young age of transcending the boundaries of her class: "So it was that although throughout her infancy and girlhood she was compelled to hear of and share a depriving and toilsome poverty, still, because of her innate imagination, she was always thinking of something better" (p. 269). Thus, to Clyde's "innate" ambition, Roberta offers an "innate" dreamy nature that puts her squarely into the Cinderella mold. It is, in fact, to satisfy this yearning for "something better" that Roberta develops so swiftly an attachment to Clyde: "sensing the superior world in which she imagined he moved . . . [Roberta] was seized with the very virus of ambition and unrest that afflicted him" (p. 275). Thus, Roberta's passion is based, to a large extent, on a falsely imagined notion of Clyde's status, just as Clyde, in the very manner that deceives Walter Dillard, is illegitimately lifted from his class of origin into the Lycurgus aristocracy on the basis of familial relationships.

The real class alliance that exists between Clyde and Roberta is scarcely broached by Dreiser, except when Clyde vaguely wonders "how strange it was that this girl and he, whose origin had been strikingly similar, should have been so drawn to each other in the beginning. Why should it have been?" (p. 464). Eisenstein, on the other hand, will greatly develop a tiny scene from the novel, where Sondra, Clyde, and companions, out for a ride in the country, ask for directions from Roberta's father. In the novel, we are mainly made aware of Clyde's embarrassment, his repulsion at the sight of the dilapidated Alden farmhouse he must approach to get directions. In the scenario, the irony of the chance encounter is emphasized, as well as the magnetic attraction of Clyde for his milieu of origin and, indeed, the very place where his responsibility now lies. What is more, Titus Alden is not in the slightest bit interested in reneging on his own class allegiances. So when Roberta inquires whom he had been speaking to, Alden replies, "I don't know, Bobby. Some rich no-accounts who lost their road" (9,11). Roberta, in fact, much less the romantic status seeker in Eisenstein's version, never forgets her origins and threatens Clyde with a class hatred similar to her father's. While in the novel her letters become simply gloomier and gloomier as her pregnancy progresses, ending with a three-page letter on her loneliness and begging Clyde to write, in the scenario her pregnancy is implicitly presented as a literal shafting of the poor by the wealthy. The response of Eisenstein's Roberta is one of anger rather than of gloom. "You have allowed all this time to pass in silence," she writes to Clyde, "and unless I hear from you before noon Friday all your friends shall know how you have treated me" (9,12).

As may be noticed, the scene of Alden's class hatred is directly followed by Roberta's threatening letter in the scenario (as contrasted with the intervening of a whole chapter in the novel). It is a portion of the script that could well have been subtitled "The Revenge of the Proletariat." In this way Clyde ends up being guilty more of a class betrayal than of murder. Eisenstein maintains and underscores Clyde's own equivocalness as to class allegiance but turns Roberta from a Cinderella into a Marxist Clotho, one of the three daughters of Night. Eisenstein's *American Tragedy* is a story of ties—ties that are broken, maintained, or simply unbreakable. In cutting off Roberta's thread, Clyde is shown to be simultaneously cutting off his own, not because of any moral transgression (since it was an accident) but rather because of a class betrayal that bourgeois society has conned him into committing.

Herein lies the crux of the ideological debate generated between Eisenstein and his precursor text. Dreiser insists throughout *An American Tragedy* on the individualistic values and motives that inform Clyde Griffiths's character. He has an innate ambitiousness, a special, nonanalyzable class position, and hence an individual *hubris* that cannot (in the eyes of American justice) go unpunished. In a fascinating and altogether appropriate conversation between Dreiser and Eisenstein in 1927, Dreiser admitted that he always had and still continued to consider the drama of the individual to be first and foremost, "since only through the individual could the mass and its dreams be sensed and interpreted."[13]

Through a process of generalization, to which ends he exploits specific potentials of the film medium, such as audio-visual montage and bracket syntagmas, Eisenstein transforms Clyde into a type of misguided American *arriviste*, whose only major flaw is to have succumbed to the phony dazzle of social ascendancy and the equally illusory in-between class position. This slight but significant tilt in the presentation of Clyde's history turns Eisenstein's adaptation into a subversive rendering of the original, a true re-creation with a new point and a sharper edge. B. P. Schulberg was therefore not far from the truth when, upon Eisenstein's informing him that according to his version Clyde Griffiths was not guilty, he exclaimed, "But then your script is a monstrous challenge to American society."[14]

In light of this famous quip—itself an emblem of the ethical code underlying nearly all Hollywood production of the 1930s and even after—it might be argued that any novel that calls for adaptation requires a "monstrous" adaptation. Eisenstein pursued only those myths latent in Dreiser's text that would serve his own purpose. Why transpose into film Dreiser's essay-like exposé of the self-made man, if the target is not individual psychology but the ideological bankruptcy of an entire society? Why be faithful to Dreiser's careful obfuscation of class alliances when this challenge is aimed precisely at the contradictions latent in one particular class? Why prohibit this challenge, this monstrosity, from bursting the boundaries prescribed by its precursor?

I would argue, in fact, that the precursor should stand in relation to its adaptation as an acorn to a full-grown tree, or better still, as the principle of a whole species to a mutation of that species. The adaptation must subvert its original, perform a double and paradoxical job of masking and unveiling its source, or else the pleasure it provides will be nothing more than that of seeing words changed into images. Furthermore, the specificities of the new sign system (in this case, cinema) require that

[13] Theodore Dreiser, *Dreiser Looks at Russia* (New York: Horace Liveright, 1928), p. 208.
[14] Eisenstein, *Film Form*, p. 96.

re-production take full cognizance of the change of sign. For it is these specificities that make possible the truly radical re-production: one that exploits the semiotic transformation in order to re-distribute the formative materials of the original and to set them askew. Eisenstein produced a stillborn masterpiece which, if allowed the proper channels of generation, would have brought to light contradictions not only implicit in Dreiser's text but rampant in American society as a whole.

Bibliographical Note. For an account of the obstacles Eisenstein encountered with Paramount in negotiating acceptance of his scenario, see Sergei Eisenstein, *Film Form*, p. 95ff; Harry A. Potamkin, "Novel into Film: A Case Study of Current Practice," *Close-Up*, 8 (December, 1931), pp. 267–279; and Ivor Mantagu, *With Eisenstein in Hollywood*, (New York, 1969), pp. 110–20.

The Great Gatsby (1925), F. Scott Fitzgerald

East Egg on the Face: Gatsby 1949

While *The Great Gatsby* is a limp translation of Fitzgerald's novel about the tasteless twenties, magical mid-Westerners on Long Island, and the champion torch-bearing hero in American literature, it captures just enough of the original to make it worth your while and rekindle admiration for a wonderful book. Its characters are like great lumps of oatmeal maneuvering at random around each other, but it tepidly catches the wistful tragedy of a jilted soldier (Alan Ladd) who climbs the highest mountains of racketeering and becomes an untalented socialite, trying to win back his Daisy (Betty Field) from a hulking snob and libertine (Barry Sullivan). Etched in old MGM-Renaissance style Fitzgerald's panorama of the twenties takes on the heavy, washed-out, inaccurate dedication-to-the-past quality of a Radio City mural. Save for an occasional shot—the rear of a Long Island estate studded with country-club architecture and the bulky town cars—that shrieks of the period, the movie has little to offer of Fitzgerald's glory-struck but acrid perceptions of the period, place, and East Egg society. The cottage scene, with an added touch of Booth Tarkington, talks and moves, as little else of the movie does, with some complication and emotional development.

Editors' title. From "Films," by Manny Farber, *The Nation*, August 13, 1949, p. 162. Reprinted by permission.

Director [Elliott] Nugent's forte is the country-club set tinkling delicately against each other amidst stupified living-room furniture, but it only appears in the scenes at Daisy's and the Plaza, which have a timeless aura and show the leisure class at customary half-mast—summery weather a glitter due to Betty Field's delight with her role, and tasteful, knee-waisted dresses. The crucial lack is that Gatsby, Daisy, the cynical Jordan, don't have enough charm to explain the story; in fact, they don't have much more than the weary hulks that are currently beached on Long Island. Owing to a tired director who, however, knows the book with uncommon shrewdness, and Fitzgerald's inspired dialogue combined with slow, conservative movie images this peculiarly mixed movie draws the most vociferous, uneasy audience response.

It would take a Von Stroheim to cast Fitzgerald's characters, each as fabulous as Babe Ruth, but rendered with the fragmentary touches of a Cezanne watercolor; the cast is routine for Paramount (Ladd, Da Silva, Macdonald Carey—Frank Faylen, a studio perennial, must have been sick) and inspired only in the case of Betty Field, whose uninhibited, morbid-toned art blows a movie apart. Ladd might have solved the role of Gatsby if he had consisted, as his normal role does, of shocking, constant movement, no acting, and trench coats. An electric, gaudily graceful figure in action movies, here he has to stand still and project turbulent feeling, succeeding chiefly in giving the impression of an isinglass baby-face in the process of melting. He seems to be constantly in pain, and this, occasionally, as in the touching cottage scene, coincides with Gatsby's. As a matter of fact, he gives a pretty good impression of Gatsby's depressed, non-public moments. Barry Sullivan streamlines the aging (30) football player ("if we don't look out the white race will be—will be utterly submerged. It's all scientific stuff") into a decent, restless gentleman whose nostrils constantly seem horrified. For a dismal C-Western star, Sullivan is surprisingly deft and subtle in a role that has become meaningless without the sentimentality, fears, and shockingly comic scenes with Myrtle's circle (probably dropped because they were too cinematic).

Betty Field is no more marked by Southern aristocracy than a cheese blintz, but she plays Daisy with her usual incredible

Gatsby (Alan Ladd) and Daisy (Betty Field) share a moment together. The Great Gatsby (1949).

Daisy (Mia Farrow) and Gatsby (Robert Redford) relive their love in flashback. The Great Gatsby (1974).

daring and instinctive understanding. She hits the role (compulsive, musical voice; scared sophistication) so hard, giving Daisy a confused, ineffectual intensity, missing some of the scintillating charm, that her creation is a realistic version of the character Fitzgerald set up simply as a symbol for Gatsby to dream about. The music of the period, when it is played right, is heartbreaking, and Elisha Cook captures this nostalgia for a few minutes at Gatsby's grand piano.

Academic Broadway veteran that he is, Elliott Nugent implies in his direction that the period and terrain—so consistently primary and wondrous to Fitzgerald—are simply a backdrop. In place of the wasteland of ashes that surrounds Wilson's garage, morbidly counterpointing the story's death-ridden conclusion, there are fleeting glimpses of a humdrum dumping ground. The huge, chaotic parties are a dispiriting blur of Arthur Murray dancing, Muzak orchestrations, stock drunks with one individualized detail (the stridently sequined stage twins) in place of the dozen needed to build the atmosphere that draws New York's night life to Gatsby's door. Fitzgerald's broken story structure has been straightened so that the movie flows slowly without break through routine stage sets. In the occasional place where a contrasting shot is slashed into the "Old Man River" development, the strategy, because of its rarity, produces more excitement than the image warrants—the oculist's billboard, with the enormous spectacled eyes, steals the movie.

The Great Gatsby (1925), F. Scott Fitzgerald

Ballantine's Scotch, Glemby Haircuts, White Suits, and White Teflon: Gatsby 1974

BY JANET MASLIN

I still recall vividly the big New York unveiling of Jack Clayton's *The Great Gatsby*. Everyone was there—from Liz Smith to Andy Warhol. And everyone seemed to be having the same reactions. There was a moment when an impeccable Robert Redford turned to face the camera, delivered his first line and then smiled —separating his gestures like an escapee from a Swiss clock— that elicited startled but still vaguely admiring gasps from us all. There was another moment, when Mia Farrow first opened her mouth, that elicited gasps of a different order. Then there was the scene where Sam Waterston and Lois Chiles stopped in the valley of ashes to buy gas from Scott Wilson and it only cost 40 cents to fill their tank; coming as it did in the middle of a collossal fuel crisis, the transaction provoked a reasonably amiable guffaw. But the real laughter was reserved for the latter part of the picture, most notably for the scene in which Farrow and Redford kiss and their images are studiously reflected in a pool stocked with expensive Japanese goldfish. *That* moment launched something noisy enough to qualify as The Snicker Heard 'Round the World.

Big studio previews are usually packed with friends of the studio, who usually lead the applause at screening's end. This time it was hard to hear the ovation, if indeed there even was one, over the din of studio friends exiting before the credits were over. Outside the theater, the pavement was littered with crumpled-up programs that looked as if they'd been thrown rather than dropped. The audience straggled away looking resentful, confused and—above all else—miserably betrayed.

I saw *The Great Gatsby* again two years later in a small, grimy, and underpopulated revival house. And I was surprised to note that, while the opus hadn't exactly improved with age, at least it didn't feel like such an affront any more. For one thing, I was no longer going for blood by making line-by-line comparisons with Fitzgerald's novel. For another, Paramount's promotional hoopla (Ballantine's scotch? Glemby haircuts? White suits? White *teflon*?) was no longer enough of an irritant to obscure the picture's few minor merits. Mia Farrow's performance, while still nightmarish, at least made more sense this time; the edge of hysteria she had tried to lend Daisy might, if better developed, have provided that character with the sense of genuine frustration, and hence the human complexity, that Fitzgerald denied her in the novel. And the film wasn't as sluggish as it had initially seemed; though whatever momentum it did possess was strictly the story-line's doing and certainly not attributable to Francis Ford Coppola's tin-eared screenplay or Clayton's moribund direction. The single most intriguing aspect of the movie remained its maverick stupidity; the film is neither faithful enough to qualify as even a run-of-the-mill screen adaptation, nor is it guided by even the faintest glimmer of adaptive imagination.

The former point can be readily attested to by anyone with an emotional stake in (and an accordingly dog-eared copy of) Fitzgerald's compact, obsessively romantic masterpiece. As for the latter one, it's odd that neither the film's director nor its screenwriter seems, on the evidence of the finished product, to have given much thought to the various adaptive options open to them. They might, for example, have elected to treat the story as psychodrama and stay relatively close to the dynamics of the novel, making up in character what they sacrificed in atmosphere and thus piquing the interest of Fitzgerald devotees. Or they could have gone the all-out glamour route, even if that meant deliberately cheapening their material, suffering a barrage of bad reviews and losing the literati. They could even have stumbled onto a successful approach by coming up with a bad film whose very garishness inadvertently evoked Jazz Age attitudes. In any case, they ultimately opted for nothing more complex than one-note sobriety, committing *Gatsby* to the screen in much the same way that an elegantly boxed corpse is committed to its burial ground.

The Great Gatsby is admittedly a very difficult work to film. It is also, I think, one of the two great American romances, the other being *Gone with the Wind* (1936). The two novels are hardly comparable in terms of styles or quality, but their authors shared a number of similar values and an incontrovertible flair for storytelling. Both works have an extraordinary capacity for engaging their readers' emotions; both are set in tumultuous historical periods and draw cultural tension from geographical polarities—North/South in Margaret Mitchell's case, East/West in Fitzgerald's. Most importantly, both books understand that the eroticism of wealth is a crucial ingredient in American daydreams about love and seduction.

Each novel, of course, also creates a pair of incomparably high-spirited sparring partners whose differences can never be reconciled, couples whose illusions about one another are both their drama and their eventual undoing. Taken on their own, Scarlett, Rhett, Daisy, and Gatsby are all great and singularly American characters—but because Scarlett and Rhett stand out in such sharp counterpoint to their surroundings, they make for great dramatic roles as well. Gatsby and Daisy are more closely interwoven with the culture they inhabit, and as such they make for potentially poor dramatic material, since their efficacy depends almost entirely on how well their surroundings are drawn. The most basic and insidious of the filmed *Gatsby*'s many flaws is thus its absolute failure to create a believable Jazz Age ambience.

The human backdrop of the story, the carousers who come to Gatsby's parties and fritter their lives away, represented (in the novel) a dubious, *nouveau-riche* "Broadway" element, people so brash in their hedonism that they actively offend old-money types like Tom and Daisy. But Clayton clearly misunderstands the character of the guests and the nature of their boozy jubilation: he populates his party scenes with an impossible blend of dusty Newport bluebloods and hyperthyroid New York hoofers. The same two-dozen trained dancers are in the foreground of virtually every mass-revelry shot, yet if you glance behind them you'll make out a wall of immobile, aristocratic stiffs.

And Jazz Age elegance presupposes not just fashion-plate airs but also the inclination to raise hell without worrying about getting one's dress dirty—so when Clayton shoots a tableful of guests sitting primly at a party, each one carefully enunciating his or her remark in turn, he demolishes the whole feeling of an era in only fifteen seconds. Worst of all, even *Gatsby*'s stylishness winds up working against it, as the characters positively suffocate in their coordinated pastels. It's too pretty, stultifyingly so, and seventies-pretty at that; *Gatsby*'s brand of airless affluence is so anachronistic that whatever social commentary Clayton may have set out to make is lost in a flurry of voile and tulle. The picture has a cold, narcissistic beauty, admiring its own image without any real sense of enjoyment.

Clayton's ideas about the women who prompt the plot's romantic machinations only add to the pervasive chill. Farrow's Daisy is as dry as a dowager, with a voice about two octaves higher than the "thrilling murmur" Fitzgerald so lovingly described. (The basic unattractiveness of Farrow's screechy, brittle-wigged Daisy makes Nick, who is expected to cast admiring glances her way throughout their first few scenes together, seem all the more nonsensical.) And Farrow, unlike the somewhat underrated Redford, is unable to deliver her character's most famous lines casually; instead she gives her readings a *Bartlett's Book of Familiar Quotations* ring, forever pausing in search of the right word when the audience knows full well what that word will be. Still, she is the most bearable, even the most sympathetic of the story's three central women; if Lois Chiles's Jordan is no livelier than a mannequin, Karen Black's repellent Myrtle unfortunately fills the breach. Black is at fever pitch in a role that doesn't demand even half the histrionics, and Clayton's idea of helping her out involves accentuating the sweat on her upper lip (this is *Gatsby's* closest brush with sensuality), muting the background sound during her embarrassingly breathy monologue about first meeting Tom and, on one ignominious occasion, having her smash her hand through a window and then enthusiastically suck her own blood. None of the three, who give far worse performances than their male counterparts, seems to have been given any idea of how she fit into the film's overall scheme.

Mia Farrow violently overreacts to Clayton's and Coppola's reshaping of Gatsby's entire obsession around the dubious (and certainly incomprehensible, at least for the audience) force of Daisy's allure. In their hands, Gatsby's unattainable dream becomes literal, earthbound, and sometimes (as when Redford is seen flexing his fist in the direction of the Buchanans' green light across the bay) just plain silly. The photo in Gatsby's bedroom is now of Daisy, not of his bourgeois mentor Dan Cody; Gatsby's romanticism has been cut down from a grand illusion to simple unrequited love.

To see what the film does to perhaps the book's greatest passage is to weep: Gatsby's "wed[ding] his unutterable visions to Daisy's perishable breath" as he "saw that the blocks of the sidewalks really formed a ladder . . . to a secret place above the trees" has been reduced to a simple ten-second flashback of a kiss, including a voice-over of Farrow whispering "I love you, Jay." Taken at face value, such moments suggest that Daisy alone, rather than the whole set of values she has come to represent, has been enough to drive Gatsby to scale such dizzying capitalist heights. And taking these touches literally is almost inevitable, because Clayton seems every bit as awestruck by Gatsby's opulence as the character is himself. He turns his star filter on every available scrap of silver or crystal, and his reverence lingers on even after Gatsby is gone. The boys who defile Gatsby's mansion after his murder scrawl their obscenities in the neatest, most respectful manner imaginable.

Never lending the film a discernible viewpoint of their own, Clayton and Coppola compound the problem by doing away with that of Nick Carraway, through whose eyes Fitzgerald's story was originally filtered. First of all, Nick is robbed of his engaging stodginess (when the Gatsby of the novel tells Nick about sealing—or decreeing—his own fate with that one irrevocable kiss in Louisville, Nick silently condemns his friend's "appalling sentimentality" yet is "reminded of something—an elusive rhythm, a fragment of lost words, that [he] had heard somewhere a long time ago.") Even worse, Fitzgerald's wry, level-headed narrator has been turned into something of a portentous windbag. Coppola's three-week-wonder of a script demonstrates an appalling insensitivity to normal speech patterns, forcing Nick and others to stumble over descriptive passages from the novel that were never meant to be delivered in conversation.

The screenplay is worse than merely clumsy; it deals the film a death-blow by making an excruciating miscalculation. Coppola pieced together details about Daisy's and Gatsby's early courtship, added a "Kiss me" or an "I love the way you love me" here and there, and slapped together a series of interchanges we were never meant to see. The novel very deliberately avoids invading the couple's privacy, once they have been reunited, and it does so for reasons more important than mere tact. The whole point, the whole agonizing irreconcilability of the story, grows out of the fact that Daisy and Gatsby never do understand one another—they *can't*. Daisy is an icon to her lover, not a real woman; she herself is so ethereally drawn that it's hard to imagine what Gatsby means to her, except perhaps some vaguely bitter memory of a chance not taken. But whatever they see in one another, they don't see eye to eye; their accounts of the reunion, if stated, would certainly and tragically differ. Yet Coppola makes the incredible gaffe of trying to objectify these moments, of trying to satisfy his audience's voyeurism instead of acknowledging the lovers' heartbreaking misapprehensions.

Filling in those blanks may have been more of a business decision than an aesthetic one; audiences don't come to see an airy, expensive love story without expecting an airy, expensive clinch or two. But the change completely violates the novel, and the only consoling thing about it is that it doesn't work. Redford and Farrow never for one minute give the impression of being in love, and that's the film's single most astonishing shortcoming.

When the two of them run off conspiratorially during a huge gala, Clayton fills the moment with absurd sexual innuendo, even though Farrow is so overdressed it's impossible to imagine her taking off that diamond headgear for the sake of a mere tryst. The book handles the same moment infinitely more gently; we sense that the two of them have already tacitly re-established their physical relationship, and that they're so close all they really *need* to do right then is talk.

Ordinarily, when a novel is adapted for the screen, readers of the book have a slight edge over patrons who have simply wandered in off the street; if you've read the book, you can overcome some of the movie's inadequacies by filling in details from memory. *The Great Gatsby* expects the viewer to do a little legwork—how does Nick know the oculist is called Dr. T. J. Eckleburg, for instance, when half the billboard bearing his name is rotted away in the name of Atmosphere? But the film doesn't play fair with the viewer's instinct to fill in the blanks; it falls back on the text whimsically, unevenly, expecting the audience's help, yet playing havoc with its sense of the original meaning. Crucial images linger on, but with a slightly distorted import; in the film, the green light across the bay still exists as a symbol of Gatsby's indefatigable vision, but it has also been turned into a ring that he gives to Daisy, that Daisy then returns to him, and that Gatsby wears when he dies. Whatever else that little alteration may hint at, it certainly suggests that Coppola and Clayton sorely needed some guiding beacon of their own.

The Sun Also Rises (1926), Ernest Hemingway

Photography Does Not a Movie Make

BY PHILIP ROTH

Outside the movie a girl walked by. I looked at her, she smiled and we went across the street to the bar and sat down.

"Pernod," she said to the waiter. She did not look like a *poule* to me. She had good teeth and a gliding way about her that made me think of Willie Pep.

"You saw the movie*?" she asked. The waiter brought her a bottle of Bud. She did not make a fuss and I liked her for it.

"Yes," I said.

"Was it good?"

A good movie for me is a movie you feel good after and a bad movie a movie you feel bad after.

"It was a disappointing movie." I didn't like to say it so I reached out and touched her shoulder. "I'm sorry," I said.

"Are you sure? In *Time* they said it was a good movie. They said it was a very good movie."

She was the first street-walker I'd ever met who read *Time*. I told her this and she said there were others.

"We read it for the *People* section," she said. "It's what we have instead of God."

* *The Sun Also Rises* (1957).

From *The New Republic*, Vol. 137, No. 15, September 30, 1957. Reprinted by the permission of The New Republic, © 1957, The New Republic, Inc.

"*Time* was wrong," I said. "They thought because it was serious it was good. They get confused about that. The movie is disappointing."

"Why?" she said, "The photography, it is not gratifying?"

"It is gratifying," I said, "But photography does not a movie make." I remembered some poetry from college.

"Then tell me why?" she said.

"The picture talks a lot, and that is not so hot. That kind of dialogue on the screen winds up in long pregnant silences followed by dime-store philosophy followed by long pregnant silences. Until they get to Spain it is a bad conversation piece. It is very slow until Spain."

"And in Spain?"

"It was very fast."

"That is bad?"

"It is very exciting. The festival of the bulls is fast and colorful and good. And there was some acting to admire. Errol Flynn is funny and good, though he appears to be gaining weight. And Eddie Albert, though he has only a little to do, is good too. They play Mike Campbell and Billy Gorton. And the bull-fighter, Romero, he convinced me."

"In *Time* they say that the man who plays the matador used to own a garment factory."

"That is important to know," I said.

"And what of Tyrone Power and Ava?"

"He is not so bad. When anyone mentions Brett's name his brow furrows and a light bulb flashes on over his head, but aside from that he is not too bad. Ava is not too good. Sometimes she resembles The Snow Queen and other times Ann Rutherford in *Andy Hardy*. Lady Brett is a nice person to think about, but to see her is something else. Maybe some people cannot be shown on the screen."

"And these people, they are *lost*?" She was a very interested *poule* but not earnest.

"They say they are. But they do not seem lost to me. They all have nice clothes and money. And they do not seem upset about America. They don't seem to be expatriates. I thought it had all been a little seedier."

"But Jake has this wound—" the *poule* began.

"That's tough all right," I said, "but not seedy."

She took it for a pun. "You are a hard man."

"What the hell," I said, "what the hell."

We looked at each other's eyes for a while; it turned out there was not much to say about this movie.

Finally I said, "It does say some things about sex."

The *poule* swayed in her chair. "Sex?"

"Yes, all those bulls and horns, and Jake's wound, and Brett. And the boy-faced girl-faced bullfighter. You know," I said.

"Yes."

I knew she knew.

"That sex is good?" she said.

"No," I said, "that it is with us."

"It is," she said.

I waited until she'd finished her third bottle of Bud before I told her about the end of the picture; I wanted to make it easy for her.

"At the end they go away together, Brett and Jake. They are riding in a cab and she says, 'Jake, there must be a way for us,' and after a minute Jake says, 'There is, somewhere.'"

"What is it?" the *poule* demanded, spilling beer on to her middy front. She was turning into a sloppy *poule*.

"It's not sex," I said. "It's something else."

For all the beer, she moved in on me like a good welterweight. "What?"

I answered, "The sun also rises, and the sun goes down . . . "

We left it at that.

Finally she looked up. "I hear they are filming *A Farewell to Arms*," she said.

"I know."

"It will have Rock Hudson," she looked up hopefully; it was a drunk's kind of hope. "Maybe it will be better?"

Someone came into the bar and from across the street I could hear silver clinking on the box office window.

"Yes," I said, "isn't it pretty to think so."

Brett Ashley (Ava Garner) and Jake Barnes (Tyrone Power) enjoy the sunlight on the eve of World War I. **The Sun Also Rises (1957).**

Dodsworth (1929), Sinclair Lewis

The Virtues of Unfaithfulness

BY ALBERT J. LAVALLEY

Dodsworth, Sinclair Lewis's best-selling novel of 1929, reached the screen in 1936. What differences exist between novel and film are mostly explained by an intermediate play version of 1934, written primarily by the playwright and screenwriter Sidney Howard, but with some assistance from Lewis himself. For reasons of clarity, it is perhaps wisest to take up the themes, special emphases, and achievements of each version in the order in which they appeared.

I

Dodsworth, the novel, represents a turning point for the Lewis of *Main Street, Babbitt,* and *Arrowsmith:* both with a broader theme (the American confrontation with Europe) and a growing adherence to mainline American values (American idealism, naturalness, and the American business world are good things when contrasted to the artificially, hypocrisy, and slowness of Europe). In letting Dodsworth confront Europe, Lewis was opting for a vision of Jamesian breadth and scope and aiming to rewrite in his own way books like Mark Twain's *Innocents Abroad* and James's *The American* or *The Ambassadors.* In Lewis's version the American would still be a "hick" of sorts, but

272

ultimately he would possess the requisite energy and wisdom to judge Europe—to make use of it to grow, but not to be stymied and put down by its judgments against him.

For his American, Lewis once again turned to the mid-Western businessman from his fictional Zenith, but this time he labeled him "not a Babbitt." Sam Dodsworth, an aging and recently retired automotive designer and manufacturer, has the naturalness of many of his businessman friends (who often do appear to be Babbitts), but he is never really crude or vulgar like them. He does appreciate culture; it is only the pretensions of culture he dislikes. His basic American energy and honesty shine through at every point. Even his retirement from business stems from a desire to experience new worlds, to widen his horizons, to know himself better.

The conservatism that manifests itself in Lewis's writing with the appearance of *Dodsworth* derives from the very self-sufficiency that Lewis finds heroic in his businessman. Dodsworth is taken aback and confused by Europe. Yet ultimately, in tapping his own resources with the aid of a newer kind of woman, the liberated and supportive Edith Cortwright, he discovers dormant energies that propel him to return to America. Back in his native land, he will dedicate himself to a future technology: high quality, indigenous American-style suburban housing, and the production of motor homes and campers.

Dodsworth is less fully dramatized than previous Lewis novels mainly because of a lack of distance between Lewis and his protagonist. In the Mencken-inspired satires of *Main Street*, *Babbitt*, and *Elmer Gantry*, Lewis achieved a measure of distance through satire and irony, but in *Dodsworth* he freely gave himself over to his protagonist, letting him muse at length about the issues of business, work, aesthetic pleasure, Europe, marriage, aging, and national manners and customs. Lewis freely poured into the novel his memories of European travel and his judgments of Europe, pro and con. The novel is really a picture of Dodsworth's and Lewis's mind, embracing a great variety of weighty questions, pondering them and validating its own depth and naturalness simply by being willing to face these questions openly and honestly.

By contrast, Dodsworth's wife Fran, in her narrow-minded way, illustrates both the worst fears of the American when he confronts Europe (that he or she is uncultured and vulgar) and the worst fulfillment of all those fears: she becomes a parody of European style, all surface pretension and manners. While she often feels she is "European" in her judgment of Sam's American ways, she is ultimately rejected by Europe far more than Sam is. Europe, in fact, becomes her self-destruction. (On this level, the novel is also a not-too-concealed polemic against Lewis's wife Grace. It is said that at rehearsals of the play, Lewis kept calling "Fran" Gracie.)

The limited perspective of the Lewis-Dodsworth viewpoint and the portrayal of Fran both often defeat the dramatic mode of the novel. Certain key scenes which we would expect—and which the play and movie supply—are missing, to be replaced by Dodsworth's musings about them. And dramatically, Lewis has trouble conceiving a humanized Fran. Occasionally Dodsworth attempts to understand the psychological and social causes of her behavior, but no evidence of any complexity to her behavior exists when she appears in the novel. Her function is to bitch and whine and to demean Dodsworth. Furthermore, Fran is traitorous, lying, and deceptive about her affairs. But Dodsworth's behavior is beyond reproach; only after intense loneliness and humiliation does he slip into a brief affair with a bohemian artist's model and he conducts his relationship with Edith Cortwright with circumspect dignity.

Despite its classic reputation, *Dodsworth* is not a very satisfying novel. To readers today it is apt to appear remote in theme and dated in subject matter. Written just before the Crash and the Depression, it speaks of issues appropriate to the twenties, fresh from contact with Europe in World War I and still weighing that experience. There is no inkling, as there is in the early novels of Steinbeck and Dos Passos, of the social upheaval to come. Nor is there any sense of new values or new aesthetic forms that we find in the expatriate writers like Hemingway and Stein, who chose Europe as a place to live and write. Aesthetically, the novel is traditionalist and also seriously flawed: major scenes and confrontations are unrealized, and the novel wobbles

Fran Dodsworth (Ruth Chatterton) and her husband Sam (Walter Huston) in a tense moment in their boudoir. **Dodsworth** *(1936).*

uncomfortably between long private ruminations of Dodsworth and a detached description of the action. Its much vaunted increase in scope finally seems dubious too; the European background is rather willfully inserted. Sometimes the pages sound like Baedecker in thin disguise. Minor characters are often nothing more than sounding boards for Dodsworth or proponents of a point of view; their dialogue often turns into speeches —for which they usually apologize after having delivered them. Finally, the consistently crude anti-Semitism of the book seems to point to a narrowness of judgment that pervades all its moral issues. *Dodsworth* is at its best when Lewis and Dodsworth openly confront their own ambiguities; unfortunately, this is not as frequent as one would like.

II

Sidney Howard's adaptation of *Dodsworth* for both the stage and screen is a surprising improvement over the original. Howard, one of the best American playwrights of the twenties and thirties, was in awe of Lewis's talents as a novelist. And he tended to downgrade his own work as satisfactory only as vehicles for actors, not as serious contributions to drama. (Perhaps the modest role was willed because of the weighty reputation of his contemporary O'Neill.) Howard's judgment on the play *Dodsworth* was that it was decent enough, but that the novel was far better.[1]

In an introduction to the printed version of the play in 1934, he states that "the screen (and let no master of director's touches tell me otherwise) is virtually incapable of comment or implication and both comment and implication are important aspects of good novel writing." Consequently, he tells us, though he wanted the scope of the novel, a "panorama of two Americans in

[1] *Dodsworth* was not Howard's first contact with Lewis's writing. He had written the screenplay of *Arrowsmith* for Samuel Goldwyn's production of the movie, which was directed by John Ford in 1930. Howard received the screenwriting Oscar that year for his work on the film. His experience with *Arrowsmith* had not dimmed his desire to do *Dodsworth* but it had altered his expectations.

Europe," what he felt he achieved was considerably less, "a marital journey's end in dramatic form."

What greatness the play possessed he saw stemming from its main actors, Walter Huston as Sam Dodsworth, Fay Bainter as Fran, and Huston's wife, Nan Sunderland, as Edith Cortwright. Ironically, despite all his admiration and praise for Lewis's writing, Howard went directly to the heart of the novel's problems with his solutions in dramatizing it. He knew he had to find a way of introducing Edith Cortwright earlier and building her character. Howard also knew that Fran's affair with the slick European financier, Arnold Israel,[2] had to be dramatized and not just told in letters. Howard found ways to conquer these structural and dramatic flaws (without ever admitting that *Dodsworth* the novel could have been better served by firmer architectonics) and the resulting scenes are the core of the play and film.

Sam's meeting with Edith Cortwright takes place on the boat to Europe, and their discreet and open relationship contrasts sharply with Fran's flirtation with Clyde Lockert, which Howard has moved ahead from England to the ship. (The movie uses some clever crosscutting to underline the contrast. Sam's meeting with Edith is set on deck where he watches for Bishop's Light with boyhood excitement and ingenuousness and where the magical Mrs. Cortwright emerges from the shadows of her deck chair to recommend a soothing stout; meanwhile below deck, Fran coyly flirts with Lockert.) Howard's other key scenes, none of which have a foundation in the book, are: Fran's birthday party where Arnold Israel makes his approach to her and after which she quarrels openly with Sam for the first time; the triangle scene in which Dodsworth confronts Fran and Israel and gets her back; and the interview of Fran by her lover Kurt's regal mother (Maria Ouspenskaya in both play and film) which brings the dissolution of her hopes to marry Kurt. The only major sequence in both novel and play is Kurt's wooing of Fran and her subsequent confrontation with Sam when he realizes that divorce

[2] Interestingly, in the movie version, Arnold Israel's name is changed—probably by Samuel Goldwyn—to Arnold Iselin, and his Jewishness is left unclear.

is the next step. Thus Howard had supplied all the major scenes which Lewis had hinted at or reported but left in a sketchy dramatic shape.

Elsewhere Howard followed the principle of "dramatizing by equivalent," as he liked to call it. One instance would stand for many actions in the novel, one character for a host of minor characters. As Lewis pointed out in his part of the introduction to the play, Howard had invented one of *Dodsworth's* best scenes in the comic yet poignant moment when Sam finds himself out of place in his own house, now occupied by his daughter and son-in-law. His liquor cabinet key is in the hands of his absent son-in-law, his humidor is used to grow bulbs, and a jigsaw puzzle clutters his desk. Though he reacts with anger, we find him likeable because we understand his reasons. And even the anger modulates into a good-humored argument about the Chicago fire in the jigsaw puzzle. In the novel, a great number of scenes are used to convey the same insight: a visit to Yale to see his old classmates at their reunion, a nonproductive talk with his son (absent from the play and film); a morning with his daughter in which he sees that he plays no part in her life; a futile visit to the new automotive president; and finally, a painful tour through his empty house. Howard's one scene hints at the underlying poignance but does not bog down in Lewis's lugubriousness; its rich comedy suggests a deeper and more resilient Sam Dodsworth. Moreover, Howard does not feel as much need as Lewis does to proselytize or to justify Dodsworth's Americanism; his Sam Dodsworth is mellower and more attractive than Lewis's.

Beyond streamlining the action and building it more firmly, and softening the character of Dodsworth, Howard also intensified and centralized a theme that is subordinate in the novel: the process of aging. Such a theme is in keeping with the increased realism of the Broadway stage of the thirties and helps to make *Dodsworth* a more universal as well as an unusual Hollywood film. Dodsworth shows how to face his years with dignity and new energy, while the vain Fran, by contrast, is intent on hiding her age and her status as grandmother. As the play and film progress, her ruses become desperate and artificial, and finally turn her into a grotesque. Ghastly hats, smeared and messy cold cream, the too cute wrinkling of her nose, and other affected mannerisms only ruthlessly accentuate what she is trying to hide. At the end of each affair, her tragic empty face betrays the terrible reality.

III

On the whole, the film version of *Dodsworth* follows the text of the play fairly closely, apart from a few obvious censorship-caused omissions (Fran's refusal to let Dodsworth into her room has more explanation in the play and seems less sudden). It was Samuel Goldwyn's habit to be as faithful as possible to the major plays he purchased for production; Goldwyn stood for big production, Hollywood gloss, but he was respected for quality and some homage to culture. Consequently he was able to hire the best writers to work for him: Ben Hecht and Charles MacArthur, Robert Sherwood, Lillian Hellman, Sidney Howard. William Wyler was virtually Goldwyn's house director; he could be expected not to tamper with the product. His famed perfectionism was often spent on small touches, never on the major alteration of a play nor on a strong interpretation that would suggest a personal *auteur* like Lubitsch, say, with *The Merry Widow* (1934). His general attitude to the material was respectful of the themes of the play and its characters. The many small touches were fused into a personal style, though of a very detached sort. Wyler's European origins gave him an elegance of attitude, and this, coupled with Howard's clarity and mellowness, further softened Lewis's crudeness. Wyler's *Dodsworth* has an almost Jamesian tone—at once elegiac, comic, and rich—yet it never compromises on the robust Americanism of its main character. The grand production values of a Goldwyn movie, reflected in the vast sets which often dwarf the players, here seem to befit the material rather than to overpower it. They offer suggestions of a rich European backdrop, often falsely romantic projections of Fran's daydreams, a layer of idealization over a grim reality.

Walter Huston's Dodsworth might seem amiss here, but Wyler's respect for actors allows him full play—even when he clashes in his robust vigor and natural movements with the stylized elegance of the sets. Already an archetype of American individualism, integrity, and nobility with folksiness from his title role in *Abraham Lincoln* (1930) for Griffith and his populist bank president for Capra in *American Madness* (1932), Huston found in Dodsworth the perfect part that allowed him to express his age, energy, good humor, dignity, strength, and depth. His memorable performance also shows the strength of Howard's fine characterization compared to the novel.

What Sidney Howard did not improve over the book—and what the movie perpetuates—is a deficient view of Fran, played in the film by Ruth Chatterton. Occasionally we get glimmers of a desperation suggesting a tragic and futile life, in which marriage has never fulfilled her energies. But these are only glimmers. As in a much later study, *Sunset Boulevard* (1950), no attempt is made to understand the different social and sexual expectations that confront an aging woman. For the mature successful man, an Edith Cortwright is ready in the wings. But for the woman growing older, an Arnold Iselin or a Kurt is there as long as the affair remains frivolous—and perhaps funded by the husband's money. Neither as play or film does *Dodsworth* explore this theme, and so it remains melodramatic in its conception of Fran. She is on the whole a vain, chattering, pretentious woman who will not accept her age. She is the villain of the piece and we are meant to hate her.

As in most melodramas, events happen too quickly toward the end and while they satisfy certain expectations, they go against the dominant grain of realism in the film. *Dodsworth*'s weakest moments occur near the finale, and here they appear to be a result of too hurried a need to tidy matters up, a problem with the screenplay that Wyler cannot gloss over. Edith Cortwright (Mary Astor in the film) seems to shift to too submissive a role once Sam has proposed to her, and Sam's renewal of energy, symbolized by an out-of-the-blue idea for a Moscow-to-Seattle airline, are so sudden as to be funny. Even Edith incredulously cries "Moscow to Seattle?" But Sam has been renewed by Edith —or so we are meant to feel. His American business energy has been rekindled; he has just equipped Edith's picturesque skiff with an outboard motor and taught the peasant Italian who sails it how to operate it. (Typically, the Italian can't understand how to get the hang of it and Sam has to mime the word "choke" by seemingly strangling him. American energy is linked to machines, progress, and power.) Sam has bigger ideas that are soaring; airlines replace the novel's solution of motor homes and suburban tracts to which he dedicates himself.

We are apt to whoop with glee when Dodsworth tells Fran that love has to stop short of suicide and walks off the ship bound for America to rejoin Edith. Yet on a deeper level we feel the whole argument has been too quickly set up. The sudden intrusion of a flashy style of quick cutting between lines in the argument while passengers rush madly in the background suggests something is being over-orchestrated. Only in Fran's tragic scream, "He's going ashore," punctuated by the departing ship's whistle, do we get a sense of her tragic abandonment and desperation.

The following final shots of the movie are also a banality and have no equivalent in either novel or play: Dodsworth approaches on the motorized skiff, his wife's departing ship shown in the background. A low-angle shot of Edith waving hysterically moves to cutting back and forth as the camera zooms in on Edith. Again the romantic pitch seems to satisfy even as it embarrasses us. Wyler felt the shots were a discreet substitute for the traditional embrace at the end—and the departing vessel in the background *is* a nice and subtle touch.

These faults—traditional to many Hollywood movies of the thirties—are easy to overlook in *Dodsworth* because the realistic core of the film has been so carefully articulated. Here the birthday party in Paris for Fran and the triangle scene with Iselin, Dodsworth, and Fran go far to give the movie its rich sense of depth. Though theatrical in the strong emphasis on dialogue and the blocked-out positions the actors take, these two scenes seem to be innovative cinema too. There is the clear mark, particularly in the party sequence, of something fresh in American film.

Partly it is the adult subject matter that accounts for this. Fran is slipped a note by Iselin in contrast to Edith and Sam's open and proper friendship. Edith warns Fran about the affair and even spars humorously with her about aging. Then, to our surprise, the scene doesn't end, but Sam and Fran go to their bedroom, proceed to undress before the camera and walk around in their underclothes and nightclothes. Fran's grotesque costume gives way to even more ghastly cold cream; Dodsworth is revealed for his true age. Gradually the pleasantry of the party yields to the scarcely concealed antagonisms and bitterness it had contained. Fran and Sam quarrel loudly, and Fran finally succeeds in sending Dodsworth home alone while she and Madame de Penable—and, of course, Arnold—plan to go to a Swiss villa. The unpleasant effects of aging and marital quarrels were not the traditional fare of Hollywood films. But it is the way in which the scene is filmed that takes us by surprise and is still breathtaking today.

Here André Bazin's arguments for the increased power of depth of focus and the long take seem to have their legitimacy. While it is true that Wyler cuts quite often in the scene, he usually returns to a master long shot of the action. This is saved from being merely photographed theater by his subtle placing of characters to echo their antagonisms, a true prelude to the later Wyler works with Gregg Toland on *The Little Foxes* (1941) and *The Best Years of Our Lives* (1946) and to the Toland-Welles photography and mise-en-scène in *Citizen Kane* (1941). While Fran and Sam argue, one character remains in the foreground and another recedes to the opposite end of the room, always in clear focus and often the dominant figure in the shot.

While Bazin was right in seeing that this abetted a certain realism, we are also intensely aware of the highly stylized nature of the scene, a sense of its deliberate orchestration and significance. Dodsworth's profile in the foreground will be one moment all dark to accentuate a light Fran in the background, where a moment ago another lighting scheme prevailed. The final touching long shot of the sequence—Dodsworth walking in his robe somberly across the darkened living room, illuminated by a shaft of light from the bedroom, and going to the phone to book passage home—is also highly orchestrated.

In fact, Wyler's "realism" is also an elegant "stylism," and it is this kind of shaping of 1930s conventional theater, part drawing-room comedy and part social realism, that makes the movie significant and different from the play. The richness of suggestion is conveyed through a carefully calculated mise-en-scène that is foreign to the thirties Broadway theater from which the play emanates.

Much of the deep-focus photography seems to be an answer to avoiding the play's confinement while supplying an alternative to opening it out, since respect for the play's text is always present. Some of the deep-focus scenes are obviously a bit mechanical or merely decorative and spatial, but others enrich the texture and themes of the film. A bravura moment features the use of a mirror at the left of the frame in which Fran appears after leaving the couch where Kurt is wooing her, and exiting to the right. The elegant second frame around her befits the false glamour of the moment and its treachery. The lighting often has a bravura touch too: *e.g.*, the wonderful scene with Kurt's mother in which a cross on her bosom goes alternately light and dark as she breathes. Gradually we see what a hostile force her old world religion is to Fran. (Wyler subtly changes the text here by keeping Kurt present while his mother denounces Fran; the pain of both Fran and Kurt is excruciating.)

The opening-out of the play that movies traditionally provide occurs only in brief interludes between the major scenes, some of which are conventional, and a few of which are memorable. Particularly touching is Dodsworth's departure from Fran at the railroad station after they have agreed to divorce. For the second time the movie uses the book's much overused line "Did I remember to tell you today that I adore you?" Wyler's restraint pays off. He films the scene from Dodsworth's eyes on the train as Fran recedes in view on the platform and uses subtle plaintive music to underline it. A final shot after we think the sequence is over shows Fran falling into the comfort of Kurt's arms. We did not realize he was there; and we are only too aware of how alone Dodsworth is.

Elsewhere the film streamlines the play further. The long opening sequence of Dodsworth's retirement is encapsulated in a few shots. Dodsworth, his back to us as he looks out of his grand office at a large Deco sign of the automotive works; a newspaper headline about the sale of the business highlighted by a ray of sunlight from a raised blind; another back shot of Dodsworth walking among his employees who clearly admire him; and finally a frontal shot of Dodsworth alone in the back of his car with the factory receding out the rear window.

On the whole, however, Wyler seems to have had no over-reaching conception he wished to imprint on the play. At best, one might say that his style tends to deepen and enrich its themes and humanize its characters; there is a poignance here that one does not feel in the play text and to which isolated film shots of Sam sitting alone in cafés and in the rain contribute. (It was Wyler, characteristically, who tried to soften Ruth Chatterton's portrayal of Fran; she quarreled fiercely with him and appears to have won.)

For many years the film *Dodsworth* was little seen, its reputation eclipsed by other Goldwyn projects that seemed more ambitious in scope. In the early seventies the Los Angeles County Museum of Art rediscovered *Dodsworth* and placed it among the fifty great American films they had selected for a retrospective. Soon many people were talking about it. Though innovative and rich for the history of film, whether *Dodsworth* is a masterpiece is probably debatable. It is certainly a key film of the 1930s—a happy conjunction of big studio production values, serious adult themes, excellent ensemble playing, and directorial and photographic artistry. *Dodsworth* is also clearly an important statement about the myths of America in late thirties films, part of that general reexamination of American roots and energies and a growing awareness of American character that marks many of the late thirties films, particularly those of Frank Capra. In *Dodsworth* we encounter, as we do in Capra's work, an ideal American type. Unlike Jefferson Smith or Mr. Deeds, however, Dodsworth does not become polemical nor does he keep nudging us about his significance as an ideal type. His battle is not with mammoth external villains—big city machines and corrupt politics—but with his own loneliness, isolation, and ideals. Fran and the corrupt Europeans are indeed villains, but not in the grand Capra tradition. If Fran poses an obstacle to Sam's growth, it is in the terms of an inner test between his own resourceful energies and his twenty-year loyalty to a woman he feels the need to protect. Dodsworth offers us the picture of the typical American conquering his limits and doubts and filled with powerful energies of renewal. It was a spirit that was soon to carry America through a major war. At the same time, it is hard not to see in *Dodsworth* the brief crystallization of a unified moment. In five years a more troubled American "ideal businessman" would appear in the figure of Welles's Kane. *Dodsworth* points ahead to certain troubling aspects in that figure, and the movie seems to forecast aspects of its long-take and deep-focus style. At the same time, *Dodsworth* clearly hearkens back to its 1929 source and roots its ideal type in a more halcyon era.

Little Caesar (1929), W. R. Burnett

Rico Rising: Little Caesar
Takes Over the Screen

BY GERALD PEARY

Little Caesar was the first novel of W. R. Burnett, who was later to write *High Sierra* (1940), *The Asphalt Jungle* (1949), and other gangland classics during a prolific career. The book was researched and written in the harsh and snowy winter of 1928 in Chicago, where Burnett had migrated from his native Ohio—also the fictional birthplace of his protagonist, Rico Bandello. At the time, as Burnett explained in his preface to the novel, "Capone was King. Corruption was rampant. Big Bill Thompson, the mayor, was threatening to punch King George of England in the 'snoot.' Gangsters were shooting each other all over town."

Burnett began to read articles on crime for his book, including a volume of sociology from the University of Chicago Press. "In this coldly factual survey, I came across an account of the rise and fall of the Sam Cardinelli gang. This account served as the nucleus for the novel that was originally called *The Furies*." The temporary title, far too literary, was replaced by another in a mystical moment reminiscent of that dreary November night described in Mary Shelley's *Frankenstein*. "Rico, the leading figure, began to take on nightmare proportions. . . . I was afraid I was giving birth to a monster. But then a consoling thought

286

came to me. . . . [M]y leading figure, Rico Bandello, killer and gangleader, was no monster at all, but merely a little Napoleon, a little Caesar."

The movie of *Little Caesar* was, at its release by Warner Brothers in 1930, an instant popular success. "Doors Are Smashed at Strand in Rush to See Gang Film" headlined a story in the New York *Daily Mirror*, which explained how "Police reserves were summoned last night when a crowd of 3,000 persons stormed the doors of the Warner Brothers Strand Theater." *Little Caesar* surpassed the previously record financial fortunes of Warner Brothers' 1928 *The Lights of New York* and Paramount's 1927 *Underworld* and every other gangster movie produced to that time. Surely the first reason for its contemporary popularity was that audiences in 1930 attended the picture with Al Capone in mind. Edward G. Robinson had reached fame by playing a thinly disguised version of Capone in the 1928 Broadway play *The Racket*. According to Chicago Judge John Lyle in *The Dry and Lawless Years* (1960), "Scarface was . . . 5 feet 8 inches, 190 pounds. He had a large flabby face with thick lips and coarse features. His nose was flat; his brows dark and shaggy, and a bullet-shaped head was supported by a short thick neck." All in all, a passable description of Robinson.

Yet Burnett had *not* based his primary story of Rico Bandello on Capone but on the exploits of the obscure Cardinelli gang. Still, Capone's dynamic presence crossed into the novel through Burnett's characterization of the Big Boy. For Burnett, his crude, unnamed Big Boy is an oversized animal, a bull in the china shop, who has held to his lower-class crudities while moving up to take over Chicago. In the novel: "The Big Boy sat opposite . . . his derby on the side of his head, and his huge fists which had swung a pick in a section gang, lying before him . . ." "The Big Boy . . . stood leaning his huge hairy paws on the table." "The Big Boy put his head back and brayed." Burnett's Big Boy is a parvenu, a pretender to culture. "'See that picture over there?' He pointed to an imitation Velasquez. 'That baby set me back one hundred and fifty berries.'"

In the movie *Little Caesar*, a major switch occurs. The Big Boy is turned into a refined upper class gangleader, with the uncouth qualities all pushed over to Rico. Big Boy is played by poised and polished Sidney Blackmer, a gentleman all the way. When he transports Rico to his mansion for one tiny scene (Rico's sole glimpse of the "power elite"!), he also points to a fancy painting on the wall. "That cost me $15,000," he says. The price of the painting is much higher than in the novel, the vulgar talk about "berries" is eliminated, and there is no indication that the painting is fake. The movie Big Boy possesses refined artistic taste, and his talk of prices is only to bedazzle the gloating, ever-materialistic Rico.

The Blackmer character never needs to struggle the way Rico (or the novel's Big Boy) had to. In social status, he begins at the top. Explains William K. Everson in *The Bad Guys* (1964):

> The "higher-ups" were, by the very nature of things, rarely seen—and then only briefly. They represented the omnipotence of power above the law; they had a culture and veneer . . . that the self-made Robinson type of gangster could only admire and never dream of duplicating . . .

So although the film Big Boy does represent Capone in his stranglehold over the city of Chicago, his personality does not match up with "Scarface" Al's. Nor do any specific actions assigned to him in the narrative. Rather, it is around Rico that Capone analogies are woven, beginning with the lower-class Italian origins of both and their initial professions as rabidly ambitious gunmen. Perhaps the best way to view the movie is to understand that the Al Capone personage is split between Rico on the rise and the Big Boy at the top. Rico's feverish objective is to make himself and the Big Boy one and the same—a fusion which he never reaches before his Fall.

Warners went far beyond Robinson's physical resemblance to Al Capone to emphasize the fastidious and narcissistic elements in Rico's character (already noted in Burnett) that matched the sartorial Capone, typically described by *Time* as "Sleek, porcine, bejeweled and spatted . . ." And from Judge Lyle: "Capone's bedroom was elaborate with fine furniture and oriental rugs. The bed was turned down. The sheets and pillow cases were silk

Rico (Edward G. Robinson) thinks his getaway driver Tony (William Collier, Jr.) is losing his nerve. Little Caesar *(1930).*

and monogrammed 'A.C.' Silk pajamas on the bed had the same handworked initials." In the movie of *Little Caesar*, Rico ostentatiously combs his black locks, buys fancy suits, jewelry, spats, acquires a grand apartment bedecked in splendorous imitation of the domiciles of both the fictional Big Boy and the real-life Capone.

The decision of the filmmakers to emphasize Rico's resemblances to Capone are symptomatic of the *roman à clef* strategy chosen by Warners to sell their project. In fact, *Little Caesar* is certainly one of the few movies ever where the film story strives to be *closer* to real events than the novel. Here are three examples from the movie:

(1) When Rico arrives in Chicago, the city is controlled in part by "Diamond Pete" Montana, clearly meant to recall "Big Jim" or "Diamond Jim" Colosimo, the Boss of Chicago when Capone arrived there from New York. Colosimo's propensity for jewels was the stuff of legend. "He acquired his name . . . by arraying his huge check-suited body with diamonds, diamonds on fingers, clothes and accessories, and diamonds carried in leather bags in his pockets, through which he delved as he talked, like a child with a heap of coloured beads" (Kenneth Allsop's 1961 *The Bootleggers*).

In Burnett, the character is simply called Pete Montana. "He was dressed very quietly, wore no jewelry. . . ." He bears no correspondence to a real person.

(2) In both novel and film, Tony is placed "on the spot" by Rico, who machine guns him as he stands on the steps of a Catholic church. In 1926 Hymie Weiss, rosary around his neck, had been executed in these circumstances by Capone's henchmen, as "more than fifty bullets flew across the street and spattered the stonework of the Holy Name Cathedral" (Allsop).

In Burnett, the historical analogies end here. In the movie version of *Little Caesar*, Tony is given a huge funeral parade in the streets, with sanctimonious gangsters (including his killers) united to pay last respects. This motor caravan seems meant to recall the notorious processional in memory of Dion O'Banion in 1924, which brought Capone and gang, his alleged assassins, into Chicago's Loop for the ostentatious wake.

(3) Rico shoots and kills the new Crime Commissioner, Mc-Clure. This incident of violence in the movie has its recognizable basis in the famous unsolved 1926 death of William McSwiggin, Assistant State's Attorney of Cook County, while he allegedly was conducting investigations into Capone's crime capitol of Cairo, Illinois. Capone had denied any involvement with the murder by issuing a statement of classical cynicism: "Of course I didn't kill him. Why should I? I liked the kid. Only the day before he got killed he was up to my place and when he went home I gave him a bottle of Scotch. . . . I paid McSwiggin and I paid him plenty, and I got what I was paying for." Charges were levied at Capone for a time, but then he was exonerated of any complicity in the murder. Still, memories of this incident persisted—and were incorporated into the film.

In the novel, Rico murders a character referred to as "Courtney, the bull." That is all the information offered, so again Burnett refers to no specific historical individual.

When Jack Warner read *Little Caesar* in 1929, he was attracted to the project because he thought that "the book was a thinly disguised portrait of Al Capone. . . ." The concern with maintaining Capone's presence in the Warners' film was in order to take advantage of public curiosity about the life of the racketeer. This interest could be translated into profits for the film studio. But there was more: the life of Capone was also borrowed by the filmmakers for its rich metaphoric possibilities.

Warner Brothers' earlier 1930 film, *The Doorway to Hell*, had utilized Capone as the deflated and failed symbol of the Depression age—reduced, in the enervated figure of Louis Ricarno (Lew Ayres), to a state of complete stagnation at the end of a futile quest for family happiness and domestic tranquility. *Little Caesar* also examines this theme, but in a totally different and indirect manner. Whereas Ricarno talks obsessively about his family, miming Capone's own public utterances ("I could bear it all if it weren't for the hurt it brings my mother and my family"), Rico Bandello never mentions his family at all, nor does bachelor Rico have any love interests.

Rico's alienation from the opposite sex can be traced to Burnett's novel:

Rico had very little to do with women. He regarded them with a sort of contempt; they seemed so silly, reckless and purposeless. . . . What he feared most in women . . . was . . . their ability to relax a man, to make him soft and slack. . . . He was given to short bursts of lust, and this lust once satisfied, he looked at women impersonally . . . as one looks at inanimate objects.

By the First Script,[1] scenarist Robert N. Lee had removed *all* heterosexual interests. For instance, Rico attended his testimonial banquet in Burnett's novel with Blondy Belle, the ex-girlfriend of Little Arnie Lorch. In the movie banquet, however, when Rico comments, "I'm glad you guys brought your molls with you," he himself is flanked conspicuously by two men.

Thematically, what is the meaning of a Rico without a female lover? A simple Freudian reading of the above quote makes Rico a repressed homosexual whose hostility toward women is combined with fear of impotence. But this interpretation, however evocative, seems inadequate to explain his familial isolation also. Lacking any loved ones, he is better understood as a perfect emblem of the Depression times, a person completely dislocated, solitary, forlorn.

In the film version, there is no past for Rico, only the dim knowledge that he has come from elsewhere than the big city. (He arrives from Youngstown, Ohio, in the novel, but references to this specific birthplace were eliminated in an earlier script.) So when he finds that his criminal career has ebbed, he cannot even attempt a return to his roots. He is condemned to wander the belly of the city until he meets his doom. In a scene invented for the movies, Rico lies around a fifteen-cents-a-night flophouse, a disheveled, alcoholic and unemployed tramp. Blatant Depression settings are thus fused onto the already basic *angst* of the gangster story.

Rico is alone, alone. Where is the traditional immigrant mother who represents some semblance of moral order in the gangster's otherwise murky life? Tom Powers in *The Public Enemy* (1931) has a kind mother who cares for him as does Tony Camonte in

---

[1] A series of *Little Caesar* scripts are located in the United Artists Collection, State Historical Society, Madison, Wisconsin. Robert N. Lee, uncredited in the screen version, wrote the early *Caesar* scripts.

Scarface (1932). (There is one mother in *Little Caesar*, novel and film, but she is Tony's, not Rico's.)

Hardly noticed in *Little Caesar* is perhaps a greater irony: that Rico is rewarded with a "surrogate mother," a nightmare version of maternity. This is the filthy, witchlike hag "Ma" Magdalena, who hides Rico from the police—for a price. She is a "fence"—greedy, untrustworthy, different from the normal Madonna-like mothers of other gangster movies. If these others withdraw from the Depression morality, "Ma" thrives in the shyster, "dog-eat-dog" environment, where everyone scraps for a living.

When Rico is pursued, he runs, in both novel and film, to his "Ma." A *real* mother in such stories takes in her son, no questions asked, no matter what his crime. Family always comes first. But "Ma" Magdalena cares only for Rico's money. With $150 in her hand, "Ma" takes Rico behind her fruit store through a labyrinth of walkways into a clandestine, tiny back room. Mervyn LeRoy based his movie set on this description from Burnett's novel: "She led him through a dark tunnel and back into the hide-out. A small, round opening just large enough to admit one person had been pierced in the wall." The symbolism is evident —Rico's flight back to the womb, even a surrogate womb, a temporary respite before being thrust back out onto the streets.

Little Caesar's concentration on Rico's familial dissociation seems partly borrowed from the publicized domestic turmoils of Capone. But the movie of *Little Caesar* uses the Capone legend metaphorically in another way, foreign to gangster films up to this time. The auspicious rise of Rico Bandello proves the most dynamic point of Capone's life—that crime can pay, and handsomely. A young thug like Capone—or Rico—with the right temperament and plenty of "drive," can rise high, much as a young businessman with the right blend of personality credentials. As Burnett described his protagonist, "Rico's great strength lay in his single-mindedness, his energy and his self-discipline." And later, "Rico made decisions quickly, seldom asked for advice, and was nearly always right. . . . Rico had been in the game long enough to know that to make money you've got to spend money."

Like his prototype Capone, Rico climbs to wealth and power within the gangland hierarchy. How does Rico differ from previous film gangsters who began low in the criminal organizations? Most had turned virtuous and quit racketeering. James Cagney in *Sinners Holiday* (1930) was the first to murder his boss. But Rico is the first to step on his bosses—Vittori, Arnie Lorch, "Diamond Pete" Montana—and over them, on the way to the top, until he has earned the title of Boss himself. "The illicitness of his incontrovertible power corresponds to the illicitness of the employee who would like to tell his boss to go to hell," theorized Parker Tyler in *The Hollywood Hallucination* (1944).

For film director Mervyn LeRoy, Rico's obsessive drive to get higher and higher was his dominant theme for the movie:

> Rico . . . was a man with a driving ambition to be on top. . . .
> He always tried to copy the man higher up, in hopes that he would
> thus assume the characteristics and eventually the job of that man.
> —(*Take One*, 1974)

In almost all previous movies (except a 1928 Raoul Walsh film *Me, Gangster*), the gangster's rise to the top would be non-existent or very brief. But *Little Caesar* concentrates the prime time of its story on carefully plotting Rico's advancement, dwelling on his acquisition of fine clothes and a fancy suite of rooms. His fall is only in the last minutes, a total reversal of fortune, a shock to Rico and maybe to viewers as well. *Time* described these final moments: "[H]is luck changes. He loses his power, his money, becomes a flop-house derelict, and finally dies behind a billboard chewed by bullets from a machine-gun."

What went wrong? Certainly there was no precedent in the Horatio Alger story, which held only the prospect for even greater success for a hero who has followed the rules of conduct correct in his milieu. "Ragged Dick," for instance, finishes as "Richard Hunter, Esq. . . . a young gentleman on the way to fame and fortune. . . ."

Why did the real-life gangster Al Capone fall? Many have theorized that he was too devoted to the limelight. He was the last major figure of organized crime to seek celebrity and he probably paid for insisting that the world know his name. Said social historian Andrew Sinclair: "His successors are harder fish to net. They have heeded Brecht's rhetorical question, 'What is robbing a bank compared with founding a bank?' And they have been rewarded with both the millions and the ease and the semirespectability that Alphonse Capone wanted all his life and never found. . . . " (*Era of Excess*, 1964).

Rico Bandello likewise was finished because he *had* to respond to the insults to his name, planted in the newspaper by Flaherty the policeman. Defending his wilted honor, a ragged and derelict Rico returns to the open, where he is shot and killed. As he dies, his magnificent creation dies with him. "Mother of Grace, is this the end of Rico?" His name is his last word.

What does death mean for Rico? In the standard twenties gangster movie, *Underworld* for example, a gangleader who commited terrible deeds, including murder, was allowed to absolve himself gracefully of his sins through heroic sacrifice, often to save the sacred love of a young and innocent couple. By giving up his life for this moral cause, he would instantly bring meaning to his existence by showing knowledge of his sins and a desire for reformation. As Parker Tyler talks of the prototype crime story, *Crime and Punishment*, "Raskolnikoff's behavior . . . is a *moral* suicide, a true expiation, an exchange of a sense of Hell for a sense of Purgatory, and therefore not self-extinction. . . ."

But Rico Bandello reaches no moral understanding. Despite his murders and unmitigated brutality, he is shocked when mortally wounded and cannot understand why he has been robbed of his life. He cannot be expected to reach the articulation of a Robert Warshow, who noted accurately that

> Every attempt to succeed is an act of aggression leaving one alone and guilty and defenseless among enemies: one is *punished* for success. This is our intolerable dilemma: that failure is a kind of death and success is evil and dangerous and—ultimately—impossible ("The gangster as Tragic Hero," 1948).

While this message applies both to Al Capone and Rico Bandello, finally there is a point where the two part company. Capone, for all his complaints, had it infinitely better. In October, 1930, W. R. Burnett himself offered this exalted view of Capone for *The Saturday Review*: "Capone is immune. He has a villa in Florida; he is a millionaire; his name has become a household word. The old pre-Prohibition slogan, 'you can't win,' is shown to be pure nonsense." But this slogan is the very essence of *Little Caesar*, the cinema's ultimate antisuccess story. As film critic Creighton Peet described the opening night for the readers of *Outlook and Independent*:

> (T)his film seems to bring out the sturdier and more aggressive members of the community who have come to see a story about the Boy Who Made Good. And let me tell you that when Sergeant Flaherty's machine guns cut him down at the end, the audience goes home mighty quiet and depressed.

Little Caesar's last question, "Is this the end of Rico?" is addressed desperately to "the Mother of Grace"—perhaps because he hasn't an earthly mother. He receives no answer, but succumbs in cosmic silence, as cruel and potent as the indifferent world of the naturalistic novel.

A *Farewell to Arms* (1929), Ernest Hemingway

Dying Without Death: Borzage's
A Farewell to Arms

BY WILLIAM HORRIGAN

The critical esteem granted Ernest Hemingway is incomparably more generous than that given Frank Borzage. For more than forty years, Borzage worked at making films. Successful they were, some of them, but he made nearly 100 films, sixty-four of them before A *Farewell to Arms* in 1932, and more of his work is likely to be lost or forgotten than remembered or revived. But for a time he was eminently visible, winning the first Academy Award in 1927 for *Seventh Heaven,* a second in 1931 for *Bad Girl,* and, in 1933, a nomination for *Farewell to Arms.*

It would be overstatement to say Borzage fell into obscurity; he worked more or less continuously through 1959, up to *The Big Fisherman.* But it is perhaps accurate to say that when the "one film"—in Jean Renoir's sense, of a director's preoccupations resulting again and again, variously guised and transformed, in the same film—on which he elaborated all his life fell into ideological/commercial recession, his critical valuation, at least in the mainstream of taste, accordingly descended. Melodrama, both as a form and as a position adopted to comprehend experience, has become historically retrograde, ideologically inadmissible.

That Borzage should occupy a central position in the surrealist pantheon (Ado Kyrou characterized him in his *Amour, Erotisme, et Cinema* as "the greatest poet of the cinematographic couple") suggests the marginality of his concerns vis-à-vis Hollywood's dominant trend, with its preference for action, its vocation of "realism," its behaviorist bent. Obviously, Borzage participates in these tendencies, but essentially he is elsewhere: in explicit versions of spirituality and the transcendent (the nonrational, the imaginary struggling with the real), in repeatedly situating woman as central, and in his commitment to what is commonly understood as "romantic melodrama." (This latter term is meant to suggest, for example, reliance on coincidence or the improbable in light of a naturalist aesthetic, or the practice of defining any conflict by its most drastic variation, and so on.)

If Borzage must, in one sense, be re-possessed, a gloss of his situation, evidently antithetical to that of Hemingway, can be offered: Hemingway writing the man's novel, Borzage filming the woman's picture; Hemingway emotionally distancing himself from "l'affaire de coeur," Borzage reviving himself in it; Hemingway's opting for action against the tendency in Borzage's melodrama to turn from action and the world. One cannot here systematically penetrate the terms of these antitheses; rather, they suggest what the most apparent version of the relationship might look like.

In 1929 the "new novel" was being written, in one register, by Hemingway. *A Farewell to Arms* secured his reputation not only as a popular writer but indeed as a vanguard one. According to one critical enterprise, this novel—his third—can be taken as a progression beyond Gertrude Stein's reading of the nineteenth-century novel, with its scrupulous concern for explanation—a progression for which the way was prepared by Stein's teacher, William James, who maintained consciousness not as fixed and gridlike but as fluvial and, above all, continuous. *A Farewell to Arms* is manifestly an account of an individual consciousness, a first-person discourse engaged in narrative elaboration. The style of this discourse persistently expresses itself as style-as-perception, differentiating it from much third-person narrative in which perceptions as such are suppressed by the self-speaking, self-referring image of the real.

Catherine Barkley (Helen Hayes) enraptured by Lieutenant Frederick Henry (Gary Cooper). A Farewell to Arms (1932).

Perceptions of the narrator, Lieutenant Frederick Henry, are voiced in short sentences unburdened by syntactical nuance, recognized frequently as the enduring lesson of Hemingway's prose. Preference for the monosyllabic word cluster and the tendency toward its repetition collaborate with the sentence design to minimize connotation (extending ultimately to ideogram—but there Hemingway does not venture).

Hemingway's prose has been characterized as cinematic in that it reveals not motive, but existence's result. Not: why or what is this?, but: this is. As the language of literature it would be as though newly born, merely recording the primally unstructured real, were it not for the various rhythms and constructions, eventually highly artificial, indicative of privileged consciousness. Any correspondence one wants to specify between his prose and cinema's capabilities has to reckon as well with the extensive metaphoric design of *A Farewell to Arms*, chiefly clustered about images of terrain and climate. As for the narrative persona—necessarily construed as detached, impassive—one finds therein the unification of one subjective vantage point, offering the perceptions of a character having weathered World War I, with the perceptions of a writer having witnessed the spectacle of America's postwar transformation. The Hollywood film has to find its own means to convey such anxious subjectivity (assuming it so desires), which is invariably problematic, given the practice of converting first-person narrators into the film's "main character." Borzage seems occasionally to recognize this difficulty.

One instance, the most spectacular: following his injury from a bomb explosion, Frederick/Gary Cooper is evacuated to Milan, and the sequence offers the simulation of the patient's view lying on a stretcher as he is wheeled down a corridor, which is to say the view of the hospital's vaulted ceilings and of nurses bending over to speak. The sequence is logically uninterrupted by cuts, even explicitly by racking focus to accommodate objects entering and leaving on different planes within the image. As Frederick is placed in bed the subjective vision is maintained, with smooth panning movements signifying his gaze as he watches a nurse. The door opens and nurse Catherine Barkley/Helen Hayes, Frederick's lover, enters. Here, when one might expect finally a reaction shot of Frederick responding to Catherine's arrival, Borzage persists in the established vantage point, carrying it to its reduction, which is of Catherine drawing progressively nearer Frederick and finally kissing him/kissing the camera. She pulls back slightly following the kiss, but remains suffocatingly close so as only one of her eyes is visible, the remainder of her face blurred from the extreme proximity to his eye/the camera's lens. Following this shot—which is, in Andrew Sarris's estimation, "as intensely Orphic as anything in the entire cinema" —Borzage recedes to offer more orthodox close-up two-shots.

This sequence offers perhaps the most radical insistence on subjectivity in the film. Indeed, along with a use of cross-cutting signifying romantic telepathy in earlier films such as *Seventh Heaven* (1927) and *Street Angel* (1928), this is likely Borzage's most audacious attempt to subvert the mundane, to make strange, for the time being, what has become impoverished, made transparent, by habit and time. In terms of adaptation procedure, however, the sequence offers a vision through the narrator's "eyes," yet the degree of contextual fissure attained is utterly distant from the level tone maintained by Hemingway. Elsewhere, Borzage performs some instructive variations that seem more truly his own.

Hemingway concludes with Catherine dying in childbirth and Frederick, typically, remarking, "After a while I went out and left the hospital and walked back to the hotel in the rain." Catherine's death, though precipitated solely by her physical complications, is linked associatively by Hemingway to the misery and ravages of war, thereby forcing her death to be viewed as especially consequential.

Borzage rejects Hemingway's undifferentiating, romantic pessimism as proper cause for generating Catherine's death. While his Catherine similarly dies in childbirth, her death follows months of separation, she in Switzerland, Frederick in Italy, neither aware of the other's location, with communication ultimately impeded by Rinaldi's meddling. During this period Catherine is seen progressively more distraught, finally collapsing when her letters are returned unopened. Frederick, in Brissago, learns of her whereabouts, and, after rowing across to Switzerland during a storm (with Borzage cross-cutting between his hands at the oars and her hands clutched as she lies unconcious in the hospital), he arrives at the hospital just as she is wheeled out of the operating chamber where she has lost their child. The melodramatic coincidence is fortuitous but it is not bound up in Hemingway's causal model (*i.e.*, the general malaise, of which war is exemplary, infecting all in its path); instead, it points to an alternate, less secular, vision seeing romance as imperiled by its own intensity, the birth of romance being the first movement in its history of tribulations.

Hemingway's death scene has Frederick and Catherine exchanging the same kind of uninflected dialogue used throughout —for example, "You're all right, Cat. You're going to be all right." —"I'm going to die . . . I hate it," etc. Borzage orchestrates this differently. Catherine, aware of death, is made up by nurses. Frederick enters, and, as in the novel, Catherine tells him she wants him "to have other girls." In alternate close-up two-shots of Oscar-winning soft-focus photography, she speaks as though she were not going to die: "When I get well, we'll take a little house in the mountains . . . and we'll live in it until the war is over, and then we'll go back to America and you'll be a splendid architect." Then she panics: "Oh, darling, I'm going to die, don't let me die, I'm afraid to be alone." Frederick responds, "We've never been apart, not really, not since we met . . . in life and death we'll never be parted. You do believe that, Catherine." Catherine's last gasps: "I do believe it, and I'm not afraid."

As she dies, Borzage cuts to a succession of shots of whistles blowing, bells pealing, and doves flying, with the Liebestod from *Tristan and Isolde* swelling up on the soundtrack. Borzage then cuts back to a medium shot of Frederick taking Catherine, dressed in a long white gown, in his arms and walking, his back to camera, towards a huge window. He stands away from the camera at the window holding Catherine, the exterior indistinct, and finally says, barely audibly, "Peace—peace!" His image then dissolves into ones of doves flying to clouds, accompanied still by strains of Wagner.

A paraphrasing such as this scarcely conveys the sequence's affective, delirious properties, but what it does suggest is a temperament foreign, to say the least, to Hemingway's. The death of the novel's Catherine arrives only after she has been transformed into Woman, into—to quote Georges Bataille—"a feminine reflection of the light emanating from her lover." To Hemingway's Frederick, the loss of Catherine is the loss of an ideal, and it serves as natural summation of the pessimistic vision offered. Borzage retains Hemingway's pessimistic "ideas" to some extent by having Rinaldi and Nurse Ferguson voice them, but he makes no systematic effort, for example, to compose the images in a single tonal key, assuming this to be an accurate translation of the prose's monotonal qualities.

John Belton reports in *The Hollywood Professionals* (1974) that *A Farewell to Arms* was released in two versions, with respectively happy (Catherine recovers) and sad endings. Evidence pertinent to this is conflicting but what can be noted is the debatable estimation of the version with Catherine dying as ending "unhappily." What Borzage is proposing, typically and paradoxically, is not death as initiation into a "lack," but as an avenue toward spiritual transcendence for the surviving partner. The sudden series of images of celebration effectively spring from Catherine's death, as though she were sacrificing herself for armistice, and the luminosity of the penultimate tableau of Frederick standing before the window holding the dead Catherine tends to reinforce this. The irony of Frederick losing (Catherine) even as he is winning (the war) is mediated by Borzage's recourse to a version of the transcendent in which romantic love is understood as an eternal balm, free from the exigencies of material circumstance. In effect, the world—and World War I—is denied.

Hemingway's lovers pull themselves out of it all to flee to Switzerland but Borzage's narrative transpositions preclude such an idyllic respite. He instead suggests not only that home is wherever it is that they are together, but is conceivable even when they are apart—Catherine, alone in Switzerland, writing to Frederick as the camera roams about the flat, clearly shabby but described by her as luxurious. The deprivations of the real are endurable, says Borzage, to those who have ascended into the privileged realm of the imaginary. Hemingway can eventually establish the sense of home simply by the appearance of

Catherine because it is her appearance *to* Frederick, the regulator of the viewpoint, but since Borzage has not given priority in this sense to Frederick, he is free to suggest her passion—indeed, her existence—as well as Frederick's on her own terms, even when they are apart. Her fictive existence is not dependent on Frederick's gaze, as in the novel; indeed, introduced in the film before Frederick appears, she can claim, in this slight sense, an existence prior to his.

Whereas Hemingway heavily emphasizes scenes of war, Borzage minimizes them, reducing them to an expressionistic montage conveying less Frederick's involvement in battle than the generalized horrors of war—lines of refugees marching through rainy nights while being strafed by enemy planes, white-crossed cemeteries being bombed, etc. What Hemingway achieves cumulatively, invisibly, Borzage pursues by this sequence's remarkable condensing operations. Clearly, he is not interested in Frederick alone, but only as Frederick exists in conjunction to Catherine—and vice versa.

Borzage's paradoxes continue to accumulate. How, for further example, could a film with Helen Hayes and Gary Cooper—James Agee's "high-priced male beauty"—ever aspire to convey the deliberately enervated, unexceptional tone of the novel? The task of a certain school of novelist to make his/her characters "exceptional" is invariably realized by a Hollywood adaptation. The characters are now stars, hence already eternally exceptional.

Further caveats. Does it follow that those valuing Hemingway look to nominal adaptations of his work for its cinematic equivalent? Might it not be more pleasurable for this purpose to study Antonioni in light of Cesare Pavese? Hollywood is nothing if not pragmatic; Hemingway means a collection of titles, a series of variably cherished situations: demanding more might be rewarding, and so might requesting less.

In the end—before that—to deal with Borzage's *A Farewell to Arms* is to deal, precisely, with Borzage. Hemingway was reportedly not pleased with the figure his novel assumed, though the partisans of, among others, Helen Hayes and Gary Cooper, most certainly were. Different dispositions, different myths.

The Sound and the Fury (1929), William Faulkner

Signifying Nothing?

BY STANLEY KAUFFMANN

A recurrent debate about criticism of films and plays is whether adaptations ought to be considered in relation to their originals or as entities in themselves. Where the original is a work of little importance or reputation, the question can be begged. Otherwise, in my view, reference to the original is unavoidable. Imagine going to see a film advertised as Chekhov's *Sea Gull* and finding that in it Trigorin has been made a Mongol (to suit a Mongolian star), that he does not seduce Nina but has taken a Daddy Longlegs interest in her which blossoms into cozy marriage, and that the character of Konstantine has been excised.

Far-fetched as that sounds, it is a fair analogy with what has been done in the film of Faulkner's *The Sound and the Fury.* Quentin (Caddy's brother) has been completely eliminated, along with about half the novel. Jason has been made a Cajun to fit Yul Brynner's accent. He is no longer Caddy's brother; he is the son of Father Compson's second wife by her previous marriage. Thus there is no blood relationship between him and the younger Quentin (Caddy's daughter), and the antagonism between them can blossom into love and probably marriage.

This from a novel which Irving Howe calls one of the three or four twentieth-century works of prose fiction in which the impact of tragedy is felt and sustained, a novel which ends with Quentin's flight with a carnival showman and the certainty that, whatever happens to her, the Compson family is doomed.

Make every allowance for the legitimate needs of screen adaptation. Even then, if words mean anything at all, how can this occasionally touching movie of a declining family's regeneration be called a film of Faulkner's work—a book which (to quote Howe again) records "the fall of a house, the death of a society"? If black is white and right is left, which way is up?

An editorial in the current *Esquire* [March 1959] suggests a double standard for criticizing films made from novels: that reviewers should treat such films as complete in themselves because most people haven't read the originals and a review that points out divergences is only spoiling their fun. It is a stirring little crusade for the sacredness of ignorance, and if only our culture can continue to keep most people from reading books, it may prevail.

But let us temporarily adopt *Esquire*'s suggestion. This film, then, was made by the same producer and director (Jerry Wald and Martin Ritt) who made an earlier Faulkner derivative, *The Long Hot Summer* [1957]. It has the same false Technicolor prettiness, the same generally competent direction. Joanne Woodward, who was in the other film, gives us more of the same quite good performance of a young Southern girl of independent spirit. Ethel Waters is comforting as Dilsey. Yul Brynner does his too-often-seen best as Jason. John Beal is pathetic as the sodden brother, Howard—a character invented for the film, presumably to take up some of the slack caused by dropping (the older) Quentin.

But the only really interesting performance is the Caddy of Margaret Leighton. Miss Leighton seems somewhat worried by the Southern accent, as if she had to carry a bothersome parcel while performing, but she is an artist whose neurotic palette is perfectly suited to the role. Her smallest move is charged with purebred emotion; she can make us feel, in a poignant way, the very fineness of her bones.

The Compsons at home: Jason (Yul Brynner), Quentin (Joanne Woodward) and Caddy (Margaret Leighton). The Sound and the Fury (1959).

Within its own context, the script has inconsistencies and loose ends. How does Jason, who boasts that he is the family mainstay, support them after he hits his employer Earl Snopes? What happened to Quentin's resentment of Caddy because of her mother's reluctance to defend her? Why did Jason tear furiously after the thieving Quentin and her lover only to tell her that she could do what she chose and then leave her? These questions are posed by the script, not the novel.

Still it must be admitted that the screen writers have nibbled around busily enough in the book to come up with a script of superficial intelligence which contains some good scenes. Most of the sequences with the idiot Benjy (Jack Warden) are effective; several of Miss Woodward's and Miss Leighton's scenes are well composed. But they seem pages from a family album, not elements of a unified progressive drama. The net result of the film, aside from its final note of optimism, is of a sprawling, occasionally gripping fourth carbon copy of Chekhov in Dixie— just another ambling "study" of Southern social disintegration and transition.

What is missing? If *Esquire* will pardon us, Faulkner is missing. The gigantic, death-destined tension is missing. So the point of the work—the force that knits the pieces fiercely together and hurls them forward—is missing. The effect of the film is like hearing snatches of a symphony through closed concert-hall doors.

In the same issue of *Esquire*, Wald is quoted as saying: "Mass audiences are hep now. There are 25 million college graduates." He must be banking on a belief—possibly well founded—that few of them have read one of the most highly regarded of all American novels and that those few won't care about its perversion. "I'm gonna do Lawrence's *Sons and Lovers* next," he says, "and I just bought *Winesburg.*" He adds that he also has an option on *Ulysses.*

Why not? With the technique of evisceration and trimming and substitute stuffing that he has perfected, he can make a good neighborhood movie out of any book he chooses. How about Nietzsche's *Beyond Good and Evil?* Gad, what a title!

JEANNE THOMAS ALLEN is on the faculty of the Department of Communication Arts, the University of Wisconsin at Madison. She obtained her doctorate from the University of Iowa's American Civilization Program after completing her thesis on narration in *The Turn of the Screw* and *The Innocents*.

THOMAS ATKINS is chairman of the Theatre Arts Department at Hollins College, Virginia, and editor-publisher of *The Film Journal*. He edited *Sexuality in the Movies* for Indiana University Press and four film books for Simon & Schuster, and he co-authored *The Fire Came By*, published by Doubleday.

PETER BRUNETTE is an Assistant Professor of English at George Mason University in Virginia. He has published articles and interviews in *The Chronicle of Higher Education*, *Cineaste*, and *Film Comment* and has edited a book of American readings for French university students.

JERRY W. CARLSON was raised in Texas and educated at Williams College and the University of Chicago. He teaches literature and film at DePaul University in Chicago.

KEITH COHEN teaches comparative literature at the University of Wisconsin at Madison. He is the American translator of the French essayist-novelist Hélène Cixous, and his fiction and criticism have appeared in *The Paris Review*, *Poetique*, and in *Revista de Occidente*.

JOHN DAVIS is the editor of *The Velvet Light Trap*.

JAN DAWSON is a long-time contributor to the British film journal *Sight and Sound*. Recently she was an organizer of the Toronto International Film Festival.

KATE ELLIS teaches English and Women's Studies at Livingston College, Rutgers University, and is a practicing poet. She is presently at work on a major study of the gothic novel.

MARK W. ESTRIN is Professor of English and Director of Film Studies at Rhode Island College. His articles have appeared in *Modern Drama, Literature/Film Quarterly* and *The Journal of Narrative Technique.* He is currently compiling bibliographies on Lillian Hellman and Edward Albee for G.K. Hall and Co.

MANNY FARBER has been film critic for both *The New Republic* and *The Nation* and now teaches film courses at San Diego State University. A collection of his criticism, *Negative Space* (1971), was published by Praeger.

TOM FLINN teaches film at the University of Wisconsin at Stevens Point and is the book editor of *The Velvet Light Trap.*

BRANDON FRENCH is an Assistant Professor of English at Yale University and Curator of the Yale College of Classic Films. Her independently produced film, *Brandy in the Wilderness* (1969), won prizes at Ann Arbor and Cannes. She is now writing a book on women and the movies for Frederick Ungar Publishing Co.

DAN FULLER is an Assistant Professor of English at Kent State University's Tuscarawas Campus in Ohio. He is an expert on American popular culture, from the works of Horatio Alger, Jr. to modern sports novels.

CAROLYN GEDULD is the author of *Bernard Wolfe, Filmguide to 2001: A Space Odyssey, Women's Films: A Critical Guide,* and numerous articles on film and literature. She teaches film at Indiana University.

JAN-CHRISTOPHER HORAK has completed his postgraduate internship at the George Eastman House and returned to his native Germany to prepare a book on the German silent cinema. His film criticism has appeared in *Image* and *The Village Voice.*

WILLIAM HORRIGAN is co-editor of *Film Reader* and is preparing a doctoral dissertation at Northwestern University on melodrama in the American cinema.

JANET JUHNKE has lived in Kansas almost all her life. She received her doctorate in English from the University of Kansas, and she is presently Assistant Professor of English and chairman of the Humanities Division at Kansas Wesleyan University in Salina.

E. ANN KAPLAN, an Assistant Professor of English at University College, Rutgers University, has published numerous articles on film and women's studies and co-authored *Talking About the Cinema* for the British Film Institute. She is preparing a volume on Fritz Lang for G.K. Hall and Co.

STANLEY KAUFFMANN has published three volumes of his film criticism with Harper & Row. He has been Visiting Professor of Drama at Yale University and co-edited the Liveright anthology, *American Film Criticism: From the Beginnings to Citizen Kane* (1972).

ALBERT J. LAVALLEY has taught film and literature at Yale, San Francisco State, University of California at Santa Barbara, and Rutgers. Editor of *Focus on Hitchcock* (1972) for Prentice-Hall, he is currently running a new film and theater bookstore, the Limelight, at 1803 Market Street in San Francisco.

JANET MASLIN has written for *Rolling Stone, The Village Voice*, and *New Times*. She was film editor of the Boston *Phoenix* and is currently an associate editor at *Newsweek*.

KATHLEEN MURPHY teaches film at the University of Washington in Seattle, contributes regularly to *Movietone News*, and is completing a doctoral dissertation on Howard Hawks and Ernest Hemingway.

ROBERT L. NADEAU is Assistant Professor of English and American Studies at George Mason University. He has published critical studies of William Melvin Kelley and Djuna Barnes and is working on a book-length study of William Faulkner.

PHILIP ROTH numbers among his novels *Goodbye Columbus, Portnoy's Complaint*, and *My Life as a Man*. He served a brief stint as film reviewer for *The New Republic* in 1957.

NANCY L. SCHWARTZ has contributed to *The Village Voice, The Soho Weekly News, The Real Paper, Film Comment*, and other cinema magazines. She is writing a study of the Screen Writers Guild to be published by Knopf.

FRED SILVA is an Associate Professor of American Literature and Film at the State University of New York at Albany. He edited *Focus on Birth of a Nation* for Prentice-Hall, is a consultant to the New York Council on the Arts, and is Editor-Publisher of *Film Literature Index*.

SANFORD J. SMOLLER is the author of *Adrift Among Geniuses: Robert McAlmon, Writer and Publisher of the Twenties* for Pennsylvania

State University Press. His articles have appeared in *Modern Fiction Studies* and *Pembroke Magazine*, among others.

JOSEPH F. TRIMMER is Associate Professor of English and Coordinator of General Education English at Ball State University. His most recent book is *American Oblique: Writings About the American Experience* for Houghton-Mifflin.

MAUREEN TURIM is a doctoral student in film at the University of Wisconsin. Her film criticism has appeared in *The Velvet Light Trap* and *Wideangle*.

GEORGE WEAD is an Assistant Professor of Film at the University of Texas at Austin and broadcasts a weekly film report on KLRN-TV, San Antonio. His film criticism has appeared in *The Velvet Light Trap* and *The Village Voice* and his book, *Buster Keaton and the Dynamics of Visual Wit*, has been published by the Arno Press.

THE EDITORS

GERALD PEARY teaches film at Livingston College, Rutgers University, and is the author of *Rita Hayworth* for Pyramid Books and co-editor of *Women and the Cinema* for E.P. Dutton. He is an associate editor of *Film Heritage* and *The Velvet Light Trap* and book editor of *Jump Cut*.

ROGER SHATZKIN has taught film and literature at Rutgers College, University College, and Livingston College of Rutgers University. He has published in *Society, The Velvet Light Trap, Rolling Stone*, and other periodicals.

SOURCES FOR FILMS LISTED
IN FILM CREDITS AND FILMOGRAPHY

AB
Audio Brandon Films (Macmillan)
34 MacQuesten Parkway South
Mount Vernon, New York 10550
(914) 664-5051
or
1619 North Cherokee
Los Angeles, California 90028
(213) 463-0357
or
Branch offices in Oakland,
Dallas, and Brookfield, Illinois

BLA
Blackhawk Films
Eastin-Phelan Corp.
Davenport, Iowa 52808
(319) 323-9736

BUD
Budget Films
4590 Santa Monica Blvd.
Los Angeles, California 90029
(213) 660-0187

CIV
Cinema 5—16mm.
595 Madison Avenue
New York, New York 10022
(212) 421-5555

CLA
Classic Film Museum, Inc.
4 Union Square
Dover-Foxcroft, Maine 04426
(207) 564-8371

CON
Contemporary/McGraw Hill
Films
Princeton Road
Hightstown, New Jersey 08520
(609) 448-1700
or
828 Custer Avenue
Evanston, Illinois 60202
(312) 869-5010
or
1714 Stockton Street
San Francisco, California 94133
(415) 362-3115

CSV
Cine Service Vintage Films
85 Exeter Street
Bridgeport, Connecticut 06606
(203) 372-7785

CWF
Clem Williams Films, Inc.
2240 Noblestown Road
Pittsburgh, Pennsylvania 15205
(412) 921-5810
or
Branch offices in Atlanta,
Chicago, and Houston

EMG
Em Gee Film Library
4931 Gloria Avenue
Encino, California 91316
(213) 981-5506

FCE
Film Classic Exchange
1926 South Vermont Avenue
Los Angeles, California 90007
(213) 731-3854

FI
Films Incorporated
4420 Oakton Street
Skokie, Illinois 60076
(312) 676-1088
or
440 Park Avenue South
New York, New York 10016
(212) 889-7910
or
5625 Hollywood Boulevard
Hollywood, California 90028
(213) 466-5481
or
Branch offices in Atlanta, Boston,
Salt Lake City, and San Diego

FIM
Film Images
(A Division of Radim Films, Inc.)
71 West 60th Street
New York, New York 10023
(212) 279-6653
or

1034 Lake Street
Oak Park, Illinois 60301
(312) 386-4826

HUR
Hurlock Cine World, Inc.
13 Arcadia Road
Greenwich, Connecticut 06870
(203) 637-4319

IVY
IVY Film
165 West 46th Street
New York, New York 10036
(212) 765-3940

KPF
Kit Parker Films
Box 227
Carmel Valley, California 93924
(408) 659-4131

MMA
Museum of Modern Art
11 West 53rd Street
New York, New York 10019
(212) 956-4205

MOG
Mogull's
235 West 46th Street
New York, New York 10036
(212) 757-1414

TFC
"The" Film Center
915 12th Street, N.W.
Washington, D.C. 20005
(202) 393-1205

TMC
The Movie Center
57 Baldwin Street
Charlestown, Massachusetts
02129
(617) 242-3456

TWY
Twyman Films
321 Salem Avenue
Dayton, Ohio 45401
(513) 222-4014

UA
United Artists Sixteen
729 Seventh Avenue
New York, New York 10019
(212) 575-3000

UF
United Films
1425 South Main
Tulsa, Oklahoma 74119
(918) 583-2681

UNI
Universal Sixteen
445 Park Avenue
New York, New York 10022
(212) 759-7500
or
2001 South Vermont Avenue
Los Angeles, California 90007
(213) 731-2151
or
Branch offices in Atlanta,
Chicago, and Dallas

WCF
Westcoast Films
25 Lusk Street
San Francisco, California 94107
(415) 362-4700

NOTE: For further information on film rental sources, see James L. Limbacher, ed., *Feature Films on 8mm and 16mm*, 5th ed. N.Y.: R. R. Bowker, 1977 and Kathleen Weaver, ed., *Film Programmer's Guide to 16mm Rentals*, 2nd ed. Berkeley, Calif.: Reel Research, 1975.

FILM CREDITS

CODE: Si: Silent; P: Production Company/Producer (when pertinent); D: Director; Sc: Screenplay; Adapt: Adaptation; Ph: Photography; M: Music; C: Cast; (RENTAL SOURCE[S]).* Films are listed in order of discussion in this volume.

The Last of the Mohicans (Si 1920). P: Associated Producers/ Maurice Tourneur. D: Maurice Tourneur, Clarence Brown. Sc: Robert A. Dillon. Ph: Phillip R. Dubois, Charles J. Van Enger. C: Barbara Bedford, Lillian Hall, Wallace Beery, Albert Roscoe, Henry Woodward, George Hackathorne, Henry Lorraine, Theodore Lerch, James Gordon, Nelson McDowell. (FCE)
The Scarlet Letter (Si 1926). P: MGM. D: Victor Sjöström. Sc: Frances Marion. Ph: Hendrik Sartov. C: Lillian Gish, Lars Hanson, Henry B. Walthall, Karl Dane, Joyce Coad. (FI)
The House of the Seven Gables (1940). P: Universal Pictures. D: Joe May. Sc: Lester Cole. Adapt: Harold Greene. C: George Sanders, Margaret Lindsay, Vincent Price, Nan Grey, Dick Foran, Miles Mander, Charles Trowbridge. (UNI)
Moby Dick (1956). P: United Artists, Moulin Pictures. D: John Huston. Sc: Ray Bradbury, John Huston. Ph: Oswald Morris (in Technicolor). M: Philip Stainton. C: Gregory Peck, Richard Basehart, Leo Genn, Orson Welles, Harry Andrews, Frederick Ledebur. (UA)
Little Women (1933). P: RKO. D: George Cukor. Sc: Sarah Y. Mason, Victor Heerman. Ph: Henry Gerrard. M: Max Steiner, C: Katharine Hepburn, Frances Dee, Jean Parker, Joan Bennett, Edna May Oliver, Paul Lukas, Douglass Montgomery. (FI)
Little Women (1949). P: MGM. D: Mervyn LeRoy. Sc: Andrew Salt, Sarah Y. Mason, Victor Heerman. M: Adolph Deutsch. C: June

* See p. 313 for key to abbreviations used.

317

Allyson, Peter Lawford, Margaret O'Brien, Elizabeth Taylor, Janet Leigh, Rossano Brazzi, Mary Astor, Leon Ames. (FI)

Tom Sawyer (1930). P: Paramount-Publix. D: John Cromwell. Sc: Sam Mintz, Grover Jones, William Slavens McNutt. Ph: Charles Lang. C: Jackie Coogan, Junior Durkin, Mitzi Green, Clara Bandick, Jackie Searle, Jane Darwell, Charles Stevens. (UNI, TMC)

Daisy Miller (1974). P: Paramount. D: Peter Bogdanovich. Sc: Frederic Raphael, (Bogdanovich—not officially credited). Ph: Alberto Spagnoli (in Technicolor). M: Bach, Mozart, Strauss, Boccherini, Haydn, Schubert, Verdi. C: Cybill Shepherd, Barry Brown, Cloris Leachman, Mildred Natwick, Eileen Brennan, Duilio Del Prete. (FI)

The Heiress (1949). P: Paramount. D: William Wyler. Sc: Ruth and Augustus Goetz (based on their own dramatization). Ph: Leo Tover. M: Aaron Copland. C: Olivia de Havilland, Ralph Richardson, Montgomery Clift, Miriam Hopkins, Vanessa Brown. (UNI, TWY, TMC)

The Prince and the Pauper (1937). P: Warner Brothers. D: William Keighley. Sc: Laird Doyle, Catherine Chishold Cushing. M: Erich Wolfgang Korngold. C: Errol Flynn, Claude Rains, Barton MacLane, Billy Mauch, Bobby Mauch, Alan Hale, Montagu Love, Henry Stephenson. (UA)

The Red Badge of Courage (1951). P: MGM/Gottfried Reinhardt. D: John Huston. Sc: John Huston (adapt: Albert Band). Ph: Harold Rosson. M: Bronislau Caper. C: Audie Murphy, Bill Mauldin, John Dierkes, Royal Dano, Tim Durant. (FI)

Billy Budd (1962). P: Anglo Allied, Allied Artists. D: Peter Ustinov. Sc: Peter Ustinov, DeWitt Bodeen, (Robert Rossen—not officially credited). Ph: Robert Krasker (in Cinemascope). M: Anthony Hopkins. C: Terence Stamp, Peter Ustinov, Robert Ryan, Melvyn Douglas, Ronald Lewis, David McCallum. (HUR)

The Innocents (1961 Great Britain). P: Twentieth Century-Fox. D: Jack Clayton. Sc: Truman Capote, William Archibald. Ph: Freddie Francis. M: George Auric. C: Deborah Kerr, Peter Wyngarde, Megs Jenkins, Michael Redgrave, Pamela Franklin, Martin Stephens. (FI)

Greed (Si 1925). P: Metro-Goldwyn. D, Sc, Adapt: Erich von Stroheim. Titles: June Mathis. Ph: William Daniels, Ben Reynolds, Ernest B. Schoesdack. (Release version edited by Rex Ingram, June Mathis.) C: Gibson Gowland, ZaSu Pitts, Jean Hersholt, Chester Conklin, Sylvia Ashton, Dale Fuller, Joan Standing, Austin Jewel, Cesare Gravina. (FI)

Carrie (1952). P: Paramount. D: William Wyler. Sc: Ruth and Augustus Goetz. Ph: Victor Milner. M: David Raksin. C: Laurence Olivier, Jennifer Jones, Miriam Hopkins, Eddie Albert, Basil Ruysdale, Mary Murphy. (FI)

The Wizard of Oz (1939). P: MGM/Mervyn LeRoy. D: Victor Fleming. Sc and Adapt: Noel Langley. Sc: Florence Ryerson, Edgar Allan Woolf. Ph: Harold Rosson (in Technicolor). M: Herbert Stathart. Songs: E. Y. Harburg, Harold Arlen. C: Judy Garland, Frank Morgan, Ray Bolger, Bert Lahr, Jack Haley, Billie Burke, Margaret Hamilton, Charles Grapewin, Clara Bandick. (FI)

The Virginian (1929). P: Paramount, Famous-Lasky. D: Victor Fleming, Dialogue: Edward E. Paramore, Jr. Adapt: Howard Estabrook (from novel by Wister and *The Virginian: A Play in Four Acts* by Owen Wister and Kirk LeShelle [1923]). Ph: J. Roy Hunt. C: Gary Cooper, Walter Huston, Richard Arlen, Mary Brian, Chester Conklin, Eugene Pallette. (MMA, UNI)

The Virginian (1946). P: Paramount. D: Stuart Gilmore. Sc: Frances Goodrich, Albert Hackett. Adapt: Howard Estabrook. M: Daniele Amfitheatrof. C: Joel McCrea, Brian Donlevy, Sonny Tufts, Barbara Britton, Fay Bainter, Henry O'Neill, William Frawley, Vince Barnett, Paul Guilfoyle. (UNI)

The Sea Wolf (1941). P: Warner Brothers. D: Michael Curtiz. Sc: Robert Rossen. Ph: Sol Polito. M: Erich Wolfgang Korngold. C: Edward G. Robinson, Ida Lupino, John Garfield, Alexander Knox, Gene Lockhart, Barry Fitzgerald, Howard da Silva, Stanley Ridges. (UA)

I Married a Doctor (1936). P: Warner Brothers. D: Archie Mayo. Sc: Casey Robinson (from a dramatization by Harriet Ford and Harvey O'Higgins). C: Pat O'Brien, Josephine Hutchinson, Ross Alexander, Guy Kibbee, Louise Fazenda, Olin Howland, Margaret Irving, Maxine Doyle, Glen Bales. (UA)

Alice Adams (1935). P: RKO/Pandro S. Berman. D: George Stevens. Sc: Dorothy Yost, Mortimer Offner. Adapt: Jane Murfin. M: Roy Webb. C: Katharine Hepburn, Fred MacMurray, Fred Stone, Evelyn Venable, Frank Albertson, Charles Grapewin. (FI)

Babbitt (1934). P: First National, Warner Brothers. D: William Keighley. Sc: Mary McCall, Jr. (with additional dialogue by Ben Markson). Adapt: Tom Reed, Niven Busch. Ph: Arthur Todd. C: Guy Kibbee, Aline MacMahon, Claire Dodd, Nan Grey, Mary Treen, Minor Watson, Alan Hale, Glen Bayles, Maxine Doyle. (UA)

The Great Gatsby (1949). P: Paramount. D: Elliott Nugent. Sc:

Cyril Hume, Richard Maibaum (from Fitzgerald's novel and play by Owen Davis [1926]). C: Alan Ladd, Betty Field, MacDonald Carey, Barry Sullivan, Ruth Hussey, Shelley Winters. (withdrawn from circulation in 1974)

The Great Gatsby (1974). P: Paramount/David Merrick. D: Jack Clayton. Sc: Francis Ford Coppola. Ph: Douglas Slocombe (in color). M: Nelson Riddle. C: Robert Redford, Mia Farrow, Bruce Dern, Karen Black, Scott Wilson, Sam Waterston, Lois Chiles, Howard da Silva. (FI)

The Sun Also Rises (1957). P: Twentieth Century-Fox/Darryl F. Zanuck. D: Henry King. Sc: Peter Viertel. (Wide screen and color). C: Tyrone Power, Ava Gardner, Mel Ferrer, Gregory Ratoff, Robert Evans, Juliette Greco. (FI)

Dodsworth (1936). P: Goldwyn. D: William Wyler. Sc and Adapt: Sidney Howard (from his play version of 1934). Ph: Rudolph Maté. M: Alfred Newman. C: Walter Huston, Ruth Chatterton, Paul Lukas, Mary Astor, David Niven, Gregory Gaye, Maria Ouspenskaya. (AB, BUD)

Little Caesar (1930). P: Warner Brothers/Hal B. Wallis. D: Mervyn LeRoy. Sc: Francis Faragoh. Ph: Tony Gaudio. C: Edward G. Robinson, Douglas Fairbanks, Jr., William Collier, Jr., Ralph Ince, Glenda Farrell, George Stone, Thomas Jackson. (UA)

A Farewell to Arms (1932). P: Paramount-Publix. D: Frank Borzage. Sc: Benjamin Glazer, Oliver H. P. Garrett. C: Helen Hayes, Gary Cooper, Adolphe Menjou, Mary Phillips, Jack LaRue. (CLA)

The Sound and the Fury (1959). P: Twentieth Century-Fox/Jerry Wald. D: Martin Ritt. Sc: Irving Ravetch, Harriet Frank, Jr. Ph: Charles G. Clarke (in Cinemascope and color). M: Alex North. C: Yul Brynner, Joanne Woodward, Margaret Leighton, Stuart Whitman, Ethel Waters, Jack Warden, Albert Dekker. (FI)

SELECTED FILMOGRAPHY

Film Adaptations of American Novels, 1826–1929

For reasons of space, we have neither listed authors whose works are too numerous to cite (*e.g.*, Edgar Rice Burroughs and Zane Grey), nor have we included under each entry all the films that may apply (*e.g.*, there are very minor novels of Booth Tarkington that have been filmed, additional versions of *The Scarlet Letter* and *The Wonderful Wizard of Oz*, etc. that are not listed). Silent film adaptations before 1921 are especially difficult to document. Our general principle has been to include those novels and films we think will be of immediate interest to film and literary scholars, to archivists and librarians. At present, there are no comprehensive reference guides for filmed adaptations, although the eventual completion of the American Film Institute Catalogues should help fill that gap. In the meantime, further information can be culled from: A.G.S. Unser, *Filmed Books and Plays 1928–1974*, London: Andre Deutsch, 1975; Richard B. Dimmitt, *A Title Guide to the Talkies*, 2 vols., Metuchen, N.J.: Scarecrow Press, 1970, 1971, 1973; *The American Film Institute Catalogue of Motion Pictures, Feature Films 1921–1930*, ed. by Kenneth W. Munden, 2 vols., N.Y.: R. R. Bowker, 1971; and *Feature Films 1961–70*, ed. by Richard P. Krafsur, 2 vols., N.Y.: R. R. Bowker, 1976.

If no rental source is indicated it does not necessarily mean that the film is positively unavailable, only that current reference sources had no listings (see note at end of "Sources for Films Listed in Film Credits and Filmography").

The following list is alphabetical by author.

Author–Title	Film Version: Title (if changed), Production Company, Release Date Director (d)	Rental Source(s)
ALCOTT, Louisa May (1832–88)		
Little Women (1868–69)	Brady, 1918—silent (d) Harley Knowles	—
	RKO, 1933 (d) George Cukor	FI
	MGM, 1949 (d) Mervyn LeRoy	FI
An Old Fashioned Girl (1870)	Eagle Lion, 1948 (d) Arthur Dreifuss	IVY
Little Men (1971)	Mascot, 1934 (d) Phil Rosen	FCE
BAUM, L. Frank (1856–1919)		
The Wonderful Wizard of Oz (1900)	The Wizard of Oz, Chadwick Pictures, 1925—silent (d) Larry Semon	BUD, EMG, KPF
	The Wizard of Oz, MGM, 1939 (d) Victor Fleming	FI

BURNETT, W. R. (1899–)		
Little Caesar (1929)	Warners, 1930 (d) Mervyn LeRoy	UA
CAHAN, Abraham (1860–1951)		
Yekl, a Tale of the New York Ghetto (1896)	*Hester Street,* Midwest, 1975 (d) Joan Micklin Silver	CIV
CATHER, Willa (1873–1947)		
A Lost Lady (1923)	Warners, 1924—silent (d) Harry Beaumont	—
	Warners, 1934 (d) Alfred E. Green	—
COOPER, James Fenimore (1789–1851)		
The Last of the Mohicans (1826)	Associated Producers, 1920—silent (d) Maurice Tourneur, Clarence Brown	FCE
	United Artists, 1936 (d) George B. Seitz	FCE, TWY, WCF
The Prairie (1827)	Screen Guild, 1948 (d) Frank Wisbar	FCE, TFC, WCF

Author–Title	Film Version: Title (if changed), Production Company, Release Date Director (d)	Rental Source(s)
The Pathfinder (1840)	Columbia, 1954 (d) Sidney Salkow	CWF, TFC
The Deerslayer (1841)	Selznick, 1923—silent (d) Arthur Wellin	FCE, MOG
	20th Century-Fox, 1957 (d) Kurt Neumann	BUD, IVY, WCF
CRANE, Stephen (1871–1900)		
The Red Badge of Courage (1895)	MGM, 1951 (d) John Huston	FI
DANA, Richard Henry, Jr. (1815–82)		
Two Years Before the Mast (1840)	Paramount, 1946 (d) John Farrow	TFC, TMC, UNI
DIXON, Thomas (1864–1946)		
The Clansman (1905)	*The Birth of a Nation,* Epoch, 1915 (d) D. W. Griffith	AB, JAN

DREISER, Theodore (1871–1945)

  Sister Carrie (1900)

    Carrie,
    Paramount, 1952
    (d) William Wyler   FI

  Jennie Gerhardt (1911)

    Paramount, 1933
    (d) Marion Gering   UNI

  An American Tragedy (1925)

    Paramount, 1931
    (d) Josef von Sternberg   CON, TMC, UNI

    A Place in the Sun,
    Paramount, 1951
    (d) George Stevens   FI

FAULKNER, William (1897–1962)

  The Sound and the Fury (1929)

    20th Century-Fox, 1959
    (d) Martin Ritt   FI

FERBER, Edna (1887–1968)

  So Big (1924)

    Warners, 1932
    (d) William A. Wellman   —

    Warners, 1953
    (d) Robert Wise   —

  Show Boat (1926)

    Universal, 1929
    (d) Harry Pollard   —

Author–Title	Film Version: Title (if changed), Production Company, Release Date Director (d)	Rental Source(s)
(*Show Boat*)	Universal, 1936 (d) James Whale	FI
	MGM, 1951 (d) George Sidney	FI
FITZGERALD, F. Scott (1896–1940)		
The Great Gatsby (1925)	Paramount, 1926—silent (d) Herbert Brenon	—
	Paramount, 1949 (d) Elliott Nugent	FI (withdrawn)
	Paramount, 1974 (d) Jack Clayton	FI
HAWTHORNE, Nathaniel (1804–64)		
The Scarlet Letter (1850)	Fox, 1917—silent (d) Carl Harbaugh	FCE
	MGM, 1926—silent (d) Victor Sjöström	FI

The House of the Seven Gables (1851)

Majestic, 1934
(d) Robert Vignola — BUD, EMG, FCE, KPF, TMC

Universal, 1940
(d) Joe May — UNI

Twice Told Tales,
United Artists, 1963 (one episode of three)
(d) Sidney Salkow — UA

HEMINGWAY, Ernest (1899–1961)

The Sun Also Rises (1926)

20th Century-Fox, 1957
(d) Henry King — FI

A Farewell to Arms (1929)

Paramount, 1932
(d) Frank Borzage — CLA

20th Century-Fox, 1958
(d) Charles Vidor — FI

JAMES, Henry (1843–1916)

Daisy Miller (1878)

Paramount, 1974
(d) Peter Bogdanovich — FI

Washington Square (1881)

The Heiress,
Paramount, 1949
(d) William Wyler — TWY, UNI

Author–Title	Film Version: Title (if changed), Production Company, Release Date Director (d)	Rental Source(s)
The Aspern Papers (1888)	*The Lost Moment,* Universal, 1947 (d) Martin Gabel	BUD, IVY
What Maisie Knew (1897)	Independently produced, 1975 (d) Barbette Mangolte	c/o Barbette Mangolte 319 Greenwich Street New York, New York 10013 (212) 925-6329
The Turn of the Screw (1898)	*The Innocents,* 20th Century-Fox, 1961 (d) Jack Clayton	FI
LEWIS, Sinclair (1885–1951)		
Main Street (1920)	Warners, 1923—silent (d) Harry Beaumont	—
	I Married a Doctor, Warners, 1936 (d) Archie Mayo	UA
Babbitt (1922)	Warners, 1924—silent (d) Harry Beaumont	—

	Production	
	Warners, 1934 (d) William Keighley	UA
Arrowsmith (1925)	Goldwyn, 1931 (d) John Ford	—
Elmer Gantry (1927)	United Artists, 1960 (d) Richard Brooks	UA
Dodsworth (1929)	Goldwyn, 1936 (d) William Wyler	AB, BUD
LONDON, Jack (1876–1916)		
The Call of the Wild (1903)	United Artists, 1935 (d) William A. Wellman	FI
The Sea Wolf (1904)	Ince/Triangle, 1926—silent (d) Ralph Ince	CSV (sale)
	Fox, 1930 (d) Alfred Santell	—
	Warners, 1941 (d) Michael Curtiz	UA
	Wolf Larsen, Allied Artists, 1958 (d) Harmon Jones	IVY
White Fang (1906)	20th Century-Fox, 1936 (d) David Butler	—

Author–Title	*Film Version:* *Title (if changed),* *Production Company, Release Date* *Director (d)*	*Rental* *Source(s)*
Martin Eden (1909)	*The Adventures of Martin Eden,* Columbia, 1942 (d) Sidney Salkow	FCE, TFC
Loos, Anita (1893–)		
Gentlemen Prefer Blondes (1925)	20th Century-Fox, 1953 (d) Howard Hawks	FI
But Gentlemen Marry Brunettes (1928)	*Gentlemen Marry Brunettes,* United Artists, 1955 (d) Richard Sale	UA
MELVILLE, Herman (1819–91)		
Typee (1846)	*Enchanted Island,* Warners, 1958 (d) Allan Dwan	UF
Moby Dick (1851)	*The Sea Beast,* Warners, 1926—silent (d) Millard Webb	UA
	Warners, 1930 (d) Lloyd Bacon	UA

Billy Budd (1886–91, 1924)	United Artists, 1956 (d) John Huston	UA
	Anglo Allied, 1962 (d) Peter Ustinov	HUR
NORRIS, Frank (1870–1902)		
Moran of the Lady Letty (1898)	Paramount, 1922—silent (d) George Melford	—
McTeague (1899)	*Greed,* MGM, 1925—silent (d) Erich von Stroheim	FI
SINCLAIR, Upton (1878–1968)		
Jimmie Higgins (1919)	Ukrain Films (Russian) 1933—silent (d) George Tassim	—
STOWE, Harriet Beecher (1811–96)		
Uncle Tom's Cabin (1852)	Edison, 1903—silent (d) Edwin S. Porter	FIM
	Laemmle, 1914—silent	KPF
	Famous Players-Lasky, 1918—silent (d) J. Searle Dawley	—

Author–Title	Film Version: Title (if changed), Production Company, Release Date Director (d)	Rental Source(s)
(*Uncle Tom's Cabin*)	Universal, 1928—silent with musical score (d) Harry Pollard	—
My Wife and I (1871)	Warners, 1925—silent (d) Millard Webb	—
TARKINGTON, Booth (1869–1946)		
Monsieur Beaucaire (1900)	Paramount, 1946 (d) George Marshall	TMC, UNI
Penrod (1914)	Associated First National, 1922—silent (d) Marshall Neilan	—
Penrod and Sam (1916)	Associated First National, 1923—silent (d) William Beaudine	—
Seventeen (1916)	Warners, 1937 (d) William McGann	UA
	Paramount, 1940 (d) Louis King	—
The Magnificent Ambersons (1918)	RKO, 1942 (d) Orson Welles	FI, JAN

Alice Adams (1921)

RKO, 1935
(d) George Stevens — FI

TWAIN, Mark (1835–1910)

The Adventures of Tom Sawyer (1876)

Morosco-Lasky, 1917—silent
(d) William Desmond Taylor — —

Tom Sawyer,
Paramount, 1930
(d) John Cromwell — TMC, UNI

Selznick/United Artists, 1938
(d) Norman Taurog — AB, BUD, CWF, TWY

Tom Sawyer,
Reader's Digest, 1973
(d) Don Taylor — —

The Prince and the Pauper (1882)

Edison, 1909—silent — —

Famous Players-Paramount, 1915—silent
(d) Edwin S. Porter, Hugh Ford — —

(Austria) 1923—silent
(d) Alexander Korda — FCE

Warners, 1937
(d) William Keighley — UA

Author–Title	Film Version: Title (if changed), Production Company, Release Date Director (d)	Rental Source(s)
(The Prince and the Pauper)	Disney, 1962 (d) Don Chaffey	AB, CWF, FI, TWY
The Adventures of Huckleberry Finn (1884)	Morosco-Lasky, 1919—silent (d) William Desmond Taylor	—
	Huckleberry Finn, Paramount, 1931 (d) Norman Taurog	TMC, UNI
	MGM, 1939 (d) Richard Thorpe	FI
	MGM, 1960 (d) Michael Curtiz	FI
A Connecticut Yankee in King Arthur's Court (1889)	Fox, 1921—silent (d) Emmett J. Flynn	—
	A Connecticut Yankee, Fox, 1931 (d) David Butler	—
	Paramount, 1949 (d) Tay Garnett	AB, TWY, UNI

The Tragedy of Pudd'nhead Wilson (1894)

   Pudd'n Head Wilson,
   Famous Players-Paramount, 1916—silent
   (d) undetermined   —

WALLACE, Lew (1827–1905)

   Ben-Hur (1880)

   MGM, 1926—silent
   (d) Fred Niblo   FI

   MGM, 1959
   (d) William Wyler   FI

WHARTON, Edith (1862–1937)

   The Age of Innocence (1920)

   RKO, 1934
   (d) Philip Moeller   —

   The Old Maid (1924)

   Warners, 1939
   (d) Edmund Goulding   UA

   The Children (1928)

   Marriage Playground,
   Paramount, 1929
   (d) Lothar Mendes   —

WILDER, Thornton (1897–)

   The Bridge of San Luis Rey (1927)

   MGM, 1929—sound sequences
   (d) Charles Brabin   —

   United Artists, 1944
   (d) Rowland V. Lee   IVY

Author–Title	Film Version: Title (if changed), Production Company, Release Date Director (d)	Rental Source(s)
WISTER, Owen (1860–1938)		
The Virginian (1902)	Lasky Feature Play Co., 1914—silent (d) Cecil B. DeMille	—
	Preferred, 1923—silent (d) Tom Forman	BLA (sale)
	Paramount, 1929 (d) Victor Fleming	MMA, UNI
	Paramount, 1946 (d) Stuart Gilmore	TFC, TMC, UNI

I / Covering Film Adaptations of Individual American Novels, 1826–1929

Archer, Eugene. "George Stevens and the American Dream" [*A Place in the Sun, Alice Adams*], *Film Culture*, 3, No. 1 (1957), pp. 3–4+.

Atkins, Irene Kahn. "In Search of the Greatest Gatsby," *Literature/Film Quarterly*, II, No. 3 (Summer 1974), pp. 216–228.

Bergman, Andrew. "The Gangsters" [*Little Caesar*], *We're in the Money*. New York: New York University Press, 1971.

Bluestone, George. "Adaptation or Evasion: *Elmer Gantry*," *Film Quarterly*, 14, No. 3 (Spring 1961), pp. 15–19.

Bluestone, George. *Novels into Film*. Berkeley: University of California Press, 1966 (reprint of 1957 ed.).

Brownlow, Kevin. "The Heroic Fiasco: *Ben Hur*," *The Parade's Gone By*. New York: Ballantine Books, 1969, pp. 441–475.

Cawelti, John. "Zane Grey and W.S. Hart: The Romantic Western of the 1920s" [*The Virginian*], *The Velvet Light Trap*, No. 12 (Spring 1974), pp. 9–11.

de Laurot, Edouard. "An Encounter with John Huston" [*Moby Dick*], *Film Culture*, 2, No. 8 (1956), pp. 1–4.

Dreiser, Theodore, "The Real Sins of Hollywood" [*An American Tragedy*], *Liberty*, IX (June 11, 1932), pp. 6–11.

Faragoh, Francis Edward. *Little Caesar*, in *Twenty Best Film Plays*, ed. John Gassner. New York: Crown, 1943, pp. 477–520.

Farber, Stephen. "*The Magnificent Ambersons*," *Film Comment*, 7, No. 2 (Summer 1971), pp. 48–50.

Fuller, Stanley. "Melville on the Screen" [*Moby Dick, Billy Budd*], *Films in Review*, 19, No. 6 (June–July 1968), pp 358–377.

Fulton, R.A. "Stroheim's *Greed*," *Films in Review*, 6 (June–July 1955), pp. 263–268.

Geist, Kenneth. *"Carrie," Film Comment,* 6, No. 3 (Fall 1970), pp. 26–27.

Gianetti, Louis. "The Gatsby Flap," *Literature/Film Quarterly,* 3, No. 1 (Winter 1975), pp. 13–22.

Heston,Charlton. "The Questions No One Asks about Willy" [*Ben Hur*], *Films and Filming,* 4, No. 11 (August 1958), p. 9.

Hill, Derek. *"Moby Dick* Sets New Style in Color Photography," *American Cinematographer,* 37, No. 9 (September 1956), pp. 534–535[+].

Horner, Harry. "Designing *The Heiress"* [*Washington Square*], *Hollywood Quarterly,* 5, No. 1 (Fall 1950), pp. 1–7.

Houston, Penelope. "Gatsby," *Sight and Sound,* 43, No. 2 (Spring 1974), pp. 78–79.

Houston, Penelope. "The Innocents," *Sight and Sound,* 30, No. 3 (Summer 1961), pp. 114–115.

Howard, Sidney. *Sinclair Lewis's "Dodsworth".* New York: Harcourt, Brace and Co., 1934.

Johnson, Albert. *"Studs Lonigan* and *Elmer Gantry," Sight and Sound,* 29, No. 4 (Autumn 1960), pp. 173–175.

Jones, Edward T. "Green Thoughts in Technicolor Shade: A Reevaluation of *The Great Gatsby," Literature/Film Quarterly,* 2, No. 3 (Summer 1974), pp. 229–236.

Kael, Pauline. *"Billy Budd," I Lost It at the Movies.* Boston: Little Brown and Co., 1965.

Kraft, H.S. "Dreiser's War in Hollywood" [*An American Tragedy*], *Screen Writer,* 1 (March 1946), pp. 9–13.

Kunert, Arnold. "Ray Bradbury on Hitchcock, Huston and Other Magic of the Screen" [*Moby Dick*], *Take One,* 3, No. 11 (1973), pp. 15–24.

Laurence, Frank. "Death in the Matinee: The Film Endings of Hemingway's Fiction" [*A Farewell to Arms,* 1932], *Literature/Film Quarterly,* II, No. 1 (Winter 1974), pp. 44–51.

Lawson, John Howard. "Hollywood History Lesson" [*The Red Badge of Courage*], *Film and the Battle of Ideas.* New York: Masses and Mainstream, 1953, pp. 29–38.

Lennig, Arthur. *"Greed," Classics of the Film.* Madison: Wisconsin Film Society Press, 1965, pp. 41–50.

Leonard, Neil. "Theodore Dreiser and the Film" [*An American Tragedy*], *Film Heritage,* 2, No. 1 (Fall 1966), pp. 7–16.

Leyda, Jay. "Modesty and Pretension in Two New Films" [*Moby Dick*], *Film Culture,* 2, No. 4 (1956), pp. 3–7[+].

McBride, Joseph. "The Magnificent Ambersons," *Orson Welles*. New York: Viking Press, 1972, pp. 52–86.

Newhall, Beaumont. "Miracle of Observation" [*Greed*], *Image*, 5, No. 4 (April 1956), pp. 88–91.

Oakes, Philip. "A Seat at the Circus" [*Ben Hur*, 1960], *Sight and Sound*, 29 (Spring 1960), pp. 94–95.

Pichel, Irving. "Revivals, Reissues, Remarks, and *A Place in the Sun*" [*An American Tragedy*], *Quarterly of Film, Radio, and Television*, 6, No. 4 (Summer 1952), pp. 388–393.

Potamkin, Harry A. "Novel into Film: A Case Study of Current Practice" [*An American Tragedy*], *Close Up*, 8, No. 4 (December 1931), pp. 267–279.

Rosen, Marjorie. "Francis Ford Coppola Interviewed" and "Jack Clayton—'I'm Proud of that Film,' " [*The Great Gatsby*], *Film Comment*, 10, No. 4 (July–August 1974), pp. 43–52.

Ross, Lillian. *Picture* [*The Red Badge of Courage*]. Garden City, N.Y.: Doubleday, 1962.

Sacks, Arthur. "An Analysis of Gangster Movies of the Early Thirties" [*Little Caesar*], *The Velvet Light Trap*, No. 1 (June 1971), pp. 5–12.

Selznick, David O. "Making a Movie" [*A Farewell to Arms*, 1958], *Life*, 44 (March 17, 1958), pp. 92–94+.

Shivas, Mark. "Blondes" [*Gentlemen Prefer Blondes*], *Movie*, 5 (December 1962), pp. 23–24.

Sirkin, Elliott. "*Alice Adams*," *Film Comment*, 7, No. 4 (Winter 1971–72), pp. 66–69.

Slout, William L. "*Uncle Tom's Cabin* in American Film History," *Journal of Popular Film*, 2, No. 2 (Spring 1973), pp. 137–151.

Smith, Julian. "Hester, Sweet Hester Prynne—*The Scarlet Letter* in the Movie Market Place," *Literature/Film Quarterly*, 2, No. 2 (Spring 1974), p. 100–110.

Smith, Julian. "Orson Welles and the Great American Dummy" [*The Magnificent Ambersons*], *Literature/Film Quarterly*, 2, No. 3 (Summer 1974), pp. 196–206.

Sternfeld, Frederick. "Copland as a Film Composer" [*The Heiress*], *Musical Quarterly*, 37, No. 2 (April 1951), pp. 161–175.

Stone, Edward. "Ahab Gets Girl, or Herman Melville Goes to the Movies," *Literature/Film Quarterly*, 3, No. 2 (Spring 1975), pp. 160–171.

Weinberg, Herman G. *The Complete "Greed,"* New York: Arno Press, 1972.

II / General Entries

Archer, Eugene. "John Huston—The Hemingway Tradition in American Film," *Film Culture*, 19 (1959), pp. 66–101.

Armes, Roy. *Film and Reality: An Historical Survey*. London: Penguin, 1974.

Arnheim, Rudolf. *Film as Art*. Berkeley: University of California Press, 1966.

Asheim, Lester. "From Book to Film," Four articles in *Hollywood Quarterly*, 5, No. 3 (Spring 1951), pp. 289–304; 5, No. 4 (Summer 1951), pp. 334–349; 6, No. 1 (Fall 1951), pp. 54–68; 6, No. 3 (Spring 1952), pp. 258–273.

Bachmann, Gideon. "How I Make Films: An Interview with John Huston," *Film Quarterly*, 19, No. 1 (Fall 1965), pp. 3–13.

Bachmann, Gideon. "Ustinov," *Film*, 30 (Winter 1961), pp. 18–21.

Balázs, Béla. *Theory of the Film*. New York: Dover, 1971.

Bazin, André. *What Is Cinema?* Vol. I. Trans. by Hugh Gray. Berkeley: University of California Press, 1967.

Bazin André. *What Is Cinema?* Vol. II. Trans. by Hugh Gray. Berkeley: University of California Press, 1971.

Benjamin, Walter. "The Work of Art in the Age of Mechanical Production," *Illuminations*. Ed. by Hannah Arendt. New York: Harcourt, Brace, 1968.

Bergman, Ingmar. "Film Has Nothing to do with Literature," Introduction to *Four Screenplays of Ingmar Bergman*. Trans. by Lars Malmstrom and David Kushner. New York: Simon and Schuster, 1960.

Bond, Kirk. "Film as Literature," *Bookman*, 84 (July 1933), pp. 188–189.

Buscombe, Edward. "Dickens and Hitchcock," *Screen*, II, Nos. 4–5 (1970), pp. 97–114.

Cahiers Du Cinema, 185 (December 1966), issue devoted to novels and film.

Cavell, Stanley. *The World Viewed: Reflections on the Ontology of Film*. New York: Viking, 1971.

Cawelti, John G. *The Six-Gun Mystique*. Bowling Green, Ohio: Bowling Green University Press, 1971.

Cohen, Keith. *Novel and Movies: Dynamics of Artistic Exchange in the Early Twentieth Century*. Unpublished dissertation. Princeton, N.J.: 1974.

Connor, Edward. "Of Time and Movies," *Films in Review*, 12, No. 3 (March 1961), pp. 131–143.

de Saussure, Ferdinand. *Course in General Linguistics*. Trans. by Wade Baskin. New York: McGraw-Hill, 1966.

Durgnat, Raymond. "This Damned Eternal Triangle," *Films and Filming*, 11, No. 3 (December 1964), pp. 15–19.

Durgnat, Raymond. "The Mongrel Muse," *Films and Feeling*. Cambridge, Mass.: MIT Press, 1971, pp. 13–30.

Eidsvik, Charles. "Soft Edges: The Art of Literature, the Medium of Film," *Literature/Film Quarterly*, II, No. 1 (Winter 1974), pp. 16–21.

Eidsvik, Charles. "Toward a 'Politique des Adaptations,'" *Literature/Film Quarterly*, III, No. 3 (Summer 1975), pp. 255–263.

Eisenstein, Sergei. "Dickens, Griffith, and the Film Today," *Film Form*. Ed. by Jay Leyda. New York: Harcourt, Brace, 1949.

Eisenstein, Sergei. *Film Sense*. Ed. by Jay Leyda. New York: Harcourt, Brace, 1957.

Eisenstein, Sergei. "Lessons from Literature," *Film Essays and A Lecture*. Ed. by Jay Leyda. N.Y.: Praeger, 1970.

Enser, A.G.S. *Filmed Books and Plays*. Revised edition. Kent, England: Andre Deutsch, 1975.

Fell, John L. *Film and the Narrative Tradition*. Norman, Oklahoma: University of Oklahoma Press, 1974.

Geduld, Harry M., ed. *Authors on Film*. Bloomington, Indiana: Indiana University Press, 1972.

Godfrey, Lionel. "It Wasn't Like That in the Book," *Films and Filming*, 13, No. 7 (April 1967), pp. 12–16.

Gotteman, Ronald and Harry M. Geduld. "Adaptation [Annotated Bibliography]," *Guidebook to Film*. New York: Holt, Rinehart and Winston, 1972, pp. 30–35.

Hanson, Curtis Lee. "William Wyler," *Cinema* (Calif.), 3, No. 5 (Summer 1967), pp. 22–28.

Hartley, Dean Wilson. "'How Do We Teach It?' A Primer for the Basic Literature/Film Course," *Literature/Film Quarterly*, III, No. 1 (Winter 1975), pp. 60–68.

Hauser, Arnold. "The Film Age," *The Social History of Art*. Trans. by Stanley Goodman. New York: Alfred Knopf, 1951, pp. 927–959.

Kael, Pauline. "Notes on Heart and Mind," *Deeper into Movies*. Boston: Little Brown and Co., pp. 230–238.

Katz, John. "An Integrated Approach to the Teaching of Film and

Literature," *Screen*, 11, Nos. 4–5 (August–September 1970), pp. 55–60.

Knight, Arthur. "Hemingway into Film," *The Saturday Review* (July 29, 1961), pp. 33–34.

Koch, Stephen. "Fiction and Film: A Study for New Sources," *The Saturday Review* (December 27, 1969), pp. 12–14.

Koszarski, Richard. "Maurice Tourneur, the First of the Visual Stylists," *Film Comment*, 9, No. 2 (March–April 1973), pp. 24–31.

Kracauer, Siegfried. *Theory of Film*. New York: Oxford University Press, 1960.

Langer, Susanne K. "A Note on Film," *Feeling and Form*. New York: Scribners, 1953, pp. 411–415.

Lillich, Richard B. "Hemingway on the Screen," *Films in Review*, 10 (April 1959), pp. 208–218.

Lindsay, Vachel. *The Art of the Moving Picture*. New York: MacMillan, 1952 (reprint of 1915 ed.).

McConnell, Frank. "Film and Writing: The Political Dimension," *Massachusetts Review*, 13, No. 4 (Autumn 1972), pp. 543–562.

Madson, Axel. *William Wyler: The Authorized Biography*. New York: Thomas Y. Crowell, 1973.

Magny, Claude-Edmonde. *The Age of the American Novel: The Film Aesthetic of Fiction Between the Two Wars*. Trans. by Eleanor Hochman. New York: Frederick Ungar, 1972.

Mason, Ronald. "The Film of the Book," *Film*, 16 (March–April 1958), pp. 18–20.

Mast, Gerald and Marshall Cohen, ed. *Film Theory and Criticism*. New York: Oxford University Press, 1974.

Metz, Christian. *Film Language: A Semiotics of the Cinema*. Trans. by Michael Taylor. New York: Oxford University Press, 1974.

Moreno, Julio L. "Subjective Cinema: And the Problem of Film in the First Person," *The Quarterly of Film Radio and Television*, 7, No. 4 (Summer 1953), pp. 341–358.

Munsterberg, Hugo. *The Film: A Psychological Study*. New York: Dover Press, 1969.

Murray, Edward. *The Cinematic Imagination: Writers and the Motion Pictures*. New York: Frederick Ungar, 1972.

Nathan, Robert. "A Novelist Looks at Hollywood," *Hollywood Quarterly*, 1, No. 2 (1945), pp. 146–147.

Nicoll, Allardyce. "Literature and the Film," *English Journal*, 26 (January 1937), pp. 1–9.

Ortman, Marguerite G. *Fiction and the Screen*. Boston: Marshall Jones, 1935.

Panofsky, Erwin. "Style and Medium in the Moving Pictures," *Critique*, 1, No. 3 (January–February 1947).

Peary, Gerald. "Selected Sound Westerns and Their Novel Sources," *The Velvet Light Trap*, 12 (Spring 1974), pp. 15–19.

Perkins, V.F. *Film as Film*. London: Penguin, 1972.

Pingaud, Bernard. "The Aquarium," *Sight and Sound*, 32, No. 3 (Summer 1963), pp. 136–139.

Purdy, Strother B. "Can the Novel and the Film Disappear?" *Literature/Film Quarterly*, II, No. 3 (Fall 1974), pp. 237–255.

Read, Herbert. "Towards a Film Aesthetic," *Cinema Quarterly*, 1, No. 4 (Summer 1933), pp. 197–202.

Richardson, Robert. *Literature and Film*. Bloomington, Indiana: Indiana University Press, 1969.

Riesman, Evelyn. "Film and Fiction," *Antioch Review*, 17 (Fall 1957), pp. 353–363.

Roman, Robert C. "Mark Twain on the Screen," *Films in Review*, 12, No. 1 (January 1961), pp. 20–35.

Roud, Richard. "Novel Novel; Fable Fable?" *Sight and Sound*, 31 (Spring 1962), pp. 84–88.

Ruhe, Edward. "Film: The 'Literary' Approach," *Literature/Film Quarterly*, 1, No. 1 (January 1973), pp. 76–83.

Scott, Kenneth W. "Hawkeye in Hollywood," *Films in Review*, 9 (December 1958), pp. 575–579.

Schneider, Harold W. "Literature and Film: Marking Out Some Boundaries," *Literature/Film Quarterly*, 3, No. 1 (Winter 1975), pp. 30–44.

Seldes, Gilbert. "Vandals of Hollywood," *The Saturday Review of Literature* (October 17, 1936), pp. 3–4.

Silke, James. "A Monograph of George Stevens's Films," *Cinema* (Calif.), 2, No. 4 (December–January 1964–65), pp 8–16.

Sobchack, Vivian C. "Tradition and Cinematic Allusion," *Literature/Film Quarterly*, II, No. 1 (Winter 1974), pp. 59–65.

Sontag, Susan. "A Note on Novels and Films," *Against Interpretation*. New York: Dell, 1972, pp. 245–250.

Thorp, Margaret. "The Motion Picture and the Novel," *American Quarterly*, 3, No. 3 (1951), pp. 195–203.

Tudor, Andrew. *Theories of Film*. New York: Viking, 1974.

Wagner, Geoffrey. *The Novel and the Cinema*. Cranbury, N.J.: Farleigh Dickinson University Press, 1975.

Warshow, Robert. *The Immediate Experience.* New York: Atheneum, 1964.

Weinberg, Herman G. "Novel into Film," *Literature/Film Quarterly,* 1, No. 2 (April 1973), pp. 99–102.

Wollen, Peter. *Signs and Meaning in the Cinema.* Revised edition. Bloomington, Indiana: Indiana University Press, 1972.

Wollen, Peter, ed. *Working Papers on the Cinema: Sociology and Semiology.* London: British Film Institute, 1969.

Index